Stonewycke trilogy 2

W9-CFV-708

Flight from
Stonewycke.

$5.99

Books by the Phillips/Pella Writing Team

The Journals of Corrie Belle Hollister

My Father's World
Daughter of Grace
On the Trail of the Truth
A Place in the Sun
Sea to Shining Sea
Into the Long Dark Night
Land of the Brave and the Free

Grayfox

The Stonewycke Trilogy

The Heather Hills of Stonewycke
Flight from Stonewycke
Lady of Stonewycke

The Stonewycke Legacy

Stranger at Stonewycke
Shadows over Stonewycke
Treasure of Stonewycke

The Highland Collection

Jamie MacLeod: Highland Lass
Robbie Taggart: Highland Sailor

The Russians

The Crown and the Crucible
A House Divided
Travail and Triumph
Heirs of the Motherland
Dawning of Deliverance

HAMPSHIRE BOOKS ™

FLIGHT FROM STONEWYCKE

MICHAEL PHILLIPS
JUDITH PELLA

BETHANY HOUSE PUBLISHERS
MINNEAPOLIS, MINNESOTA 55438

Flight From Stonewycke
Michael Phillips and Judith Pella

Cover by Dan Thornberg,
Bethany House Publishers staff artist.

Library of Congress Catalog Card Number 93-74540

ISBN 0-87123-837-3 (trade paper edition)
ISBN 1-55661-453-5 (Hampshire Books Edition)

Published by Bethany House Publishers
A Division of Bethany Fellowship, Inc.
11300 Hampshire Avenue South
Minneapolis, Minnesota 55438

Printed in the United States of America

Dedication

To five special boys:

Michael
Jonathan
Gregory
Robin
Patrick

The Authors

The PHILLIPS/PELLA writing team had its beginning in the long-standing friendship of Michael and Judy Phillips with Judith Pella. Michael Phillips, with a number of non-fiction books to his credit, had been writing for several years. During a Bible study at Pella's home he chanced upon a half-completed sheet of paper sticking out of a typewriter. His author's instincts aroused, he inspected it more closely and asked their friend, "Do you write?" A discussion followed, common interests were explored, and it was not long before the Phillips invited Pella to their home for dinner to discuss collaboration on a proposed series of novels. Thus, the best-selling "Stonewycke" books were born, which led in turn to "The High-land Collection," and the "Journals of Corrie Belle Hollister."

Judith Pella holds a nursing degree and B.A. in Social Sciences. Her background as a writer stems from her avid reading and researching in historical, adventure, and geographical venues. Pella, with her two sons, resides in Eureka, California. Michael Phillips, who holds a degree from Humboldt State University and continues his post-graduate studies in history, owns and operates Christian bookstores on the West Coast. He is the editor of the best-selling George MacDonald Classic Reprint Series and is also MacDonald's biographer. The Phillips also live in Eureka with their three sons.

Contents

Introduction

To America they came!

From every background, every economic status, every corner of the world. America was the land of hope and promise, opportunity and new beginnings. They assaulted its shores, blending and mixing into one, until a mighty nation was formed.

The reasons for migrating were as countless as the 35 million daring souls who left their homelands in the 19th century to make for themselves new lives in the melting pot over the Atlantic to the west. America offered a haven from troubles left behind, an unexplored corner of the world in which the bold adventurer could strike out and seek his fortune. Each voyager had his own private story to tell. Some fled poverty, others the inevitable shrinking of the family plot of land in the old country, still others were lured by tales of wealth. But all had visions of better times ahead and hoped in the prosperous new world to find them come true.

More often than not, however, reality dimmed the dream.

The journey by sea took most of the capital a willing immigrant could raise, usually his whole life's savings. Those who had no savings had to sell what they possessed, even themselves, if there were nothing else left. But the lure of "the dream" was great and they did what they had to do. The fortunate and enterprising ones among them found the resources.

Boarding a clipper, however, was only the beginning of a new life. The weeks which followed were enough to daunt the hopes of even the strongest and most optimistic. The majority found they had only sufficient funds to travel steerage; scores of immigrants were crammed into the hulls of a ship; food was in short supply, sanitation almost nil, and disease ran rampant. Many died en route, and their dreams with them.

Yet the financial cost and physical suffering often did not represent the greatest sacrifice to this budding new generation of Americans. Most painful of all for many was the emotional sacrifice of being uprooted from all that had been dear—the country of their birth, the villages where generations of ancestors had been born and raised and died. They said good-bye to familiar homes and loved ones with scant hope of ever seeing them again. A one-way ticket had taxed their meager resources to the limit; there would likely be no return voyages. Parents, grandparents, brothers, sisters, homes, inheritances—all had to be left behind. Such was the price of new life in a new land.

Such sacrifice was indeed great among the Scots who left their beloved and enchanting homeland. For those who left the Highland fields—the primrose, the heather hills—for them the land had always held special significance, for nobleman and peasant farmer alike. The land was everything. The land had bound their ancient clans together and had torn them apart. They were a proud people, these Celts who settled the land more than 25 centuries earlier. And now as they left it for new frontiers, the parting could never be without sorrow. The earth gave meaning. Only one's land offered a permanence to the heritage which could be passed on to one's offspring. The land held the community together as a whole, as it had for centuries.

No one left such a heritage without personal and inward sacrifice. Even as they left, full of hope, what they left behind could never be erased from memory. Well might their voices have echoed the Irish poet's lament:

> Farewell to thee, Erin mavourneen,
> Thy valleys I'll tread never more;
> This heart that now bleeds for thy sorrows
> Will waste on a far distant shore.
> Thy green sods lie cold on my parents,
> A cross marks the place of their rest—

The wind that moans sadly above them
Will waft their poor child to the West.

Notwithstanding, there was an allure in the very word *America*
which helped remove some of the sting of parting. Here was a land
so rich, so immense that there was opportunity for all to make
their dreams come true.

But when the ships bearing them landed, practical obstacles of
a more difficult nature had to be faced. Suddenly they were alone,
cast upon their own resources. Now they had to discover their own
inner resources. Those who pulled themselves up in the face of
insurmountable heartbreak were able to forge a new life for themselves in this new land. Others failed. But rarely did the reality
match the idealism of the dream.

For those increasing numbers who sought their new life to the
west of the Ohio Valley and the Mississippi River, in the expanding
American West, the ties to the past were usually severed completely. Communication was severely limited. Many were illiterate,
and mail was slow and undependable.

Still they came—undaunted.

From New York they moved slowly west, the more adventur-
ous by wagon train to the wild American frontier. Some, indeed,
discovered the green pastures they had come seeking. Others
found further disappointment, and even death. For this was a raw
and untamed land. The life of the midwestern prairie offered no
pot of gold at the end of a mythical rainbow. And rare, indeed, was
the opportunity to look back to the homelands they had left. When
their hearts yearned once more toward the lands of their birth,
the practicality of struggling for life in the new west was always
more pressing.

Yet by their very ability to wrench themselves away from home
and kin and heritage, to courageously face the hurdles thrown in
their path, they proved themselves a special breed. Out of their
sorrows, their hopes, their dreams, their valor, their private ex-
ultations and agonies, a nation was forged. Each one lived out his
personal and unique drama and so carved out a future in what
became his new homeland.

Thus the proud Ramsey lineage, one of Scotland's ancient and honored names, sent a new strain of the noble dynasty across the sea to root itself in a new land. As former generations of the Ramsey descent had given their lives and blood to Scotland and to the family estate of Stonewycke, so now would future generations give themselves to this new land.

1 The Father and the Vicar

It was going to be one of those pale days of autumn in which the chill hung almost visibly in the air. A breeze portended from the ocean, as yet a mere hint that somewhere over the horizon to the north winter had already come and would soon engulf this coast in its icy grip. Before this day was over the breeze would increase and rush over the forested cliffs overlooking the craggy coastlines of northeast Scotland. But for now the morning was a quiet one.

In the distance the sound of galloping horses intruded into the stillness. As they approached the village the hoofbeats grew louder, and now and then a shout could be heard. The three riders were oblivious to the tranquil scene into which they tore in a frenzy of speed and determination. As they crested the hill and came into view, the pulsating rhythm of pounding hoofbeats thundered down the hill unheralded by dust clouds, for the road was still wet from days of rain.

The lead rider, a slight man, sat his horse firmly, like the lord he aspired to be. James Duncan's shoulders were square, his back straight. And as his black eyes bore down on the road in front of him with a steely malice, one sensed he was not the sort to let anything stand in his way. He was clearly not a man who would swerve from his purpose. His mission on this chilly fall morning was to find the man who had had the audacity to block the success of the scheme he had been working toward for years. The man he sought had not only run off with his daughter, he was also in hiding for the murder of the man Duncan had planned to make his son-in-law. Now Falkirk was dead, removing from James' reach the Falkirk fortune which Duncan had been greedily eyeing for the furtherance of his financial empire. And the man who had thwarted his ambitions and seduced his daughter—the son of his hated cousin, the Earl of Landsbury—must be found and brought to justice.

The horses rounded a bend in the road and were suddenly upon the environs of the little Scottish village of Fraserburgh. The town was awake, to be sure, but the wild pursuit of the three horsemen caused such a storm as they sped through the normally quiet street that the few persons who happened to be out quickly took shelter; children's hands were grabbed and the youngsters yanked to the safety of whatever buildings were closest at hand. The look in the leader's eye could be felt as much as seen, and no one dared impede his flight.

Through the streets they raced, and around two corners; then the pace slackened. Their destination was at hand. They rode up to the front of a homely stone manse standing within thirty yards of the ancient parish Presbyterian church, "the muckle kirk," as it was referred to by the local inhabitants. Duncan leapt from his foaming bay gelding and stalked briskly toward the house. He lifted a clenched fist, but before he had a chance to begin pounding on it, the door opened.

The elderly vicar had heard the approaching commotion, had risen to investigate, and now stood facing a glaring James Duncan.

"Oh, dear me!" he said, nervously straightening his spectacles.

"I'm looking for a man," James bellowed without pausing for any of the common amenities, "—a scoundrel trying to pass himself off as a gentleman! I have reason to believe he may have come to you."

"I have seen no such man," returned the vicar, regaining his composure. "Though in truth, it is well he would seek out the church, and I hope that I may have the opportunity—"

"He was with a girl!" James broke in, ignoring the vicar's speech. "The impudent—they would have wanted to be married!"

"Oh-h-h," breathed the vicar slowly and thoughtfully. Now he knew the couple, but he was less than certain he should tell this man, whom he was all but certain could be none other than the girl's father. He was clearly in a very dangerous mood.

For a moment his mind spun. He liked the young couple who had come to him two nights earlier to be married. Not only were they well-mannered and obviously in love, in addition the vicar had been given to believe, through a note from the girl's mother, that they had the parents' blessing. Jeremy Littlefield was an inch or two shorter even than James Duncan, and a good many inches rounder. But while his figure and ready smile were considered jolly by the people of his parish, the vicar was a staunchly principled man, and once his mind was set he could appear as stiffnecked as several of the hearty fishermen who listened to him preach on Sunday. For all he knew, this man might *not* be the girl's father, or might, indeed, be the scoundrel himself. The look in his eye told clearly enough that his was not an errand of love.

"Well?" James demanded. "Have you seen them?"

"Sir, I must tell you," Littlefield began cautiously, "there are certain privileges of my calling . . . certain, shall we say, confidentialities—"

"I give not a bloody hang about your calling! I am James Duncan, laird of Stonewycke—and the girl's father. You will tell me *now* all you know!"

"Sir," replied the vicar, the back of his neck growing stiffer by the moment, "the authority of Stonewycke does not extend to Fraserburgh."

"Why you contemptuous old . . ." As he spoke James stepped forward toward the vicar, still standing in the open door, raising his hand slightly as he did so.

"Your lordship!" said the vicar sharply. "I must warn you that even though I am not a strong man, I am well respected in this town, and there are even now on the street men observing our conversation—men who would come swiftly to my defense, and ask questions later. I caution you, for your own safety, nothing more."

If James had intended to harm the little man, he made no further move in that direction. "Sir," Littlefield continued, "I can see you are distraught. Please come in, and we can discuss the matter privately over a cup of tea."

"I want none of your tea," James replied in a lower but no less menacing tone. "Tell me what you know, or I swear you will never see the inside of a church again."

"I do not take kindly to threats," stated the vicar firmly, rising to his full height.

"And *I* do not take kindly to your stalling!" rejoined James sharply. "I must warn you of the repercussions of your unprincipled harboring of a man who has kidnapped an innocent girl." James paused, allowing time for his words to have their full impact on this stubborn clergyman. "Besides which," he went on, "the man is a fugitive from the law."

Though he did not let his face show it, the angry man's statement did indeed impress the vicar and stimulated a reevaluation of his position. Although the girl, Lady Margaret Duncan, had appeared in no way coerced into the marriage, there was still the point to be considered that she had acted in disobedience to her father's will. Yet, the marriage had apparently been arranged by the girl's mother. And if the boy was indeed fleeing from some crime, how could he—as an agent of God's righteousness—withhold what he knew? The thing had come to a most confusing pass!

Deep in his heart the vicar saw good in his fellowmen. Evil existed in the world, to be sure, but it was found in dark and disreputable drinking houses and back alleys of large cities, not in the hearts of fathers toward their children. Littlefield was the father of three daughters, whom he loved and had doted upon since their earliest days. What father could feel differently toward a daughter? Furthermore, the marriage he had recently performed was over, in the eyes of God and man a legal and spiritual reality. Thus there was little this man Duncan could do to change that fact. Undoubtedly the children would be able to reason with the overwrought father, and in light of the fact of the marriage, he would in the end follow the mother's blessing with his own. And if there was some difficulty with the law, the father, as laird, certainly possessed every legal right to look into the matter on behalf of the authorities.

When Littlefield at length spoke, his words came from a heart which was certain he was doing the right thing, given the unusual circumstances facing him. "Your lordship," he said, "I will direct you to where I believe they may be, though I cannot guarantee they will still be there—it has been two days since I last saw them."

"Where, then?" James barked, moderating his cold tone but slightly.

The vicar hesitated. There was something in this man's eyes he could not identify, a hard emptiness he had never seen before, something which reminded him of the angry sea in the middle of the winter.

Their eyes met for a brief instant, then the vicar glanced quickly away. *It must be nothing,* he thought to himself. *The man is merely worked up, and it will pass. Soon all will be mended and healed.*

He directed James Duncan to the humble little cottage some four miles down the road. Without a word of thanks James spun around, jumped onto his horse, and rode off with his two companions in the manner in which they had come.

The vicar stared after them, exhaled a long sigh, closed the door of his home, and turned back inside.

2 The Daughter and Her Man

The morning sun pierced the wood with fragments of light dancing against the leafless birch and rowan and the green stands of fir. The face of approaching winter was evident, but a few tenacious orange and yellow leaves still clung to their branches, flickering colorfully in the sunlight. Most of the foliage, however, lay on the ground, a dying bed of autumnal splendor.

Laughter rang through the wood overlooking the sea, roaring

far below the top of the bluff. The three riders heading eastward on the bordering road did not hear the happy voices, perhaps because the laughter blended so sweetly with the serenity of the wood; perhaps, too, because the reverberating hoofbeats of their steeds drowned out all other sounds as they passed.

Two figures, concealed from the riders' eyes as their laughter had been from their ears, stood at the far end of the wood, at the very edge where the tall cliffs began to fall away to meet the beach below. They had heard the horses approach, pass, then die away in the distance. The galloping rang with urgency. But they could not have guessed that they were themselves in the very eye of the storm whose fomenter was now disappearing toward their own honeymoon cottage over the next rise—a storm whose thunder-clouds threatened to engulf them and destroy the bliss they had shared so briefly. The man and the woman stood hand in hand overlooking the sea, gazing toward the distant horizon. Had James Duncan known that the very people he was searching for stood so close within his grasp, the peaceful little grove would have rung with dissonant sounds of strife. As it was, Lady Margaret and her new husband Ian Duncan stood alone, taking in the scene before them, as if by peering far enough they might see far ahead into their own lives.

"It's out there, you know," said Ian at last. "That's where our future lies."

"That's north, silly," replied Maggie, still in a cheerful mood.

"You know what I mean," returned Ian. "Away from Scotland. Not north, maybe, but over the sea."

"I know," said Maggie with a sigh. "But I want to go, Ian. As much as I am torn about having to leave this land I love, our future is westward, in America."

"And you're still sure?"

"Ian ... we made the right decision."

"No second thoughts about fleeing the country with an accused killer?"

"Of course not! When Falkirk's murderer is found and once my father gets used to our being married, we can return, just as we agreed. Maybe in a few years. But for now, this is best. We must get away and start our life together afresh. There's no other way."

She paused and looked her new husband full in the face. Then, as if to divert his attention from forebodings about their future, she grabbed his hand. "Come, I think I know a way down to the beach!"

"You do know this whole coastline!" exclaimed Ian in disbelief.

"I told you, before you came into my life, I rode every inch of this ground with Cinder and then with Raven."

She laughed, then tugged at his hand and led the way to a steep, narrow path strewn with rocks and dead leaves and debris. It was clearly seldom used. And no wonder, for it wound steeply downward back and forth down the edge of the precipice.

When they at last reached the bottom, with only a few smudges on their faces and a scratch or two, they turned back to look up at the wood from which they had come. From this perspective the trees looked as if they had rushed up to the cliff and then frozen before hurtling over the edge. Their attention then turned out to the sea, where a lone fishing vessel was fighting the rising sea about a mile offshore. The surface of the water was glassy calm, but its pale gray seemed to indicate that it was only holding the grand storm in check for a few moments more. And indeed, on the horizon a mass of dark clouds threatened to swallow the blue which remained overhead. A solitary gull winged overhead, swooping down to the water for a moment, then quickly arching upward again.

"I can hardly believe we're actually married!" said Maggie with a sigh.

"Believe it, my dear. 'Tis true," said Ian, bending over to kiss her.

"It's so peaceful here. Just think, Ian, not a soul knows where we are." Maggie paused, then added, "I wonder if he knows?"

"Your father?"

"Yes. What do you suppose he thinks now that it's too late to stop us?"

"It matters little what he thinks," stated Ian. "We are married, and I love you."

Suddenly he jumped to his feet from where he had been sitting.

"Do you hear!" he shouted toward the cliff and along the shore, "I love her!" The sound of his voice was quickly lost in the crash of the surf on the rocky shoreline.

Maggie laughed. "You always did believe in expressing yourself to the fullest, didn't you, my goose of a husband!"

"Of course," replied Ian gaily. "If you have something to say, everyone might as well know it."

"Digory was right," remarked Maggie. "He said all things work out for good when you believe God. It's true. It's happened for us."

Ian smiled and merely nodded. The mention of God suddenly brought back to him the painful memory of that desolate ride to Stonewycke Castle only a few days ago when, thinking he had lost Maggie forever, he had shouted curses at the very God Maggie now spoke of. It would not be easy for him to regain his hold on that God—whoever or wherever He was. Even at its best any belief he had once possessed had been fragile. He was glad Maggie could forget those days so easily and know everything had worked out for good. But he still had to live with the horrible burden that perhaps he was, in fact, the murderer of the heir to the Earl of Kairn.

He could laugh with Maggie and speak of the future. But that cold fear was never far from him—fear that his mind had blocked out what he did not want to remember. Yet for her sake he masked it, as he had masked his deepest feelings all his life.

"A storm is moving in," he finally said. "I hope that little fishing boat makes it back to shore before it breaks." He continued to fix his gaze on the white sail in the distance, bulging in the mounting wind.

"The sea can be so friendly one moment," Maggie said, "and the next—"

She left the sentence unfinished. As with Ian, the sea had made her pensive and her thoughts had wandered. She had lived her entire life within sight of this mighty Scottish coast. And now the thought of sailing to America, living away from the sea, perhaps never to—

No, she told herself. *None of that matters. The important thing is that Ian and I are together, and safe. We can live anywhere and be happy.*

Suddenly Maggie became aware that Ian was staring at her. "Confused?" he asked. "Having more doubts?"

"No," she answered. "Perhaps a little sad, but never confused. We have done the right thing. I am happy, and my future is with you."

They climbed back up the rugged path, but the ascent was far more taxing than coming down, and when they finally reached the top they both fell onto the soft floor of the forest, breathing hard. They lay for some time as the shadows shifted in the swaying tree-tops. When they stirred into activity again, the sun had reached the midpoint of its arch.

Ian pulled Maggie to her feet and they walked toward their horses, the silky black Raven and Maukin, the chestnut mare. "You probably thought we were never coming back," Maggie murmured into the ear of her friend from childhood, her closest companion since she had been fourteen. So many changes had come into her life since then, but Raven had been an important and deeply loved source of stability. A momentary stab of bitterness raced through her at the thought of Cinder, the first horse she had loved, and what her father had done. But just as quickly it passed, and they mounted and rode out of the forest and back onto the dirt road which wound along the high coastline.

The highway was empty now; it had been two hours since the three riders had passed. Maggie and Ian rode eastward, the way they had come, in silence. The few belongings they had brought with them on the night of their hasty wedding in Fraserburgh were tied to their saddles. Yet as if by common consent they followed the road back toward the cottage where they had spent the last two nights. The wind had picked up, and conversation was difficult. At length Ian reined Maukin to a stop.

"Maggie," he said, "I think we should ride straight to Aberdeen and seek passage immediately."

"I wish we could go back to the cottage for a few days longer," said Maggie.

"So do I. But I have an uneasy feeling about it. If your father does try to follow us, he won't have far to look. Our presence there was not altogether unknown."

"The vicar would never tell, do you think?"

"Perhaps not. But word spreads in a place like Fraserburgh. And your father can be very persuasive. I think we should ride for the coast without any further delay." Ian knew what he was asking of his new wife. Yet Maggie had shown herself strong, an̄ ̄e knew the time had finally come for decisions. "Maggie," he said at length, "if this is going to be too difficult, we don't *have* to go to America. We could be happy closer, someplace—"

"No, Ian. It's our only hope. It's the only way. I *want* to go, to be safe and with you. But . . ."

"What is it, my love?"

"When I said good-bye to my mother, I hadn't known it might be forever. Maybe that's what is making me hesitate, the thought of never seeing her again."

"We can go back to Stonewycke," Ian broke in quickly. "Besides, maybe they have found the killer by this time."

"Oh, Ian, you would risk going back, for me?"

"Of course."

"But it's too dangerous. What if—?"

"Nonsense!" said Ian, reeling Maukin around in the road. "I'd do anything for you! Besides, we'll just slip in, see your mother, tell her of our plans, and be gone before your father lays an eye on us. We'll go to the inn. Queenie will help us."

"We'll have to be careful," cautioned Maggie.

"Don't worry. Everything will be fine. But you're right, we do have to be careful. And if your father is looking for us or hears any rumor of us in connection with Fraserburgh, this very road is the one he'd use to follow us. Is there any other way back to Port Strathy?"

"There's a road—hardly more than a trail actually—a mile or two west of here that cuts across to the Inland Highway. That would be a long way around though."

"Better than being seen," said Ian. "Lead the way!"

Maggie swung Raven around, dug her heels into the mare's flanks, and the two galloped back up the hill, passed the wood where they had spent the morning, and in less than fifteen minutes were heading south away from the sea on the trail Maggie had spoken of.

They had scarcely left the Coast Road when three riders, returning from the abandoned cottage, thundered past the inland cutoff and descended once again upon Fraserburgh. Their second interview with the vicar was brief and terse. Satisfied that he knew no more than he had told them earlier, the riders spurred their exhausted mounts back through the streets and again toward Port Strathy, to the estate of Stonewycke, where the leader of the three would have to rethink his strategy against the son of his hated cousin.

3   Flight from Stonewycke

Queenie Rankin moved her stout bulk deftly among the tables of the Common Room of her inn. With a strong arm she polished each one until it shone. She was proud of the inn she and her husband had built, and all the more now that he had died so shortly after its completion. Perhaps the *Bluster 'N Blow* stood as a memorial to the only man that had ever loved her, and the only man she had trusted enough to love in return. Some characterized the woman as cold, and the hard businesslike gleam in her eye attested to that image. But there was more to Queenie than most of her customers ever guessed, for she had kept what lay underneath hidden from all except her husband. Even he had seen only glimpses of it.

Evening shadows had begun to fall across the glistening tables. Queenie stood back from her work, cast a quick eye about, and deemed the place at last fit for her evening patrons. With winter coming on and the herring season completed, times at the inn were busier; they would be coming soon. There was just time to clean up a bit behind the counter where the glasses and most of her cheaper stock of liquor were kept. But she had barely reached the counter when the door unexpectedly opened behind her. Turning around, her eyes opened wide and the glass she had been holding nearly dropped to the floor.

"I canna believe my auld eyes!" she exclaimed, hurrying out to greet the new arrivals. "An' the leddy too!" she added. "Whatever ye'll be doin' here I don't know, but a hearty welcome t' the both o' ye!"

Ian glanced quickly around and was obviously relieved to find the place empty.

"Hello, Queenie," said Ian almost in a whisper, as if he feared being heard despite the fact that the three of them were alone in the inn. "I don't want to bring more trouble upon you, but—"

"Hold yer tongue, lad!" interrupted Queenie. "I'll be the one t' say when trouble's bein' brought upon me. Now, come in an' sit ye doon."

Queenie led them to a secluded bench near the hearth. A cheerful fire was blazing away in anticipation of the evening guests, and the two travelers welcomed its warmth. Noting the anxiety on Ian's face, Queenie was reluctant to be the one to confirm the news Maggie and Ian dreaded most to hear: the murderer had not been found, rumors were still circulating (rumors which had grown to conviction in the minds of many of the townspeople) that Ian was the guilty party, an incriminating knife had been discovered, and James Duncan had been ravaging the town for three days in search of any stray clue that might lead him to wherever Ian was hiding.

Maggie fell back heavily against the wall. How desperately she had forced herself to believe that all would be resolved once they returned to Stonewycke! Now it seemed to return at all would be suicide if they encountered her father. Once again, there seemed no alternative but to get as far away from Port Strathy, and Scotland, as possible.

Into the blur of Maggie's consciousness drifted the urgent sound of Ian's voice, hurriedly making arrangements with Queenie. She struggled to pay attention but could barely concentrate; her confused brain could only tell her that he was making arrangements with Queenie for Atlanta, her mother, to come to the village to see them. *I have to see her,* she thought. In that instant nothing else mattered to Maggie except being able to see her mother one last time.

"...an' I'll fix up a room fer ye upstairs, until then," Queenie was saying, but Maggie scarcely heard.

A full moon illuminated the tall grasses behind the inn. The clouds that had hung threatening in the sky all day parted for a time, allowing the night light to shine through. A short distance away the waves crashed against the shore, their foamy tops an eerie phosphorescence in the moonlight. Atlanta Duncan quickly surveyed the scene. But her mind was not on its beauty, but upon the clandestine reunion with her daughter. Her heart ached; she, too, had hoped it would not come to this. Yet when she had sent Maggie and Ian off to be married, a dark premonition had told her their flight would be more permanent than any of the three had dared openly admit. She was a pragmatic woman, and had hardened herself against that possibility. Still, she had hoped. Now she knew the inevitable moment had come. Why else would they send for her so soon? And in the dead of night? Why else but to say good-bye? So Atlanta had prepared herself to bid her only daughter farewell, knowing she might never see her again.

Maggie stepped out of the cover of the grasses when she saw Atlanta approach.

"Mother!" she said in an urgent whisper.

"Oh, dear child!" cried Atlanta, turning toward her and taking her daughter in her arms.

"I had to see you again," Maggie said.

"I know," Atlanta replied, holding her close.

"Mother," began Maggie, "we're going—Ian's still in danger ... we have to—"

"I know, I know. Ian's note said you were going away."

"Mother, we've decided—we're going to America."

"Oh, Lord!" gasped Atlanta.

"It's the only way."

Recovering herself, Atlanta brushed an unseen tear from her eye, took a deep breath, and replied. "You are married now. You and Ian must begin a new life. He will take care of you."

"I wish you could come with us."

"No, Maggie. My life is here. Yours is with Ian now. You will be happy."

"I know," said Maggie, clinging to Atlanta. "I am happy."

Atlanta eased Maggie away from her, then held her at arm's length and gazed into her face. She reached up and arrested a tear that had begun to drop down her daughter's cheek. "You are strong, my dear daughter. And you have a husband who loves you. You will have the happiness you deserve. And perhaps you will return some day, when all this is—"

A sob caught in Atlanta's throat. Even as she spoke, she could feel the hollowness of her words. She swallowed hard and closed her eyes for an instant in an attempt to regain her desperately needed reserve.

Maggie embraced Atlanta again. "Mother," she said, "we'll let you know where we are—we'll write."

"That may not be advisable at first," said Atlanta, the practicality of her nature speaking out before the urgings of her mother's heart. She drew a deep breath. "Only until this thing with Ian is cleared up, of course."

"You can reach us through Drew Mackinaw," said Ian, speaking for the first time. "You should at least know that much. He has a small farm in Chatham, New York."

"Thank you, Ian," said Atlanta, turning to her son-in-law. "I want you to know, regardless of what has happened, that I have faith in you. I know you will do what is best for Maggie."

"Thank you, my lady," Ian replied. "That means a great deal to me. I will try to be worthy of your trust and—"

The rest of his reply was lost in a wild volley of shouts which erupted behind them.

"I swore you would not get away with this!" shrieked James as he approached hurriedly, his eyes flashing. His outstretched hand held a pistol poised dangerously at Ian's head.

"Father, no!" screamed Maggie.

"You'll thank me for this later!" Turning toward Ian, James continued his threats. "The constable may not have thought there to be enough evidence to hang you, but, by Jove! I'll not have a murderer abducting my daughter!"

"Don't be a fool, James!" Atlanta interrupted.

"Trying to undermine me again, my dear wife?" James sneered. "But you'll not win this time."

Ian stood gaping in shock and disbelief. When at length he came to his senses, a resolve rose within him. He would stand his ground and make James Duncan know that he was not a murderer. He opened his mouth to speak, but all the words he would utter caught in his throat.

"I'm—I'm no killer," he stammered out, but the speech was weak and strained. How could he convince this man of something he was not even certain of himself?

"Ha!" returned James with a fiendish laugh. "And whose blood was that on your hand, your own? Ha! ha!"

Unconsciously Ian shot a quick glance at his hand as if the blood might still be clinging to his skin. His eyes saw only the remaining bandage over the wound he had received that awful night—the wound he could not remember how he had received.

"I'm warning you, Duncan," James went on. "Leave this town immediately! I'll not give you another chance. If I ever see your face around Stonewycke again, I'll kill you, do you hear?"

"Father!" cried Maggie, running to Ian and standing by his side, "you cannot shoot my *husband*!"

At the word a fury of rage swept over James's face.

"Husband!" he shrieked. "He's a scoundrel!" Again he raised the pistol and took deadly aim down its barrel.

"Run, Ian!" Maggie screamed, rushing toward her father. "Run!"

For a brief instant Ian stood transfixed. Maggie slammed into her father, sending him reeling backward. Without further thought, Ian turned and sprinted toward the chestnut mare. He was barely astride when a shot rang out. Astonished by the suddenness of her attack, James had been dazed by the jolt of his daughter's body. Coming quickly to himself he threw her aside and let fly a hasty round after Ian. The crack of the gun made the horse bolt forward just as Ian had found his seat.

"You'll not destroy my family again, Landsbury!" James yelled, firing once more, this time nearly finding his mark. In his wild frenzy he never realized he had called Ian by the hated name of the lad's father.

Quickly James reloaded. Just as he was setting himself to fire a second round, Atlanta rushed to him and grabbed his arm. The shot went wild.

"Go after him, Maggie!" Atlanta cried.

Maggie cast a forlorn glance of farewell toward her mother, then sprang onto Raven and bolted in the direction Maukin had taken Ian.

James easily broke free from Atlanta's grasp and flung her viciously to the ground. The gun shook in his hand as he glowered like a crazed animal at his wife.

For one of the few times in her life, Atlanta trembled with fear. But she directed a cold, penetrating stare at her husband.

"Would you kill me, James?" she said softly. "Or your own daughter? Has your madness gone that far?"

The shots had been heard, and by this time a small group of locals were straggling down the path to investigate. The surprise was evident on their faces finding Lady Atlanta lying on the ground with the laird above her holding a gun. Realizing the delicacy of his position, given the local tendency toward gossip, James hastened to explain that the fugitive who had killed Master Falkirk had dared to show his face and that he had frightened him off. No one thought of questioning the laird, although not a few wondered to themselves why they had heard the sound of two horses.

Atlanta silently rose as the group disbanded, saying nothing—for she could hardly refute her husband's word in public. She was only glad that Maggie and Ian had escaped safely and soon would be out of danger for good. How fortunate it was that James knew nothing of their plans!

4   A Knife in the Night

Raven and Maukin galloped through that entire night, carrying their masters faithfully despite their exhaustion. The few stops for rest were all too brief before their riders once more urged them on. For another day Ian and Maggie continued their urgent flight, stopping to sleep but twice, and even then only for an hour or two.

Ian was sullen and morose. Maggie tried to bring back his merriment, but her efforts proved useless. He refused to say what was troubling him.

"I just have to think," he had insisted.

"But can't you tell me, Ian?" Maggie pleaded. "I am your wife now."

"I can't talk about it, that's all. I just can't! I have to work it out myself."

Finally she stopped pressing him.

On the second evening out, just as the sun was setting, they stopped the haggard horses and dismounted. For the first time in days Ian looked at Maggie. He suddenly saw how pale she had grown. Dark circles outlined her lovely eyes.

"Oh, my Maggie!" he said. "I'm sorry. It's been thoughtless of me to push you so hard, as tired as you are."

"I'm fine," she replied, trying to smile. But in truth she had never been more exhausted in her life. Twice she had nearly fallen asleep in the saddle.

"We'll stay here tonight," he said. "We've covered enough ground to relax somewhat. No one's after us."

A small search revealed a secluded spot some hundred feet from the roadside, nestled among the trees. The ground was soft with fallen leaves, though moist from a shower the day before, but rain did not appear likely tonight. They spread out the blankets Queenie had provided, and brought out a half-eaten loaf of bread, several oatcakes, a round of cheese, and the last of two bottles of wine—all of which had also been graciously provided by the innkeeper. They enjoyed their dinner greatly; if not the most luxurious they had partaken of in their lives, at least one of the most appreciated. The two horses munched peacefully at what grass they could find, as if they too sensed that this stop would be a little longer than the others.

At length, darkness having fallen in earnest, Maggie lay out on one of the blankets and stretched to her full length. "This *is* nice!" she said dreamily. And scarcely had the words parted her lips before she was sound asleep. Ian gently laid two more blankets over her. The night was chilly and a steady breeze whistled through the trees. Perhaps they should have sought out an inn, but Ian judged it better that they not take that risk. Especially with Aberdeen so close, then America, and their freedom!

Yet what good would it be if Maggie became sick? he argued with himself. *What good was anything?* he thought with despair.

In those days of silence, his tormented mind had not given him a moment's peace. He was beginning to hate himself as he never had before. He had *run* from James Duncan! Like a coward, he had left two women to defend him, and he had *run away*! The mere memory made him recoil in shame.

Yet his cowardly flight was not the only memory gnawing at him. For as he had galloped away in terror, the thought had driven itself into his brain that James had won, after all. In his panic the conviction shouted out to him that Maggie would stay with her father. She would realize she had married a hopeless weakling, unable even to speak like a man to her father. When he had looked back to see his new wife riding up behind him, he had actually found himself surprised. And thus what troubled him more than anything was the simple fact that he had not believed in Maggie. He had forgotten how strong she was.

Ian lay down next to Maggie and put his arm around her as if to protect her from the cold—the only danger he had any power against. Tossing and turning in the confused corners of his tired mind, he soon fell into a deep sleep.

A sharp cry pierced the night, and Ian started awake. His protective arm was no longer around Maggie, and his shoulder ached, for it had been pressed against a rock underneath him. Groggily he rubbed it, then lay his head back down, forgetting the cry as if it had been part of some hazy dream.

But again a terrified scream rent the air and this time Maggie's voice pulled Ian fully to his senses.

"Maggie!" he yelled, turning around where he lay.

A huge form hovered over her. Ian could see the gleam of steel in the darkness. He sprang on the enemy with a howl, knocking the man away from his prey. Maggie leapt to safety while the two men rolled on the ground, the crude knife looming inches from Ian's throat. Whoever the man was, his intent was clearly evil, and he would stop at nothing short of the death of his antagonist.

With all the might he could muster, Ian held the murderous weapon at bay. Somehow he forced the attacker onto his back, then smashed the wrist of the hand holding the knife against the ground. At last the man's grip loosened and the knife fell to the ground. Unconsciously Ian relaxed momentarily and the attacker quickly seized the advantage, sending his fist into Ian's face. Stunned, Ian staggered backward. The man bent down to look for the knife, caught its gleam in the moonlight, and reached for it. His hand never reached its target, however. With a dull groan he fell backward from the weight of Ian's booted foot in his midsection. Crying in pain, his hand sought his two cracked ribs, then he lumbered forward like an angry wounded bear. But Ian had followed the line of the man's hand to the knife and now held the treacherous weapon. Not seeing the advantage his enemy held, the man threw himself toward Ian, and the knife sliced his arm.

"Bastard!" he yelled, then tore off into the shadows.

Ian took two steps after him, then stopped. He turned and sought Maggie where she stood alone in the darkness, sobbing with terrified relief.

"Maggie, my dear!" Ian cried, enveloping her in his embrace. He shuddered at the thought of what might have happened. Hardly realizing that he had saved her life, he could only berate himself that he had not waked sooner.

At length Maggie's panic eased and she found her voice.

"It was him, Ian," she said in tremulous tone. "The man from before. That voice! I would know it anywhere—it had to be him!"

"Oh, God!" wailed Ian. In the seconds since the attack, he had hoped the man was nothing but a passing vagrant, a thief, or marauder passing along this same road. But Maggie's words confirmed what he had been afraid of all along: they had been followed, and by the man who had already attacked her once, on the very grounds of Stonewycke. If it was indeed Falkirk's money he sought, he would try again, and again. He would not leave them alone until he had it. And even then, would their lives be safe?

He must get Maggie away from this place! Far away! But he groaned within himself at the conflict in his heart. For now he knew a decision must be made, a decision Maggie would never willingly accept. Yet he knew it was the decision he must make if he would be the man he longed to be.

5   A Change in Plans

Maggie tried to focus on Ian's words, but her mind screamed out against them.

"...*Alone*..." She heard nothing else he had said. Riding along the quiet road late the next morning, it seemed as if the terrors of the night were far behind them. She would have no fear as long as he was beside her. But now he was telling her he couldn't be there.

"Don't you see?" he had just stated. "I can't run anymore."

"You said we would both go away together until we were out of danger," Maggie argued.

"I know ... *I know*!" he replied, his voice revealing the strain from the decision he felt compelled to make. "But I despise myself for running from your father. What kind of man—what kind of a husband is such a coward?" The muscles in his neck rippled with tension, and there was an emptiness in his tone and bearing.

"Ian, please don't say that. You're not a coward. My father had a gun!"

"But *you* faced him. You ran at him—to save me."

"You would have done the same," she replied with urgent tone. "And you stood up to that awful man last night."

"Maggie," he said, paying little heed to her arguments, "I had no choice last night. And maybe I could stand up to your father now. Anyway, I would rather he kill me than to run again."

"Ian, how can you say that?"

"Try to understand. I have to learn to be a man, to stand on my own two feet, to face what comes at me—to face your father."

"What does all that matter, Ian? As long as we are together, the opinion of my father means nothing."

"Maggie," said Ian in a more thoughtful tone, "there was a time when I tried to bring derision on my name. I hated it. I hated my father, my family. I suppose I hated myself, too. But it's different now. Since meeting you, something has risen within me—a pride, a self-respect. For your sake—and for my own sake too—I must restore the integrity of my name ... of who I am. I cannot be a coward. I have to face whatever comes squarely—like a man."

Maggie was silent. There was no other sound in the morning than the gentle clop-clop-clop of the hooves of the two horses on the hard-packed dirt road.

At length she reached over toward Ian and placed her hand on his arm where he rode beside her.

"Ian," she said, "I am proud of you. You *are* a man—a good man—a strong man. We can face this—together! If you want to stay until you are cleared, I'll stay with you. If you want to go, I'll go with you. But please, don't send me on without you. I can't bear it."

"There's no other way. I am afraid for you. Your life is in danger."

"If I'm with you, I won't be afraid of anything."

"I'm your husband now, Maggie. I must protect you. And getting you away from here is the safest thing. We know one man followed us. There could be others. What if your father—"

"Oh, Ian!"

"It's the only way, Maggie. If that man finds you, he will kill you. I can't let you stay here after what happened last night."

"Then come with me," Maggie pleaded, "like we planned!"

"No, Maggie. I have to clear my name. Please try to understand. I *must* restore my honor. Besides you, all I have left is the integrity of what I stand for. All my life I've amounted to nothing. Now I'm accused of a murder I don't even know if I committed. If my life is to mean anything, if my love for you is to mean anything, then I have to stay until my name is cleared. There is nothing a man has left but his honor."

"But isn't our love just as important?"

"Maggie," insisted Ian, "I won't expose you to danger because of me. I must know that you are safe. Then I have to face this alone."

"Oh, Ian," begged Maggie, "don't do this to me. Don't leave me alone!"

Ian focused his eyes straight ahead, fighting within himself to control the tears and the screaming agony in his soul. How he wanted to find some way to avoid inflicting this pain on the one he loved so dearly! Yet in the depths of his heart he was still driven by another fear which he could not tell Maggie, and barely could face himself: that if Maggie did remain behind, somehow James would find a way to wrest her from him—or kill them both trying.

"It's the only way," he said, swallowing hard and closing his eyes to shut back the tears of desperation. "And you will not be alone. Drew Mackinaw will be there to help you until I come. Hector says Drew has been longing to see someone from the homeland for ten years. He knows he will be anxious to open his home to us and put us up until we are settled on our own. He gave me a letter to take to him."

"I've never even met Drew Mackinaw."

"Maggie, you're from Stonewycke. That's all that matters. They will welcome you as family."

"But—"

"And I will be there before you realize it! Almost before you set foot in New York a month from now, I'll be getting ready to board the next ship. We'll be apart a month or two at the most!"

"If I stayed with you, I could help," insisted Maggie.

"No, my Maggie. It's too risky. Please—trust me. It's only because I love you."

"Two months, and no longer?" she questioned, evoking a promise.

"No longer," he replied with more confidence than his sickened heart felt certain of. "You take the train up to Chatham, stay with the Mackinaws until the next ship arrives, and I will be there to meet you. Think of it, Maggie—America! A new life for us!"

"It will seem like forever," she replied, still far from convinced about her husband's optimistic words.

"But it won't be forever," he said. "The time will pass so quickly you'll hardly realize we're apart."

He drew Maukin up close to Raven, stretched out his arm and pulled Maggie gently toward him. He leaned over and kissed her as the two horses walked peacefully side by side. Then he released her and they rode along together in silence.

Maggie wiped her face, looked toward Ian, and forced a smile, but a vague apprehension still lingered in her eyes.

6 Aberdeen

It was another day to Aberdeen. Their stops continued brief, and though Maggie dozed occasionally Ian never once allowed himself to sleep. His mood vacillated between carefree joviality and intense disquietude; the spirit Maggie had seen in him when first he came to Scotland gave way to the opposite melancholy half of his personality.

Twice on the road he had sensed they were being followed. But try as he might, without giving away his suspicions and alarming Maggie, he could never gain a clear sight of anyone tracking them. Eventually they reached the city without incident.

Darkness had closed in upon the streets by the time of their arrival, and the sound of their horses' hoofbeats echoed crisply into the stillness of the night. They easily located an inn, but they could not make time stand still; morning arrived too soon for a couple dreading their parting.

Ian had slept fitfully, never escaping the gnawing anxiety that all was not well. When they descended the staircase for breakfast, the innkeeper casually mentioned a stranger who had arrived in the middle of the night.

"But I gave the two o' ye my last room," he said, "so I had t' send the bloke away. Dinna ken why folk canna arrive at a decent hour o' the evenin'."

Ian was relieved Maggie had not heard these words, and that she did not comment on his restiveness. He could hardly eat and continued to glance about nervously. When breakfast was over Ian rushed Maggie to the waiting horses, anxious to complete the final leg of their journey to the dock before anything could happen to stop them. When they arrived, passengers were already mounting the gang plank while seamen busily hoisted the riggings, loaded luggage and stores onto the deck, and made the final preparations for departure.

Suddenly Maggie thrust her hand into the pocket of her cloak and realized her mother's envelope was missing. This couldn't be! It had been in her pocket constantly since the night she and Ian had left to be married.

"Ian ... it's gone!" she exclaimed as her hand frantically searched the empty pocket.

"What?" asked Ian in the detached tone of one whose mind is on other matters.

"The envelope. My mother gave it to me before I left," she answered. "It's not here. I took it out for a moment at the inn, just to look at it. I thought I put it back in my coat. Perhaps it fell out somewhere in the room. I have to go back for it."

"But the ship is ready to sail!" replied Ian, forcing his attention now on this new crisis.

"I have to have it! Mother said it was important."

"I'll go," said Ian.

He mounted Maukin and wheeled her around.

"Ian," cried Maggie. "Hurry! I can't leave without it ... nor without seeing you. Hurry!"

Ian dug his heels into the mare's sides and galloped off through the streets, hounded by a growing sense of foreboding. But his fears proved groundless. He easily found the packet on the floor beside the bed. He caught it up quickly, flew back down the stairs three at a time, and ran across the inn's common room to the door. He hastened toward Maukin, and almost instantly felt a pair of eyes on his back. Yet he forced himself forward, never once betraying the stab of dread which hit him.

Maggie had climbed the gang plank for a better vantagepoint. Most of the passengers had boarded, and from all indications the crew's final preparations for departure were underway. She paced back and forth anxiously.

Ian, where are you? She couldn't sail without seeing him. The packet hardly mattered now. She had to hold him in her arms once more and feel his reassurance that this was indeed the best way. Something inside still shouted out to her that she should refuse to go. Even as a child she had always made up her own mind, never letting people tell her what to do. But however strong her doubts, he had been so insistent that this was best. She had to hear once more his promise that they would again be together in two months.

The final call for passengers to board was given.

Oh, Ian, Maggie thought, *where are you? Please come!*

"Miss!" one of the sailors yelled. "I've got my orders t' pull away the plank. Are ye stayin' or goin'?"

"Please," Maggie answered, "just another moment."

Her eyes strained down the dirt street she and Ian had come down only a short time ago. All about the dock there remained a bustle of activity, though by now all the passengers were on board.

She alone remained—uncertain, staring over the crowd into the maze which was Aberdeen.

Oh, Ian ... why don't you come?

Ian hesitated momentarily when the stranger called his name. Then without glancing back he broke into a run, raced to Maukin, leapt onto the mare's back, dug his heels into her sides, and galloped off. He did not look back, but heard the immediate flurry of footsteps in quick pursuit.

His impulse was to race directly for the dock. But he could not bring the danger there. Maggie's safety remained foremost in his mind. If this was indeed the man whose dagger sought to end her life, he must not let him near her.

Instead, he wheeled Maukin to the right, through a short street, then left, across a broad thoroughfare, down several blocks, right again into a deserted alley, out the far end, and left. Back and forth through the unfamiliar streets he raced, desperately hoping to elude his pursuer.

At length he stole a backward glance over his shoulder. It appeared he was not being followed—for the moment at least. Now if only he could find the pier in time. He turned toward the sea and sped in that direction, not daring to slow his pace. He remained oblivious to obstacles, wagons, other riders, and passersby and allowed Maukin every inch of the wild freedom she desired. As he came in view of the dock his heart gave a leap: the ship was still anchored firm! Still he did not slow his frenzied ride until he nearly collided with a loaded vegetable wagon.

Reaching the edge of the gathered crowd, he hastily dismounted and flailed through on foot. His eyes darted back and forth until he saw her standing peering in a different direction. She had been looking elsewhere and had not yet seen him.

She spotted the mare first. Then she heard Ian's shout.

"Maggie!" he cried.

She rushed down the empty gangplank, heedless of the warnings of the sailors who had been trying to urge her aboard. She was only aware of her husband's outstretched arms; she cared for nothing else until they were firmly around her.

"Ian," she said, "I was so afraid . . ."

"It's all right now, my little Maggie," he said, trying to calm her, as he handed her the envelope. Yet both were painfully aware that their hurried words could never convey the depth of the feelings hidden in their hearts.

"Ian . . . there's so much I want to say—so much I want to give you."

"We will have time," Ian reassured. "But it will have to wait. We must just hold on to the promise of the future."

With her head pressed against his chest, Maggie could tell Ian had been riding hard. But she asked him no questions; neither did he tell her of the man outside the inn. They only remained locked in each other's silent embrace.

At last the moment came.

In the background rose the urgent cries of the seamen. Still Maggie wanted to scream, "No, I can't leave you . . . I won't go!"

But this bitter parting was Ian's wish. There was danger at home, and this was the course he had chosen. He was now her husband; from the very beginning she had known she was willing to sacrifice all for him. This, then, would be her sacrifice of affection for the man she loved. And she must do it joyfully, leaving the memory of a smiling face in Ian's heart.

She gazed deeply into his brown eyes one last time, then held her face up and kissed his lips. He returned the kiss fervently, squeezed her close once more, then released her and choked out the words, "It's time for you to go."

"Ian . . ."

"Two months," he said, forcing a cheery smile reminiscent of old. "I'll be on the next ship."

Reluctantly Maggie took her place on the ship's deck as Ian slowly descended the gangplank. She stood clutching the rail until her hand ached, and watched as Ian dragged his sleeve across his brow. She knew his tears were flowing as were hers.

Suddenly she felt the movement of the ship, its first jerky motions causing her insides to lurch in one final moment of uncertain anguish. Gradually it moved away from the dock. She tried to call out, but her husband's name caught in her throat. Words were no longer possible. Thoughts were no longer possible . . . save the one piercing realization that he was slipping farther and farther away.

At last she could bear the torment of his gradually shrinking figure no longer. The ship was out of the harbor now and gathering speed. She would rather remember his face standing there reaching out to her than to see it fade slowly into oblivion. She turned away from the rail. Immediately she wheeled around and ran back. A glimpse—any glimpse—was better than nothing at all!

The crowd had now become but a distant blur. To one side she saw a horse speeding away from the pier, leading another which had no rider. Ian's face was nowhere to be seen.

At last she turned away, walked to the bow of the ship, and cast her eyes out toward the open sea and what lay ahead.

7 Capture

Standing on the dock, Ian stared after the retreating ship. The desolate gray of the sea suited his mood, but he was scarcely aware of it. Already the crowds had begun to disperse and the crew of longshoremen were hard at work lugging several giant crates from the pier.

Still he remained transfixed, gazing after the ship as if somehow his intensity might bring it back. He could just barely make out what seemed to be a single figure standing on the ship's deck. Was it his imagination, or was it returning his wave?

At length, when the ship had receded into the distance, appearing the size of a child's toy, he turned, mounted Maukin, took Raven's reins in his free hand, and said, "Come on, you two, it's time to go."

If Ian Duncan had ever known tragedy in his life, he had faced it with a hard laugh and a cynical sneer. But in the mere three months since he had come to Scotland, he had learned that life could be sweet, and with that realization the hard veneer which many had thought to be his true personality had been stripped away. He hadn't known, however, that happiness and sorrow were reverse sides of the same emotion. With the joy had also come an inroad for pain, for the greater one's joy, the greater the capacity for sorrow. Hence, when the painful tragedy had assailed him, it had come so suddenly that there had been no time for him to pull his protective shield around him. As his heart opened to the joy of love, so too he had become vulnerable to the devastation of loss and heartache. Now, the strength and determination he had possessed only a short time ago slowly drained from him. For all his confidence and reassuring words to Maggie, he wondered how he could go on. Half his being and all his soul had disappeared over the horizon on that ship.

Oh, Maggie! Why did I let you go?

He shook his head as the reality of the truth dawned upon him. *I did not let you go; I made you go,* he thought. *How could I have been such a fool!*

He rode aimlessly from the dock, hardly caring in which direction he proceeded. He had formulated no plan to free himself and restore his honor, as he had told Maggie he would do. On he rode, letting Maukin determine his direction while his mind wandered equally at random. Storekeepers were setting out their wares on the sidewalks, shoppers were beginning to gather for the morning's activity, children were darting in and out of open doors.

But Ian was only vaguely cognizant of the city's bustle.

Maggie was gone!

Yes, they were going to meet again in two months—everything had been arranged. But that hope seemed all too tenuous to him, like a man grasping at a branch to keep him from falling over a cliff. The branch might break at any time, and what then? For what purpose had he stayed behind in Scotland? To restore his integrity? What honor was possible when even he could not be certain he *was* innocent! The night of the murder was still a horrible blur in his mind, and he looked down at his wounded hand—another reminder. It was healing now, and Queenie's fears that he would lose two of his fingers were unfounded. But the wound called out to him again and again, reminding him he could not recall where the gash had come from. *Could he have had another fight with Falkirk?* What if this second fight had involved a weapon which had cut his hand and fatally wounded Falkirk? Surely he would be able to remember such a thing—surely! But he had been drinking...

Dear God! The words caught like bile in his throat. There could be no God. It was all a cruel joke, a twisted irony with him at its center. The world was mad!

Yes, he thought, *perhaps I could have murdered that night.* But Maggie's father would have been the more likely victim. For did not James Duncan stand irredeemably at the core of his pain? He had forced Ian and Maggie apart and had threatened to kill him. James had tried to manipulate their lives as if they were mere pawns in his grand business schemes. He was no doubt at this very moment plotting further how he might destroy his own daughter's husband.

But you won't touch Maggie, thought Ian grimly. *She is out of your reach now. And although I may have lost her too, for a while, at least you won't turn her love for me away.* In his misery Ian, even after she had left her beloved homeland for him, sorely underestimated Maggie's love for him. Her very act of obedience in leaving her dear home stood as everlasting proof that she placed her love for her husband above whatever affection may have remained for her father. But Ian had no way of grasping the depth of such a love, for in all his twenty years never had such devotion been expressed toward *him*. No wonder, then, that he could little understand such a giving and sacrificial love.

Ian continued on through the town, so absorbed in his thoughts that he took no particular notice of the three horsemen approaching him. One of the three cut sharply in front of him, bringing him up short; Maukin reared in alarm. Ian pulled in the rein, brought her under control, and then stared at the riders with a gaze which registered neither emotion nor question. He recognized none of them. They were dressed in coarse woolens and wore wide-brimmed hats and heavy coats.

"Ye be Theodore Duncan?" asked the man who had directed his horse to cut in front of Ian. His voice was gruff with the tone of one who was tired and most likely hungry. "That right?"

"Yes," answered Ian.

"I'm the constable up Strathy way, Tom Lancaster. Ye led us a merry chase this mornin'. But 'tis o'er now."

Ian had all but forgotten his frantic ride through the city trying to elude the stranger who had tried to accost him at the inn. Now he recognized that this was the very same man.

"What happened to Duff?" asked Ian, dull fear rising to panic within him.

"Seems the laird thought it time fer him to be thinkin' o' retirin'," Lancaster replied. "Too old t' do his job properly's how I heard it. But I'm none too old, ye see, an' I don't plan on retirin' fer a good long time. So ye jist come along wi' us nice an' peaceable."

"What—what for?" asked Ian, knowing all too well the man's mission. Again James Duncan's hand had reached out toward him. Suddenly he realized that with Maggie gone, James could do anything he pleased. He would have no more strength to resist the man if he did not take it now. Without waiting for an answer to his question, he let go of Raven's rein, jerked Maukin's head around, and dug in his heels. But the constable's two men were on the watch, drew up the same instant, and wrenched Maukin's reins from his hands.

"I was hopin' ye'd be a reasonable man," said Lancaster.

"You can't do this!" cried Ian. "You have no proof against me! Duff knew that, and let me go."

"Well, Duff's not the constable anymore. An' since I came to the job, I've uncovered new evidence."

Lancaster paused for effect, then went on. "Seems we found the murder weapon—right where his lordship was killed. Guess Duff's failin' eyesight o'erlooked it. 'Twas a real handsome-lookin' dirk too." Lancaster fumbled in one of his saddlebags for a moment, and finally withdrew a jewel-handled dagger. He held it toward Ian triumphantly while an evil grin spread over his face.

Ian stared in disbelief. It was his own knife. His father had given it to him years ago. The best one, the family heirloom, had of course gone to his brother. But though only a cheap copy, Ian had nevertheless treasured this knife and had discovered it missing shortly before he and Maggie had left Stonewycke. Then he shuddered—the tip of the knife was stained with dried blood.

"Well, I can see, Mr. Duncan," Lancaster continued, "without yer sayin' a word, that ye hae seen this afore."

"What are you planning to do with me?" asked Ian coldly.

"Why, I thought ye knew, lad," replied Lancaster with a laugh. "I'm puttin' ye under arrest. I'll be takin' ye to the choky here in Aberdeen, since there's no jail in Strathy. Ye made my job a bit easier in comin' here yersel' so I can forgive ye fer givin' me the slip this mornin'." Again he laughed, this time without restraint, joined by his two companions. "Abner," he directed one of the other men, "I think ye better tie Mr. Duncan's hands behind him." Then he looked back at Ian. "Jist so ye don't get any more ideas aboot diggin' yer heels into that frolicksome mare o' yers."

Abner did his deed. He yanked the rope tight, apparently enjoying his assignment, until the cords cut into Ian's wrists.

Ian offered no resistance. James Duncan had indeed won, after all. It was useless to fight against a man whose power was so vast it even controlled the law. Submissively he sat while they turned and led him back toward the middle of Aberdeen.

Maggie! he cried out inside. *Maggie, I'm so sorry. But how could I ask you to spend your life with a murderer? At least this way you are safe.*

Ian's heart sank, and any last hope that things would work out died within him. For what hope was possible now but a belief in a power greater than the futility of this life? And Ian no longer possessed any such belief.

8   Mid-Sea

Maggie drew in deep gulps of the tangy salt air. For three days she had remained cabinbound with violent seasickness. Longing for fresh air, this morning she had forced herself out of her bunk and dragged herself onto the deck. But she could hardly keep her feet under her, and the gentle swaying back and forth of the ship in rhythm with the swelling sea was more than her queasy stomach could handle.

She had been fine at first. The voyage to London was uneventful, and the seas were calm around and through the channel and westward. Six days out of Brighton they had encountered a brief but blustery autumn squall; the ship had pitched about unmercifully, and she had been unable to recover. When the captain had looked in on her last night, she had asked how long the storm would go on.

"Why, we left that little tempest behind yesterday morning, my lady!" Captain Sievers laughed. "Why, we haven't begun to see anything like a real storm yet!" Noting the dismay on Maggie's face, and recalling that the purpose of his visit was to console his young passenger, he hastily added, "But no doubt we'll avoid any others completely, so you need not worry yourself."

This morning the sea did seem somewhat gentler. But whatever the change, it apparently had no effect on her tormented stomach. She had scarcely eaten in three days and even the captain had grown concerned.

But today she would fight this thing. With determination she gripped the cold metal railing until her knuckles were white, repeatedly breathing in deep draughts of the healthy sea air as if it were a medicine she had been ordered to take. Her mind cast up rumors she had heard of people dying on such voyages, but she was not going to be one of them! *Oh, Lord, please, I'm not ... I refuse ...* A new wave of nausea assailed her and she lurched over the rail in silent agony.

A few minutes later Maggie raised her eyes and tried to focus on the horizon. Everywhere was the sea, in all directions. *Oh, Ian,* she thought, *why did we part?* She had to stay healthy, for soon she would see him again! The handsome visage of her husband rose before her face—his laughing brown eyes and tender lips and disarming smile. The hint of an involuntary smile crossed her mouth as she recalled their first meeting. How his brash impudence had galled her! But he had been able to make her laugh at the same time. He had opened his troubled heart to her, and taught her to open herself in return. Together they had grown, and discovered strengths and a love neither could have believed possible.

How I need you, Ian! Maggie thought. Yet as the very thought formed, the nightmare of her departure from Scotland flooded through her like the remembrance of a half-forgotten dream. How could such horrors happen? The murder ... the man who had attacked them in the forest ... having to part from the man she loved? Yet all dimmed beside the treachery of her father's contemptuous outburst. His incensed threats against Ian made her shudder. What wellsprings of maniacal self-centeredness could cause any man to so hate his own flesh and blood?

Perhaps Ian was right, leaving Scotland was the only way. But she would never forgive her father for making it come to this!

Then out from the depths of the past crept that old gnawing uncertainty, the question that had so often plagued her. *What did I do to make you hate me so?*

"I see you're coming a bit more to yourself, my lady." Captain Sievers' resonant voice drew her back to the present. His eyes, above sun-reddened cheeks, smiled, revealing deep crows' feet at the corners of each.

Maggie turned, relieved to be diverted from her melancholy thoughts. "I'm trying." Her voice was thin and weak.

"Well, you're still a bit pale, but you look a mite less green about the gills, as we say on the sea. I'll wager by tonight you will be able to join me at my table for dinner."

The mere thought of food brought Maggie's stomach halfway back up her throat. She forced a smile and said, "Thank you, Captain. I'll make my best effort."

"Don't feel you're alone in your misery, my lady," Sievers went on cheerfully. "Why, I remember my first voyage. I was but twelve, and stowed away in the hull of a clipper bound for the Barbados. I don't know which is worse during a storm, to be up top-mast or down in the belly of the ship. But at the time I was sure it was the latter. Finally, I didn't care if they hung me up by my thumbs—anything was worth the risk of a breath of fresh air. I crawled up on deck and was nearly washed overboard by a wave which crashed over the starboard side right at that moment."

"But you stayed with the sea?"

"I got better about a week later and figured it would be foolish to throw away all that agony for nothing. And besides, I'd always loved the sea. It gets under your skin, you know."

"I do know what you mean," said Maggie, warming to the captain's enthusiastic manner.

"Do you, now?" Sievers replied, leaning forward on the rail and giving his stubbly beard a scratch, fully interested in any tale this young lass might have to share with him.

"I live—that is, I used to live by the sea," began Maggie. But before she could go on she felt warm tears rising in her eyes. She turned her gaze back to the open sea. The pain was still too raw. Maybe in time she would be able to talk about her homeland again with composure. But today she could say no more.

"Whereabouts was that, my lady?"

"I'm sorry, Captain—I'm afraid I'm not feeling very well. I think I had better return to my cabin and lie down." Maggie turned and hurried away without awaiting further response.

Would she ever be able to think of her wild and rocky seashore again, or see the heather bloom, or look into the face of a lovely yellow primrose ... How Ian had loved them!

Dear God, she wept into her pillow, *how can I do this thing? Everything I love is in Scotland! Why must I leave? Why couldn't you help us?*

Maggie did not make it to the captain's table for dinner that evening, and for two more days lay on her bunk. Even death, it seemed, had to be better than the misery of the constantly pitching ship. On the ninth day of the voyage she emerged from her cabin again, noticeably thinner and her face drawn and pale. But her nerves had quieted down and the hint of an appetite sent occasional stabs of hunger rumbling through the empty cavities of her stomach. The thought of solid food was for the first time in nearly a week an appealing notion.

If only her heart might heal as quickly! But in her mind she could find no peace, not even in the joyous prospect of her reunion with Ian. For there was always the fear—though she fought against it whenever it threatened to take shape in her mind—the fear that something would go wrong.

9   Chatham

New-fallen snow lay in drifts against the little farmhouse. Staring out the kitchen window, Maggie could not help wondering if the first snows of winter had yet fallen in Port Strathy. Right after a snowstorm was one of the few times the massive stone towers of Stonewycke could be truly beautiful.

Winter had come early to Chatham, the little village in eastern New York where Maggie's journey had come to an end. Snow did not usually fall until after Thanksgiving, the townsfolk said; this year it was already ankle-deep with the autumn holiday still two days away. But the weather was of little consequence to Maggie. Let it snow, let it rain, let the wind blow, let it do whatever it liked, just as long as it did not keep Ian from arriving on schedule!

She herself had arrived only three weeks ago. How intimidated she felt the moment she first stepped off the ship in the vast harbor of New York City! How different the people sounded, how fast everything moved—and not a single familiar face. But at least the ground was not moving under her feet! She had recovered from her seasickness; fortunately, Captain Sievers had been right and they had encountered no more stormy weather. Nevertheless, the journey had not been an altogether pleasant one, and she was relieved it was over.

What she would have done had it not been for the assistance of the cab driver, she didn't know. An old man with a cherry-pie face and a broad, toothy grin, his mission, it seemed, was to help foreign strangers get over their initial fears after setting foot in America, the great land of promise. Taking the uncertainty on Maggie's face as a challenge, he stepped toward her, assisted her with her things, and within moments had won over a new friend. He took her to a respectable boarding house, with whose mistress he was apparently on good terms, helped her make arrangements for travel to Chatham by train, and investigated for her the timetable for all future arrivals in the harbor from England. She breathed a deep sigh and smiled her thanks. Just knowing that information was all the world to her!

Maggie was in such a daze from the rapid flow of events that it was not until the following morning that she realized she did not even know the man's name. Too weak from the effects of the sea voyage, she had hardly stopped to consider how it seemed her path had all been prepared for her in advance—everything had progressed as smoothly as clockwork ever since her farewell to Ian on the Aberdeen dock.

Perhaps the most difficult hurdle would be facing the Mackinaws themselves. There had been no time to send word of her arrival, and while Maggie knew very little about them, they knew nothing of her. Drew had been forced to migrate from Scotland some twelve years earlier; three harsh winters and poor harvests in succession had not left enough to feed the mouths on the scraggly Mackinaw homestead on Braenock Ridge. As the eldest of the children, his lot had been to seek a new beginning elsewhere, and he had chosen to do so in America. As Maggie had neared the village of Chatham, she wondered if Drew Mackinaw harbored any resentments toward the lordly family of Stonewycke who knew no want, yet did so little to help the people of the land.

As the train began to slow, Maggie's misgivings rose defiantly to the surface, telling her to stay in her seat and keep riding . . . riding . . . But where else was there to go? As disagreeable as was the idea of imposing upon people she had never met, there were no other options open to her. Therefore, when the clickety-clack of the wheels on the iron rails finally ground to a halt and the shrill whistle blew, Maggie rose from her seat, picked up her belongings, made her way to the door at the front of the passenger car, and then timidly stepped down.

How strange and foreign everything looked! The hilly region probably compared in many ways to her native Scotland, but it was somehow different. She glanced about the small town. There were only a few buildings and not a great deal of activity. Chatham was probably even smaller than Port Strathy, she thought with relief. Just as long as all American cities weren't like New York!

Well, thought Maggie, *here I am. I might as well make the best of it.* She took a deep breath, then walked toward what appeared to be the center of town, if town it could even be called. She passed a feed store, then a livery stable. Most of the activity seemed to be coming from within one building. "S-A-L-O-O-N," Maggie read. "Whatever can that mean? I suppose it could be the proprietor's name," she speculated. "Still, it is a rather odd-sounding name for a store."

At the end of the street, running out of buildings, Maggie walked into a friendly looking establishment whose sign called it a "General Store." A couple of farmers were milling around and chatting with a man behind the counter.

"Howdy, ma'am," he said, leaving his friends and approaching her with a broad smile. "What might I help you with today?"

"I just got off the train," Maggie began. "I'm looking for someone in your town, and I wondered if you might be able to help me."

"I reckon Jeb here knows just about everybody in these parts for miles," put in one of the farmers, nodding toward the owner of the store.

"Well, I'll sure help you if I can, ma'am," said the man they called Jeb. "I been selling goods to the farmers hereabouts for nigh onto twenty year, so I guess I know most of 'em."

"I am looking for the Mackinaws ... Drew Mackinaw."

"Oh, sure, Drew's a good man. Walked into town twelve years ago with nothing to his name but a few dollars and a strong back and willing heart. A good worker, that man. He's built him up a nice place. Lives out yonder, mile east of town, past the bridge over the wash."

"I'm headin' out thataway, ma'am," said the third man, who had not yet spoken. "Drew's my neighbor. Mine's the spread just yonder o' his'n. If you'd be likin' a ride, my wagon's got a heap o' spare room. I just have to load up my supplies here from Jeb; then I'm on my way."

"Why, thank you. Thank you all," said Maggie. "That's very kind of you. Yes, I would like a ride."

Warmed by the genuine hospitality of the three men, Maggie enjoyed the fifteen-minute ride on the bumpy wagon. Her host pointed out all the landmarks he deemed interesting, and by the time he drew rein on his plow horse at the gate to the Mackinaw place, Maggie felt she knew almost as much about the little farming village of Chatham, New York, as she did about her own Port Strathy. When he drew the horses to a stop she descended, thanking him again, and with a carpet bag in one hand and smaller parcels under each arm, Maggie approached the house.

The farmhouse was not exactly what she had anticipated. She had half-expected every dwelling in America to resemble the drawing of the one-room log cabin she had seen in a book one of her childhood tutors had shown her. Instead, the four-room house was constructed from rough-hewn pine, whitewashed and trimmed with brown around the windows. A dozen chickens pecked about in the yard, scattering wildly in all directions as she walked up. Besides the house and barn, there were two or three smaller outbuildings. Had she been able to identify them, she would have known them as a chicken coop, a smokehouse, and a woodshed. Though she knew absolutely nothing about American farming, by Scottish standards at least, humble as the dwelling was, it appeared to be a farm with plentiful provision. In addition to the chickens, Maggie caught evidence of cows, goats, and a few pigs as well. She could not help but compare this sturdy house with the poor one on Braenock Ridge Drew had been born in. It certainly seemed the elder Mackinaw had benefited from his move.

The only train to Chatham came in midafternoon two days a week, and Drew was out in the fields when Maggie arrived. All Maggie's last-minute fears of intruding were quickly dispelled by the greeting she received from Ellie Mackinaw, Drew's wife.

After Maggie's awkward attempt to explain why a stranger was standing on her front porch with bags in hand, the light suddenly seemed to dawn on Ellie's face.

"All the way from Scotland!" she exclaimed. "Why . . . I don't believe—but how. . . ?" she stammered through beaming eyes that sparkled with all the welcome Maggie needed. She placed a strong, loving hand around Maggie's shoulder and drew her inside while Maggie attempted to explain the circumstances as best she could. Ellie's immediate warmth reminded Maggie of Bess Mackinaw, and she could not help noting the coincidence that Drew had married a woman so like his own mother. But the comparison between this American housewife and the mother-in-law she had never seen ended with their warm personalities. Unlike the large-framed, plain-looking Bess, Ellie was short and plump. Soft blue eyes highlighted a pretty face, with creamy skin and full lips that never ceased either smiling or laughing. Ellie had been raised but twenty miles on the other side of the Hudson, high in the Catskill mountains, and was as thoroughly American as Maggie was Scottish.

Immediately Ellie began preparations to find a place for Maggie in their home. The four rooms were spacious, to be sure, but with five children, ranging in age from three to nine, living quarters were already tight. Conscious of Maggie's uncertainty, Ellie simply laughed and said, "Why, with five young'uns running about, you're a gift right from the Lord!"

The home was snug and warm despite the gathering signs of approaching winter. The large potbellied cookstove was the hub of household activity where Ellie spent a good portion of her time. The kitchen opened into a huge room containing a table, a great stone hearth where a fire would be blazing later in the evening, a bench which sat under the only window, and three rockers.

"The children sit on the floor, me and Drew each sit in one of the rockers, and the other one's for a guest," Ellie explained with a smile. "If there's more'n one guest, we make do some other way."

One by one the children made their appearance: Bess, 7, and Darren, 5, from their chores outside; the two older boys, Bobby,

9, and Tommy Joe, 8, home from school; and finally little three-year-old Sarah, wandering in sleepily from her afternoon nap.

Despite her protests against displacing Bobby and Tommy, a little loft above one of the bedrooms was prepared for Maggie's sleeping quarters. The two boys were eager for the opportunity to sleep out in the barn and ran out excitedly to begin their boyish preparations.

When Drew walked in just after sunset, his welcome may have been less exuberant than his wife's, but in no way would it be called less sincere. He was a large hulk of a man with red hair and beard. Young wiry Stevie flashed through Maggie's mind, and she wondered if she were seeing a vision of what he would look like as a full grown man. In many ways Drew resembled old Hector. Quiet and reserved like his father, it seemed to require the greatest part of his bodily energy simply to keep his large frame in motion. And like Hector, Drew was a compassionate man of few words. Had Maggie known of his widespread local reputation for never turning his back on a man or woman or child in any kind of trouble, she would never have spent a moment worrying about her reception into this big man's home.

Maggie's report of Bess Mackinaw's death was the first of it they had heard. Observing the reaction of her loving son, Maggie could not keep herself from weeping. As the color drained from his ruddy cheeks, at first he merely stared blankly ahead, the knuckles of his hand turning white as they gripped the arms of his wooden chair. Back and forth he slowly rocked. The only sound in the somber room was the gentle creaking of the chair on the hardwood floor.

He had known when he had left Scotland that it was unlikely he would ever see any of his family again in this life, and his struggling faith often doubted whether he would see them in the next. Therefore, when the news came, his human heart was torn. At length he heaved himself up and walked outside without a word. Whether he wept or not, no one would ever know. But when he returned an hour later, his voice was husky and strained.

"I'm glad ye were wi' her, my leddy," said Drew. "It means a lot t' be able t' talk wi' one who was there at the last. I'm happy that now we can see our way t' do ye a small favor in return.

Although just havin' ye here in our home is a great pleasure fer us all!"

"I need nothing in return," Maggie replied. "It was a privilege to be with her. She was a special woman. But if there is any other favor I could ask of you, it would be that you simply call me Maggie, and not *my lady*."

"But ye be a leddy, aren't ye, an' not folk like us?"

"This is America, and I am no different than anyone else. I left Scotland and any claim to title behind. In fact, while I am under your roof, it is you who are the master."

The grief seemed to have done its work, and the sorrow had passed. Drew laughed, so deep it rumbled like a roll of thunder.

"Hoots!" he said. "Wouldn't my auld daddy get a chuckle out o' that? His son a laird o'er a Duncan!"

"I'll stay under no other condition," Maggie persisted.

"Well," he agreed at length, "let's just say we are equal an' leave it at that. An' I'll try t' call ye Maggie."

"The Lord is the only master we need in this house, anyway," added Ellie buoyantly.

Her husband tossed her a curious glance as if to say, "Not now, dear." Then he threw another log on the fire and stood staring as it crackled into bright orange flames. Maggie wondered if perhaps Drew had abandoned the faith of his parents when he came to America. But she took no time to dwell on the thought, for it seemed enough that he was warm and kind and had welcomed her, a stranger, into the home of his family with open arms.

Now, three weeks after her arrival, Maggie was jolted from her reverie by the scamper of a light-footed young deer across the fresh meadow of snow. She gave a sigh and turned her eyes from the kitchen window back into the house. Thanks to Ellie's open heart and Drew's generosity, she had been made to feel as much at home as could be expected under the circumstances. The gentle snowflakes again began to fall and the sound of rising activity indicated that breakfast was nearly at hand. *I wonder what Ian is doing now,* Maggie wondered. But of course, he was on the ship. There were only two weeks yet to wait. She hoped he didn't get seasick. But no matter, she would take care of him when he arrived!

"Child," called out Ellie's voice into the midst of her thoughts. "Watching won't make the snow stop, nor make your man get here one day sooner. Besides, the ship will float along with or without the snow."

Maggie turned and smiled. "You read my thoughts, Ellie."

"Well, I know you're thinking of that husband of yours most of the time!" Ellie chuckled.

"But my daydreaming certainly isn't helping much with breakfast, is it?"

"Never you mind about that," said Ellie. "You'll still be our guest, for a little while yet. But if you really want something to do, you can help little Bess with the dishes. They're a mite too heavy for her to carry."

Maggie lifted the stack of plates the youngster was attempting to carry and took them over to the table. Bess, a pale, willowy child of seven, followed with the flatware. The girl's hair was deep auburn like Maggie's; perhaps it was this similarity that had drawn her to their visitor from Scotland. Since Maggie's arrival Bess had been her shadow, following her everywhere. She was a quiet child, her large eyes ever attentive.

As the two set the table, Ellie busily hovered around the cookstove. Suddenly a sharp crackle set the kitchen ablaze with sound as she tossed a handful of bacon ends into a large cast-iron skillet. The fragrance of frying bacon filled the room, but as the pleasing aroma drifted past Maggie it had just the opposite effect it was meant to. The same awful nausea she had experienced on the ship assailed her. She threw her hand over her mouth and dashed outside into the snow. A few moments later, pale and trembling, she returned.

"Good heavens, child!" exclaimed Ellie with a questioning look on her face.

"I must not be quite over the seasickness," Maggie said weakly.

Scrutinizing her, Ellie momentarily forgot the bacon. Then, catching a whiff of burning edges, she quickly returned her attention to the stove, stirred the bacon in the rising grease, then removed it from the heat. Finally she wiped her hands on her apron.

"Maggie," she said, "I doubt that's seasickness."

"What do you mean?"

"When was it you and Ian were married?"

Puzzled, Maggie answered, "About two months ago."

"Dear girl!" Ellie grinned. "You're—"

She stopped suddenly.

"Boys!" she called to her sons who were in the next room. "Go out and tell your pa breakfast is ready."

"All of us?" nine-year-old Bobby protested.

"Yes, all of you. Now scat!"

The three boys grabbed up their coats and marched obediently from the house.

Ellie approached Maggie, took her hand, and led her to a chair at the table. Still grinning from ear to ear, she seemed hardly able to contain the excitement which had suddenly risen within her.

"Dear," she began, "have you ever considered that you may be—in the family way?"

"Family way?" Maggie repeated.

"You know ... with *child*!"

Unable to keep calm a moment longer, Ellie giggled as if she were a girl again and threw her arms about Maggie's neck.

Bewildered, Maggie sat as if in a trance. The thought of being pregnant had never so much as crossed her mind. She tried to open her mouth to speak, but words refused to come. Instead, she felt tears rising in her eyes.

"Why, Maggie," laughed Ellie, "you're going to have Ian's baby!"

Now came the tears in earnest, to both women. And Maggie would not have stopped them even if she could. Her womanly instincts knew that Ellie was right, and she let the tears of joy flow, for this was the first moment of real joy she had felt since she and Ian had been together.

Ellie slackened her embrace, sat back, and smiled radiantly at Maggie.

"I'm so happy for you!" she beamed. "There's nothing more wonderful for a woman—and I should know!"

"Oh, I wonder what Ian will think," said Maggie.

"He'll be delighted," assured Ellie. "What a wonderful gift for you to present to him when he arrives!"

They laughed again, then Ellie said, "Now let's figure out when you're going to be due."

Maggie provided the knowledgeable wife the necessary information, then Ellie spent a few moments counting on her fingers, and finally announced, "July!" Then she added as an afterthought, "Maybe your first child will be born on the Fourth of July—the birthday of our country. That would make him a true American baby!"

Beaming as if the child-to-be were her own, Ellie could hardly keep from sharing her great practical wisdom, and for the first time could see a hint of happiness shining in Maggie's eyes—eyes which till this day had always seemed haunted and sad. Feeling well-satisfied with the turn of the day, Ellie rose and continued with her breakfast chores, singing softly the verses of "Rock of Ages."

Maggie remained at the table in a contented daze. The nausea had passed for the time, and suddenly she felt Ian's presence with her in a way she hadn't since their painful parting on the dock. The words *first child* echoed in her mind. She and Ian would have such a wonderful life here with their children! For the first time since leaving Scotland the hope of a new life seemed actually possible. This life around her seemed so inviting; how could even the title of marquise compare to it? Maybe she and Ian would even out-do the Mackinaws and have six or seven "young'uns" of their own. Lots of children and a cozy farm like this . . . with Ian beside her in his own oak rocker. It was all Maggie had wanted and yearned for.

10   Giles Kellermann

The man stood gazing out his large picture window over the expansive valley of green farmland. On a clear day the slowly moving Hudson River could just be seen in the distance to the west.

In the other direction an afternoon's ride on horseback brought him to the Massachusetts border. It was good land, he thought, and he had done well for himself. It would not be long before he owned a great deal more of it. His name was already prominent in Columbia Country, and if this drought continued another year his dream of occupying a position in Albany's legislature could become a reality. He would by then hold power over a large financial base of prime land. And what he didn't want to keep for himself, he would resell for a handsome profit.

He could hardly believe his good fortune. When he had begun diverting some of his investment capital into mortgages for local farmers, his goal had merely been the high interest he was able to receive on notes for their farms and equipment. Too poor to obtain loans from any bank in the area, many immigrants had seen his Mortgage Company as a way for them to expand, get new tools and equipment, and plant new crops they wouldn't have been able to afford otherwise. Times had been plentiful, hopes ran high, and even though the 7% interest of his terms was almost double the 4¼% being offered by the banks in Hudson, Albany, and Catskill, most of these people had no collateral with which to secure financing any other way than with him. He required no cash investment on the part of the farmers, as the banks did. The poor were more than willing to place whatever they had—homes, livestock, acreage, future profits on crops—on the line in exchange for capital to expand.

But with the drought the bottom had fallen out, and one by one the local farmers had been forced to the painful realization that their visions of prosperity had been only dreams.

A tentative knock on the door to his office interrupted his reverie. He turned, walked across the floor, and opened it. There stood a farmer in his faded blue dungarees with suspenders, plaid workshirt, and heavy worn boots. "I brung you the wagon, Mr. Kellermann," he said with his hat held between both hands. Seeing no response on the face of the man opposite him, he nervously went on, "It's out back. I unhitched the team. But I got t' keep them oxen, Mr. Kellermann. Surely you kin understand. I got t' have 'em or I can't nohow plow my fields."

"Yes, yes, of course, I understand, Homer," said the other, finally speaking but revealing no other sign of communication. "As we agreed, you have another month before the oxen are—well, you understand."

"Yes, sir! And don't you worry, I'll have the money by then. Yes, sir, I'll git it sure!"

"Good, Homer. That's just fine. Now you give my best to your wife."

He closed the door and the farmer slowly walked outside, untied the team of two oxen where they stood at the side of the building, and led them home on foot.

Inside, Kellermann watched Homer Wilson through the window. He didn't like to have to repossess something as small as the poor man's wagon. But business was business, and Wilson was already two payments behind. He could never allow word to get out that he was soft.

At length he went to his desk and sat down. Giles Kellermann carried a frame of average height with dark brown hair, tinged with gray. His build, in his younger days, would have been termed stocky. But the life of comparative ease with which he had accustomed himself had turned him soft, and now instead of athletic he simply had the appearance of one comfortably overweight.

But what arrested one's attention more than his build was the piercing look of his face. His deep-set dark eyes were surrounded by a firm, square face; his mouth, on the rare occasions when it lent itself to a smile, seemed to resist every movement of the exercise. The natural resting place of the facial muscles set the wide mouth and strong chin in a perpetual look of hard-boiled offense. Whether this stern visage, with just a hint of cunning about the corners of the lips, had been physically inherited or had been acquired through years of practice as a crafty businessman would have been difficult to determine.

Kellermann had started his investments in the financial centers of Boston. But competing with men older, wiser, and more unscrupulous than himself had proved too upsetting for his vanity. Realizing he could achieve his ends to greater purpose where he held a superior advantage over those he had to deal with, he migrated westward, working for a brokerage firm in Albany for a time. A brief sojourn south a few years ago had alerted him to the unlimited possibilities for gain among the farming community. When he settled here in Chatham, his coming had at first been viewed by the inhabitants as a godsend. But with the failure of the crops two years ago, they first began to realize how much power they had foolishly given him. By then, of course, it was too late, the documents had been signed.

Another knock on the door followed, but this time the door opened without waiting for Kellermann's answer.

Glancing up, the businessman's face broke, not into a smile, but at least into a sign of recognition.

"Oh, it's you, Harry. What did you find out?"

"Old man Simpson doesn't have a cent to his name. It looks like we'll be moving on his place next month."

"Good! Add it to the auction list. I want to get that list of properties over to Albany by next week. There are some prized plums on it this time. We should get handsome prices. What about the widow Rodman up in New Lebanon?"

"She paid me. Everything, in fact. Two months back interest, and next month's besides."

"Blast it! How'd she come up with that kind of money?"

"Rumor had it some of her friends chipped in. They're really upset around there. They hate us. There's talk of banding together."

"Let the clodhoppers talk!" said Kellermann. "There's nothing any of them can do. They signed the deeds over to me and if they don't pay, the law's with us. By the way, Homer Wilson was by to leave his wagon."

"Fine," said his associate. "I'll take care of it."

"You know I don't like dealing with these people face-to-face, Harry. I don't want you to let this kind of thing happen again."

"I'm sorry. I was going out to Homer's for the wagon this afternoon. I suppose he thought bringing it here himself might make us more sympathetic about his oxen."

"Yes, he did mention them. And I can be as sympathetic as the next guy, as long as he keeps up the payments on his loan. And what about that Scottish fellow?"

"Mackinaw?"

"Yes, Mackinaw."

"He has some time left."

"But what does it look like?"

"He's not doing well. His should fall in time, like the others."

"Good. That farm of his is a choice piece. I want it. And I'd like to get rid of him anyway. That phoney accent of his drives me crazy. He's been nothing but a nuisance, always taking people in, trying to help them. It goes against what we're trying to do. Things will run a lot more smoothly when he's gone."

"They've just brought in someone else from what I hear."

"Who?" asked Kellermann.

"I don't know," answered Harry. "I'll try to find out. Someone said it was a noble lady from Scotland."

"Just so long as she doesn't get any ideas about making his payments for him. Find out what you can, Harry. We need to be ahead of him on this. We can't take any chances on getting his acreage."

"I'll see what I can find out. In the meantime, I think it might be a good idea for you to talk with him, sir."

"Why?"

"I've been out there a few times, for payments, half-payments, and so on. He's none too cordial with me."

"You expect him to be cordial when we're about to repossess his farm?"

"The folks hereabouts don't like me none too much since I went to work for you, Mr. Kellermann."

"Do you want to be liked or rich, Harry?"

"I just think Mackinaw could be a problem, if it gets into his mind to challenge you. He's pretty highly thought of. He could raise the rest of the folks around here. So I thought if you talked to him—firmly and decisively—it might lay any ideas he might have to rest. I think he'd be afraid of you if you really laid it down to him."

"I understand, Harry. I'll talk to him and we'll make him see the futility of trying to fight us on this. He either pays or he's off the land."

11 The Long-Awaited Day

It was all Maggie could do to still herself long enough for Ellie to offer thanks for the breakfast.

". . . and now, Lord," Ellie was praying, "we ask that you watch over us while we travel down to the big city, and bless Drew and the children till we get back. And thank you, Lord, for your bounty and provision in this food you have given us. Amen."

The day had finally come!

Somehow the interminable weeks had passed; now it seemed it had not been so long after all! And in one hour she and Ellie would board the train which would take her to New York and—

Oh, the thought was too wonderful!

"I declare, Maggie, you're in another world!" laughed Ellie.

"I know," beamed Maggie. "I'm sorry. I just can't concentrate on anything else. I've forgotten everything you've said these last couple days and—"

"No need to apologize, dear. We all understand. We're excited about Ian's coming, too. Have you considered Allen Smith's offer of his springhouse for the two of you?"

"Oh, yes," Maggie replied. "I'm sure it would be perfect. It's so kind of him."

"Nothin' fancy," Drew added, "I mean, fer the likes o' ye an' yer gentleman husband. 'Tis a rough-hewn place."

"It's just what we want, Drew. We've left the other life behind us. I only wish," she added, a serious look crossing her face for the first time, "I only wish you would be here to share our new life with us."

Ellie glanced toward Maggie, then quickly away and down at the floor. Drew also said nothing. It was clear the subject Maggie had opened was a painful one to both of them.

" 'Tis fer the best, Maggie. We have no choice," said Drew.

"Oh, Drew," said Ellie, almost in a pleading tone, "we could manage, we could find a new place. My family would—"

"Ellie," interrupted Drew, "I know how ye're feelin', but I thought all that was settled."

"It is," replied Ellie with a submissive sigh.

"I've told ye before," Drew went on, but the firmness in his voice was touched with his own uncertainty, "that I dinna want handouts from yer family. If we can't keep up the mortgage on the place, 'tis best we move on. An' ye know as well as I that old Kellermann's been lookin' fer a way t' get the place back from us."

"I know, but it just seems that there must be something—"

"I've been t' the bank down t' Hudson, an' everyone in Chatham's in the same fix as us. It's jist been a poor two years an' there's nothin' more we can do aboot it."

The remainder of the meal continued in subdued silence with only the sound of the chattering of three-year-old Sarah, who was oblivious to the vague tension about the table. As soon as breakfast was over everyone scurried in different directions. Ellie remained subdued and Drew went outside to bring the wagon around for the short trip to town.

"I'm sorry, Maggie," Ellie said at last, "for spoiling your special day."

"Nothing can spoil it, Ellie," Maggie replied, gently stroking little Bess's hair; the girl had shyly sidled up for a farewell hug. "But," she went on, "if there's anything I can do ... I mean if you think you ought to stay here, I can go to New York—"

"No," Ellie answered quickly. "This is the best thing for me. There's no way I could sleep knowin' you were off on that train and in that huge city by yourself." She sighed. "Besides," she added, "a couple days away will be good for me, give me a chance to think. And this is somethin' I have to work out for myself, I suppose. The Scriptures talk about a woman leavin' her kin to become one with her husband. Maybe it's a choice all women have to face some time or other. And maybe this is my time."

"Moving west you mean?"

"I knew it was comin'. He's been a wantin' to go west since he set foot on this land. Then he married me, and I kept gettin' in the family way. I had two stillbirths besides these five. Well, he kept puttin' it off, an' then we got this here little farm, which was a good thing them first few years. And he kept puttin' it off and puttin' it off, but I knew it was always on his mind. Then these last two years were so bad. The crops nearly failed completely and all the smaller farms around these parts are in trouble. Drew tried to keep it up. He worked hard, fourteen hours a day, and he tried to find money to keep up our payments on the place."

Ellie paused and sighed, then rushed on, "But when there's no rain and when you've got little mouths to feed, sometimes there just ain't much a body can do. I see the strain on his face. I know he's just trying to do what's best. And he has his pride as a man, too. I try to be a good Christian wife—but my whole family's here, and we're awful close, and I sometimes think I can't bear to leave. I might never see 'em again."

She stopped and glanced away and Maggie felt the tears she could not see. She set Bess down and stretched out her hand to Ellie's shoulder.

"But listen to me!" said Ellie after a moment, wiping her eyes with her sleeve and forcing a smile. "That's exactly what you did, isn't it? Why, *you* are the good Christian wife."

"It was much different for us," replied Maggie wistfully. "We had little choice."

"But still, you did it."

"It wasn't easy for me either, Ellie. Leaving to follow your husband can't be easy for any woman when she's got to leave her family and home behind. And here I had to leave *without* my husband," she laughed, trying to lighten the mood. "But the wait's almost over!"

"Your trial's nearly past; mine's just beginnin'," said Ellie.

"But when the time comes you will be strong for it. And perhaps something will happen ... maybe Drew will find a way for you to stay."

"I don't know, Maggie. It's gone so far now I think there's no turnin' back. I can see the far-off look in his eyes. He's saddened by the turn of things here. But at the same time I can tell he's buildin' with excitement about what may lie for us west somewhere. California and Oregon—that's all he and Evan McCollough seem to talk about anymore. Evan's got picture books of how it is. And he says the ground there is so rich anybody can grow anythin' they like."

"And you think it's certain, then?"

"Might as well be. All we're waitin' on is to find out the *when*. Mr. Kellermann was by the place two days ago. I saw him and Drew talking out in the fields. Drew, he didn't say nothin' about it later. But I could see it on his face. I knew it was all settled."

Just then the sound of the wagon interrupted their voices. As Drew brought the horse up to a stop in front of the house, the four older children ran outside and scampered up into the large flatbed. Drew jumped down, picked up little Sarah and set her up. Lastly he offered Maggie his hand, then Ellie, and in a few moments the seven Mackinaws and their new friend from the old country were on their way into Chatham to meet the New York Central on its way south.

"Maybe the two o' ye will be wantin' to come west wi' us," said Drew, trying to make conversation. "That's where the opportunities in America are now, they say."

"I don't know, Drew," replied Maggie. "I don't want to get too far from New York. You know, we're going to want to return to Scotland someday, after . . ."

Her voice trailed off and she fell silent.

"After what?" asked Ellie.

"It's a long story," replied Maggie. "Let's just say we won't be able to return for some time. But after a few years, hopefully it will all have blown over by then and it will be safe to go back."

No one felt inclined to pursue the conversation further, and the rest of the ride into Chatham was dominated by the sounds of the five happy children in the back of the wagon.

12   New York

All Maggie would ever remember of that train trip was its length. When she had taken it a month ago, it hadn't been slow enough. She had blankly stared out the window, neither noticing nor caring as they passed through Jersey City, Rockland, New-burgh, Poughkeepsie, and Hudson. Now the southbound train could not move fast enough, and the miles seemed endless.

They did not arrive until late afternoon, as dusk was starting to descend on the great metropolis. The ship was not scheduled to arrive until the following morning and the two women stayed at the boarding house where Maggie had spent her first night in America, close to both the train station and the harbor, a four-story brownstone on Vanguard Street. The stairs creaked as they climbed to the second floor behind the tall, austere figure of the elderly landlady.

"She reminds me of an old teacher I once had," giggled Ellie once they were alone in their room. "You couldn't blink without her knowing it. And believe me, you didn't try!"

"I'm so glad you came with me," said Maggie. "Somehow the city isn't quite so intimidating with someone to share it with."

"Do you suppose," asked Ellie, "that we could have a look around the city after we meet Ian? I've only been here once before, and I was only ten. We have to wait till day after tomorrow for the train north, anyway."

"Oh, that would be fun," agreed Maggie. "But to tell you the truth, all I can think of now is seeing him again!"

"I know. Perhaps he will want to stay here a little longer. He's from London, didn't you say?"

"Yes."

"Well, the big city won't be anything new to him. He might want to wait until the train four days from now. You know how men are—sometimes they're attracted by all the lights and bustle of a city."

"What about the children?"

"Drew'll be fine. Besides, didn't I tell you? My mother's comin' over for a visit, and to help him out a bit. And maybe I'll just go back to Chatham myself and let you and Ian be alone."

"Oh, Ellie!" said Maggie. "Stop teasing!"

"Come now, child, I remember what it was like bein' just married!"

"Your Drew is a good man," said Maggie. "You must feel very fortunate."

"Yes, I do," replied Ellie with a long sigh. "Only it's such a heartache to me that he can't bring himself to share my faith."

"What? He's such a kind man. I assumed . . ."

"Drew's a good man. The best. And he accepts my faith in God just fine. Down in his heart I know he believes. There's somethin' gnawin' at him that keeps him from bein' able to accept it fully. But his day will come."

"I'm surprised," said Maggie. "If only you could have known his mother. She positively radiated her love for God."

"Oh," exclaimed Ellie joyfully, "that's so wonderful to hear! Drew doesn't talk much about his family."

"It was Bess Mackinaw who got me really thinking about spiritual things. She and our old groom, Digory."

"Maggie, you don't know what that means to me, to know that Drew comes from a godly background like that. I pray for him, of course. But that helps me know that somewhere down inside he must believe. The Word says, you know, that when children are raised in the faith they won't depart from it. Who knows but maybe that's why the Lord's wantin' us to be movin' west. Maybe a change like that's what's needed to rekindle his faith."

Maggie found herself touched by her new friend's openness. Would she understand if Maggie told her about her own father? As they dressed for bed, twice she opened her mouth to try to share some of her own feelings and uncertainties, but each time found that she could not make a beginning. The words, along with the painful resentments of the past, remained locked inside. Perhaps when she and Ian were finally together—maybe then all the hurts would finally heal. Maybe she would be able to forget what her father had done, once she and her husband were out of his reach forever.

Only a few hours left to wait! Maggie thought.

A flurry of light snow fell on New York during the night, and when the two women woke, the dingy city streets were covered with a thin layer of purity. Maggie sprang out of the old four-poster feather bed as if she hadn't slept at all. Ellie yawned, stretched to her full length, and lay back again, thinking what a change it was not to have to get up, stoke the fire, prepare breakfast, change a diaper, or dress children.

"Oh, this *is* nice!" she groaned sleepily as she rolled back over on her pillow.

"No more sleep, Ellie," said Maggie cheerfully. "This is the day!"

"You're right. And I suppose I ought to go downstairs to help that dour old landlady prepare breakfast."

"Ellie!" Maggie laughed. "This may not be an expensive hotel, but even in a boarding house like this they do those things for you. Have a bath instead."

"A bath! They charge extra for that."

"This is New York, Ellie! How many chances do you get to do something like this? I'll pay for the bath. Enjoy yourself!"

Reluctantly Ellie complied.

"That was the most wonderful bath I've ever had," she said as they sat down to breakfast, "except for when I was a kid up in the swimmin' hole on Gorsett's Creek. Just think, I didn't have to hurry so one of the kids could use the water."

"Mine was nice too," said Maggie, "but rather cold."

"All we try to do is take a little of the chill off," said the landlady, who had overheard the last of the conversation. "And that's only for the women. Men have to wash in the cold as best they can. Can you imagine the cost of providing *hot* baths!"

Sheepishly Maggie glanced toward Ellie and grinned.

"You look so nice," said Ellie. "Ian won't be able to keep his eyes off you. You're just beautiful today."

Maggie had been relieved when she awoke to find that most of the wrinkles had fallen out of the navy blue taffeta she had hung up as soon as they had arrived. The dress was so plain despite its pearl buttons. She thought of all her lovely dresses back in her wardrobe in Scotland. But they had left in such haste, there had only been time to pack three. And these had to be practical and versatile; there was no room for the colorful silks and satins with their yards of lace and ruffles. She had wanted to buy a new dress for this important occasion, but she knew she and Ian were going to have to conserve their money in order to make a start in America. Besides, there weren't many fancy dresses to be found in the rural shops in Chatham or any of the nearby villages. This taffeta was her best, and might have to remain so for a long time.

"Thank you, Ellie," Maggie replied with a smile.

"Before long you'll be havin' to borrow some of my dresses," giggled Ellie. "That is, when your young'un starts pushin' out."

"I appreciate the offer, Ellie, but I'm glad I'm not showing just yet. I want to look my best for Ian."

"Oh, child! Do you think he'll care what you look like? Remember, he's been countin' the days just like you." Then she added brightly, "But you do look lovely, just the same!"

After breakfast they informed the landlady that they would need a second room when they returned that evening. Then they opened the door and walked out into the glistening sunlight of the new day. The thin snow cover and the clear, wintery brightness could not have matched the exuberant mood of Maggie's heart more perfectly.

"Oh, it's a glorious day!" she exclaimed.

Travel through the streets, however, was slow. Twice the hired carriage nearly skidded out of control on the icy streets, and thereafter the driver refused to listen to Maggie's urgent appeals to hurry.

"Look, lady," he said, "I take people down to the dock all the time, and I tell you that ship don't arrive till 11 o'clock."

"But I don't want to be late," Maggie insisted.

"Late! You got almost two hours before those passengers are even going to see the harbor."

Maggie said nothing more, thinking instead of the kindness of the driver she had had on her first day in New York a month earlier.

At last the shipyards came into sight. The streets here were so alive with activity that the snow had been long since trampled away. The driver obviously knew the harbor well, waving greetings to other carriage drivers and directing his horse straight to the pier where the great steamer, *H.M.S. Fairgate*, was expected from London.

"Well, if that don't beat all!" exclaimed the driver. "There she is heading in already."

Maggie looked in the direction he pointed. To her great excitement she could see the ship in the distance. By the time they had reached the roped-off waiting area, the ship had covered half the remaining distance and was already beginning the gradual turn which would end as the captain maneuvered her gently into the waiting slip.

Anxiously Maggie scanned the faces onboard. The passengers crowded about the railings, as eager to get off the ship as Maggie had been to meet it, but she could not find Ian among them. It took nearly another hour for the dock hands and ship's crew to make the *Fairgate* secure. Frantically Maggie continued her visual search, but there were so many faces.

At long last the gangplank was slowly lowered, and in a surge of bodies the passengers made their way onto land. Maggie and Ellie found themselves nearly smothered in the confusion. Customs officials ushered the great rush of humanity into narrow roped-off lines and began the tedious process of checking each one's papers. Some were allowed to go their way quickly. The greater number, however, those who had come third or fourth class, were subject to close scrutiny, disinfection, even de-licing. Maggie knew that Ian would be holding a second-class ticket, as she had, and concentrated her attention on those who were passed through customs most hurriedly.

One by one, men and women passed by, and the growing uneasiness became more and more apparent on her face. Once or twice she cast an apprehensive glance toward Ellie. The older woman tried to remain calm, returning Maggie's pleading looks with as much calm and reassurance as she could muster. But inside she could not ignore her own concern, visibly mirrored on Maggie's panic-stricken face.

Finally, after more than an hour, the gangplank was empty. In a frenzy of agitation Maggie turned this way and that, scanning the ship with the imploring eyes of a caged animal.

"Oh, Ellie!" she cried, "I'm—I'm so afraid. I don't—"

"Best go speak to one of the men on the ship," said Ellie with measured calm. "I'll go ask about him if you like."

"No," replied Maggie. "I can manage. But come with me, please."

Desperately hoping that Ian had been somehow detained on board and would any moment wander from somewhere within the ship with the other laggers who one by one were disembarking,

Maggie and Ellie tentatively approached the ship, walked up the steep gangplank onto the deck.

"Hoy, ladies," hollered out a crusty voice with heavy Irish accent. Maggie turned to see a grizzled sailor with a deep scar across his forehead. "Ready t' set sail again, are ye?" He laughed good-humoredly, but it did little to ease her anxiety. His banter was joined by several of his shipmates before being abruptly cut short by a commanding voice approaching behind Maggie and Ellie.

"All right, you lubbers!" it snapped. "Any more of that sort of rudeness and I'll dock your pay. Now get back to your chores!"

Recognizing the voice, Maggie turned quickly.

"Captain Sievers! I didn't expect to see you!"

"We made good time on the return voyage, Lady Duncan, after we left you in New York. The Captain of the *Fairgate* took sick, so I filled in for him, turned right back around, and here I am."

"Oh, I'm so glad you are," said Maggie, seeming to suddenly remember why she was here. "I'm here to meet my husband, Captain. He's supposed to be on the ship, but I haven't been able to find him."

"Well, my lady, give me a name and I'll check the roster," he replied. "You're sure it was this ship?"

"Yes ... well, this was the day I thought he was to arrive. You've taken on the passengers from Aberdeen, haven't you?"

"Aye, just as when you made the voyage."

"Then he has to be here."

"Let me check the list—what was the name?"

"Theodore Duncan—perhaps Ian Duncan."

The captain turned, disappeared for about ten minutes, then returned carrying a sheaf of papers. The frown on his face revealed the news Maggie had dreaded to hear. She could not even bring herself to ask the question.

"I'm sorry, Lady Duncan," he said.

"Ellie, could he possibly have got past us? There were so many passengers."

But then without waiting for an answer, she turned again to the captain. "Did you check the entire list? Maybe he was in steerage."

"I hardly think so, my lady."

"He could be!" returned Maggie sharply, forgetting the captain's kindness.

Sievers checked the list once more, then shook his head.

"You must have missed his name! He *has* to be there. I'm going to look—I know he's here!"

In tears Maggie pulled herself away from Ellie and began running along the deck of the ship.

"My lady! Please . . . Lady Duncan!" the captain called out after her. But Maggie was heedless of his voice. Ellie attempted to follow her, to calm and comfort her. But it was no use.

Hysterically Maggie ran along the deck, then inside and along the inside corridors of the ship, toward the kitchen, then to the sick bay. Weeping she ran, calling out his name between choking sobs, "Ian . . . Ian . . . please—please be here!"

At last, exhausted and broken, Maggie slumped to the floor in the middle of a deserted hallway on the second deck, and—still weeping—murmured the words, "Oh, Ian . . . Ian—where are you?"

It was there Ellie and the captain found her some time later, still on the floor, weeping and calling out Ian's name in a barely audible voice. Gently Ellie eased her to her feet and led her off the ship and home.

13 Incommunicado

Somehow he had to keep the panic from overpowering him. He couldn't lose his grip on reality.

Ian jumped to his feet and once again began pacing the tiny cell. It was cold and dark, and the ancient stones indicated that he was being held in some massive city prison of great age. He supposed it was Glasgow but had no way to be certain. What did it matter where he was, anyway? He was not on board the ship, and that is all Maggie would know. Somewhere around this time—but how could he keep track of the passage of days and weeks?—she would go to New York expecting to meet him.

God, he thought, *I've got to get out of here! Maggie will think I've deserted her!*

He paced for a few more minutes, then sat down again on the floor. He had been here only two days. But he could not escape the growing obsession of panic which threatened to master him. All he could think of was Maggie in New York, waiting . . . waiting.

For three or four weeks they had held him in Aberdeen. He had seen no living soul other than the jailer. At first he had been angry. Then he had grown morose and despondent. But as the days passed into weeks it finally began to dawn on him that he was in serious trouble which could well keep him from Maggie. The time dragged by slowly and there was no word, no sign of release, no sign of a trial or official charges. No lawyer was sent to interview him or review his case. There was no sign of anything whatsoever! He had been allowed to send no communications to the outside— nothing!

Then one night four or five days ago something did happen. Two men came for him, dragged him from the jail and outside where a light rain was falling. How delicious the fresh air had tasted! But he had little time to enjoy it. Rudely they shoved him into the back of a carriage, his hands tied, and immediately took off into the night. Only minimal stops were made during the journey; each time he was given a new jug of water and half a loaf of dry bread. Sleeping while jostling about was impossible, but he did manage to doze off frequently.

The destination was reached in the dead of night. He heard voices he did not recognize talking outside in subdued tones. Then the carriage door was opened, he was pulled roughly outside, and with the words "We'll show ye how we takes care o' low-life aroun' here!" Ian was hauled into the great stone building, down several flights of stairs, and at last deposited in the tiny cell in which he now sat. From the length of the trip he judged himself in Glasgow. There was no window, and when the terror of his position overcame his attempt to remain calm, he was alternately seized by the cold sweat of dread or the hysterical desire to scream his way to freedom. But whenever the latter took hold, his voice echoed against the dull stone walls and fell again to silence, and Ian knew no living soul had even heard. He had been used to brief stints in London, but never in a place like this. There was an evil irony about this turn of events which did not look hopeful.

The sound of the jailer approaching from the end of the dark passageway interrupted his despondency. The decrepit old man was his only link with the world, and each time he heard the jangle of the guard's keys mingled with the faint shuffle of a leg that had gone lame, his spirits came to life. He leaped to his feet and pounded on the great, unyielding iron door.

"Get me out of here!" Ian shouted. "I'll do anything—I have money!"

"Ha!" replied the jailer with a cruel laugh as a key fumbled in the rusty lock. "I've heard that one afore, guv'nor. Ye tell me that every time I come an' I no more believe ye than t' think ye could fly through these walls. Now, get back against the wall so I can bring ye these fine victuals!"

The door swung open and the man slipped a tray in on the floor. Ian stormed toward him, kicked the tray, scattering the contents, and threw himself against the man. In other circumstances he would surely have overpowered such a one. But he had grown weak and his despair had not been accompanied by prudence. The wary jailer was experienced and cannily on his guard. He whisked the heavy cudgel from his side and swung it deftly at Ian's head. Ian fell senseless back against the wall.

"Now ye gone an' done it, ye rotter!" swore the man.

Still dazed from the blow, Ian felt himself being dragged toward the adjacent wall where a thick chain hung from an iron ring. He clasped the manacle around Ian's wrist. "Why don't ye take t' some manners, yer lairdship! I got my orders t' keep ye chained as long as ye've a mind t' cause trouble!"

"Please!" Ian pleaded, coming to himself, "help me! For God's sake, at least let me have some paper to write a letter. No one knows I'm here."

"Oh, I'll help ye, guv'nor!" the man laughed, shoving the tray toward Ian with his foot. "There, enjoy yer supper! Ha! ha!" He turned to go, then called out after him, "Ask me fer help again,

yer lairdship, when ye got some o' that money jinglin' in yer
pocket! Ha! ha!"

The door slammed shut with a final metallic thud. Ian fell back
on the dirty straw mattress, while a bold rat approached the sour
oatmeal which had spilled on the floor.

As the days passed, Ian's body continued to weaken and his
mind wandered. Often his imagination convinced him he was back
in his own room in London and the crippled guard was his butler.
More frequently he awoke to find himself calling out Maggie's
name, having dreamed himself with her again in the little cottage
near Fraserburgh. And each time his mind wandered, it was more
difficult to pull himself back to reality. For whenever his wild-eyed
countenance focused with renewed reality on the filth and squalor
about him, and when his nose brought his senses fully awake to
the stench of his own private dungeon, the horror of this utter
helplessness nearly drove him mad.

Days, weeks passed. There was no change. There was no night
or day, no light or darkness; only a pale glint of faded yellow from
the candle-flame down the corridor seeped in through the small
barred opening in his door. He lost all track of time. The guard
came and went, bringing the nauseating provisions designed
merely to keep him alive, of which the rats took more than their
fair share. At length the iron wrist bar was removed and Ian accepted his newfound freedom with indifference. His body was depleted and his tormented brain plagued with forlorn thoughts of
Maggie and his own impotence; more often than not the guard
found him sitting in a heap in a corner, staring straight ahead into
the darkness, mumbling incoherently.

Honor! He cursed the thought. What a fool he had been! If only
he had gone with Maggie all this would never have happened. What
an imbecile to think he could throw away the past and suddenly
become an honorable man. Then the face of Maggie rose in the
vision of his blurred consciousness. Her face was despairing, looking this way and that. As the vision faded in and out he could see
her standing forlorn on a dock, peering toward an empty ship,
looking, searching, tears of anguish streaming down her face. *Oh,
Maggie! I never meant to put you through this. What will you do
... can you ever forgive ... Maggie, I'm still coming—don't desert*

*me—Oh, Maggie, help me! Maggie ... Maggie ... I'm sorry—I'm
so sorry!*

Guilt assailed him. Not only was he a stupid fool, he was a
rogue, possibly even a murderer. He had killed Falkirk, and now
he had ruined Maggie's life besides, forced her away from her
homeland, her family, her inheritance, and from a marriage and a
future with a gentleman. Perhaps she would have been happy with
Falkirk. But he had ruined it all! What was honor to such a wretch
as he? For so-called honor he had given up happiness and ruined
lives besides.

Why did I send Maggie away! Why? Why ...

The familiar sounds slowly penetrated his dazed brain. *Jingle
... shuffle ... shuffle ... jingle ... jingle ...*

It was a sweet sound, a gentle sound. Soon his mother would
be back in to tuck him in. She always set the little bell ringing in
his room just before she came in to say good night. Usually with
the ringing came a bedtime story, a special moment, for even his
brother didn't often get one. He hardly needed it, with the attentions showered upon him by their father. Then when the story was
over, she would pull the satin comforter over him and gently kiss
his forehead. *Good night, my little Theodore ... pleasant
dreams ...*

Jingle ... jingle ... shuffle.

The cell door creaked open. Ian looked up. The face standing
over him wasn't his mother's. He couldn't quite remember ... he
had seen it someplace before ... if only he could remember.
*Mother ... where are—Mother, won't you come back? I heard the
little bell ...*

"Don't ye know me by now, yer lairdship?" the face asked. It
wasn't his mother's voice at all, but a gruff masculine one.

"Huh?" said Ian, staring blankly ahead.

"Ye're lookin' at me like ye never seed me afore."

"Get me out of here," said Ian dully, through the parting fog
of reality.

"Same ol' story, eh, guv'nor?" stated the guard, shoving the
tray toward him on the floor.

"At least tell me what day it is."

"Tuesday."

"The date," said Ian sleepily. "What is the date? When is my mother coming for me? She said she'd be back soon—"

"Yer mother!" roared the jailer. "That's a good one, guv'nor! But seein' as they call this the season o' good will an' all, I guess no harm could come o' tellin' ye. Mind ye, I'm breakin' strict orders, for we're s'posed t' tell ye nothin'. But if ye'll have it, why 'tis Christmas Eve!"

Ian started forward with a wild look in his eyes. The jailer jumped back, his hand instantly on the handle of his cudgel. But he did not have to use it. For just as suddenly Ian slumped back against the wall and slowly fell again to the floor.

"Oh, God, no!" he wailed, hardly aware that he had long since told himself he no longer believed in such a being.

"'Tis the season t' be jolly, yer lairdship!" mocked the guard.

With sudden energy, Ian grabbed at the tray, which today in addition to the customary gruel and dried bread contained something resembling a slice of meat. He flung it at the man.

"There you go again! An' I was just about t' tell ye that if ye behaved yersel' I had instructions t' take ye up fer an airin' outside. Now ye can rot in this stinkin' miserable cell!"

Ian heard nothing of the jailer's words, nor did he even notice when the door clanged shut with the finality of death. He only heard the echoing ring of the words he had just heard.

Christmas Eve!

He and Maggie were to spend Christmas together. He had *promised* he would meet her. What must she think of his honor now that he had broken every vow he had made to her? Oh, the cruelty of this fate which seemed to be punishing him for trying to change his ways and start a new life! Now there was no way to tell her that he had meant every word, that he truly loved her. What futility lay ahead! *Oh, Maggie, what have I done to you? Can you ever forgive me? Will I ever see your smiling face again? Oh, gentle, sweet Maggie . . . I never meant to hurt you. I love you! Maggie, how I loved you! Oh, why did I do it, why did I send you away? What a fool I was . . . I didn't trust your love for me, and yet you went to a strange land because you trusted me. And now you are alone. I failed you, Maggie!*

Ian fell back against the stone wall, pressing his hands against his head. At length his eyes rested on the tray and the food scattered about the floor. He crawled across the cell and retrieved the crusty hunk of bread and slowly raised it to his mouth. As his teeth bit into it he suddenly realized to what pathetic depths he had sunk—he had scarcely bothered to brush off the dirt and mold. He looked down at the frayed rag which had once been a white shirt, and his filthy breeches which had come from one of London's finest shops.

This was his true self! He had finally sunk to the reality to which he had been destined since birth. He had tried to cover it up through the years with his quick wit and winning smile and fine clothes—playing the part of a gentleman. But he had played false with the world. He was no gentleman. He was not even a man! All the while, deep inside, lurked this ghastly illusion of manhood—wasted, impotent, waiting for the right moment to surface and destroy him and those around him.

In the distance the familiar sound of the jailer's shuffle again approached, but this time Ian detected the additional sounds of someone with him. Probably another prisoner, he thought. Christmas or not, it could certainly be no visitor. Who would visit him? His father? Ha! If his father ever found out where he was, he would probably rejoice, thought Ian cynically.

The steps drew closer, then stopped. Ian heard the jingling of keys outside the cell door. His heart quickened!

All at once an unbelievable thought pierced the fog. This *was* Christmas Eve. Perhaps this was the season for miracles after all! Could someone have finally realized it was all a mistake? Had the real murderer been found? It could only be a matter of time before this horrible mistake would be undone. Yes, of course, they were coming to release him! *Maggie ... Maggie ... I'm coming after all! Don't give up, Maggie—I'll be there!*

The door opened and a man entered, well dressed; although of slight stature, he carried himself with a straight back like a military officer. He was attired in an impeccable brown pinstriped suit, probably of cashmere, clearly not the usual garb of a prison official. His shirt was snowy white and boasted a silk tie. There was something in his bearing of authority Ian recognized, but the light was poor and his visitor held a handkerchief to his nose, partially obscuring his face.

Coughing lightly, he lowered the handkerchief and finally spoke.

"How do you stand the stench?" he asked.

At the sound of the man's voice, the scales fell from Ian's eyes and his ears were opened. He started forward, uncertain whether his mind was not playing another vile trick. But he could never mistake that voice, and the loathsome face was unchanged. This was no Christmas miracle, only a shattered mirage of justice.

"What do you want?" snarled Ian, flooded with anger at the remembrance of past cruelties.

"I heard of your . . . er, your misfortune," James began in measured tones. "You can imagine my dismay. I felt it my duty, as this trouble befell you while you were under my roof, to inquire into your welfare. I see I have come none too soon!"

"What do you want, I asked!" repeated Ian, still doubting whether the figure before him might be but some fiendish specter of his insanity.

"I wish to do what I can for you," James replied, and coughed again, as if to further punctuate the magnanimity of his gesture. "Of course, I can do nothing to alter the facts of your guilt, but you need not remain in"—he waved his hand disdainfully in a circular motion about the cell—"in such abject straits."

Ian continued to stare blankly at Maggie's father.

"I have here a document," James continued, removing a paper from the vest pocket inside his coat. "You need only to sign it, and I'm certain funds could become available and certain, shall we say, *arrangements* could be made to—ah—procure such comforts as might make your stay here more tolerable." James stepped forward toward Ian and handed him the paper.

Mechanically, Ian took it from his hand, opened it, and tried to focus his eyes in the dim light. Mingled anger and apathy combined to make him resist anything James Duncan might suggest, while at the same time he felt that he had little recourse but to act in a foreordained manner as events came to him.

Then his eyes fell on the single word—*annulment*. Nothing more was necessary to stir the passion simmering within him. In one swift motion he crushed the paper, dashed it under his foot, and flew at his adversary's throat.

For the first time in weeks Ian felt fully alive. He threw James to the floor, his blood boiling hot within him. If he would rot in this hole for murder, then let it be for good reason!

The jailer had stepped into the corridor to allow the distinguished visitor privacy. And even when he heard the first sounds of trouble, he still waited before interfering. If the gentleman wanted to rough up his prisoner, what was that to him? But at length he realized the sounds from within the cell were not what he had expected.

He rushed inside and found James on the floor struggling wildly, Ian beating at him with clenched fists.

"You fool! Didn't you hear me yelling at you?" shouted James enraged. "Get this bastard off me!"

The guard rushed at Ian, knocking him aside, then turned to help James to his feet. But Ian, awake now, turned, and rushed the guard, kicking him to his knees, then made another lunge at James. But his fury was ill-advised, for the guard, recovering himself quickly, sent him sprawling backward with a punishing blow to his midsection with the brutal cudgel.

James stood, brushed off his clothing, and attempted to pull his coat back into some semblance of order. Once he had put a safe distance between himself and this wild man, he cast Ian a hateful look of scorn.

"You shall regret this!"

"I regret only that it was Falkirk who died that night, and not you!" cried Ian.

"You shall die a thousand deaths in this stink-hole as payment for that error!" replied James with a sneer. "I'll not try to help you again!" With these words he spun and stalked from the cell, followed by the jailer.

Ian slumped back onto his cot. Every ounce of strength was drained from his limbs, and with the fight had gone his fleeting Christmas hope.

Slowly Ian's head sank onto his hands. Every fiber of his being told him that James was right, that he would die in this miserable pit and never see Maggie again. The tears rose in his eyes, and Ian wept.

14 Evil Designs

The perceptive eye of any who knew James Duncan well would have seen that the preceding months had taken their toll. But few, if any, knew James well. Atlanta had noticed, but said nothing.

The gray streaks in his black hair had grown more pronounced, and a hollowness about the eyes had shown itself. He was thinner and there was a slight slump to his formerly poker-straight shoulders. Despite all this, the fire of his former self still burned in his eyes and the hard force of his drive was ever present.

George Falkirk's death had been a difficult blow. Not that he cared a trifle for the man, either as a friend or as a suitor for his daughter and potential son-in-law. The real blow had come because the anticipated funds from the lad's father—intrinsically linked to the marriage of the young couple—would never be forthcoming. When he had exchanged his daughter's hand for certain financial gratuities, James had never dreamed the intended bridegroom would be violently struck down. So certain had he been of the match that he had stretched his resources to the limit in prospect of laying his hands on the elder Falkirk's investment capital, foolishly putting up earnest money for a new brewery. When the marriage, and thus the deal with Falkirk, fell through, the deposit had been lost and James suddenly found himself in financial difficulty.

Times have definitely not been good, thought James. He reflected on his own father who had squandered a fortune and brought ruin on the whole family. Of course, James stood to lose only his private reserve; there still remained his share in Atlanta's inheritance. But it bitterly galled him to crawl to her for help. As yet he had avoided having to do so. But every farthing of the profits from the old brewery was now having to go toward paying off debts incurred in the loss of the earnest money. Lord Browhurst had turned surly and demanding. Sales of his fine Scottish ale had dropped. His reputation in economic circles had grown shaky. And he had even been forced to dip into the profits of his shareholders in order to keep things afloat, though he remained confident he would be able to turn the business back around and repay these amounts before he was discovered.

James rose from his chair and walked toward a small table which held a tray and two crystal decanters. He opened the one containing brandy and poured out a generous portion into a glass. He took one swift gulp, then began coughing.

"What in heaven's name is in this brandy!" he said, trying to catch his breath.

He managed to force down another swallow as the fit subsided. "Terrible stuff," he reiterated. "If only I could have got that brewery for myself."

James had been drinking a bit more than usual of late. He was an intensely proud man and could not face the erosion of his self-confidence. But if anything within James Duncan was giving way, it was not yet evident to others—and was certainly something he would never admit to himself. He remained a powerful man, but he was walking a narrow ledge.

Stonewycke had begun to mean more to him than ever. Of course it would never be for him what it was to Atlanta. But now, for the first time, he saw the estate and his presumed standing as its so-called *laird* as his only link to a future in the world of the rich and powerful.

The face of Maggie came before his mind. Her leaving had been one of the few positive events of late. But so surrounded was her departure by the whole predicament concerning that cousin of his that his blood boiled just to think of it. He had actually been surprised she would go so far. Had it been fatherly compunction and regret he had felt when he had heard the news? Whatever it may have been, the feeling was overshadowed by the thought that she had actually spurned him for that scoundrel of a lover! She— his own daughter!—had practically ruined him.

Any remaining glimmer of fatherhood was quickly put to rest in the memory of that thought. How dare she! *Regrets are for the weak,* James thought. *A strong man takes tragic events and disappointing setbacks and turns them to his advantage.* Maggie knew how to take care of herself; she would not suffer in America. Meanwhile, James could see how her absence might prove fortuitous indeed. Would it not make Stonewycke all the easier to secure for himself—not to mention his son? Atlanta would no doubt prove as difficult as ever. But a present husband and heir would be able to exercise a great deal more power than an absent heiress.

There remained sticky details to work out, however. James reminded himself he had often faced greater obstacles than these, and had surmounted them. The challenge would be invigorating! He had already taken care of the one crucial detail, and he was confident the news he had arranged about Ian would have just the impact Atlanta feared most. But if it put any ideas in Maggie's head about returning, he would just have to come up with something else.

He tossed his head back and emptied the brandy glass, then poured himself another.

There was always a way to get what you wanted. He was as confident that Maggie would never return as he was that this was inferior brandy. Unless, of course, she returned to put a gun to his own head. He laughed a dry, barking laugh which quickly gave way to another fit of coughing.

No, he thought, *she has that Ramsey pride flowing through her veins, and it would never let her return to the arms of the people she will most certainly despise!*

He would just have to wait and see. It was a nasty turn when that blackguard of a boy refused to sign the annulment papers. That could have made things so much easier. When he had first been informed of their intentions to marry, he had been certain he would have little difficulty effecting a swift end to any such plans. But he had underestimated Atlanta's power. And when she had threatened to bare that power and use it against him, James realized his only recourse was to force that criminal cousin of his to agree to an annulment. Thus, James had arranged for a change in magistrates, had planted evidence against the lad, and thereby forced an arrest.

It had not been difficult, with his remaining influence in the lower circles of the law, to delay a trial and keep Ian incommunicado, while at the same time preventing any information about him from reaching Atlanta. He wanted her to hear nothing until the time was right. He had judged the boy weak-willed enough to agree to anything in order to escape from that rat-infested dungeon of a prison where he was being kept. But he had been wrong, and that miscalculation would cost Ian Duncan dearly.

In his heart, James did not believe Ian a murderer. Certain factors which only James knew pointed in other directions. In addition, James simply didn't think the boy man enough to commit such a brutal act. Cold and calculating as he was, James wanted to avoid the stain of innocent blood on his hands. His future—and whatever the temporary setbacks, he still had the future to consider—demanded that his record be as unblemished as reasonably possible. But though the evidence leading to Ian's arrest had been entirely fabricated, James still hoped further evidence—*true* evidence!—would eventually be found against him, sufficient to hang him. So much the better if he actually *was* guilty!

And soon it would not matter anyway whether the boy was alive or dead. By then Stonewycke would be firmly within his grasp.

15   A Letter to America

It had been well over a hundred years since the careless laird Iver Ramsey had nearly lost Stonewycke. His poor management had in the end reduced the awesome stone castle to an empty shell dominated by cobwebs, empty hallways, and scavenger rats.

Why should Atlanta Duncan, the mistress of Stonewycke, be thinking of these things today? Surely on this winter's day in early 1864 the house stood as grand as ever, reclaimed in all its glory from Iver's carelessness. The walls were adorned with flocked red and blue paper and golden sconces. Velvet hung from the windows. The furnishings were the best to be found in Europe. Though at times an overlooked cobweb might be found in some dark corner, no scavenger rat dared show its face in those halls these days.

But for Atlanta the house might as well have been as empty as in Iver's time. She walked down the hall, her black taffeta sending a ghostly echo into the damp air. There were duties to be performed as mistress of a grand Scottish estate, and she would never have dreamed of shirking even the most trivial. But her heart had gone from her. She had once considered Stonewycke her heart and soul. But when her daughter had left, Atlanta gradually began to realize that Stonewycke was only part of what gave her life meaning. The greater part had been Maggie. She had been the reason for it all. Without her, everything suddenly had grown meaningless.

The vague melancholy which had settled over Atlanta stemmed no doubt from the uneasy conviction that Maggie might never return and that the land would instead go to her brother Alastair, who cared nothing for it. It was bad enough that not a drop of Ramsey blood flowed through the boy's veins, but infinitely worse was the obvious fact that Alastair was cut straight from his father's mold. The boy was only fifteen, but Atlanta could already see that his sole interest in Stonewycke lay in gaining prestige, power, and wealth. When he came into the inheritance, Stonewycke would at first fulfill such temporal cravings. But the moment it ceased to enhance his schemes, she was certain he would have no qualms about disposing of it.

At first Atlanta had harbored the hope that Maggie would return. But when Mistress Rankin had brought Maggie's letter written after her arrival, the inferences from her daughter did not bode well. Clearly it had been written when she first arrived in America, for Atlanta had received it a mere month after the girl's departure. Atlanta had been staggered by the news that Maggie had at the last minute sailed alone and that Ian had remained behind to clear his name. The news had been inconceivable! Especially since in that time she had heard nothing from Ian. Certainly he would have tried to contact her despite James's threats. Yet even now, over a month later, she had still received no word from him. What it all meant, she dared not guess. Had he sent Maggie on alone, only to desert her, as part of some cruel revenge against her family?

Of only one thing could she be certain: the fact that Maggie had gone to America alone signified a depth of devotion and loyalty to her husband which was unequaled. Whether Ian was, in light of his disappearance, worthy of that devotion was perhaps a question to be considered. But the point was that in Maggie's heart all ties with Stonewycke had surely been severed. The mere suggestion brought a wince of pain into Atlanta's well-controlled face. There was a pride in Atlanta's bosom of motherhood for her daughter's courage, but it was a pride not unclouded with agony. Maggie was a Ramsey, with roots in an ancestry which had maintained the family continuity for over 300 years. She exhibited the same strength that had carried other Ramseys through war, poverty, and betrayal. Yet now that very strength had wrenched her from the beloved land.

Atlanta turned down another corridor and paused by a closed door. Gingerly she reached for the knob. Her hand trembled slightly as she gripped the ornate brass. Slowly the door swung open to reveal the room which had been Maggie's. Atlanta had not entered it since the day Maggie had left.

She stepped into the room and tears rose quickly to her eyes as she glanced upon everything just as Maggie had left it. It had been a night of hasty flight—Atlanta, being forced without preparation to sever the ties of motherhood all too quickly; Maggie, excited yet terrified, beginning the adventure of her new life with the husband she loved.

A dress still lay across a chair where Maggie had tossed it when it wouldn't fit into her carpet bag. The bed was rumpled where she had sat sifting through her belongings trying to decide which to take and which to leave behind. Now it was all so still; the silent ghosts of that night flitted to and fro through Atlanta's memory. Maggie seemed so very present in the room. And yet the dim intimation of her presence made her seem even farther away.

"Oh, Maggie," Atlanta sighed. "Did we do the right thing?"

Atlanta's gaze fell on the tapestry hanging over the bed. She recalled so vividly the day she had given Maggie the intricate needlepoint of the Ramsey family tree. Her daughter had been glowing in her newfound love for Ian and had at last found the courage to share the secret with her mother. Fresh tears rose in Atlanta's eyes at the remembrance of the tender moment between mother and daughter—a moment all the more touching in that for so many years there had been such distance between them.

When Atlanta had presented the tapestry to Maggie, she had not known how much it would mean to her daughter. When she had suggested moving it to Maggie's present room, Maggie had been reluctant.

"But it has always hung here," she had said. "It seems like it belongs in the nursery."

In the end they had moved it, and here it still hung.

Suddenly Atlanta reached up and took the large tapestry from the wall. She was not an impulsive woman, and later might well look on her action as silly and sentimental. But right now she felt sentimental! For this moment, in her present reminiscing mood she wanted to again see the tapestry in the place where perhaps it was the most natural—in the room where Maggie would always be remembered. Maggie was a grown woman now, married and far from home. But for her mother, she would always think of her daughter in relation to those happier times before womanhood and sorrow closed in upon them.

Still holding the great framed tapestry between her hands, Atlanta turned, left the room, and made her way to the nursery.

Later that afternoon, sitting at her desk sorting through some papers, Atlanta was interrupted by the butler knocking softly at her door.

"A message just came to the house, my lady," he said.

"A message? From whom?"

"'Tis from Glasgow, my lady. It came on the schooner this morning."

Atlanta took it, dismissed the man, then broke the seal on the envelope and unfolded the letter inside. The only sign of reaction as she read was a gradual whitening of her lips and increasing tautness in her composure. The message was brief and took but a few seconds to read.

She immediately rose, went to the door, and called out to the butler retreating down the corridor,

"Where is my husband?" she asked sharply.

"I saw him last in the library, my lady," he replied, half-turning toward her.

Atlanta swiftly made her way down the stairs to the second floor and to the library, which she entered with a single rapid motion. James was seated at his desk. He glanced up casually, but immediately a look of concern passed over his face.

"My dear, whatever is wrong? You look positively ashen. Are you ill?"

"Since when were you concerned with my health?" she snapped in return, her voice shaking as she tried to maintain her composure.

"You are being unfair, Atlanta. I *am* concerned. You need to take things more in stride. You have seemed so overwrought of late."

"And I have no reason to be?" she fumed. "You have driven away my daughter, your bastard son stands to inherit my land ... and now this!"

She flung the letter down in front of James.

He replied with nothing more than a puzzled look, then picked up the paper, and briefly scanned the lines.

"My God!" he breathed, appearing shaken.

"You knew nothing of this?"

"What do you take me for? I confess I did know the boy was in prison—"

"And you said nothing?"

"I knew how upset it would make you," replied James. "And there was nothing we could do."

"You knew I would tell Maggie and were afraid she would come home!"

"How dare you!" James retorted. "She is my daughter, too. The last thing I wanted was for her to leave. I fully intended to inform her of his ... his—plight. But she was so worked up over this whole thing. The boy turned her against me. I had hoped to give her enough time to reconsider her actions, to cool off, as it were, and to get fully over her silly infatuation."

"That *silly infatuation* was her husband!"

"It's no secret I bore the boy no love. But this news grieves me as much as anyone." James's tone had calmed and over his face spread a look of grief. "I am deeply sorry for the boy, especially in that he was so troubled. But I cannot say I am equally sorry that our daughter is once and for all free from him. Now maybe she will come to her senses and come home where she belongs. If you know where she can be reached, you should notify her of this news at once."

"Yes, I will have to write her," Atlanta said with a candor in her tone not often displayed for James. "But I am afraid ... I'm afraid my letter may produce just the opposite effect. What if it drives her farther from us? But she must be told."

Slowly Atlanta turned and walked heavily from the room. Gradually the terrible burden facing her came to focus in her thoughts. She must write a letter that could be her only and final hope of getting her daughter back. Yet at the same time it could push Maggie into self-imposed oblivion. Maggie was a strong-willed girl; she could well blame everyone for Ian's fate. And she would be well within her rights to do so.

Dear Lord, Atlanta prayed, *please give me strength and wisdom to do this thing I must do.*

16 Thoughts of the West

The weeks following her futile trip to New York were anguish for Maggie. To have anticipated a moment with every fiber of her strength, only to have its joyous object dissolve into nothingness, was a crushing blow. Had she not been physically strong, it is doubtful her emotions could have withstood the devastating impact of that awful moment. Now she was truly alone in a strange land, with the hope which had sustained her thus far crumbled into doubt and apprehension. Worst of all, she did not know *why* Ian had not come, and was left to the confused and frenzied night-mares of her vivid imagination.

With every approaching rider or wagon, she found herself stopping in the middle of her drudgery, heart pounding wildly. Each time she would jump up, rush to the window and look out, only to return again, each time more disappointed than before. The days passed on and on, one into the next. She gave scarce a thought to her future, only built back her hope again, one tiny piece at a time, that Ian would be on the next ship, and would notify her however he was able. She could wait, she thought. Even if it took two or three more ships from Scotland without Ian, still she could wait. Any wait was worth the joyful thought of once again holding him in her arms, of seeing his smiling face, of listening to his ex-uberant laugh. Just so long as he arrived before their baby was born!

One afternoon shortly before Christmas, Drew burst into the house, his face red—not only with cold but with excitement.

"Evan's got himsel' a Conestoga!" he announced. "Why, 'tis the prettiest thing ye ever saw!"

The response on the part of his wife was considerably less enthusiastic than Drew had anticipated, and his expression quickly sobered.

"What's a Conestoga?" asked Maggie.

"It's a covered wagon. Remember, I showed ye a picture o' one the other day."

"So that's what they're called," replied Maggie. "And you put all your things in them and that's where you live?"

"*A few* of your things is more like it!" said Ellie, speaking out of her cool silence for the first time since Drew had burst in. "Mostly folks have to decide what to leave behind."

"That doesn't sound very appealing," said Maggie.

Ellie merely nodded, while casting Drew a knowing glance as if to say, "You see, I'm not the only one who thinks the whole idea's hairbrained!"

Not to be put off so easily, Drew went on enthusiastically, "It's not so bad. Especially for a new life out west. His wagon'll be Evan's home for several months."

"His whole family!" Maggie exclaimed. "But they're just tiny little things!"

"Ye'd be surprised, Maggie. 'Course, 'cept in poor weather, most o' the folk sleep outside under the wagon itsel'. But when it's cold or rainin', they're right cozy an' snug."

"Well, I don't envy them," Maggie replied. "But I suppose it's no worse than that ship I sailed on."

Drew laughed. "They call 'em *prairie schooners*," he said. "An' maybe that'll be just why. Ye an' yer husband ought t' give it some thought."

Maggie exhaled a sharp sigh. She was silent and everyone in the room, most of all Drew himself, realized he had opened the painful subject of Ian's absence with the word *husband*. In spite of her own troubled and subdued spirit, Ellie walked to Maggie and placed a reassuring arm about her.

"Who knows?" said Maggie at length, "it may be just the thing for us . . . you may be right."

"So," said Ellie, with forced nonchalance, "the McCollough's are movin' out west?"

"They're leavin' in a month," Drew replied. He was in no way oblivious to Ellie's reluctance and spoke cautiously, keeping his enthusiasm in check for the moment.

"Seems a foolhardy thing to do," remarked Ellie, "in the dead of winter and with a war goin' on."

"Ellie," answered Drew, trying to reason with his wife without arguing, "ye know the war's not goin' t' have any effect on that, so long's they stay far enough north t' avoid the fightin'. Why do ye think they passed that Homestead Act? They want t' make sure the west is solidly Union."

"Sometimes these American terms are completely foreign to me," Maggie interrupted. "What is the Homestead Act?"

" 'Tis a law the Congress passed," Drew answered. "Says they'll give ye a hundred an' sixty acres o' land if ye but work it an' live on it fer five years."

"Just give it to you? Free?"

"Aye! Ye see, Maggie, America is a huge land. There's millions o' acres just lyin' fallow belongin' t' the government. 'Tis nothin' like in Scotland wi' all its estates. It would be impossible fer the government t' control that much land. An' they figure the best way fer it t' be productive is fer each person t' own his own piece. A man will work his life out on his own parcel o' dirt—take real pride in it."

"That may explain leavin' in the middle of a war," Ellie said briskly. "'Course, that doesn't bother me so much since I nearly lost you at Bull Run. Nothin' could be like that again. But what about the winter? You explain that, Drew Mackinaw!"

Drew smiled, for he had been waiting for the opportunity to explain that very thing.

"Seems crazy, I ken," he began, "but if we don't leave now, we won't get t' Independence in time t' hook up wi' the wagon trains. Ye got t' cross the prairie in a caravan, Ellie. Wouldn't do no other way, what wi'—"

He stopped short, realizing suddenly what impact his words would likely have on the force of his argument. Yet he was not a deceptive man and would not persuade others by telling them only half-truths. Especially those he loved.

"Well," he continued after a moment, "what wi' Indians an' all. Ellie, I'll not lie t' ye. 'Tis a dangerous trip, an' maybe folks are a wee bit off their chump t' make it. But think o' what's waitin' at the other end! The pick o' the choicest land in the whole country—an' a hundred an' sixty acres is just the start. The land is so cheap, we'd be able t' buy more in no time. Rich pastures an' fields o' wheat as far as the eye can see!"

"The land of milk and honey," said Ellie, more in the tone of a reflection than a criticism.

"Oh, yes, Ellie! Can't ye see it? We're not makin' it here, with the drought an' Kellermann an' all. It's a chance t' start over."

Maggie could not help noticing the similarity of Drew's arguments in favor of moving west with those with which she and Ian had convinced themselves of the wisdom of leaving Scotland for America.

Ellie found herself gazing steadily into Drew's face, alive with the fire which comes with a man's vision. An intense joy gathered in his countenance and she could not help being moved by it. She was, after all, his wife and partner, the woman given this man by the Lord to share the adventure of his life. Gradually she felt her doubts dissolving in the strength of his fervor. She stepped toward him and placed a loving hand on his arm.

"Drew," she said softly. "I think I'm beginnin' to understand how you feel. Can you forgive me for holdin' you back? Wherever you go, I'll follow."

"It wasn't ye holdin' me back, not really. The time just hasn't been right. But now—if ye're willin', I mean truly willin'—I think the time is right. I told ye, Kellermann's given us notice. So I think that's just some kind o' sign that this be the time."

"I'm willin'," answered Ellie simply.

Maggie watched, happy for her new friends. She knew Ellie had taken a great step forward and she was glad for her victory. She wondered if she would ever be so lucky as to have the opportunity to surrender to her own husband in such a loving manner. And she wondered, too, what Drew and Ellie's decision would mean for her own future.

17 A Message from Atlanta

Christmas came to the little farmhouse in Chatham with mingled gaiety and sorrow. For Ellie it signified the last she would spend with her mother and father and the rest of the family for a long time, if not forever. And despite the fact that she had begun preparations for their move with preliminary packing and arranging, she insisted on having her parents and her two sisters with their families—a total of twenty people—to their home for Christmas Day. Besides, she thought, it would give her the chance to dispose of some of their belongings, for she was certain her sisters' families would not turn down any handouts. Having made up her mind that moving west was indeed for the best did not, however, keep Ellie from occasional outbursts of tears at the thought of never seeing her loved ones again.

Maggie welcomed the bustle of the festive day because, for

her, Christmas was merely one more lonely day without Ian—one more day of waiting, one more day of wondering where he was, one more day filled with dreams of their being together once again. She was thankful for the furor of activity to keep her mind occupied. For several days before there had been constant Christmas baking. Even with their precarious finances, Ellie had wanted to hold nothing back for this very special holiday. And when Maggie went to the store for her, she added several things to the list of purchases which she knew the Mackinaws would be unable to afford. It was the least she could do to repay their hospitality and kindness. She only wished she had enough to pay their mortgage. *If Ian would only come*, she thought. *He might be able to help.*

All in all, the two women baked mince and pumpkin pies, fruit bread, and four varieties of cookies, in addition to the staples of a magnificent Christmas feast. Ellie's mother brought a ham, her sisters fresh yams, carrots, and potatoes, and Ellie's father supplied the arm-power—one of the few things he could contribute, he said—to make fresh-churned butter out of the cream from Drew's cows. It was one of the last meals they would contribute toward, for the livestock were scheduled to be sold at auction the following month, the proceeds from which Drew would use to settle his accounts in town and outfit his Conestoga for the journey west.

Both Ellie and Maggie tried, through the activity, each in her own way, to forget the individual trials of their hearts. Yet neither could keep the tears from occasionally flowing in the midst of the frantic pace.

Seeing his wife brush back the tears as she stood in front of the stove on the day before Christmas, Drew went to her and gently drew her aside.

"I'm sorry, Ellie," he murmured softly, "'t' be bringin' this on ye. I know 'tis a hard time."

"This is what the Lord wants for us," she answered firmly, sniffing and wiping her eyes and nose with her apron.

"Well, I'm glad He an' I agree fer a change."

"I'll get over it, Drew. Once we're on our way I won't have time to give it another thought."

Ellie turned to return to the kitchen but was stopped by Drew's hand on her arm.

"Ellie," he said hesitantly. "I know I don't say this t' ye enough, but . . . well, ye'er a good wife—an' I'm thankful fer ye—an'—an' I love ye."

He turned quickly and lumbered from the house before Ellie could throw her arms about his great frame and give him the kiss her heart felt. Ellie smiled and watched him go, her tears now tears of joy. *He is a good man too*, she thought, *and I have much to thank the Lord for*.

Maggie had not been prepared for the difficulty of Christmas Day. Her stoic facade had served her well up till then, masking much of the pain in her heart. But surrounded by Ellie's family, with children and happy shouts all about her, she was barely able to keep from weeping every moment. But her protection gave way entirely when little Bess stepped up to her from the tree with a carefully wrapped package tenderly tied with a single strand of blue yarn.

"What's this?" asked Maggie huskily as tears began to fill her eyes.

"It's for you," the girl said shyly, staring down at the ground.

Suddenly the image of Lucy Krueger rose before Maggie's eyes. This was so like that humble gift she had received so many months ago—in another lifetime, in another world—a gift from a poor peasant girl who had begun to be Maggie's friend.

With trembling fingers, Maggie slipped off the yarn, then opened the paper, her eyes blinking rapidly in order to see. Inside was a pale blue knitted neckscarf. Instantly Maggie realized the girl had made it with her own hands and the last wall of resistance broke. The flow of tears broke through, and she wept in choking sobs, pulling the slender child into her arms as she did.

"Well, I declare, Bess!" Ellie exclaimed. "Aren't you full of surprises? Whenever did you manage to make that?"

"I seen her hidin' out in the barn doin' somethin'," said Tommy Joe.

At last Maggie released Bess and smoothed the girl's hair away from her face. "Bess . . . Bess," she said, trying to stop her crying, "don't you know you could have caught a dreadful cold out there in this weather?"

The girl merely stood and nodded with a half-smile on her face.

"Well, I thank you even if you do," said Maggie, hugging her again. "This is the most special Christmas gift I've ever received. I will treasure this always."

The climax of the day came in midafternoon, after the Christmas meal had ended, when Ellie's sister stood and cleared her throat.

"I have an announcement," Leila said.

Ellie clapped her hands. "Another baby!" she cried.

"At my age!" laughed Leila, not embarrassed at the subject in mixed company. She was taller than Ellie and older by five years. Her appearance was more imposing and her face wore a look of austerity, but she retained the family trait of good humor.

"No. I'm just waitin' for grandchildren now," she replied. "My announcement is this—" She took a deep breath, then turned to her husband. "Maybe you want to tell this, Frank?"

"You're doin' just fine," he replied.

"Well then," she continued, "Frank and I have been a-talkin' an', well . . . we've decided—that is, we think we'll move out west with Drew an'—"

She never had the chance to finish for the scream of joy coming from Ellie's mouth as she jumped up and clasped her hands over her mouth in disbelief.

The remainder of the day proved to be one of renewed mayhem in the little house. Suddenly everything had changed for Ellie—she would have *kinfolk* with her, and that made all the difference in the world. God had answered a prayer, she told Maggie later, that she hadn't even dared to pray. She would still miss her parents and her other brother and sister. But with Leila, the best friend she had ever had, besides being a good sister, the journey would be more wonderful than ever.

The first weeks of the new year were full of anticipation and excitement in the Mackinaw household. Ellie and the children proceeded with the slow process of deciding what could go and what couldn't, while Drew sold, gave away, or traded for provisions what he could of his livestock and equipment—those items which weren't pledged already to Kellermann. For Maggie, however, the weeks were more difficult than ever. Another ship had been scheduled to arrive in January and she fought within herself the urge to travel again to New York to meet it. She knew Ian would come immediately to the farm the instant he set foot in America, but somehow she longed to be standing on the dock when he sailed in.

Ellie talked her out of the journey, however, realizing that another disappointment would devastate her already fragile emotional state.

"He'll come, child," she reassured. "And when he does, he'll be *here* the next day. One afternoon you'll look down the road, and there'll by your Ian runnin' toward you with open arms!"

Maggie tried to smile her thanks for Ellie's comfort.

"And you know we won't leave you here alone. We'll wait as long as we can before we have to go, till he comes. We'll find out every ship due in if we have to, so we will know when to be a-lookin' for him."

Maggie nodded her appreciation, but was unable to say anything.

One afternoon toward the middle of January, Drew approached Maggie, hesitated a moment, then said, "Why don't you and Ian come with us ... out west?"

Maggie merely looked down toward the ground.

"That is," Drew went on, "I just wanted ye t' know that ye'd be welcome, and that we'd love t' have ye join us, fer as far as ye'd want t' be goin'."

"Thank you, Drew," Maggie answered. "Perhaps we will, that is if—" Maggie's voice caught on the remainder of her sentence, for she could not bring herself to say *if he comes*.

Approaching them where they stood, Ellie had heard the last of the conversation. She put her arm around Maggie and said, "He'll come. I know he will. And like I told you before. Don't you worry. We're not goin' to leave you all alone. Drew an' I've decided we're goin' to wait till your Ian's here."

Maggie thanked them both, then turned and walked toward the bare winter fields to be alone and to think. Ellie's words were comforting, but Maggie could find little hope in them. Aside from the farfetched fear that Ian had simply decided not to come, there were other more awful considerations which Ellie and Drew knew nothing about. She had tried to push them from her mind, but they refused to go. What if Ian had not been able to clear his name of that terrible crime? What if her father had had his way? What if he had been tried and convicted, even hanged? *Oh, Lord! no ... please no!* Maggie wailed in bitter agony.

She thought of returning to Scotland. But the risk that Ian had already set out for America was too great. If they missed one another on passing ships, the torment of uncertainty would be magnified all the more.

Oh, God, what should I do? Help me, Lord. Help me!

In the confusion of tormenting thoughts and half-prayers, Maggie threw her shawl about her shoulders and continued down the dirt path. Remnants of the last snowstorm lay in the fields, but on the walkways it had long since turned to mud. The chill bit through to her skin, and Maggie shivered. Yet the crisp air felt good; it reminded her of home, and she suddenly realized how little she had been out-of-doors since arriving in Chatham. Maybe this was just the sort of exercise she needed. In Scotland she had spent nearly every possible moment outside. She thought of Raven, the sleek black mare that had carried her for years over the endless miles of moors and hillsides and sandy beach west of Port Strathy. She could almost feel the Scottish wind whipping through her hair and the spray of salt-water in her face.

Those were wonderful times, she thought, *even though often those long rides had been designed to escape life at home.*

Home ... Maggie smiled wanly as she thought of the place she had called home. A grim, three-hundred-year-old castle with more rooms and corridors than even she had been able to explore in her entire childhood. She had alternately hated and loved it. A tear dampened the corner of her eye. It may never have been home, not in the same sense that this little place in Chatham was home for the Mackinaws. But Stonewycke was such a part of her. *Stonewycke will always be part of me,* she had once told her mother. *I will never forget it.* And what was it her mother had said the day they parted—"It will always be *yours,* Maggie!"

What is a home? she wondered. Was Stonewycke her home? Was it part of her, as she had told her mother? Was that what Atlanta had meant when she said it would always be hers?

Or was her home now with the Mackinaws? Yet they didn't even have a home at all—at least they wouldn't in a few months. Their home would be nothing but a tiny wagon covered with canvas.

When Ian had asked her if she could leave her beloved homeland, Maggie had replied that her home was with Ian. She loved Stonewycke, but it meant nothing without Ian. She loved Scotland, but it too held no meaning apart from him. And now here she was in America, with a family she had known only two or three months. How could she make this her home without Ian?

"Oh, God," she prayed, "are you so cruel that you would take it *all* away from me! Am I to go back? *Oh, what are you trying to tell me!*"

Yet she could never go back. Not without Ian. The strife at Stonewycke, with her father in its midst, was too great. Since her earliest memories she had always had the sense of being caught in the middle, the root of the family contention. Who could tell, perhaps now that she was gone, things were happy again at Stonewycke. How could she ever go back? How could she face her father again? That would be the most bitter pill of all, to go to him, hat in hand, and admit his victory over the love she and Ian had shared. No, she would never do that! She would never forgive him for what he had done to them!

Ian *would* come. They *would* have the life together they dreamed of. And *this* new land would become their home!

As Maggie returned to the house and approached the barn, she saw Drew talking with a man she recognized from her first day in Chatham. The man then turned, climbed onto his wagon, and headed back toward town.

"Maggie!" called Drew as he saw her in the distance.

He ran toward her with something in his hand. "Funny ye should be out here," he said. "I was just headin' into the house t' get ye."

"I needed some fresh air."

" 'Tis a fine day fer it," he replied, reaching her, then stopping to catch his breath. "I just had a visit from Jeb Cramer o'er at the General Store. He brought this fer ye. Looks like it came all the way from Scotland."

Maggie's heart leapt and she took the envelope from Drew's hand with a face that radiated hope.

"Figured ye might feel that way," Drew stated with a smile.

Maggie quickly scanned the envelope. It was smudged and crumpled, and had obviously passed through many hands before finally coming to rest in Maggie's cold, pale fingers. She studied it for a moment, then realized with a sinking feeling that it was not Ian's but her mother's handwriting she recognized.

"Maybe ye'd be wantin' t' be alone," added Drew, sensing her hesitation.

"Yes . . ." she replied. "I think so. I'll go into the barn."

She turned and walked in that direction; Drew gazed after her, then went toward the house.

The familiar smells of animal flesh, manure, and hay greeted Maggie like old friends from the past and she welcomed them. She thought of old Digory with his kind visage and soft, loving voice; a fleeting remembrance of all the time she had spent with him crossed through her mind. She found a mound of hay and nestled down into it.

She looked again at the letter she held in her hand. The precisely elegant script was so descriptive of her mother. Slowly she tore an edge of the paper and then opened the rest of the envelope. Two sheets of fine paper slipped out into Maggie's hand.

With trembling fingers she lifted the pages and, with emotions surging through her, began to read the words which had caused Atlanta such agony to write:

My dearest Maggie,

I was not certain if I could write this letter, but it had to be written and it is best, though it pains me more than you can imagine, that I be the one to impart this news to you.

I thought when you left that your troubles would end and you would finally find the happiness I longed for you to have. I had prayed and hoped for it more fervently than I had ever desired anything in my life. But now I must place upon you instead the greatest of all sorrows. I must tell you, my dearest daughter, that your husband is gone. Gone, I hope, to a final peace, into a final rest for his troubled spirit.

I doubt that it has come to your knowledge that he was arrested shortly after your departure. (What a shock it was for me to learn that you had sailed for America alone!) It appears that while Ian was in prison he refused all attempts at assistance. Even your father made an attempt but it was violently rebuffed (and who could blame the poor boy after the things your father said to him!). Finally there was an accident—a fire.

Oh, dear child! How my heart aches! When the news came of his death, I could not make myself believe it. It simply did not seem possible. But, alas! There can be no doubt—he is gone.

Oh, dear Maggie, I so regret that you must be alone at this terrible moment. How I yearn to put my arms around you and give you what comfort it is within my power to offer. If I cannot do this for you now, let me at least do it for you soon. You will find that I have enclosed some money to secure your passage home. Please come as soon as you can—there is no need for you to be alone. Ian may be gone, but your family is still here at Stonewycke.

> With all my love,
> Mother

The letter fell from Maggie's hand onto the hay-strewn dirt floor. For endless moments she sat motionless, staring straight ahead as if into a void of space. Her brain ceased to function. There were no feelings, no sensations, no tears. All within her had gone numb.

How long she sat there Maggie could not tell, and whether at last she fainted or simply fell into a stupefied sleep she never knew. But just before she slipped from consciousness, the visage of her father rose in her mind.

An hour later Ellie found her curled up in the straw. She awakened her gently, realizing at once from the deathly pallor of her face that some dreadful calamity had befallen her. Maggie stared blankly up at her out of dull, unseeing eyes, and when Ellie reached down to help her to her feet, Maggie could barely stand, her strength spent. Leaning on the mature woman like one of her small children, Maggie allowed Ellie to lead her from the barn. Neither woman spoke as they walked slowly back toward the house.

18   A Grief-Stricken Resolve

For three days Maggie neither spoke nor rose from her bed. Little Bess tended her friend, brought Maggie meals which remained mostly untouched; often she just sat next to the bedside offering her childlike comfort.

On the fourth day, Maggie awoke to find Bess beside her again; only this time the child's head was bowed as she softly murmured what Maggie recognized as an innocent childhood prayer. Keeping still so as not to disturb her, Maggie listened as the child said, "Dear Jesus . . . please help Maggie to be happy again."

As simple words often do, Bess's prayer somehow penetrated the shell of Maggie's pent-up grief. But from beyond the words came the realization that they would never be fulfilled. She never *would* be happy again. The child's faith was naive and misplaced. *All faith was misplaced!* Maggie thought, as tears at last swelled in her eyes. She covered her face with her hands and wept.

Thinking she had caused the outpouring of Maggie's grief, Bess jumped up and scurried downstairs in alarm. Ellie climbed up into the loft and looked upon the scene of heartbreak with relief. She knew there was good in the release of tears, and that often healing could begin no other way. But what she did not realize was that with Maggie's tears of mourning for Ian were mingled the bitter tears of anger and hatred.

"Bess," Ellie called back down, "fetch Maggie a cup of tea. I think it'll help her feel better. An' watch them steps comin' back up."

Ellie turned and sat down on the edge of the bed next to Maggie. She placed a gentle hand on Maggie's shoulder. "Cry, dear Maggie. Just go ahead an' cry it all out."

Still sobbing, Maggie turned a tear-streaked face toward Ellie. "He killed him! It was no fire—my father killed him!"

Knowing practically nothing of Maggie's former life in Scotland, Ellie hid her momentary dismay at the harsh words and continued to soothe the young widow the Lord had placed in her care. In the anguish of the moment, she thought, the girl was raving. She would settle down and accept the reality in time. Until then, she would minister to her as if she were her own kin. Still, Ellie could not hold back an involuntary shiver from the cold tremor of loathing she had detected in Maggie's voice.

Sleep did not come to Maggie that night to block out the pain for a few blessed hours. The tears which had begun in the afternoon continued to flow. Whenever a moment of respite came and she began to doze off, almost immediately a vision from the past would follow and crowd out the moment of calm. Dominating the confused torment of her overwrought brain was not the face of Ian and the awful emptiness she felt, but rather visions of her father. The vague sense of bitterness she had carried through the years intensified, and before the night was through she had heaped upon him blame for every bad thing that had ever happened to her. Visions of Cinder exploded upon her memory, mingled with her father's words to Ian—shouting vicious, threatening, evil words—the night of their flight from Stonewycke. She tried to force herself to think of Ian, to remember his laugh, his voice, the tenderness he had shown her. But always James pushed Ian from her mind, just as he had tried to push him from her life.

And had he not now succeeded? In the end, James Duncan had *won,* just as he said he would. He had always been set on destroying her. His wrath had not been set against Ian at all—it had been directed at her! *It was always me you despised, wasn't it? Me, not Ian.*

The face of her father loomed large in her mind, laughing, toasting his success with his friends ... laughing, laughing. The vision took on grotesque proportions as the lips grew and grew— laughing still—taking over the whole face, and turning evil in their intent. Still he laughed ... she could hear the sinister voice as if it were in the same room.

Of course! He *was* in the same room, for there she sat in the corner. She could see herself just like it was yesterday, sitting in that old wooden chair in her nursery, sitting in the corner watching. Her father was talking with a big man about something. They were talking about Cinder! Now she could hear them perfectly. He was giving the man her horse! *No, Daddy ... no!* she cried. But she could not speak. She couldn't open her mouth or move from the chair. *No, please—Daddy don't!* she shouted. But he didn't hear her. He just threw back his head and laughed, then glanced in the direction of where she sat, gesturing toward her, and said to his companion, "You see, my daughter won't mind. She doesn't care about horses!"

Suddenly the laugh changed and an evil sneer took over her father's face. Still she sat immobile, watching—watching ... powerless to move, to speak, to stand. He was no longer laughing with the horseman but shouting threatening and horrible things. But who was that man he was yelling at? His face was too obscure. If she could just get a little closer. Unable to move from her chair, she squinted, and—yes, it was Ian. *Ian, Ian!* She opened her mouth and tried to force out the words, but they strangled in her throat in a chilling, stifling silence. Still her father was yelling, screaming. Ian was backing away, pleading with him in gentle tones. Suddenly her father pulled a gun from his pocket. *No! no! Daddy, please ... no!* But it was too late. A deafening explosion sounded and Ian slumped to the ground.

At last her muscles were freed and the little girl sprang from the chair and ran toward the dying form. He lay in a pool of red blood, still flowing from the open wound in his chest. On his face was a look of peace, but there was no life left in it. She spun around to face the villain, but the room was empty. She was alone ... alone with the corpse of the only man she had ever loved.

She turned again toward the dead man, but the face which only moments ago had looked so contented to have passed out of the world of the living was fading ... fading. She reached out to touch the beloved face one more time, but her hand sunk to the floor and she was left with only the red pool of blood, still wet where he had fallen and now was no more. From above and around her came the hateful voice, the sound of death—laughing . . . laughing . . . laughing in his triumph, laughing in his final victory. *I hate you . . . I hate you!* she screamed, and now her voice returned—*I hate you!*

Suddenly Maggie started awake in her bed, roused from the nightmare by the sound of her own voice, cold sweat dripping from her body. *Oh, God!* she cried silently, *God . . . help me!* Then she lay back down as new sobs shook her frame.

Maggie turned on to her side, aching for sleep—peaceful, dreamless sleep—to enfold her and deliver her from the prison of her thoughts. All at once a strange fluttering stirred within her.

The child! Her hand sought the place where the new life was growing inside, eager to feel the tiny movement again. Then she realized for the first time—*this child will never see its father.* "Oh, why?" she moaned. "It should not have been this way. We were supposed to have a happy life together. Oh, God, why? What purpose can there be in this heartache and anguish?"

Now Atlanta intruded upon her mind, urging her to return, to come back to the home of her childhood, to the land of her ancestors, to return to be comforted by her family. But what comfort could there ever be at Stonewycke? Yes, she longed to feel the embrace of her mother's arms again. And perhaps there would be some small comfort there. But there would also be the abhorrent presence of James Duncan hovering over her, no specter from her dreams but a living and malefic presence, bent on completing his destruction of her in order to further his own ends. And would not his treacherous intent extend—as it had begun with her and reached to Ian—to her child? Her child! No, she could never let him near the child of her marriage. He would destroy the child as he had destroyed them! He did not care for family, ancestry, the estate, or the future of Stonewycke. He only wanted to secure his own empire, whose future he would place in Alastair's hands. Should her child ever stand in his way, he would stop at nothing to remove any barriers to the execution of his plan. Had he not already demonstrated how far he was willing to go?

But she would not let this child stand in his way. He had won. He could have Stonewycke! But she would keep this baby as far from James Duncan's lethal tentacles as possible, even if it meant keeping the child from Atlanta. For if Atlanta knew where the child was, surely James would find out, and would seek to destroy it. Maggie had been helpless to save Ian, but she would let nothing happen to his child.

"You will never," she determined, voicing her thoughts, "lay eyes on us again!"

Verbalizing her resolve silenced Maggie's trembling thoughts and stilled the flow of her tears. An icy calm stole over her, followed by an uneasy sleep.

She awoke just as the first streaks of dawn were breaking through the night sky. Downstairs the hushed voices of Drew and Ellie filtered up to the loft where she lay.

"... but I don't want to press the poor child," Ellie was saying. "She's already been through so much."

"But—" Drew hesitated in his uncertainty.

"I know, I know," Ellie went on. "The time is drawing so near."

"Harry was by yesterday. He says if we're not out, Kellermann's goin' t' send men o'er t' pack up our things an' haul 'em away. An' we just can't hold the others up much longer."

"I'll talk to her today," promised Ellie.

Maggie slid from the bed, wrapped herself in a blanket, and descended the steps. As the wood floor from the loft creaked beneath her feet, the voices immediately ceased. Drew and Ellie both glanced up, more surprised that she had at last risen from her bed than that they had been caught talking about her.

"I didn't mean to eavesdrop," said Maggie.

"We weren't likin' t' talk about ye," said Drew sheepishly. "But—"

"I've been a real burden for you," interrupted Maggie. "And I'm sorry."

"No, no, my leddy—I mean, Maggie," Drew answered quickly. "Never that. 'Tis just that ... well, we're wonderin' what ye'll be doin' now. I ken 'tis a terrible time t' be thinkin' about such things."

"It may be a terrible time for me," said Maggie, moving fully into the room where the light of the fire seemed to accentuate her pale frailty all the more. "But I realize you have to decide what you're going to do."

There was something in Maggie's tone which was new to her. Ellie saw the same look in Maggie's eyes that Atlanta had seen on the night of their mother-daughter farewell. There was in the set of her face a strength, a determination, a fearlessness of new resolve. It both alarmed and relieved Ellie, for it was a resoluteness of will which could either carry her victoriously forward or plunge her into destruction.

When Maggie opened her mouth to speak again, her voice was steady and clear. "If you are willing to put up with me," she said, "I want to travel west with your family."

19 Dermott Connell

Dermott Connell rested his chin in his folded hands. On the desk before him were piled several huge law books, their leather spines brittle with age, and a half-dozen scattered sheets of paper. They represented, however, not merely a great deal of work but a perplexing legal dilemma. He sighed deeply, rubbed the sleep from his eyes, and looked once more at his desk.

A tall, muscular man in his late thirties, he might easily be mistaken for a common laborer. Indeed, he was no stranger to Scotland's factories and coal mines. But he had given them up long ago to follow the profession of a lawyer. Therefore his labor these days was most often focused on tasks of the mind. One of the city's most respected yet misunderstood lawyers, Dermott Connell had the reputation in the legal community of a maverick, a loner whose penchant for exposing falsehood and proclaiming truth went beyond the bounds of propriety and tradition. The moment Connell caught the faintest hint of a compromise of the truth, his high-principled instincts sprang into action—no matter whom he opposed in the process. To him, principles were everything; practical considerations, if they could not be carried out with integrity, were nothing.

Today, on this gray Glasgow morning, his mind was focused on the dismal state of one of his clients. He had spent half the night obtaining the troubling bit of information; now perhaps it would be better if he had never found out—or never taken the case in the first place. His client, one Harvey Bidwell, was a poor man whose work in the shipyards was more off than on, and whose large family depended on him for their sustenance. Not a man given to hasty conclusions, Dermott had finally come to believe the man's pleas of innocence and had committed himself to his defense when no one else had given him so much as a nod. Harvey's crime was not an especially heinous one—he had been accused of embezzling a few shillings from his employer, A. P. Carey. Now he was locked up in prison, and doomed to remain there for some time unless something was done to help him.

For half the night Dermott had trudged about the grimy back alleys of the Glasgow Saltmarket. He had questioned dozens of the city's more seamy inhabitants, hoping to find a witness to corroborate Harvey's story that he was nowhere near Carey's Coffee House on the Trongate at the time of the burglary. But he had, in fact, learned just the opposite. Harvey had been seen slipping into the shop's rear door a short time after closing. The witness seemed reliable. But in that part of town, of course, virtue was not always the motivating factor in things that were said.

All at once Connell's door burst open and the lawyer's head jerked up from its tired reverie.

"Didn't mean to startle you, old boy," said the visitor, a stocky well-dressed man about Dermott's own age.

"I'm afraid I was deep in thought," Connell replied with a smile. "Though I admit after last night it wouldn't take a great deal to put me to sleep." He ran a hand through his thick black hair and leaned back in his chair.

"You waste too much time thinking, Connell," laughed the visitor.

"Time spent thinking is never time wasted, Langley," he replied, the serious, almost intense timbre of his voice contrasting sharply to the other's light joviality. "The Lord gave us minds to think with and wills to move mountains with. But you can't move the mountains without thinking first what to do."

"Well, I still say it's no way to start out the day—so serious and pensive."

Connell smiled, but his upturned lips seemed to oppose the melancholy depths of his cobalt-blue eyes. He bore heavily the troubles of Harvey Bidwell and those of a half-dozen others in similar straits.

"You've been up all night, haven't you, Connell?" Langley went on. "No doubt tromping after one of those poor devils you call clients." Langley Howard was a competent barrister, and in his own way given to compassion now and then. But he would never dream of staying out past seven o'clock on a case.

"They have as much right to representation as any," replied Connell calmly, "and perhaps more need of it than most."

"I only wish I could afford your benevolence," Langley said. "But I'm a family man now, and I need more from my clients than promises of good faith."

"Not everyone is called to follow such a course, Langley, my friend. But he would be a fool who spurned his calling."

"Quite right," Langley replied more thoughtfully. Then resuming his jovial tone, he continued. "Now, as to why I barged in on you in the first place. Agatha has asked me to invite you to dinner this evening. It would seem my wife's calling is akin to yours— taking in stray cats and poor bachelors!"

"Then it would be foolish indeed of me to refuse Agatha's kindness and her wonderful cooking!" replied Connell with a good-natured laugh. "I would not want to stand in the way of *her* calling."

Langley opened the door to let himself out, then as if only remembering an afterthought, turned once more toward his friend.

"One more thing," he said, then hesitated before going on. "You've heard that Lord Crowley has been making inquiries into engaging a permanent advisor to manage the affairs of his estate?"

"I heard nothing of specifics," Connell answered. "Though I did understand he was in Glasgow."

Langley eyed his friend a moment before speaking. "You're not capable of false modesty," he said at length, still with a hint of the question in his eye, "so you must indeed not have heard." He closed the door, stepped back inside, and approached Connell in a confidential manner. "Rumor has it that Crowley has his eye on you."

An amused flicker awoke in Connell's eye, which grew, giving way to a wide grin, then a mighty laugh. Almost immediately his serious look returned, but the twinkle in his eye remained.

"Me?" he chuckled. "What use could a man like him possibly have for a malcontent like me?"

"Go ahead, laugh, Dermott," said Langley, taking his turn to be sober. "But it is true. He was observing you yesterday in the courtroom, and I've heard he was impressed. It's no secret that it would be a highly prestigious position. This could be quite a coup for you, Dermott—a real advance in your career."

"Langley, you said I was not one given to false modesty, and I thank you for that compliment. And in that light, I can only assume that Crowley must certainly have been eyeing someone else. And even if what you say is true, can you imagine a man more unfit for such—a—calling? My methods would not fit in with the sort of thing he is used to. And I most certainly would not alter my convictions. Lord Crowley's circles are a bit removed from my realm. I can assure you, I possess no such career aspirations as you allude to."

"Your realm being the back streets and gutters where—"

"Where people need help," replied Connell almost sharply. "Certainly more good can be done there than in advising a wealthy lord how to make still greater fortunes."

"I have a feeling you would be able to do great good there, for I doubt you would be intimidated or bedazzled by it all. A man like you would—"

Langley stopped, suddenly realizing that arguing Connell against his conscience was futile. He smiled and turned the conversation into a light vein.

"You'd surely set the Glasgow Bar a-talking, that much would be certain!"

"Well, regardless of that," Dermott replied good-naturedly, "Crowley will have to look elsewhere for his pigeon. I have no intention of denying the calling the Lord has given me. And I have more important matters to occupy my time as it is."

When the door finally closed behind his friend, Connell returned his thoughts to the predicament which had been occupying him before Langley's visit, the news of Lord Crowley dimming perceptibly in light of the hard luck of a penniless embezzler.

He had always known the day would come when he would find himself in just such a scrape, though he had tried to avoid it by judiciously reviewing every potential case beforehand. It had always been part of his creed never to take on a case he did not thoroughly believe in, so that there would be no disparity between his client's success and his own convictions. But now here he was facing that dreaded dilemma he had sought to avoid: Could he defend a man he knew was guilty?

Certainly he could aid his family and offer comfort to them. And he could do his best to lighten the rigors of the man's prison sentence. But he faced a more pressing question: Could he use his lawyer's wiles and deductive skills to fight for the release of a man, knowing all the while he was arguing against justice and truth? He had given the man his pledge; he had *taken* the case.

Was not doing his best to secure the man's release inherent in having taken the case upon himself? Was not that the essence of being a lawyer? Had he not so pledged himself when standing before the judges of the Bar? Was not that how every lawyer in the land viewed his calling? Was not that principle at the root of a free society where every man, however guilty he may appear, deserved the right to a solid defense?

To every question he would answer *yes*. Then why was this uncertainty still gnawing at his gut?

As he turned the dilemma over in his mind, arriving at no apparent solution, gradually his thoughts awoke into prayer.

"What would you do, Father? Your Son knew the hearts of men and knew what was best for them. And you must constantly face this situation, for all men are to you as Harvey Bidwell is to me. How do you respond, Lord? You forgive, you love. How I wish all society could respond thus to Harvey Bidwell! Oh, Lord Jesus, show me what *is* in Harvey's best interest. Show me, Lord, what you would have me do."

Dermott sighed, inwardly calmed by the prayer, though he knew an answer would not come easily. He removed his watch from his pocket, glanced at it briefly, then replaced it. He closed the books, straightened the papers, and rose to leave.

His office was located on the second floor and toward the rear of the drab but stately stone building on the Trongate. This particular street represented the hub of the Glasgow business community where sat dozens of such buildings containing hundreds of offices, Connell's being undoubtedly one of the least pretentious.

He often mused that he had not been placed toward the back of the building by mere chance, but rather by the specific design of the more respectable occupants. And it suited him perfectly, for most of his clients were glad to be able to slip in and out, using the back stairway unnoticed. Yet in truth, very few of Dermott's *people,* as they were sometimes called, ever came near his office. Most were either already in prison, or close to it, and had all but given up hope—never even considering the luxury of professional legal counsel. Dermott usually sought out his clients rather than the reverse.

Today he would have to visit the tollbooth again. But this time it would be to confront Harvey Bidwell with the truth.

Dermott stepped out into the street, then stopped briefly to button his old tweed coat against the winter chill. A fine mist fell from the sky, destined to soak his thick dark hair long before he reached his destination. He had never been able to develop the habit of wearing a hat, though Dr. Townsend, his landlord and a retired physician, had often remonstrated him for this. He had tried to do so early in life, but found he was forever removing his hat and leaving it someplace or other. Townsend would laugh over his excuse, saying a forgetful memory when it came to the misplacements of hats was at least one sure way of keeping poverty from the door of the milliner's. But the good doctor realized Connell's mental lapses rarely extended beyond the loss of hats, and had come to greatly respect the keen instincts and sharp mind of his young friend. The thought of Townsend reminded the lawyer that he must inform the doctor that he would not be in for dinner this evening. He would send a message when he finished at the prison.

Even at this hour of the morning, traffic was heavy along the wide street. Public horse cars, carriages, and people with an infinite variety of business on their minds pursued their daily activities despite the steadily increasing drizzle. Dermott walked briskly east past the row of great stone buildings darkened by the perpetual soot of the city. Within fifteen minutes he had reached the Saltmarket at the fringes of the slum where Harvey Bidwell lived. How fitting that the tollbooth should be located so near, to house the city's ne'er-do-wells until a more permanent place could be found for them. The building itself was far less noble, a structure of hewn stone with a tower considerably too lofty and imposing for the infamous place.

Dermott breathed deeply before entering. This would be his last breath of fresh air for some time and he used it to full advantage, filling his great lungs full. More, however, he used the moment's pause to whisper a quick prayer for grace and wisdom. *If ever I needed the mind of Christ,* thought Dermott, *now is that time.*

The main entryway bore the appearance of many similar buildings on the Trongate, conducting their enterprises from day to day with various clerks and employees milling about. However, the business of this place was of a considerably different nature.

Dermott paused to speak with the chief wardman who then called another wardman to assist Dermott to his destination.

"Well, guv'nor," the second man said as he led the way down a long corridor, "ye think the rain'll gi' us a breather?"

"It doesn't appear so, Willie."

"What wi' the snow an' all a fortnight past, my wife's near her death o' cold."

"I'm sorry to hear that. If there's anything I can do . . ."

"Thank ye, sir. We jist need a few days o' sunshine t' dry out her bones."

"Well, you and your wife say your prayers then, Willie."

"Are ye thinkin' the Lord'd trouble himsel' wi' the likes o' such a prayer?"

"I'm more sure of it than I am of anything, my friend. And you let me know if I can be of help to you."

They had by now walked along the main hall and passed through two great iron doors into the heart of the gaols. The stone walls and floor became increasingly dingy as they walked and the fresh outside air had given way to an inundating stench. They passed a stair winding steeply downward into the belly of the building, and at last Willie unlocked and shoved open another heavy iron door. This opened into a large room where several men were variously lying about on mats or pacing aimlessly to and fro. No man without a strong constitution could long have withstood the sight and smell of such deprivation.

"Bidwell!" Willie called. "Harvey Bidwell, ye got ye a visitor."

From the far end of the room a man slowly stepped forward. He was tall and gangly, stooped at the shoulders, and with his tousled hair and squinted eyes, he looked easily twenty years beyond his age of thirty-one. The ankle-irons prevented him from approaching more than a step or two toward his visitor.

"Harvey," Dermott said, stepping toward the man and extending his hand. "How is it with you?"

"Fair t' middlin', sir," Harvey replied without enthusiasm.

Willie unlocked the ankle-irons and the lawyer led the prisoner to a bench in the hallway where they could talk in semi-privacy. As they sat down on the ancient splintered wood, Dermott caught an uneasy glance from Harvey, as if he had some premonition of the sort of pointed questions which were about to be put to him. It was a difficult, even agonizing interview for Connell.

Midway through he suddenly came to the realization that Harvey Bidwell was indeed one of Glasgow's most skilled actors. He still refused to admit guilt, but now Dermott could see and hear in him those subtle signs betraying true motive which he had missed on previous occasions. There was in the convict's voice a timbre of belabored sincerity and in his eye a nervous glint. The light was so dim he could scarcely see it. Yet he could somehow *feel* it all the while they talked.

Dermott had long since risen above the petty feelings of insecurity over his own initial mistaken judgment of the man's intent. Lawyers were taken in. It had happened before and it would no doubt happen again. He was not hurt or angered by Bidwell's dishonesty; he was profoundly saddened by the man's inability to see his own folly.

When he finished the interview and was waiting for Willie to lock him back into the dingy room, he still had come to no decision regarding Bidwell's disposition. Forever clouding his judgment was the impoverished picture of Harvey's wife and three innocent children. He could perhaps leave Bidwell to the mercies of the state, but then what of the family that depended on him?

He and Willie were progressing down the dim corridor when they heard a jangling of keys and a mild commotion. All at once two figures emerged from the stairwell rising from the lower depths of the building. The one in the lead, though clearly not the leader, was pushed headlong into Connell.

"Watch yer step, ye miserable cuddy!" shouted the other, a jailer. "Sorry, yer honor," he added in Dermott's direction.

The lawyer barely heard the hasty apology, for his attention had been arrested by the prisoner who had stumbled into him. Like all inmates in this place, he was lean and gaunt. His light sandy hair was unwashed and hung to his shoulders as his clothing hung in rags from his body. He would have remained to Dermott indistinguishable, except that as he was pushed, their eyes met. In that passing instant Connell saw a different kind of desperation than he had ever seen. There was something in those silently pleading eyes that spoke, not just of innocence, but of heartbreaking confusion. And there was the hint of a spark of love which had not yet been fully extinguished.

This indefinable something arresting Dermott's gaze caused him to take in additional details which would otherwise have slipped by him. The prisoner was little more than a lad. Even in his wretched state it was clear he could be no older than nineteen or twenty. Then there were his clothes. Rags to be sure, but they had once been the garb of a gentleman. And still those eyes—a mute appeal, a hopelessness, the look of life slowly fading, but not dead yet.

Before Dermott could say a word or offer even the hand of hope the man so desperately needed, the jailer nudged the prisoner forward with a sharp poke from his cudgel and away down the corridor he shuffled with his guard limping after him.

"Who was that?" Connell asked as if waking from a daze.

"I dinna ken," replied Willie.

"Surely you must know his name," the lawyer persisted.

"Not that one," said Willie. "Everythin's real hush-hush about him."

"Why?"

"I axt na questions, but jist do my job."

"What do they call him?"

"Well, Jerry there is in charge o' the de'ils doonstairs. He'd be the one fer ye t' talk to. I heard Jerry call him yer lairdship sometimes."

"What is he in here for?" Dermott asked as he watched an iron door clang shut behind the two retreating figures with a finality that made him shiver.

"Now *that* I can tell ye, sir," Willie answered, glad for the chance to vindicate his appearance of ignorance. "He's here for murder!"

"Murder!" Dermott exclaimed in an astonished voice. "But why is he *here*? He's obviously been here a long time. Has he been brought to trial?"

"I'm afraid I canna answer any more questions, Mr. Connell. Ever since the fire down in that part o' the prison, they been keepin' a closer guard on that bloke than ever, an' nobody's sayin' nothin'. Maybe ye ought t' talk wi' Jerry—though I'm doubtin' he'd be knowin' more'n me."

That evening Dermott was a less than entertaining dinner guest. He could not erase the young prisoner's eyes from his memory. At length he broached the subject with his host.

"Langley," he said, "have you heard of any gentleman being imprisoned down at the Saltmarket? I'd say in the last two or three months?"

Langley laughed. "Some of them are in and out of it constantly."

"I don't mean for disturbing the peace or welching on a debt. Have you heard of a murder?"

"Hmm," Langley pondered, sipping his brandy slowly. "A murder ... no—and I doubt that something of that magnitude would slip past me. I say, Connell, are you finally giving some thought to the upgrading of your clientele? A gentleman, you say?"

"I would certainly never dream of prejudicing myself against our nobility," Dermott replied soberly, without the slightest hint of a jest. "I would take on the defense of any king's son as readily as any beggar's if the man turned to me for the sort of help I could give. And of course, if I felt the Lord's prompting me to do so."

"Yes, yes ... quite. Well, in any case, have a brandy, Connell?"

Dermott shook his head while Langley poured himself another. Suddenly he thumped his head. "That's it!" he cried. "I knew it couldn't get by me! Surely you remember? Lord Byron Falkirk's son—you know, the Falkirks from the estate of Kairn up north. It happened about four months ago. He was murdered under very odd circumstances. I was in Aberdeen shortly after it happened. Perhaps that's why I heard about it. Now that I think of it, it is rather strange how the whole thing was kept so quiet."

"You think intentionally so?"

"I don't know. The whole affair dropped quickly out of the news. I know there were suspicions floating about which the authorities couldn't substantiate. There was another local laird involved too. There was something about his daughter being involved with the younger Falkirk."

"What happened?" Dermott asked, leaning forward in his chair. "Do they know who killed him?"

"I don't believe it was proven conclusively, but the rumor I heard involved the Earl of Landsbury's son—a typical love triangle, a fight over the girl. I suppose we never heard more because he died in prison after they finally caught up with the boy."

"Died?" Dermott queried. Again the visage of the bedraggled youth rose in his mind. "He was never brought to trial?"

"I never heard anything of it."

Dermott pondered his friend's words. Yes, there could be no doubt that a trial such as that would have been widely publicized and could hardly have escaped the attention of the two barristers. He thought about the evening's events over and over as he walked home later that night. He climbed the steps of Dr. Townsend's stately residence near George Square, then suddenly remembered he had never sent the good doctor a message about his dinner plans.

20 The House at George Square

A tiny sliver of pale light in the gray sky was the only sign that morning had ascended over Glasgow. The light struck the high dormer window in the garret of Dr. Elijah Townsend's ancient brick house at just the proper angle to reflect down across Dermott Connell's bed.

He started awake, and for a man who had had one nearly sleepless night followed by another late one, he greeted the morning energetically. He swung his feet out of bed in order to gain a better look out the window. The light had fooled him into thinking the sun had broken through. But what he saw was only a small streak of sunlight across the sky, surrounded by the massive gray clouds that had hung over the city for days.

He smiled and softly murmured one of his favorite passages from the twenty-eighth chapter of Deuteronomy: "The Lord shall open unto thee his good treasure, the heaven to give rain unto thy land in his season, and to bless all the work of thine hand."

The rain had its good work to do and Dermott could therefore welcome it gladly. The night had been a restless one, disturbed by dreams of haunted youths and gloating judges and penniless thieves. But as the rain washed the dingy city, so the new morning renewed Dermott's spirit.

The room was small but comfortable in its plain way. In addition to the bed with its quilt which Mrs. Townsend had made him some years ago before her death, a desk and chair sat under the dormer, and a bookcase stood against the wall, jammed with an assortment of volumes: *Ivanhoe* and other favorites of Sir Walter Scott's, poetry, some sermons, a first novel by a fellow Scotsman by the name of MacDonald, and a number of ancient volumes on Roman law. On the desk, Dermott's Bible lay open where he had left it the previous night on returning from Langley's. The particular passage which had sparked his interest had not been on forgiveness, for he had already resolved to do whatever he could for Harvey Bidwell, in or out of prison, if for no other reason than because he could not yet give up on the man's spiritual regeneration. Whether this help would come in the courtroom or after Bidwell's probable conviction, he didn't know. But he would continue to pray, and the Lord would do His work; Dermott Connell was again at peace in that regard.

But instead of Harvey, Dermott's mind had been elsewhere, and the book was still opened to the fourth chapter of Luke. The desperate image of that poor youth he had seen so briefly in the prison had never once left his mind during his every waking hour since, and had even intruded into his dreams. As Dermott dressed, he paused to look at the passage once more. *The Spirit of the Lord is upon me, because he hath anointed me to preach the gospel to the poor; he hath sent me to heal the brokenhearted, to preach deliverance to the captives, and recovering of sight to the blind, to set at liberty them that are bruised . . .*

Here certainly was hope for the despairing. And if he never again saw that young gentleman, at least Dermott was comforted that hope existed for such as he. Those very words had comforted Dermott as he neared the end of his own search for faith.

He finished dressing, then descended the three flights of stairs to the main body of the house. He could have had any other room in the great place, many with much finer appointments than the garret. But he had chosen his present quarters because of their simplicity and because he liked its high aspect, with a broad view of the city reaching, upon occasion, even as far as the Clyde.

Dr. Townsend was already in the dining room, seated at the table in his usual place near the hearth.

"Up with the chickens as usual, Elijah," said Connell, greeting the old gentleman warmly.

"Yes," the doctor replied. "But on my feet before you as well, and that is not so usual!"

"I have been something of a sluggard," said Dermott, seating himself at the table.

Dr. Townsend laughed. He knew Dermott all too well and did not even attempt a response.

At sixty-two, Dr. Elijah Townsend was one of those rare individuals who combined a youthful vitality with such a depth of wisdom and venerability that he was both respected and loved by all whom he met. Beneath thick white brows, his eyes sparkled with life, and the white fringes of hair circled his balding head like a halo. Spare in girth, his slightly bent frame stood only a few inches shorter than Dermott's. The lawyer had lived with the older man for eight years and still could not say whether Dr. Townsend was more a father, a brother, or a best friend to him. Indeed, he occupied each of those roles in relation to his young companion. For it was the doctor who knew Dermott best, who had been part of his past struggles and victories. It was the doctor who had nurtured him through more than one crisis as he was slowly gaining his spiritual feet. It was the doctor who had laughed with him, cried with him, talked him through times of weakness, and more than any other single person was responsible for the man of God Dermott Connell had in the end become. And it was now the doctor to whom Dermott could most fully open his heart and share the burdens of his vision of service to Glasgow's downtrodden.

"You were in late last night," Dr. Townsend commented, noting a hollowness in the lawyer's eyes that perhaps only he could have detected.

Before Dermott could reply, Tillie, the housekeeper, scurried into the room carrying two steaming bowls of porridge on a tray.

"Och! 'Tis you is it, Mr. Connell. There ye be at last!" she said with no attempt to disguise her scolding tone. "Yer dinner still sits untouched on the sideboard there, as cold as stone."

"I'm sorry, Tillie," replied Dermott with true contriteness in his voice. "I will try to repent of such thoughtless actions in the future."

"Hoots! 'Tis rich, that!" Her round face changed in an instant from the former sternness to a look of good-humored embarrassment. "Ye were no doubt out doin' some good, an' what's a cold dinner t' that!" She set the bowls down in front of the men and returned to the kitchen, calling over her shoulder as she went, "I'll hae some fresh bannocks for ye in a minute."

The men turned their attention to their meal and nothing was said for a few moments. At length Dermott was the first to speak.

"I apologize to you also, Elijah," he said, "for failing to send you word that I planned to be absent for dinner. I was with Langley."

"No need, my boy. Such things happen, and we have over the years learned to remain flexible with the rise and fall of circumstances."

"Yes, but this was simply pure thoughtlessness on my part." Dermott paused to sprinkle salt over his porridge, then stirred the hot cereal before continuing. "But I must admit, though, something has happened which has quite overtaken my mind. I can seem to find no mental rest since it happened."

"I could tell there was some trouble behind those eyes of yours."

"The incident itself covered the span of merely a few seconds. Yet I still cannot escape the impression it made on me."

"There may be good reason for this," said Dr. Townsend. "Is not that frequently how *He* speaks to us?"

"Exactly! And that is precisely why I have been wondering—"

Just at that moment Tillie burst into the room again bearing a tray of bannocks and thick slices of cheese. She served her two charges, then poured out for them cups of the strong black coffee they both enjoyed. Dermott commented on the wonderful nature of the meal and Tillie beamed as she again retreated into the kitchen.

"I don't know what I'd do, Dermott," mused Dr. Townsend as he lowered his cup from his lips, "if you disdained my preference for this foreign drink as so many of our countrymen do."

"There are moments when a soothing cup of tea is the perfect thing. But on a morning such as this, I heartily endorse the coffee for which this house is known!"

"I suppose you're right; they each have their place. Now, go on with what you were telling me."

"I was at the gaols on Saltmarket yesterday visiting one of my clients," Dermott resumed, "when I *chanced* to bump into another prisoner. Elijah, I shall never forget that face! So tragic, so hopeless, yet with the ray of something unknown, the glimmer of love and the life he had left behind. So desperate were the eyes crying out, yet they seemed to know they would never be heard. Without hope, yet with a glint of life that could not be extinguished."

"Nothing is *chance* in our lives, my friend," said the doctor with a smile.

"How well I know! Don't forget, you taught me to see the Lord's hand in every circumstance."

"You should say, we learned it together. Please go on. I am intrigued."

"Mind you, everything I have just recounted transpired in but a few seconds. Later that evening I dined with Langley Howard and questioned him about the youth I had seen."

"How did you come to question Langley?"

"I forgot to mention, the bearing and aspect of the man, despite his ragged appearance, indicated high birth. Langley would be likely to know of such a one being imprisoned."

"A gentleman in rags, imprisoned in the Saltmarket gaols!" Townsend exclaimed. "The case grows more and more curious. That alone could well pique the curiosity of such a one as you. Did you learn who this unfortunate is?"

"Now comes the puzzling part of the whole question. One would think that the imprisonment of such a one would have come to our attention, especially for a crime as hideous as murder, of which this youth has been accused. But neither Langley nor myself could recall any talk of it among the legal community of the city. And when I asked Willie, one of the wards of the place, about him, he said things had been kept secretive about the young man and his case."

"Hmm," voiced the doctor with a puzzled expression. "I think I begin to understand why your inquisitive mind latched onto this and can't seem to let it loose."

"Langley remembered a crime up north several months back. A certain George Falkirk was killed."

"Certainly," said the doctor. "I recall reading of it, the heir to the estate of Kairn, up near Aberdeen somewhere—nearer Banff, actually. I have heard the old earl has accumulated a sizeable fortune. Though with his son gone I doubt it will bring much happiness. Money never does, as the Lord said. But I am beginning to ramble. Back to your prisoner. You think he is connected somehow to the death of Falkirk?"

"That is one of the troubling elements. The son of the Earl of

Landsbury was arrested for the crime."

"Are you certain?" asked the doctor. "Landsbury is a powerful man. He is not unfamiliar to me. And he would certainly have the power to keep something like this out of the papers. So you think the lad you saw might be Landsbury's son?"

"The thought did occur to me. But Landsbury's son is reported to have died in prison. There was a fire shortly after Christmas."

"Then you do have something of a mystery on your hands," Townsend remarked with a sigh, settling back on his chair to reflect on the full implications of all he had just heard.

"Yes—and I am afraid it is definitely on my hands," said Dermott with a curious mixture of humor and sobriety, "for I doubt I shall find a moment's rest until I get to the bottom of it." He made another attempt at his meal, growing cold like its predecessor on the sideboard. But the doctor could already see the signs of restlessness overtaking him. "What do you know of Landsbury?" Dermott asked after a lengthy pause.

"I met him last year in London," Dr. Townsend replied, thinking over each word as he spoke. "I can think of nothing particularly striking about the man. He sits in the House of Lords and is quite influential, from what I understand. Much of the talk, upon that occasion, did in fact turn upon his sons, though none of the talk was in Landsbury's presence. It seems the elder has distinguished himself in the Navy and will no doubt follow his father into Parliament. The younger son, Theodore, was something of a troublemaker, the subject of the unquenchable gossip of those London circles. The father has on numerous occasions bailed his son out of difficulties which were an embarrassment to his reputation."

"Then the earl is the benevolent sort?" Dermott offered.

"Not the Landsbury I met, I'm afraid to say. Quite the opposite, I believe. It is far more likely it is the mother who has championed the son's cause."

There followed another lengthy pause, during which neither man touched his food and both sat absorbed in thought.

"I wonder why Landsbury's son would kill Falkirk?" Dr. Townsend mused, half to himself.

"Langley said there was a girl involved."

"Ah! Not an unfamiliar motive for murder."

"Not unfamiliar. Yet not common among gentlemen. And from such well-known families."

"If I might offer you some counsel, Dermott," said the doctor seriously, "I would say that if you choose to follow this course— that is, if you feel the Lord prompting you forward in it—you must prepare yourself for stiff opposition from Lord Kairn, or perhaps Landsbury himself."

"Yes, I know," replied Connell, drawing the words out slowly. "But I sense that my hand is already set to the plow, and that it is too late for me to alter the course before me."

"I thought as much," said Elijah. "Then I will pray all the harder for you."

21   Stone Walls

"I tell you, Connell, the man you're looking for isn't here!"

"You're sure there is no chance you overlooked—"

"None whatever!" interrupted the warden belligerently. "No murderer would sit here for two months without my knowing it!"

"I simply thought that with the unusual circumstances of the case—"

"How many times do I have to tell you, Connell? He's not here!" the man replied with steadily rising anger. "That's the trouble with you independents, you think you can just walk in and have the run of the place. Well I know your kind, Connell. And it won't work with me. Do you hear? It won't work!"

"I'm sorry, I didn't mean to—"

"Just get out!"

Slowly Dermott rose and left the warden's office. All morning he had been battling various authorities connected with the Saltmarket gaols. No one would admit to the presence of such a prisoner as he described. He had finally worked his way up to the warden himself, with the same result. Under no circumstances would they allow an arrogant young lawyer to roam about among the prisoners with nothing more to go on than a few hazy notions of thwarted justice and an unnatural desire to help society's outcasts.

Stepping from the warden's office, Dermott hesitated momentarily, trying to decide what to do next. The best thing, he concluded, would be to go home, take stock of the situation, and ask the Lord for guidance. With that resolve, he made his way toward the end of the hall toward the main entrance. About halfway down the corridor he heard a voice.

"Mr. Connell!" The tone was a labored whisper, as if the speaker wanted to be heard by no one but Dermott.

"Yes, sir," said Dermott, turning around to see the warden's assistant poking his head halfway out his office door, glancing about nervously.

"I ... that is—this is," the man began to reply as Dermott approached; "—please come into my office," he said finally, still speaking in little more than a whisper.

Dermott did not hesitate. The man closed the door behind him, saying confidentially, "This is a very delicate matter. We mustn't be heard."

Dermott did not reply, but sat down in the chair indicated by the man. He looked quickly around the office. J. Ellis Withers, the man who had summoned him, looked about thirty, with thick spectacles and thinning brown hair. He was clearly agitated, but whether that was the result of his nature or the nature of his present business was unclear.

"I have heard of your inquiry," he began, his eyes continually darting about, as if the three offices between his and his superior's were insufficient separation. "I don't know if I can help you, but ... I have kept my eyes closed long enough."

"At this point, Mr. Withers, anything would be a great help," said Dermott.

"I know you are a respectable lawyer. There are others who think your views of justice, shall we say, misplaced. They think if a man is born to poverty, then it's nothing more than he deserves if he happens to wind up in here. But I wanted to work for the prison system because I wanted to help these kinds of men. I'm sure you can understand—"

"Yes, Mr. Withers, I think I do. Perfectly, in fact."

"But there are just too many ... that is, there is no way I've found to help—the system is ... but I want you to know I have never been a party to what has happened. At first I was afraid ... now of course, I am ashamed of myself ... but with the security of my job—though it's not much of a job, now that I think of it— but I was afraid to lose it."

He paused, struggling to find words to express what was on his mind. At length he went on. "But I finally feel compelled to do something."

"Please, I don't want you to jeopardize yourself for me."

"No, Mr. Connell. I respect and admire what you do with these men. It's what I have wanted to do myself, to serve, to make a difference."

"Follow your conscience, Mr. Withers. I can ask nothing more."

Withers took a deep breath, sat down behind his desk, then began slowly in a voice of resolve and decision.

"I believe, Mr. Connell, that the man of whom you have been inquiring *is* in this prison, though I have no idea who he is. He was brought here in the dark some months ago. I did not lay eyes on him personally, but—as much as they tried to keep the matter quiet—I got wind of it through a guard. I inquired; the warden told me not to concern myself, said he would handle all the details with this prisoner, and that was the last I knew of it. But if you knew our warden you would know that he is never personally involved with any of the inmates. So I could hardly help being curious. I tried to see the prisoner myself, but was barred at all points by the guards and referred back to the warden. He left me no doubt that my job would be affected if I meddled in the affair again."

Throughout his speech, Withers fumbled with a pen on his desk, rolling it in his fingers and tapping it on the dark oak surface. All at once he rose, began pacing the room, and went on, "I fear something is amiss. And I have allowed it to continue too long. There are principles involved here. I don't know what can be done to remedy the situation ... I don't know if I—or perhaps you—I'm not really certain of—the way to ... proceed. But perhaps you—that is, you seem like a man who could do something."

"First, Mr. Withers, it is imperative I see the man. That is where we must begin if the truth is to be obtained."

"Naturally," Withers replied. He stopped his pacing, stood still for a moment, then turned toward his desk with face brightening. Hastily he pulled a paper from his drawer and began writing. When he had finished in a few moments he handed it across the desk to the lawyer. "This," he explained, "is the name of another prisoner *downstairs*, as we call it. It is also an authorization to see him. That will at least get you in the general direction of the man you seek."

"I do not like you endangering yourself—"

"I am not exceeding my authority," Withers replied, a look of satisfaction, almost enthusiasm, spreading over his face.

"I know you are acting on the best of motives. And whenever truth is served, the man upholding it cannot be hurt. I am confident the Lord will bless your intentions to help."

"Now," said Withers, "the men downstairs are brought up for an airing twice a week. I am certain the man you want is never with these, but generally two or three guards accompany this group. At these times the downstairs cells are left manned with only one guard for a space of about half an hour."

"That should give me time to make a beginning at least. Thank you, Mr. Withers. I will be in touch with you if there is news. And I will pray for the safety of your job."

"Don't worry about me. Perhaps it's time I had a new position anyway."

"Then I will pray you are led into one of service, where you clearly belong."

22   A Downstairs Interview

The descent into the bowels of the Saltmarket prison was narrow and steep. Where the stone steps were not worn smooth, they were broken and jagged and in the dim light could be treacherous to unfamiliar feet. It was not a pleasant journey under any circumstances, but Dermott felt a deep sense of purpose and satisfaction. Not only did he finally have hopes of actually laying eyes again on the wretched youth who had so occupied his thoughts of late, but also he was penetrating yet deeper into the heart of his ministry. Here were imprisoned souls he had till now never been able to reach, men so miserable that their unfortunate counterparts above trembled at the mere thought of being sent *downstairs*. The prison system was so appalling that short sentences were a blessing, even when they ended at the gallows. Death was preferable to a long sentence in one of these dungeons where even a month was considered a living death, not to mention years. The words of his Lord ran through Dermott's mind: *I was in prison and you came to me.* "Help me, Lord," he breathed. "Help me be your instrument to this man."

He strode down the narrow, dimly lit corridor at the bottom of the stairs, following Withers, while a strange mingling of fear and anticipation filled his heart. For his own safety he was not concerned. He knew he had a Protector fully equal to Daniel's of old even in this dark pit. Rather, his fear sprang from a sense of inadequacy to meet such evil as resided here. But then he reminded himself of Paul's words: *My strength is made perfect in weakness.* As always, from his personal inadequacies sprang strength—strength from One beyond himself. And from this sprang anticipation.

All at once Withers' voice broke sharply into Dermott's thoughts, though the words were not directed at him. The man had definitely changed during the preceding hours. His step was purposeful and he had mustered a certain ring of authority in his voice that had not been there earlier. In his eyes was the look of a soldier who had finally proved himself in battle.

"You, Barnes!" he commanded. "Look alive! I've a visitor for Phelps."

Barnes' head snapped up at the unexpected sound of Withers' voice. He had not been dozing, but very nearly so. Scrambling to his feet, he said, "He ain't here, they all gang up fer a airin'."

"Blast! I forgot," replied Withers. "Well, we can't keep an important man like this waiting. Go fetch him!"

"Phelps?"

"Yes, and be quick about it."

"But I'm the only one here," protested the guard. "I canna be leavin' my post—"

"Are you insinuating that I'm not capable of manning your post?" Withers retorted, his eyes flaring with outrage.

"Well, I wasn't ... what I meant was—"

"I'll have none of your excuses. Just do as you're told!"

Barnes began to stumble away down the hall as Withers bellowed after him, "And don't come back without Phelps!"

Then he turned to Dermott, cast him a knowing, almost sheepish glance, and said, "We won't have much time."

"Which is his cell?" asked Dermott.

Withers led the way down the hall a few more cells, then came to stop in front of a locked door. He fumbled through his keys, finally settled on one, and shoved it into the rusty keyhole. The door groaned as he pushed it open.

"You will have to make haste," said Withers before the lawyer disappeared inside the cell. "But don't worry about Barnes. He will slow down the minute he's out of sight."

As Dermott stepped inside it took some moments for his eyes to accustom themselves to the darkness. A cold chill crept through his body. He had seen such things before, but it was a sight he would never grow used to. A thin form of a man lay on the wooden pallet at the far end of the tiny room. The head turned slowly toward the bright light of the open door. The face was as pale as a hundred deaths, and the eyes were the same unforgettably hopeless eyes Dermott had been haunted by since he had first seen them in the corridor above. The lawyer stepped fully inside and shut the door behind him.

For a moment Dermott stared at the wasted form in silence, uncertain what beginning to make. At last he spoke, and in the silence of the ancient and foreboding walls around him, his softly spoken words seemed to resound like thunder.

"I'm Dermott Connell," he said. "May I speak with you for a moment?"

"What do you want?" the prisoner asked with a voice that rasped and grated like a rusted door.

"I'd like to help you—"

Suddenly the man lurched to his feet. The dullness of despair was suddenly fired by a fierce ember of life. "I know what you want!" he tried to shout. But his voice could not muster the force to succeed. "He sent you, didn't he?" he said, in scarcely more than a whisper.

"No one sent me," Dermott replied calmly. "I bumped into you in the hall the other day. The look in your face seemed to say you needed help and I—"

"I won't sign anything!" he yelled, half-crazed, then flew at Dermott. He had been so subdued of late that the chain had been removed from his ankle. Dermott was momentarily knocked off balance, but he easily repelled the attack and held the youth firmly, but gently, in his grasp.

"Please listen to me," said Dermott urgently, still holding him by the shoulders. "I haven't much time before the guard gets back. Let me help you. I have nothing for you to sign. I have come completely on my own. I am a lawyer—"

At the word the youth tensed and struggled to free himself from the large man's grasp. But his strength was not what it had once been.

"Perhaps you have no reason to trust me," Dermott continued, "but can it be any the worse for you? Now, I'm going to let you go. You can do what you will. But would it do any harm for you to talk with me, if there is even a small hope in it for you?"

Slowly Dermott released his captive. The lad glowered at the lawyer for a moment before slumping back down on his pallet.

"Tell me your name," Dermott said.

"My name?" he asked, his voice quiet and remote. "When was the last time I even heard my name? *My God!*" he groaned. "Was it in Aberdeen when she said good-bye?"

He paused and Dermott waited patiently in silence. At last he spoke it like an anathema. "Ian," he said. "My name is Ian—how I despise it."

"Then you're not Lord Landsbury's son?"

"Ha! ha!" Ian scoffed dryly. "Now I see your game. You hope to curry my father's favor by helping me. Ha! You are as much a fool as I, for my father doesn't care a straw for me. He would sooner see me dead than lift a finger for me. No, Mr.—Mr.—whatever your name is—"

"Connell."

"Well, Mr. Connell, as I said, my father will only scorn you for trying to help me."

The words tore at Dermott's heart and a lump rose in his throat at the thought of this man's feeling deserted by his own family. But time was too precious. If he wanted to help, he would have to use the few moments he had wisely. He swallowed hard, but the words which came from his mouth were not the ones his heart ached to speak.

"Your father? And who is your father?"

"You said you knew."

"I know only that the Earl of Landsbury has two sons, neither of whom is named Ian."

"Ian is my middle name. I am Theodore. And I am finally out of my father's hair, which must be an enormous relief to him at last," he added with a bitter laugh.

"Then you do not know," said Dermott. "Your father ... everyone—they all believe you are dead."

"Dead!"

"That is if you are Theodore Duncan, the son of the Earl of Landsbury—"

"My God!" cried Ian. "Everyone? How..." He stood up, wringing his hands and looking frantically around as if he must do something. Then suddenly realizing his impotence, he crumbled back down onto his mat. "Then she must think so also ... he would have told her ... just to punish us. Oh, God, no!" He buried his face in his hands and silent tears trickled through his fingers, tears perhaps more for his own loss than anything.

Just then a sharp rap came on the door.

"Mr. Connell!" It was Withers' urgent voice. "Are you almost through? Time is short. Barnes will be back any moment."

Dermott looked across the cell at the heap of defeated humanity which had reached out to him from the depths of some unknown bond of love. He knew that as of this moment the troubles of this young man had been placed irrevocably upon his own shoulders by the One who was the guiding power of his life. But he realized he would never learn all he needed to know in the short time left today. His final question was crucial, yet there was so little time to weigh every word in the balance of forethought.

"Ian," he asked, "did you do what they said you did?"

The lawyer felt he already knew the answer, but he had to hear it from Ian's own lips.

Ian looked up, his dirty face streaked with the tracks of his tears.

"I don't know!" His groan revealed that he had asked himself that very question a thousand times. "I could have ... I—"

He held up his left hand, showing a thick white scar across the palm. "There was blood there ... was it only my own? Why can't I remember? If only I could make the blood go away..."

"I will help you, Ian—" But Dermott's words were cut short by Withers' sharp appeal. In the distance Dermott thought he could hear the sound of faintly approaching footsteps.

"If you would help, then find *her*!" Ian implored. "Tell her I'm alive. What a fool I've been ... tell her that I need her."

"Who, Ian? Who do you want me to tell?"

But before he could answer the muted echo of voices could be heard outside and the door swung open.

"Come!" whispered Withers urgently. "They're almost here!"

"I'll be back," said Dermott. "I'll try to find her for you. Don't give up, Ian. Trust God."

Withers pulled Connell free of the door, hastily shut and locked it, and the same moment the guard Barnes and a pitiable old man, who could be none other than Walt Phelps, came into view.

Barnes swore freely and angrily at Withers' insistence he had brought the wrong man. But not about to trudge back upstairs, he locked Phelps back in his cell while Withers and Dermott made their exit. Though Dermott had promised Ian he would return, he wondered how he would keep his word, for this first visit had been difficult enough to manage. Then he remembered he was not alone—that there was Another who also cared for the lad in the depths of the Saltmarket gaol.

23 A Second Visit

Three interminable days passed before Ian's strange visitor returned. From his initial suspicions and mistrust, the quiet lonely hours worked on Ian's imagination. For the first time in what seemed an eternity, he had something hopeful to occupy his thoughts. He had no reason to, of course, but what would it hurt to trust the man? He did not seem the sort to be party to a cruel hoax, but appeared strong and reliant, even compassionate. And in his deepest heart, Ian realized he needed someone.

Thus by the end of the third day, Ian's despair had gradually changed to anticipation. When he had said, "I'll be back," there was a ring in the tone of his voice which told Ian he could trust in that promise—that he *would* return. In his wildest fancies he began to imagine freedom again. And best of all, he dreamed that somehow—defying all reason and all of James's schemes—the lawyer would be able to reunite him with Maggie.

When at long last the door once again creaked slowly open, Ian leapt to his feet.

"I'm sorry it has taken so long for me to come back," Dermott's familiar voice spoke through the dim light of the open cell door. "I have never had such difficulty getting in to see a prisoner. But God has proved faithful once again."

"How did you do it?" asked Ian.

"We have won the assistance of one of the guards," Dermott

replied. "I'm afraid Withers has bribed the man, though they both deny it completely. I'll accept Withers' word for now—he has a great heart." Dermott strode over to the pallet where Ian was seated. "May I sit down?" he asked.

"It's dirty."

"I'm no stranger to a little grime. It's better than standing, and we shall have more time today."

A shot of hope filled Ian's face. "You mean there's a chance . . ."

Reluctantly Dermott had to shake his head in answer to the unfinished question. He had labored constantly for three days on Ian's behalf but had immediately come to see that he would have to be discreet if he hoped to see the lad again. Pushing too hard would only drive Ian further into isolation and further from any hope of release. Progress would be slow, and would be made all the more painful from the hope his activity was bound to raise in Ian's heart. In this tiny cell each hour would seem as a week, while on the outside Dermott realized that weeks, even months, could go by without a single step made in the right direction.

Ian sank back against the wall, the momentary color draining again from his face.

"You didn't find her."

"No, I'm sorry," Dermott replied, wondering how much good he was going to be able to do this lad if he just raised his hopes only to dash them to pieces. "Tell me about her," he said.

Slowly Ian began to talk about Maggie. A year before, sitting in one of the many cells of London, he would never have opened his heart to a stranger. But just the thought of Maggie brought her nearer again. At times during the past months he had wondered if she had not been just some cruel figment of his imagination, a dream, a taunting vision of loveliness. But now—speaking of her, reliving in his mind their conversations and plans—she began to come alive again. And as she came near again in his memory, his heart opened and he found himself sharing more intimately with this stranger than he ever had with anyone but Maggie. There was something in the man's eyes which gave Ian confidence, confidence that all would somehow be made right in the end.

Dermott listened, reaching out at times with a comforting hand on the weeping lad's shoulder as he recounted the events of the night of the murder and then the terrible day in Aberdeen when he had sent Maggie away—alone.

"Do you understand?" Ian sobbed. "She trusted me ... she loved me ... she gave up everything for me—and I sent her away. God, how I hate myself! Will she ever be able to forgive me? Will I ever see her again?"

Dermott said little, comforting when he could, listening a great deal. When at last he had to leave, it was with anguish of soul that he rose and said, "Ian, I know it's but little comfort to you, having to stay in this cell and my dragging you back through all these unpleasant memories. But you have my solemn promise that I will pray earnestly for you. I know the Lord loves you far more than I do, even more than Maggie does. And He will show us what to do. I know He has sent me to you, and He will turn this all out for your best. I do not know how, but I will pray He will show us."

Over the next several weeks, Dermott's visits increased and he listened with growing interest to Ian's story—his former life in London, his weeks at Stonewycke, his newfound love with Maggie, the altercations with Falkirk, and finally all about James Duncan, his plots and threats and machinations against them. Dermott balanced the conversation by sharing about his own life and ministry with those in dire circumstances. Ian grew to look forward to his stories about his lively friend Langley and the buoyant housekeeper Tillie as if they were his own friends, and clung to the lawyer's words as if they were givers of life—as indeed they were.

Dermott continued to pray for an opportunity, not only to help the lad find justice and possible release but also to share the meaning of Life with him—to the lawyer an even more vital necessity. Yet whenever he began to approach the subject, a wall of ice sprang up around Ian! Dermott did not press. He knew the Giver of that life would do His work in His good time.

One day, to Dermott's great satisfaction, a momentary laugh escaped from Ian's lips—slight, yet it could have been the very music of angels. Even Ian himself seemed surprised when he heard what had come from his own mouth, then stopped short and grew quickly somber.

"Don't stop," said Dermott. "You know what they say about the healing virtues of laughter."

"I used to laugh," Ian said, "to hide the pain. That was before Maggie showed me I could laugh for pure joy."

He stopped as his lip began to quiver. "Oh, God! Will I ever know joy again? How can I laugh again without seeming to be unfaithful to her?"

"Perhaps she would rather know you are laughing than dying inside," suggested Dermott.

"But I *am* dying!" cried Ian. "I can't hide from it any longer!"

"I wouldn't ask you to hide from it. But joy can exist next to heartache. Perhaps that is even its purpose. Don't shut Him out when He desires to give you His life to sustain you in your time of pain."

"*Him!* I want nothing from God!" retorted Ian with unexpected anger, rising from the pallet and stalking across the cell. "I want none of that whitewash you try to pass off as *joy*. It only proves God is helpless to take away this agony."

"Sometimes merely removing our difficulties is not for the greater good in our lives, and the Lord knows—"

"Greater good!" spat Ian at the floor. "Ha! That's a stinking excuse! If there is a God, He can't bring Maggie back to me, and you gloss over it with that drivel about it being for the best."

"As much as you feel you need Maggie," Dermott replied, "there is even a higher need. How the one might prevent the other, only God knows. He has nothing but your good in His heart—and Maggie's also."

"Get out of here!" Ian shouted. "I'm not better off without her and I won't listen to any more of your religious nonsense. Get out! I'm sick of you!"

"I'll leave when I'm ready," Dermott replied calmly. "But I have one more matter to discuss with you."

"I was wrong to think you might be a friend," said Ian scornfully, swinging around to face the lawyer.

"I am as distressed as you over my failure to help you," Dermott replied. If Ian could have seen the pain in the lawyer's eyes, he would have known the face of true friendship. Realizing it was useless to argue against the man whose mind was made up, Ian sat back down and said nothing further, listening with disinterested resignation. "That is why I feel compelled to take more aggressive action," the lawyer went on. "Up till now I did not want to risk making things worse for you by stirring it all up. For if I was to expose this hoax that has been played upon you, it could mean an immediate trial—a fact which might not bode well for you in your present circumstances. You have sworn me to keep your family out of this, and so that avenue is closed as well—though if they knew you were alive, it might help me to—"

"My father wouldn't care," muttered Ian.

"Perhaps some other member of the family?"

"It would kill my mother to know what has happened to me."

"And what do you think it has been like for her thinking her son dead?"

That very question had crossed Ian's mind several times of late. He tried to convince himself that they were all better off without him. But in reality his steadfast refusal to contact any of his family was only his way of avoiding having to face another painful rejection. What if he appealed to his parents only to be ignored and left to rot in jail? It was better to be thought dead than to be turned away. The risk of such renunciation was too great.

"There must be another way," said Ian at length.

"If there is," Dermott replied, "perhaps I shall find it in Port Strathy."

"Port Strathy?"

"Yes. I've decided to go north. Your only hope of release may be in forcing a trial. Before that time, I must find some answers. For if it does come to that, I will have to be prepared. There is only one place I can learn what I need to know, and that is where this all took place."

"James Duncan will maul you if he discovers what you're about."

"No doubt he is a strong man. But there is power on my side, and I can be strong too."

"Not in the way he is," Ian warned.

"And he not in the way I am," Dermott replied, a smile tugging at the corners of his mouth.

Dermott rose to take his leave. As he reached the door, Ian

called after him in the most despairing voice the lawyer had yet
heard, seeming by his tone to apologize for his earlier outburst.
"Will you...?" he said, then hesitated a moment. "Will you—still
try to contact her?"

"Of course, Ian. I will do everything I can," replied Dermott,
then opened the great iron door and let himself out.

24   The Journey West Begins

May was well in bloom before the sparkling expanse of the
Missouri River came within view of the small party made up of
three covered wagons. They had set out from New York later than
planned and the snow-encrusted roads had slowed their pace considerably. Then two severe breakdowns in Pennsylvania and In-
diana had cost them an additional three weeks.

The three wagons—carrying Drew and Ellie's family, Evan
McCollough with his wife and three children, and the Wootons
(Frank and Leila and their two teenage sons)—which would later
become known as the Mackinaw Party, reached Independence
feeling already seasoned and travel-weary. Yet the bulk of their
westward trek still remained before them. Up to this point they
had traveled largely through long-settled and friendly farmlands
with towns and villages and other signs of civilization all about
them. Once they crossed the Missouri, however, all that would
change. On the Kansas plains they might easily go days—perhaps
weeks—without sight of civilization. And though the trails west
were well charted by now, the dangers of desert sun and Indian
attacks and barren waterholes were ever-present concerns. But
the spirits of the three men remained high on the crest of anticipated adventure.

With a dull countenance Maggie absorbed the changes of en-
vironment as a matter of course. The decision to travel west in
this huge and strange new land had been the one supreme effort

of will which had enabled her to get past the bitter shock of Ian's death. Once that decision had been made her once energetic emotions sank into apathy and despondency. Dressing in the morning, helping Ellie with a pot of beans for the night's meal around a campfire, bathing one of the young children in a nearby stream— Maggie did everything by rote, as if walking about in a half-dream. She spoke little, cared nothing for the changing sights of the terrain, and was the only member of the party who displayed no anticipation for what lay ahead.

Yet as impassive as her empty stare was, a look deep into her eyes could not hide the truth that Maggie was running away— away from her past, away from the memories of pain. Setting sail into the unknown world of America's western frontier was her way of severing the ties to her former life—a life at one moment she hoped she would one day forget, a life at other times she longed to run back to.

At this moment the arduous journey served her need to forget and could be nothing else for her. Only *One* greater than she could cause it to serve her highest need. But His ways take time, and Maggie could not see His hand at work. Yet as they approached the desert which would before many months burn its heat down upon their wagons, the Master's hand was lovingly moving closer to Maggie's heart through the parched and barren desert of her soul.

The three wagons entered Independence, Missouri, as the afternoon sun was melting into evening. Drew did not pull back on his reins until about a mile on the other side where they found eight covered Conestogas like theirs camped in a haphazard circle.

"Ho, there!" called out a barrel-chested man with long arms and a bushy beard. "Pull up anywhere. We got lotsa room."

Drew was first to leap down from his perch, then he helped Ellie to his side. The children needed no invitation to scurry from the confines of the wagon and join the new children already presenting themselves from behind the circle of stationary wagons. Maggie remained where she was, watching the proceedings with indifference as the others of their small party followed Drew's example.

"I'm Drew Mackinaw, and this is my wife, Ellie," Drew said,

thrusting out his hand. The big man took it and shook it vigorously.

"Glad t' make yer acquaintance," he replied in a brusque, deep voice which contrasted with his obvious friendly nature. "Pete Kramer's the name. Everyone else can take care of their own introductions."

"A man in town said we'd find ye oot here," Drew went on. "If ye be goin' west we thought ye might like the company o' three more wagons."

"I declare, where'd you all hail from, Mackinaw?" said Kramer with a booming friendly laugh. "You don't strike me as the pioneerin' type!"

"I'm from Scotland years ago," answered Drew, "but we just left New York a few months ago, where we been livin' fer ten years."

"Well, wherever you're from and whatever kind of accent your tongue's comfortable with, you're welcome t' join us. This here land's big enough for us all, I reckon. And three more wagons couldn't hurt none. Fact is, we been hung up here more'n a week. No one's willin' to take such a small train of wagons cross them plains these days."

"We were just about ready to strike out alone," put in a tall, slim man several years younger than the bearded Kramer. He ambled forward and offered Drew, Evan, and Frank his hand.

"Maybe *you* was, Williams, but I ain't so sure," said Kramer.

"What's the problem?" asked Evan.

"A few weeks makes a big difference here," Pete explained. "If we'd have arrived a little sooner there wouldn't have been no problem. But it's near the end of May and we—and now you folks—why, we're just about the last of the emigrants heading west this year. Most of the big trains left last month, on account of the fall snows and such like. You can't make it unless you start before June. So you see, we can't keep waiting to see if any others show up. But we've been warned to stay in large groups—twenty, thirty wagons at least."

A pause followed; the question *why* seemed to hang unspoken on the lips of all in the recently arrived Mackinaw Party. Finally Drew spoke the word.

At first Pete seemed reluctant to venture an answer. "Well,

139

there's always rumors like this flyin' around," he began. "It's right hard to tell just what a body should put stock in and what you should just put out of your mind altogether. Word is, there's been some Indian trouble. Seems the stage line to Denver's been attacked a couple of times. And there was a couple of wagons from the last train headin' out of here that came back with some stories to tell that'd shiver your hide."

"Come on, Pete!" interjected Williams, his voice laced with the frustration of youth toward their elders. "If anyone listened to that batch of hog feed, there'd be no settlers west of the Missouri!"

"I know you and the other young bucks around here think nothin' of a scrape with some renegade redskins," said Kramer. "But those of us with families is bound to exercise a bit more caution."

"Weel," said Drew, "eleven wagons be more'n eight."

"Maybe we can get someone to take us on now," said Kramer hopefully. "But most of the experienced wagon masters have already set out with full trains," he added, almost as an afterthought to himself.

"Stoddard's still in town," put in a new voice joining the small crowd.

"I thought we voted him down," said another.

"That was a week ago," came the reply. "Things are different now."

"We can't sit around here forever!"

As the discussion continued, Ellie, Leila, and Rebbekah McCollough glanced toward one another with some apprehension. The subject of Indian raids had come up before. But suddenly the danger loomed much closer than they had dared allow themselves to think about.

Long before the discussion between the men grew heated, Kramer's commanding voice interceded.

"This ain't gettin' us nowhere. Maybe it's worth another vote. But first, I reckon these newcomers are plumb beat and lookin' for supper."

Two hours later, once dinner was behind them, parents began settling their excited but tired children into bed. Between the Mackinaws and McColloughs there were eight youngsters, in addition to Frank and Leila's older boys. Evan was but twenty-five, and Frank was the oldest member of the group. But the party revolved around the Mackinaw wagon and around Drew Mackinaw himself. His quiet strength and vitality represented a maturity that both the other men willingly looked up to. Yet each man and woman contributed to the total fiber of the group which had already grown into a close, compatible unit. Only Maggie remained outside the circle of their oneness—by her choice, not theirs.

Once the children were asleep and the dinner gear put away, Pete Kramer sauntered over, the aromatic smoke from his pipe preceding him, and invited them all to join an impromptu meeting with the rest of the small camp. They followed him toward the large campfire already blazing away. He introduced the few who hadn't already met, then cleared his throat several times until he had the undivided attention of the group.

"Well now," he began, "it looks to me like we gotta decide what we aim to do. And soon. It's nearly June, and summer's no time to be settin' out across the plains. Some of you been talkin' 'bout goin' it alone. But since none of us has ever been across before, and with Indian trouble brewin', it strikes me that we oughta be thinkin' of somethin' else."

"There's Stoddard," said one of the men.

"Yes, there is him," returned Kramer thoughtfully.

"He's been across four times."

"Knows his stuff, that's sure."

"But we voted him down," put in another.

"Who is this Stoddard fellow?" asked Evan.

"We only know what we heard," began Kramer, but he was interrupted before he could go on.

"And what we heard is that the last train he led was massacred while he was drunk!" said one of the men.

"Is that true?" asked Drew.

"Like I told you before," Kramer replied, "rumors hereabouts are thick as swamp mosquitos on a balmy night. But the train was massacred, that's a fact."

"Seems a man ought t' have the chance t' defend himsel'," said Drew. "Things like that happen an' ye canna be holdin' it against a person the rest o' his life."

"Would you want him responsible for your wife and children?" asked the man who seemed to be head of the opposition.

"That I couldna answer till I met the man face-t'-face," answered Drew. For a moment there was no reply, for none of those present had yet met Gil Stoddard personally.

Before the discussion had ended sometime later, it had been decided that their situation was desperate enough to merit giving the man Stoddard the benefit of an interview.

The next morning Drew, Pete Kramer, and the man who had spoken against Gil Stoddard rode into Independence in search of the man who had been the object of their discussion. Their search was rewarded, for shortly before noon, four riders approached the small cluster of wagons. The fourth sat in his saddle like one weary with riding, weary with life. His wide-brimmed hat was tattered and dusty, tipping downward over his eyebrows so that it cast a melancholy shadow over his face. Yet that was perhaps only an illusion; a deeper and more permanent shadow shrouded his eyes even when his hat was removed. It might have been a handsome face once. No doubt in its younger days it had turned the eyes of more than one frontier woman. But all those past glories were dulled by dust and a three-day stubble of beard, and dark eyes that seemed to have forgotten how to smile. His clothes hung shabbily from his large but weary frame, and one could only wonder what had caused this once mighty man of the west to age before his time.

A somber group slowly gathered about the riders as they dismounted. Somehow they had hoped all the rumors were wrong about Stoddard, but one look told them this was a man about whom such rumors could certainly be true. Still, why else had Pete brought him back to camp unless he thought they should hire him to lead their group of wagons west?

"Folks," said Pete addressing the group, "this here's Gil Stoddard. He wanted to come out and have a look around before he made any decisions."

No one spoke as Stoddard began to amble in and out among the group, eyeing the wagons, seeming to count the children with growing disgust, never relaxing the scowl on his face. Suddenly he stopped in front of Maggie, who had edged toward the fringe of the onlookers.

"Good Lord!" he exclaimed rolling his eyes. "That's all we need—a pregnant woman!"

"You don't need to worry about me," Maggie replied haughtily. The defiance in her voice came as a surprise even to her. But she resented this man's tone. She'd been pushed around by circumstances enough, and she wasn't about to let this rude and dirty horseman insult her. "I can manage myself just fine!"

"A foreigner, too," he mumbled as he moved on. Finally he stopped and swung around to face Kramer. "I'll tell you all something right now. You're going to be paying me good money to do that—*worry*, that is. And you just well better let me do my job. I expect you to do what I say and when I say it. There's no room on the prairie for a bunch of greenhorns arguing with the only person around who knows what he's about. Those are my terms. I'll want a hundred and twenty-five dollars. Fifty now and the rest when we get there."

A murmur rippled through the group, and a few suppressed gasps of astonishment could be heard.

"The going rate's only fifty dollars," complained one of the men.

"That's in April," stated Stoddard roughly, "and that's not for no ten-wagon train with more kids underfoot than grown men, and pregnant women besides," he added with another glance toward Maggie.

"We have eleven wagons," said one of the wives.

"Ten ... eleven, what's it matter?" said Stoddard. "It's not enough."

"What about the rumors of your last train?"

In reply, and without a word, Stoddard swung back up on his horse, wheeled it around, and began to ride off.

"Wait!" shouted Kramer. "Where you goin'?"

Stoddard paused to shout back over his shoulder. "That's another rule I forgot to mention. If there's no trust, there's no use even making a beginning."

"We're only askin' fer a reason t' trust," answered Drew, gazing steadily after the man.

Stoddard's horse stopped; the weary trail boss returned Drew's stare, seeming to sense the younger man's desire to trust him if only he would let down his hard-bitten exterior.

"I wasn't drunk," Stoddard said at length, his voice as steady as Drew's gaze.

A moment of silence followed, during which the only sound was the shuffling of Stoddard's horse's hoofs in the dust. At length Drew's voice broke the silence: "The Mackinaw party will put in forty dollars."

With his words the trance-like hush was broken and others of the small group began likewise to pledge themselves to the task at hand. Whether they had more faith in Drew's assessment of Stoddard's character, or in Stoddard himself, no one could tell. But it did not take long before the full amount had been committed, so anxious were they all to get moving again.

In the midst of the general commotion Maggie stood, still angered over Stoddard's arrogant words. As she turned to move back toward their wagon she was startled by the presence of another man who had come up quietly behind her. Not expecting the mingled look of anger and surprise on her face, the stranger stood speechless for a brief moment.

"I hope I didn't startle you," he said at last.

"No, you didn't," Maggie replied crisply, hardly noticing that her body had stiffened again.

"I'm Dr. Carpenter," the man said. In the awkwardness of the moment, his words were reticent, yet there was also in his voice a quiet, soothing quality which could not help but dissolve a little of Maggie's tenseness. "Mr. Stoddard's less than sympathetic words compelled me to speak to you," he continued.

"Mr. Stoddard's words meant nothing to me," said Maggie coldly, hoping her lie was convincing.

"I'm glad to hear that," Carpenter said. "Still, I want you to know that I am available to assist you when it becomes necessary."

The man before Maggie was at least two inches beyond six feet tall, with most of his height in his thin gangly legs. Yet he did not appear clumsy but carried his tall frame easily, as if he had long ago conquered his lanky build because there were more important things for him to concentrate his energies on. In his mid-thirties, he had brown hair streaked here and there with strands of gray. However, the gray tended to soften his lean, angular face, almost handsome in its rugged irregularity.

"Thank you, Dr. Carpenter," said Maggie, relaxing by degrees. "That is very kind of you." She continued on her way without further word.

She did not look back again until she had reached the wagon, then cast one backward glance at the retreating doctor. A momentary pang of guilt reminded her that she had been less than courteous to him, but she brushed it aside quickly. She owed the man nothing, she thought. Still she was uncomfortable with the memory of the encounter. It had given her an almost forgotten glimpse of her old self—the child Maggie enclosed in self-imposed walls of protection, the Maggie who had shut out all love before finally allowing Ian to break through to her heart.

She thought that she had changed, but in reality the change had not worked into her fully. Perhaps the brief change had been worse than no change at all. For now Maggie felt that her childhood rejection by her father was made complete by the one man she had allowed herself to love. Even Ian—through no fault of his own—had deserted her at last, through death. Her father had had the final victory over her and the final revenge over Ian. As she climbed up into the wagon, the lonely child deep within her heart still felt the bitterness of a father's rejection, and if the woman in her refused to admit it, the child nonetheless hid once again behind the stone walls of her soul, thicker and more impenetrable than the walls of her girlhood home.

By the time Stoddard had returned to town for the few possessions he would need, a hasty lunch had been prepared and camp had been broken. By one o'clock in the afternoon, eleven wagons with billowing white canvas were creeping toward the Missouri, where a ferry was waiting to carry them to the west bank and the beginning of their long journey.

25   An Unexpected Encounter

Maggie tossed a sweaty strand of hair from her face. But it was no use—another immediately took its place. Had she ever been so hot in her life? She inhaled the tepid air, but it only stung her parched throat. Gazing out the back of the wagon, Maggie strained her eyes to see some change in the terrain. But as far as her eye could see, as it had been for days now, was nothing but the monotonous expanse of dry, grass-covered plain—barren as a desolate heath moor. For a moment her mind wandered back to the solitary wasteland she had known and loved called Braenock Ridge.

"I've heard some call it godforsaken. But I'll not be believin' that. A place like Braenock Ridge holds a tender place in His heart just because it never gives up." Digory's words rushed unbidden back into her mind. She had not thought of the old groom in weeks.

Maggie sighed. But as the sigh caught in her throat a sob rushed in to replace it, suddenly jarring her back to the present. She could not think of the past! She had to forget. Forget Digory, Braenock Ridge, Stonewycke . . .

"Oh, Ian, I can't forget you!" she murmured into the dry air.

Suddenly the rear wagon wheel jostled over a rock, almost knocking Maggie off her hard wooden seat. She glanced quickly at the bed opposite her. The three youngest Mackinaw children still slept soundly. Maggie marveled, for the constant jolting of the wagon did not seem to disturb them; yet last night, when all had been still and quiet, they had hardly slept a wink.

Perhaps last night had been too quiet. Almost eerie. If the children's cries had not kept her awake, she would undoubtedly have found sleep difficult all the same.

There had been talk of them all day. And about an hour before sunset they had actually seen four Indians on a ridge about half a mile in the distance. The Indians sat tall and proud on their brown and white horses, all except for the leader whose magnificent white stallion Maggie had particularly noticed. Still as statues they remained, watching the train in silence as it passed until slowly it had rumbled out of sight. Maggie knew she and her friends were under special scrutiny, and the incident had had a most disquieting effect on everyone in the wagon train.

For some unknown reason Maggie did not feel afraid of these savages, as all the men called them. In an odd sort of way they reminded her of her own Viking ancestors—proud and mighty warriors who would spare neither blood nor tears for the land they loved. Could these very natives of the land called America have sprung from the kindred blood of exploring Vikings who ventured to the New World centuries before the Spaniards?

Yet in the end the Scotsmen were subdued—some called it unified. Maggie supposed that these Indians, as well, would be subdued one day. The thought made her more sad than afraid. Yet glancing back toward the four grand warriors, she knew they would not allow their people to be subdued without a struggle.

Now the children were asleep, for the fears of the night had been dispelled. Another day's welcome light had arrived safely. For Maggie it meant another day to go on living, another day to watch the children, to *watch* the progress of their train and the lives that were bound up in this adventure, but never to feel a part. She wondered if she would ever feel a part of anything again.

As her thoughts drifted back to the present Maggie realized the wagon had stopped. Scrambling forward she poked her head out through the canvas opening.

"What is it, Ellie?" she asked.

"Soldiers," Ellie replied with some alarm in her tone. "Drew," she went on, turning toward her husband where he sat at her side holding the reins, "you don't suppose the war's come this far west?"

Drew did not answer for a moment, then spoke thoughtfully. "Fort Laramie's none too far from here. 'Tis most likely they're from there. I doubt 'tis the war."

With the words he swung his large hulk down from the wagon. "I'd best be goin' over t' see what it's all about. Ye stay here," he added firmly.

Most of the other men had also climbed down from their wagons and were walking toward the cluster of eight or ten mounted soldiers where they sat conferring with Gil Stoddard. As Drew came within earshot he could hear the voices of Stoddard and one referred to as Captain Henry.

"We heard talk of that in Independence," Stoddard was saying. His voice, naturally low and gruff, sounded even more serious now.

"That looks like only the beginning," replied the captain, a young man in his mid-thirties with a clean-shaven face and eyes that seemed unable to focus long on any one object. At first Drew thought him nervous, then wondered if the constantly roving eyes were actually alert and vigilant, always on the lookout for possible signs of danger.

"Evans has sent out a proclamation to the Arapaho and Cheyenne—" Captain Henry began, but was cut off by one of the men who had gathered.

"Who's Evans?"

"He's the governor of Colorado, you dimwit!" yelled another before the captain could reply.

"That's right," Henry went on. "He's warned all the friendly Indians to collect at the various forts so they don't get killed along with the bad ones."

"They're not likely to take too kindly to that," said Stoddard in the tone of one who knew his business.

"That's why we're out on patrol," replied the captain. "Evans' message just got out a couple days ago. So far none of the Indians have responded except a few of the old and sick. The worry is that they're mixing with the Sioux from up in Dakota. And they're a bloody bunch, always inciting the more peaceful tribes into war."

"You don't think the Cheyenne will listen to Evans do you?" asked Stoddard cynically.

"Not hardly. That's why we're expecting trouble. Evans is determined to put a stop to all the pillaging and raiding. He'll retaliate and the redskins will fight back."

Henry's eyes deliberately scanned the distant horizon. Unconsciously the eyes of the onlookers all followed his gaze, but all that met their looks was the dry, blazing-hot prairie grass.

"Evans has had enough," Henry went on, almost to himself. "He's vowed that no more Little Crows will turn up in his territory, even if it takes a repeat of what happened at Mankato to keep them in their place."

"Mankato?" asked one of the men.

"A small town up in Minnesota. Little Crow and thirty-nine of his followers were all hanged from a single scaffold a while back. They had killed over 700 whites before the army tracked them down."

A murmur rippled through the men as the captain wheeled his horse around. "So you all stick together, and watch yourselves," he warned. "These are perilous times to be heading across the plains, and there's not enough soldiers to defend every one of these trails."

Before the men had concluded their informal meeting with the army officer, Maggie shifted uncomfortably in her seat and realized how stiff and cramped she had become. And the sun beating down on the immobile wagon had made it like an oven inside. It was time for a little walk and some fresh air.

Without a stepping stool on the ground outside to assist her, it took Maggie some moments to maneuver her cumbersome, swelling body out of the back of the wagon. But finally her feet touched the ground, and she sighed with some satisfaction. Several of the other women were stirring about the wagons. There were no children about.

The still air outside the wagon gave Maggie little respite from the heat, and she could not help being drawn to the river less than a stone's throw away. She didn't think to tell Ellie where she was going, nor did it occur to her how foolhardy it was to wander away from the train alone. If the wagons should start up again, who would know she was missing? Still less was she aware of the tiny furtive figure that climbed out of the wagon and followed.

Before her lay the Platte, a broad expanse of muddy water running swiftly within its low banks. By summer's end it would in many places be little more than a trickle, but in this spot in early June, still swollen from the last spring runoff, it bore a strong resemblance to the more mighty rivers of its kindred land. It was certainly not the Lindow, Maggie thought carelessly, then braced herself against the pain of whatever memories the thought of that lovely Scottish river would give birth to in her mind. In defiance of those memories she sucked in a deep breath of the warm air and marched boldly down to the bank. The few cottonwoods scattered sparsely along the shore offered little promise of shade from the intense June heat. Cautiously Maggie lowered herself at the water's edge, reached down with a cupped hand, and began to splash water onto her dry face. She couldn't remember when anything had ever felt so refreshing.

Suddenly a twig snapped behind her. She froze, arresting her hand halfway to her face. She turned slowly, then let out a relieved sigh.

"Bess! What are you doing here?" she asked in a scolding tone despite her relief.

"I don't know," the child replied simply. "I just followed you."

"You shouldn't have left the wagon."

"No one told me."

Maggie eyed her for a moment, then smiled and held out her hand.

"Oh, dear little Bess," she said, "I suppose neither of us should be out alone like this. But since we are, come and let me splash some of this cool water on your face."

Bess approached her and, in a sudden playful mood, Maggie threw out a handful of water toward the young girl. Giggling, Bess ran to the water's edge and retaliated with two small splashes of her own. Maggie threw her head back and laughed, and in the brief moment of unusual abandon felt almost like a child again herself. She was, after all, only seventeen, and it had been so long—too long—since she had actually giggled. Dripping with the cool water, Maggie threw her arms around Bess and kissed her.

The brief moment of affection ended a second later with a sharp gasp from Bess as she stiffened in Maggie's arms.

"Bess, what is it?" asked Maggie with alarm.

The girl's mouth moved but she was unable to utter a word, continuing to stare over Maggie's shoulder. Maggie turned, and to her horror saw a young Indian girl not much older than herself inching toward them. Just as Maggie turned the Indian slumped down to the ground against one of the scraggly cottonwoods. Overcoming her initial shock, Maggie glanced hastily around, afraid that others might be following. She grabbed Bess by the hand and rose to leave. Still the woman sat motionless, leaning heavily against the tree. Her worn buckskin was old and dirty with several dark splotches on it. Maggie paused to stare a moment longer. The young woman was clearly too exhausted to warrant Maggie's initial fear. Her bronzed skin and large dark eyes set in a moon-shaped face must surely have once been lovely to look at. But now her features revealed only weariness and pain. Her eyes stared blankly ahead, taking no notice of the two whites who had intruded into her land. Still Maggie stood, little Bess clutching her skirts.

All at once Maggie saw that a small baby lay on the woman's lap, wrapped in rags which must have once been an Indian blanket. How she could not have noticed it sooner, despite her fear, Maggie did not know. The child remained very still, then as Maggie took notice of it, seemed to stir slightly.

Maggie took a tentative step toward the girl and her baby, and then the Indian turned her head slightly and stared toward Maggie's swollen abdomen. A sudden kinship of motherhood stirred within Maggie, the first of its kind even though her own time was drawing near.

"My—my—baby is almost due," Maggie said at last, with tentative voice.

The woman gave no indication that she understood the words.

"Ellie thinks it may be only two or three more weeks. And she's had five children, so she must know." As she spoke, Maggie took a step closer, with Bess still clinging behind.

"Is this your first?" asked Maggie. "Seems like a good sleeper."

The woman's eyes seemed to search Maggie's face, as if beseeching Maggie with her eyes because her mouth had no words.

"I don't know if I want a boy or a girl," Maggie went on, trying to put the other woman at ease. "Ellie says God knows what is right for us."

All at once the woman held the child up toward Maggie in her two hands, as if making an offering. She spoke a single word, which was as unintelligible to Maggie as Digory's Gaelic utterings of her childhood. But as with that gently spoken Gaelic, Maggie did not need to understand the words to know what was being said. The woman's pain-ridden eyes and the soft wail in her voice was interpretation enough. She was pleading for help.

Maggie approached cautiously and reached out to lay a hand gently on the baby's cheek. But even before her touch revealed the burning fever, she could see it in the flushed skin.

"Oh, dear! he's so hot," she said with alarm.

The woman repeated the word she had spoken before, imploring Maggie once more, then lowered the child again into her lap as she fell back against the tree.

"Bess!" said Maggie. "Go get the doctor!"

Bess did not move but continued to press up against Maggie's back.

"Go on, hurry!" Maggie urged. "This is important . . . do you understand, *important*!"

Bess began to edge away.

"Run, Bess, run!" Maggie called. The young girl took one last hesitating look at Maggie, then at the Indian woman, then shot up the bank and back toward the wagons at a full run.

In less than five minutes Samuel Carpenter appeared trotting down the shallow slope of the bank toward Maggie. He took in the entire scene with a single glance, not appearing in the least disturbed at the object of his call.

"What's the trouble?" he asked, kneeling down beside the two women. As he reached toward the child's reddened cheeks the mother drew her infant back, hugging the baby closer to her with a look of panic growing in her eyes.

"He wants to help," said Maggie softly. "He's a doctor. He will help . . . help . . . do you understand? *Doctor*."

She paused and glanced helplessly at Dr. Carpenter. Then an idea struck her.

She hastily repeated the single word she had thus far heard the Indian woman say. She said it over several times, and gradually a dim light seemed to dawn in the young mother's countenance and she slowly relaxed her grip on the child and allowed the doctor to touch him.

"Dear Lord!" Carpenter exclaimed. "He's burning up!"

Moving closer he peeled away the blankets and wrappings and began pressing the baby's abdomen and flexing its limp arms and legs.

"He's dreadfully dehydrated," he said, then turning to the

woman, "When was the last time he ate something? Have you any milk?"

She stared back at him blankly.

"Milk," he repeated, touching his chest, then the baby's mouth, "milk!"

The woman dismally shook her head. Maggie saw tears inching down the poor woman's cheeks. But the doctor's urgent voice was oblivious to the woman's inner sorrow. He was intent on saving her child.

"Mrs. Duncan, have you a petticoat?" he asked, then continued on before she had a chance to reply, "No ... never mind. I'll use my shirt." As he spoke he tore the shirt from his back.

"The sun will burn you to a crisp," objected Maggie.

"Never mind that. Just take my shirt to the river and get it wet, mud and all, if you have to. It'll be better for the child than nothing."

Finally understanding, Maggie complied. "How could such a thing have happened?" the doctor said to himself in frustration. "I only hope we've found her in time to do some good—"

But the rest of his words were lost on Maggie as she plunged his shirt in the dirty Platte and ran back to where the doctor still knelt at the woman's side.

He took it from her and brought the moist cloth to the baby's parched lips. Maggie placed a hand under the tiny head and before she knew it was cradling the baby in her arms. The child's mother had fallen back unconscious. Carpenter bent over her and, picking her up in his strong arms, carried her to the water's edge.

Meanwhile Maggie held the Indian child closer to her breast, as if to afford it extra protection now that its mother had gone from sight. The child made a feeble effort to suck at the wet shirt. Unconsciously she began to softly sing an old poem Digory had taught her which she had hardly thought of in years:

Ane by ane they gang awa;
The getherer gethers grit and sma':
Ane by ane maks ane and a'!

Aye what ane sets doon the cup
Ane ahint maun tak it up:
A' thegither they will sup!

Golden-heidit, ripe, and strang,
Shorn will be the hairst or lang:
Syne begins a better sang!

She sang the tune softly again, then again, until Dr. Carpenter's heavy footstep sounded behind her. She turned, surprised to see him approaching alone. His face was pale in spite of its sunburned skin, and the strain of failure was evident in his deep-set eyes.

"She's gone," he said with a husky, strained voice.

"Gone?" repeated Maggie, confused.

"She's gone . . . dead," he answered, his lips trembling slightly. "She was the one who was really sick, hemorrhaging. I saw it when I carried her to the river. She must have known she was dying and was probably trying to get to Fort Laramie for help."

He dropped to his knees beside Maggie where she sat holding the baby. "It must have depleted all her strength and dried up whatever milk she had for the poor child."

Overwhelmed with a greater sorrow than she could understand, Maggie listened dumbstruck to the doctor's words. She felt she had lost a friend. And indeed, in those brief moments, Maggie and that poor lovely Indian woman *had* shared an intimacy of sorrow and loss as perhaps no other two friends could have. A choking sob struggled to explode from her throat, but generations of Ramsey breeding kept it back and prevented the hot tears from escaping to the surface.

Maggie merely held the baby closer, and—as if to remind her of the preciousness of life—her own unborn child moved within her. It was also a reminder of sorrow.

In the midst of her private thoughts Maggie realized Dr. Carpenter was speaking, but when she looked up at him she saw that his head was bowed. He had not been addressing her.

". . . in your wisdom. Protect this child with your strength, Lord," he said earnestly. "He is in your hands, for I have no power to help him without you. Let his mother's dying wish be fulfilled."

"Did—did she say something to you?" asked Maggie when he paused.

"No. But I don't doubt that her last thoughts were for the survival of her son, even that her own death might somehow buy back the life of the child."

Maggie merely nodded. There were too many questions. Why should such an exchange of life be necessary? Why couldn't both be spared? Life could seem so cruel!

Dr. Carpenter watched her for a moment as she concentrated her attention on the small Indian child. He could detect a hidden purpose in her eyes—she seemed to be coming to life again. The doctor had observed this young Scottish mother-to-be frequently since the wagon train had left Missouri. And though the dormant beauty of her face was not lost on him, what had truly drawn his attention was the tragic sadness of her countenance and being. She seemed but going through the motions of life. He had learned that she was a recent widow and his heart ached that this joyous time, the anticipation of her first child, should have been so marred with grief.

Yet now he could almost detect a small spark igniting within Maggie. Just as the helpless little Indian child was struggling for its very life, so also the spirit which had once given life its joy and zest was fighting within Maggie to remain alive. He hoped the spark in her eyes would ignite and grow. For as she sat holding the motherless child, Dr. Carpenter could see that the success of the one struggle was intimately bound up with the progress of the other.

26   Samuel Carpenter

Voices and the clamor of approaching feet suddenly broke in upon the gentle silence of the two kneeling figures. Dr. Carpenter looked up to see several of their train companions coming toward them.

"What's keepin' you?" Gil Stoddard asked with an impatience that had clearly been simmering for some time. "We thought you musta drowned!"

"Maggie here found an Indian woman—"

"Indians!" shouted one of the others while the rest looked frantically around.

"Only a sick squaw and her child," Carpenter replied calmly, but with a hint of exasperation in his voice. "The poor woman just died and the child here is very sick."

"It ain't contagious, is it, Doc?" Stoddard asked.

"No. You needn't worry."

"Are you sure?"

"I'm a physician, of course I'm sure!" Carpenter snapped. "We'll have to take the child on—at least as far as Fort Laramie. And we need to bury the woman."

"We'll take the kid," Stoddard replied. "But we ain't stickin' around for no buryin'. There could be warriors not far behind her."

"We can't just leave her here."

"Didn't you hear those soldiers, *Doctor* Carpenter?" said Stoddard, emphasizing each syllable. "We're right plum in the middle of three or four tribes of hot-tempered redskins. We've already given them time to surround us twice over lookin' for you and the lady here."

"Surely you're not suggesting we leave the poor woman to rot in the sun?" demanded Carpenter, pulling himself to his feet. "That's inhuman."

"If you think we're going to risk our necks for a dead savage who would have thought it nothing to stab you in the heart if she had the strength—"

Carpenter stepped up to Stoddard and faced him squarely. "Then you go on ahead. I'll catch up."

"You're a crazy fool," said Stoddard spitefully. "And I thought it was *good* fortune you was with us." With the words Stoddard turned and hurried back up the bank toward the wagons. In a few moments he returned with four shovels and a scowl on his rugged face.

"Well, Kramer, Williams, Wooten," he shouted at the other men present, "if I'm goin' to lose my scalp buryin' a redskin squaw, I ain't about to do it alone!" He walked away, cursing loudly.

"Mr. Stoddard," the doctor said, his voice beginning to lose its usual even-tempered patience, "I'll also remind you there is a lady present."

Stoddard's mumbled reply was lost to the doctor's ears as he slammed the tip of his shovel into the hard, dry earth.

Samuel Carpenter was not a frontiersman. Born and raised in the Lower East side of New York City, the son of a dock-worker, Samuel was a good deal more familiar with brick and crowded tenements and noisy markets than with the dusty wagon trails, lawlessness, and sage brush so typical of life on the open prairie. Practically from the moment he could walk he had worked, first as an errand boy, then a newspaper assistant, and finally by his father's side on the grimy docks of the greatest city in the land. In his meager spare time he read incessantly and while reading about the discovery of the smallpox vaccination in England, he had been inspired by the courage of English physician Edward Jenner and decided he wanted to become a doctor. He loved helping people more than anything else. Raising himself up in society, however, especially with illiterate parents who considered his desire for an education to be frivolous, proved to be a long and strenuous achievement. But when he graduated from one of New York's medical schools as second in his class, their pride knew no bounds. Shortly thereafter he married the daughter of a wealthy New York businessman whom he had met during his hospital residency. Samuel Carpenter seemed well on his way to what was destined to be great achievement and worldly success in his career and in the glamorous life of New York society.

He was just on the verge of being appointed chief-of-staff at Bellevue when his well-ordered life began to crumble. After six childless years his wife had finally become pregnant. But their ecstasy was short-lived. The blessed news was followed shortly by the devastating revelation that she had contracted leukemia. Within six months the doctor's wife and unborn child were both dead.

For a year Carpenter's shattered life lost all meaning. Even the spiritual values which he had considered part of his life were unable to sustain him. He resigned his position at Bellevue and took to traveling—wandering throughout the east, searching for the inner strength he had thought he possessed. The tragedy of his wife's death drained away whatever scanty reserve of fortitude he had, leaving him with the firm conviction that God had deserted him altogether.

But when he finally came to terms with his loss, he realized God had never left him at all. The moment came as he stood in the biting cold before a solitary white-steepled church in the snowy Vermont hills. For the first time he was empty enough to be able to yield himself fully to the God he had kept at arm's length all this time. Coming in from the cold into the humble boarding house where he was lodging, his mind was suddenly alive again. Suddenly he saw that he could make something of his life again if he would begin relying on God rather than himself. He knew he could never return to the comfort of his previous life as a successful physician in the high society of the city. For the first time he realized that in the glamour of his success, he had forgotten his original dream to help people in need. But he determined to forget it no more.

A week later, in Boston, he chanced to hear a lecture entitled "Medicine in the Wild West." Here was a need he never knew existed! The thousands of easterners and emigrants pouring across the American plains were finding medical services in short supply. When a doctor was to be found he was often a charlatan with little or no medical training.

But the moment his talk turned to thoughts of going west, again he met with opposition. His family and friends considered him crazy even to think of turning his back on his well-established career. But more than ever before in his life he knew he was being *called* to a cause greater than himself, and he would let nothing stand in his way. He was accustomed to fighting for what mattered to him, not perhaps in the manner in which a rough westerner like Gil Stoddard would fight, but nonetheless determined. His battles were not fought with fists but with a strength of will and even, as his mother might have said, "with a streak of stubbornness a mile wide." Yet he remained a soft-spoken man who never relied heavily on words to win his battles, but rather on his immovable convictions.

Having made the decision to go west, Samuel Carpenter became more single-minded than ever in the pursuit of his goal of helping the sick. That passion had drawn him away from the city life he had known since birth with the destination of California before him. But he was in no hurry, for was there not plenty to do along the way? His sensitive nature had surfaced in his rugged surroundings more than it would ever have been able to in the confines of Bellevue. Not only did he minister soothing words and comfort to the ailing, but their cares ministered healing to his once-troubled soul in ways he was only beginning to see.

Maggie gladly took charge of the Indian child when Dr. Carpenter asked her. She had hardly considered any other course of action. In fact, she found herself surprisingly disheartened when he explained that they would give the child to the Indian agent in Fort Laramie when they arrived in two days. It hardly crossed her mind that she would soon have a newborn child of her own to care for; the mothering instinct simply reached out to the helpless little infant who had so unexpectedly dropped into her arms, and she wanted to love him as her own.

Ellie dug out a bottle from a small box of baby things she had brought along for Maggie, and their cow was still yielding a scanty supply of milk. By the end of the day the baby had taken enough to insure his survival at least through the night. By morning his fever had dropped and his eyes seemed more alert.

"It's amazing how quickly they mend," remarked Maggie as she cradled the infant in her arms.

"It is that," replied Ellie, pausing a moment in her repacking of their gear for the day's journey. "But he didn't do it alone," she added, noting the look of pride on Maggie's face. "I've been prayin' for him."

Maggie smiled. "Thank you," she said. She could not bring herself to confess that she had never once prayed for the dying child. The thought of prayer had come to her, but the words would not form on her lips. And she could not admit, especially to Ellie, that she was rapidly losing any assurance that God even heard whatever prayers she might offer.

As the two women spoke, Dr. Carpenter ambled up to the Mackinaw camp and was carefully eyeing Maggie and the baby.

"You're doing a fine job with him," he encouraged.

"It's the prayers, like Ellie said," Maggie replied, looking away.

"Yes, Mrs. Duncan, but you are the answer to those prayers. You have given the boy something he needed far more than milk. Let me examine him a moment."

The baby protested mildly as the doctor took him in his arms, and smiled. "He's getting some fight back. That's good."

"I thought we should give him a name," Maggie suggested.

"He will be here only until tomorrow."

"Yes, I know. But he ought to be called something besides 'the baby.'"

"You don't want to become too attached, Mrs. Duncan. You do know that taking him to the agency is the best thing for him."

"How can some agency take better care of him than I—we—than Ellie and I could?"

"They will return the child to his people. He deserves to be raised among them. I'm afraid, Mrs. Duncan, that it would be neither an easy nor a happy life for him among white men."

"I understand," Maggie resigned. "But I shall call him my little *Indian bairn,* nonetheless."

Dr. Carpenter tried to restrain the smile that crept to his lips. She, too, had a stubborn streak, and he realized it would serve her well as she tried to forge a new life in this rugged land.

Before anything else could be said, Drew approached with the announcement that they were ready to be on their way. Dr. Carpenter returned to his wagon, and Maggie, carrying the baby, climbed into the back of theirs, followed by Bess, Sarah, and Darren. By now Tommy Joe and Bobby had all but taken up residence in the roomier Wooten wagon.

With a shout from Gil Stoddard and the answering commands from each of the men to their teams, the wagons plodded forth into another wearisome day. The following day dawned in the same manner, each moment bringing them closer to Fort Laramie. Though Maggie understood, when the moment finally came it was no less difficult to relinquish her Indian bairn. The Indian agent was a kindly man and said the boy would be returned to his tribe to grow up among his own people, perhaps to even be reunited with his father or grandparents.

It was the best thing—Maggie knew that, but that knowledge could not keep away the empty feeling within her. That emptiness was beginning to be so ingrained in her that she wondered if she had ever been without it. The child had filled the void, but only for a few days. Now the hollow pit in her heart seemed larger than ever.

Samuel Carpenter could sense Maggie's need and tried to find ways to involve her in the needs of others. Caring for the child had been good for her, he thought, even if the parting was painful. At least she was feeling again. Even pain could be beneficial in the right doses. *Yes,* he thought, *she just needs some time, and enough opportunities to help others.* He would continue to try to draw her into his work whenever she might be useful.

West of Fort Laramie the road brought the weary train to the ascent of the Black Hills. Stories of previous trains passing through the Dakota mountains were enough in themselves to sober any overconfidence which might still have remained in the minds of any of the western migrants. Already they had seen evidences of earlier difficulties and heartbreaks strewn along the road—treasures cast aside as the stresses of travel had mounted: a weather-worn carved secretary, a rusted iron plow, an equally rusted cookstove. Stoddard had insisted that all the wagons be repacked before they left Fort Laramie, and many had found parting with at least one precious keepsake necessary.

Though low in comparison to the Rockies which the travelers would eventually cross, the road through the Black Hills was nevertheless rough and barren, surrounded on all sides with craggy bluffs and with many steep inclines. They negotiated one of these bluffs and began making their descent at a point called Mexican Hill.

Stormclouds had been massing throughout the day, and as they crossed the rolling plateau that led to the descent, cracks of thunder began splitting through the still, humid air. Almost immediately the deafening sounds were accompanied by great pounding drops of rain. The jagged streaks of lightning and strange explosions terrified the bewildered animals. The oxen pulling the wagons were easily brought under control, but the fifty or sixty head of cattle following behind bolted with the first peal of thunder. Despite the attempts of the men on horseback to bring them under control, they rampaged through the train and the oxen followed suit. The declivity of Mexican Hill gave the oxen unexpected freedom, and several of the wagons, including Frank Wooten's, were caught in the middle. For a few tense minutes, a flood of dust, animal flesh, and billowing white wagons seemed bent on racing toward certain destruction.

Tommy Joe poked his head out of his uncle Frank's wagon to catch a glimpse of all the excitement just at the moment when the wagon wheel struck a protruding rock in its wild dash down the hill. The jolt sent the boy flying from the wagon. He would almost certainly have been trampled to death had he not been thrown clear and landed in a narrow gully some ten feet off the path of the stampeding livestock.

Drew Mackinaw had managed to keep his team in tow where he followed behind Frank, but the horror of seeing his son flung to what certainly must be his death was far worse than the terrors of any stampede. With shaking arms Drew reined his team to a halt as quickly as he could and ran to where his child lay. Two other wagons, including Samuel Carpenter's, stopped as well while the remainder continued down the hill to give what aid they could to the stampeding wagons.

Near hysteria, Ellie climbed from the wagon and followed her husband. Maggie ordered the little ones to stay inside, and then joined her friends. When they reached the gully where Tommy Joe's broken body lay, they found Drew kneeling at his side, tears streaming down his cheeks, holding his son's limp head gently in his hands. Ellie's tenuous control gave way.

"He's dead!" she screamed. "My boy's dead!"

Scrambling down the gully Dr. Carpenter ran to the scene, knelt down, felt about his neck and shoulders, leaned over the boy's chest with the side of his face against his heart, then rose slowly.

"He's alive," he said, but the words were lost on Ellie's screaming mind. A moment later her form, limp and unconscious, fell into Drew's arms.

"Oh, God!" Drew wailed. "It's my fault! What have I done?"

"Stop it, Mackinaw!" the doctor said firmly. "Your son is alive! And I'm going to need you strong if you're to help me bring him around. Now, see to your wife while we get the boy back to the wagon."

Then he directed his words to the two other men who had followed them off the trail. "Help me carry him out of here. But be gentle. I still can't tell if there might be some broken bones."

The three men eased Tommy Joe's body off the ground and worked their way up the embankment, now slick with mud. Drew carried Ellie back to the top, but Maggie found that she could not climb out of the gully alone. Glancing back as he reached the top, Dr. Carpenter saw her predicament, ran back to where she stood, and gave her his hand. He did not speak until they reached the top.

"Mrs. Duncan, go to my wagon and prepare a bed for the child. And we'll need a fire," he added to no one in particular, "if one can be lit in this rain."

They carried the boy to the doctor's wagon where Maggie stood by, watching and wondering what else she should do. But the doctor did not leave her standing thus for long.

"Mrs. Duncan, come here," he said. "Sit beside the boy and speak to him—he needs someone he knows nearby. I've got to see about the fire."

Maggie sank down next to Tommy, and laid a trembling hand lightly on his head. "Tommy ... Tommy ..." she said with shaky voice. "It's ... you're going to be fine. The doctor's—"

"Mama!" the boy cried. "Mama!"

"Your mama will be here soon," Maggie soothed. "Here, take my hand."

The boy seemed to calm down and in a moment Dr. Carpenter returned. "The leg appears broken," he murmured. He began to probe gently with his hand, but when he reached a point three inches below the knee, where the skin was lacerated and his trousers were wet with blood, Tommy Joe screamed out in agony. "If only I had ether."

Just then Stoddard's voice could be heard outside. The wagon boss had galloped back up the hill after bringing the runaway wagons and stock under control. The weariness of his visage seemed even more pronounced.

Carpenter jumped from his wagon and hurried up to the trail master, who had dismounted and was barking orders to the few who were still standing out in the rain.

"Stoddard," the doctor asked without prelude, "have you some whiskey?"

Stoddard glared at the doctor.

"I need it for the boy."

Still Stoddard hesitated. The moment he and the doctor were alone, he reached into his saddlebag and withdrew a battered canteen. He shoved it into Carpenter's hand, but before the doctor could retreat to his patient, Stoddard said, "You ain't going to tell no one?"

"I'm a doctor, Mr. Stoddard. I know how to keep secrets."

"I only keep it around for times like this," the trail master added lamely. But the doctor had barely waited to hear and was already hastening back to the wagon.

Immediately Dr. Carpenter busied himself with preparations for the task ahead. He gave the whiskey to Maggie with instructions to administer it to Tommy Joe in whatever amounts he could tolerate.

It was a grueling two hours before the shattered leg was set to the doctor's satisfaction. Tommy Joe had long since passed out, both from inebriation and shock, and Maggie had been pressed into assisting the doctor more directly. While the leg was the most immediate concern, there was also a broken arm to be tended, as well as numerous cuts and scrapes. A badly bruised head also indicated the likelihood of a concussion, but Dr. Carpenter was at least relieved that no internal injuries were apparent.

When a pale and grief-stricken Ellie finally appeared at the doctor's wagon, Maggie assured her that Tommy Joe was sleeping soundly and doing well, considering what he had been through.

"I was so scared," Ellie whispered. "I couldn't even pray. But the Lord will see him through. I know He will."

Maggie smiled and put an arm around her friend.

"I'm afraid, Mrs. Mackinaw," said the doctor in a soft voice, not wanting to disturb the sleeping boy, "that the worst may still be to come. Once he wakes up, for several days the pain is going to be excruciating. He's going to need lots of comfort and sympathy, and probably a good deal more whiskey to relieve the pain. And there's always the possibility of infection, but I'll watch him closely."

"Oh, dear!" said Ellie. "Poor Drew. He worries me almost as much as Tommy Joe. He keeps blaming himself, for letting the boy go in the other wagon, for dragging us all out west. I can't seem to say anything to him."

"He'll feel better when he sees that Tommy is all right," said Maggie.

"I don't know. I've never seen him like this."

Suddenly Gil Stoddard's shout could be heard outside. "Come on, let's get movin'. We're wastin' precious time!"

Maggie's initial reaction was outrage that the man could be so insensitive. She had no way of knowing that the soldiers had decidedly warned Stoddard against even starting out through the Dakotas. The Black Hills were Sioux country. Only two weeks before, a train had been attacked and had suffered many casualties. A full-scale massacre had been averted only because an army patrol had happened along. But there could be no such guarantee of good fortune for other travelers. And Stoddard wanted to take no risks by remaining in one place too long.

Within five minutes the wagons began lurching forward and down the slope of Mexican Hill. The two women remained by the side of the injured boy in Dr. Carpenter's wagon. He awoke once and, after being comforted by the sight of his mother, fell back into a fitful sleep.

As the day progressed, Ellie and Maggie took turns remaining with Tommy Joe. Maggie made every attempt to relieve Ellie's anxiety by urging her to return to their wagon to be with Drew. And by the next day Maggie was tending the boy almost single-handedly while Dr. Carpenter eased his wagon along the rough and rocky trail as gently as he was able. Whenever he had the opportunity he turned, poking his head back through the opening in the canvas, to smile reassuringly at Maggie. He knew there was more healing taking place in the back of his wagon than in Tommy Joe's body and was gratified whenever Maggie returned his with a smile of her own. And not only was Samuel Carpenter concerned for the hurt in Maggie's heart, he knew her time was rapidly approaching; it was his responsibility to keep an ever closer eye on her condition.

After two days, the train made camp beside a grove of cottonwoods near a spring of pure, gushing water known as Warm Springs. Tommy Joe had gradually improved, and Dr. Carpenter was optimistic. He did not say, however, although the thought was heavily on his mind, that they still had to brace themselves for the possibility of infection.

Maggie climbed wearily out of the wagon. Even in her fatigued state it felt wonderful to stretch and walk about. The storm had long since passed, but it had left clouds in its wake and the respite from the earlier heat had indeed been welcome. She had hardly left the wagon in the past two days, and the fresh air and the scent from the trees and water invigorated her spirits.

"It's a wonderful place," she voiced, almost to herself.

"I wish we could stay here and recuperate for a few days," said the doctor, walking up behind her.

"Oh, Doctor," said Maggie, glancing around. "I didn't know you were there."

"The boy's sleeping. I needed to stretch my tired legs. But you must be exhausted, Mrs. Duncan. You've been so attentive to the lad. I appreciate your help."

"It's the least I could do. After all, his family's my family now too."

Just then Stoddard approached. As he passed she heard him muttering to one of the other men, "Too many trees here. I don't like it," he added in his gruff, laconic manner.

"All the wagon trains camp here," offered the other.

"Yeah. It's a fine place if the Indians don't—" He cut his words short the moment he saw Maggie nearby.

Maggie forced a thin smile. "Good evening," she said awkwardly.

"How's the kid?" Stoddard asked.

"About the same," Maggie replied.

"He'll be fine, Mr. Stoddard," added the doctor.

"Shouldn't have kids out on the trail," Stoddard muttered.

Maggie turned to walk back toward the doctor's wagon, but Stoddard addressed her once more. "Where you from anyway, Mrs. Duncan, with that peculiar accent of yours?" he asked bluntly.

"Scotland," she replied, wondering what had prompted his sudden interest. "Why do you want to know?"

"Just curious." He paused, then went on. "You about ready to have that there kid of yours?" he asked.

Maggie's cheeks reddened at his plain-spoken manner. Her embarrassment heightened because, even in the twilight, she could see that he had noticed her reaction.

"Look here, ma'am," he said. "This is a wagon train. Things are a mite different here than you may be used to. We gotta cut through all that propriety they hide behind in the East. If you're going to have a baby in the middle of Sioux territory, it's important that I know."

"Thank you for your concern," Maggie replied, still dubious but realizing he was right.

"My concern is for the whole train."

With the words Stoddard strode off in the direction he had been heading, leaving Maggie to ponder what he had said. *He'd be the last person I'll tell when my baby comes,* she thought, defiantly ignoring the sharp twinges of pain she had been feeling for the past three hours.

27   Ian's Child

As if Gil Stoddard's words had been prophetic, that night Maggie's labor came in earnest. As she lay on her bed wide awake, her eyes seemed to bore a hole through the canvas ceiling, now black with night. When the first sharp pains began to assail her with regularity, her muted cries were lost on the sleeping children.

Drew and Ellie were asleep in the doctor's wagon to be near Tommy Joe. One after another the pains came and she lay awake wondering if it were the real thing or a false alarm.

Oh, Ellie, she thought, *why aren't you here when I need you!*

Beads of perspiration gathered on her forehead and the joints of her hands ached as she gripped the bedclothes. Finally there could be no doubt. Maggie pulled herself up, rolled over, and crawled to the end of the wagon. Just then another contraction hit. She waited until it had passed, then eased her cumbersome body down from the wagon and onto the ground.

The night was still all about her. How she dreaded the thought of waking the whole train! If she could only suppress the screams that seemed bent on forcing their way out of her mouth! Slowly she walked toward the doctor's wagon, pausing every few steps to catch her breath in anticipation of the next pain. They were coming sharply now, and more quickly.

It was not far, but it seemed to take an eternity to traverse the few yards. Every step made her dizzy and nauseous. At length she fell against the wagon and tried to whisper, "Doctor . . . doctor . . ."

Dr. Carpenter was asleep under the wagonbed. A light sleeper by nature, he was awakened by the soft footsteps shuffling toward him. Pulling his suspenders over his shoulders, he crawled out just as the words reached his ears. There he saw an ashen figure braced against his wagon.

"Mrs. Duncan!" he gasped softly.

She made no reply but stepped forward as if she would continue her quest, but almost immediately she crumpled into the doctor's arms. He picked her up lightly, carried her back to the Mackinaw wagon, roused the children, and laid her back in her bed. Bess was sent to wake her father and mother, and while Drew carried Sarah and Bobby from their beds, half-asleep, and deposited them in the doctor's wagon, Ellie and Dr. Carpenter began hasty preparations which soon became a very furor of activity. A baby is not born on a wagon train in the middle of desolate Indian country without causing some stir, and before many more minutes had elapsed, several of the wives had arrived, drawn by the common bond of dawning motherhood, to lend what assistance they could.

Desperately Maggie tried to maintain the control that years of breeding had taught her. But as night wore into morning, her energy for propriety diminished. The other women at her side recalled the pain of their own labors and encouraged her with every cry, rejoicing in the agonizing ecstasy of the struggle for new life.

"Ian!" she screamed, hardly knowing what she said.

But Ian was not there. Even before the word left her lips, another cry forced its way into her throat—but this cry was not from the pain. *There was no Ian!* She was alone in this precious moment, with no one to hold her hand and caress her tangled hair.

"Oh, Ian!" she sobbed, and turned her face away from the women who were trying to comfort her.

Just then a strong hand touched her head and brushed back her hair. She looked up into deep-set, dark eyes gazing down on her with love and compassion.

"You're doing fine, Maggie," said a voice. "Just fine. We're all here to help you."

It was a voice she recognized, and the gentle eyes of Samuel Carpenter were eyes that cared. She closed her eyes and tried to relax. Ellie was there too, never leaving her side. Now her mind began to come clear again. Now she remembered. Of course, these people cared! They were her friends now. This was a new life. That other life was a long time ago, in another place.

Oh, but how could she forget the land and all it meant! Her child should have been born in the place where generations of Ramseys before it had been born. Not in this godforsaken, barren strip of land. Not out on the ridge. Nothing could grow there. It was windy and cold. And the child should have a father to receive it lovingly into its arms. And what about the child's grandmother . . .

"Oh, Mother!" Maggie cried, breaking into sobs again.

Was there to be no singing the child to sleep in the arms of a smiling grandmother? Was the proud Scottish matriarch Atlanta Ramsey to have no opportunity to look into the face of another generation of this mighty family?

Outside the sun continued its steady rise, and its heat began to penetrate the canvas roof of the wagon. Before ten o'clock the air had become stifling.

Dr. Carpenter lifted her head and placed a cup to her lips. "Here, Maggie," he said gently, "take a sip. That's good ... good. We're close to the end now. You're doing wonderfully!"

He set the cup down and silently prayed, "Lord, speed her along. Comfort her. And may this precious child work healing in the wounds of this family."

"It will be over soon," he said, "and you'll have a fine child—"

Maggie interrupted him with another scream. One look told the doctor all he needed to know.

"Mrs. Mackinaw!" he shouted to Ellie who had left the wagon for a moment, "Mrs. Mackinaw ... the moment has come!"

By late afternoon Maggie finally drifted into a sound sleep as the wagon jostled beneath her. In her arms lay her tiny daughter, as fine a child as the doctor had assured her it would be. As she had lain there before falling asleep, so many of her cares seemed to dissolve in the sweet awe of motherhood. This was *her* child, her own daughter! And for the moment, at least, all the painful memories were forgotten.

When she awoke the wagon was still and she could tell they had already made camp for the night. The voices outside were a blur, but as consciousness gradually returned she became aware that a heated debate was in progress.

"She just better be ready to go in the morning," declared Stoddard's unyielding voice.

"I tell you," began the voice of Dr. Carpenter in a measured, but less than patient tone, "there is too great a danger of another hemorrhage. She has to remain still until I can control it. The movement has already taken its toll. If the trail is rough tomorrow, there could be fatal consequences."

"I'm willing to risk it," came Stoddard's gruff reply.

"You're willing to risk it!" the doctor returned, his voice rising angrily. The past three days had been tense, sleepless ones for him; little reserve of patience was left for this mulish trail master. "No one is risking anything, do you hear! You refused to stop for the boy—"

"And I'm refusing again," Stoddard rejoined flatly.

"Then go on. I'll be staying. And that is no idle threat! We'll catch up with you as soon as we can."

Drew had walked up and heard the last two remarks of each of the men. "I know my party'll be stayin' behind wi' the doctor," he said. "An' I heard some o' the others complainin' it were time fer a rest. The oxen's hoofs are wearin' raw, an' they need t' be shod. If it's Indians ye're afraid o', ye're na goin' t' get far wi' lame animals, nor wi' only a han'ful o' wagons."

"You greenhorns just don't understand, do you?" stated Stoddard with disgust. "You don't understand the danger. You hired me to get your carcasses through safely, and that's what I'm trying to do. Okay, I give up!" With the words he turned. "Women!" he muttered as he stalked away. "They're always trouble."

Though Maggie heard fragments of their words, she was too absorbed in the daughter sleeping in her arms to care, or even to notice the pains of her own weary body. The tiny infant had given her a joy she thought she would never experience again. Words from her childhood floated into her mind, and for the first time in many months she found she could almost believe them: *"Every good gift and every perfect gift is from above, and cometh down from the Father of lights, with whom is no variableness, neither shadow of turning."*

Could it be that God had given her this wonderful gift? That was what Digory always called Him, the giver of pure and lovely gifts to His children. Ever since news of Ian's death she had been cursing God in her mind. How could He be both the giver of life— pure and innocent as this new child—and the author of death and heartache?

Could it be that God had *not* taken Ian from her? Could the sadness and destruction and death in the world be not His doing at all? Was it possible that in the midst of her heartbreak, God himself was trying to shower His love into her heart to sustain her and help her to stand in the midst of evil forces operating to destroy her life? Could He, after all, really *be* a God of love as Digory said? Might this child be more truly from Him than the heartache she had laid to His charge?

Ellie's cheerful voice, oblivious to the deeper struggles within

Maggie's heart, suddenly washed away all Maggie's thoughts as she burst into the wagon.

"As Drew would say, 'She's a braw lass!' "

"How's Tommy Joe?" asked Maggie weakly.

"Moanin' something fierce. But the doctor says he's on the mend. Have you decided on a name yet?"

Maggie had hardly given naming her child a thought. But all at once she knew what it would be. "Her name is Eleanor. After you, my dear friend."

Ellie fell to her knees by Maggie's side and, stretching her arms around Maggie, wept great tears of joy.

Later that evening, as Maggie dozed in and out of consciousness, her thoughts drifted again to Ian. How he would have loved this baby! Tears welled up in Maggie's eyes at the thought that little Eleanor would be robbed of knowing her own father.

Father.

With the word, confused and bitter images tumbled into Maggie's mind. *He* was the one who had brought this ruin on her and Ian! It hadn't been God at all! He was the cruel man responsible—her own father!

How she hated him for what he had done!

But even if he had brought destruction to the love that she and Ian had shared so briefly, at least he would be powerless to reach out and take this precious child from her.

Maggie hugged her daughter close.

No, she thought, *you will never see this child, James Duncan! She will never know how cruel your selfishness can be. I will protect her! I will love her. And you can never take that away from me!*

28 The Master of the House

Digory was a good deal slower these days. It took twice as long for him to move his arthritic body about the stable to feed the horses. But every morning, without fail, he was there about his tasks, and never was a single animal slighted. If he seemed to dote particularly on the coal-black Raven and the chestnut mare Maukin, he could perhaps be forgiven. They were reminders to him of happier times.

Digory had never been a man to dwell on the past. He knew that God's hand was in every season of life, regardless if the weather of the soul was sunny or frostbitten. But Stonewycke had become so bleak of late that he often was reminded that, truly, God's ways were not his ways.

"An' fer that truth I do truly gi' ye thanks," he murmured that crisp, late-spring afternoon. "I'd hae things all braw an' pleasant, an' then we might ne'er see oor need fer ye, Lord."

The depth of his own dependence on his Father above was a truth never far from aging Digory's mind. Thus his old heart ached when he saw others reject his Lord. And how his heart did ache every time he looked upon his master!

If a man's inward degeneration could be denoted by his outward appearance, then James Duncan was truly a lost man. Each time Digory's loving eyes rested on the laird of Stonewycke, he seemed to have aged several years. The hollowness about his visage reminded Digory of a grand cathedral gutted by a raging fire. Digory knew the fire which was slowly consuming James Duncan was an internal one no eyes would ever see. But he was not one to speculate on what was in his master's heart. All he could do was pray that the laird would one day yield to the purifying fires of Love's forgiveness before the self-willed fires of hell took him to his death.

Digory hobbled up to the black mare's stall, carrying a pail of oats which he poured liberally into the trough. The mare gave his arm an amiable nudge before she began the business of devouring her lunch.

"Ye're a braw one, Raven," Digory said softly to the animal. " 'Twas a glad day when ye an' yer chestnut friend came back home. I only wish ... eh, but what's the use o' it? Yer mistress is gane an' if the Lord wants her back, then 'twill be. A fine day like this is when I'm missin' her the most, an' I don't doubt but ye'll be missin' her too. Ye're needin' a good run, ye are. If only the master—"

"What about your master?" came an icy voice behind Digory. If James had intended his words to impart scorn to his groom, Digory did not notice.

Digory slowly turned his bent frame to face the laird. "I was jist wonderin' when auld Raven here might get oot fer a run, my lord."

"I told you, no one's to ride that horse!"

"An' no one has, sir," Digory replied. "Not since—well, not since the lass hersel' gang away."

"That's over and done with, do you hear?" James barked. "And I'll not hear any more of it. Nor will I stand for your turning around and disobeying my orders behind my back!"

"That I couldn't dream o' doin', sir," Digory replied earnestly. " 'Tis just that sometimes I canna help thinkin' aboot those happier times."

"So, now you're complaining?" James accused.

"Oh, no, yer lairdship, at least no fer mysel'."

"For whom, then?" James's question was phrased as a challenge, and a man with less humility and more guile would have backed down from it. But Digory knew only how to hear a question, and answer it, from his heart.

"I canna help but t' see that ye yersel' hae seemed sorely troubled since the Lady Margaret left. An' my heart truly hurts fer ye, an' I wish there was somethin' I could do fer ye."

"You leave that little tramp out of it!" James exploded. "It'll be a cold day in hell," he spat, "when a measly groom could do anything for *me*! Except saddle up the bay—which is all you're good for." His dry laugh was unmistakably full of derision, and might have indeed stung the groom if it had not immediately been followed by a pathetic fit of coughing.

Digory could feel no malice toward his master, only regret that he had himself brought it on. "Are ye sure, sir, that ye ought t' be oot wi' sich a cough?"

"And I'll not be treated like a doddering old man, either!" shrieked James in a rage. "Especially by an old fool who can walk no better than you!" Without awaiting a reply James stalked outside to await his servant's compliance to his orders.

Digory left Raven's stall and shuffled with all the speed he could muster toward the bay. He hitched on the reins, then led the horse to the saddle rack where the laird's finest English saddle lay. If he had not had so many other things occupying his mind, he might have wondered that the laird had come to the stable with such a request at all.

For three weeks James had not set foot outside the ancient stone castle. The servants had more than once discussed the peculiarity of this change from the man who had previously seemed bent on remaining away from his home as much as possible.

But Stonewycke had become a place of refuge for James, a shelter where he did not have to face the wagging tongues of his business associates, nor embarrassment from his creditors. Rumors had begun to spread about the laird of Stonewycke. Many had begun to guess the truth about his pilfered funds from the accounts of the stockholders. Others had noted his alarming increase in alcohol consumption. Still more wondered when long-overdue accounts would be settled.

Stonewycke had become a convenient hiding place. But for James it symbolized more than that. Here he could hold his head high, here he could still maintain the ruse of his lordship. If his ambitious dreams of grandeur and power had slipped because of these temporary setbacks, his servants and these locals need never know. He was still the mightiest man in Strathy. This was his domain, and he still ruled with an iron hand and a word which was the law.

Yet such assurances did not completely mollify his apprehensions about his difficulties outside Stonewycke, for in the depths of his soul James knew the foundations of his lordship remained in place only through the sufferance of his wife. He couldn't help wondering why she was suddenly allowing him to have his way so easily. Had she stopped caring? Had the disappearance of their daughter affected her so greatly that she had even ceased to care about who controlled her beloved Stonewycke?

It didn't matter. He was beyond trying to analyze it. He never looked things straight in the eye anymore.

All that was important to James was that he never had to come face-to-face with his horrible failure. And to maintain this thin gloss over what remained of his life, another requirement became tantamount—Atlanta must never know that he had fabricated the entire story of their son-in-law's death.

To this end went a good deal of the money James had not already lost on his erstwhile brewery. Bribes were costly, and he prided himself on being able to keep it a secret this long. If only that blackguard son-in-law *would* die in prison! But now it only mattered that Atlanta never find out. For James knew with cold certainty that if she did, her recent lassitude would explode with more vengeance and wrath than a dozen generations of Ramseys could contain.

To this end his current ride had become necessary. More money had to be sent to Glasgow. An assistant wardman had found out about Ian—how close he was to the truth James hadn't been able to determine. There were rumors another man had become involved as well. He couldn't let it unravel now. He would have to buy their silence; every man had his price, and these men were no different. But it came at a difficult time. He hoped their price was not too high, for he was drawing dangerously near to the end of his resources.

What James did not know was that one of these men had no price. And he was at that very moment in temporary residence at the inn less than two miles from Stonewycke.

29 The Lad on the Moor

Dermott had been in Port Strathy only two days and was becoming more and more convinced that his task was not going to be easy—not that he had ever expected it would be.

This was a small, closely bound community, and he had immediately discovered that it was unwise to barge in with questions which might be taken to be accusations. Especially where the laird's family was concerned. The day after his arrival he had asked an innocuous question about Ian of the innkeeper. The woman's small eyes had sharpened and her hands sought her hips in unconscious defiance.

"What d'ye want t' ken fer?" she asked in something less than friendly tones.

"I made his acquaintance some time ago," Dermott replied honestly enough. "I heard he stayed in Port Strathy for a time, and I hoped I might avail myself of his friendship while I was here."

"Well, he had precious few friends," she said gruffly. There was an odd catch around the edges of her voice, as if she knew more than she was telling. But before Dermott could comment further, she scurried out of the common room where they had been talking, and disappeared into the confines of the kitchen.

Further queries among other townsfolk yielded similar responses. The few who acknowledged Ian acted as if there were some ban on revealing anything about him. With every encounter Dermott probed the eyes of each person he met, trying to ascertain whether this might be someone in whom he could confide his purpose. But a voice inside kept saying, *Wait.* From scattered remarks the boy had made, Dermott had assumed the woman known as "Queenie" was his friend. However, upon arriving in Port Strathy he wasn't so sure. Her eyes had contained a suspicious glare since the moment he walked into the inn, and Dermott had been reluctant to open his mind to her. *Time will tell,* he thought, *whether this past acquaintance of Ian's is truly to be relied on as an ally*. For all he knew she could be part of the elaborate frame which had caught Ian in its grip. He would have to be discreet with his questions and watch that whatever plot that was afoot did not ensnare him as well.

For the next several days he walked about the village, listening, observing, learning what he could of its people and their ways. He learned a good deal about the family of Stonewycke and heard many reports—not always consistent with one another—concerning the laird, the James Duncan Ian had spoken of. But nothing came his way which revealed where he should direct his attentions. Finally, after a week, a chance conversation with a feisty old fisherman down at the harbor yielded a bit of information which he thought worth exploring. The man told Dermott he had seen a young couple the previous fall on horseback heading toward a desolate moorland ridge south of town.

"Used t' visit wi' a fellow by the name o' Kruger, I did," the man said. "Kin o' my wife's. They lived on a sparse patch o' ground two or three mile from here. They was havin' trouble wi' a couple o' their animals last year. My wife an' me, we rode oot t' see 'em every week or so, t' see if we could help. That's when I seen the young lad from Lonnon, wi' Lady Margaret. More'n once I saw 'em ridin' out toward the ridge."

The following morning, having received what directions the man had been able to give, Dermott decided to ride out into the countryside. The solitude would be restful; he needed time to seek guidance for what he should do, and in addition, he thought, an idea might unfold as he followed Ian's paths of the previous autumn.

He headed south on the old, slow-plodding gelding Queenie Rankin, the innkeeper, had provided. As she had handed him the reins a puzzled look came over her face, and she opened her mouth as if she was about to tell him something. Then apparently she thought better of it and turned away. If she had something to say, Dermott thought, she would have to learn to trust him first—and he her. If it was meant to be, that would come in time. They would have to continue testing the waters of each other's loyalties.

About a mile out of the village, the terrain began to rise slightly into gently rolling meadows. Summer was gradually revealing its face to the land held so long in winter's harsh grasp. The meadow lay green before him with the soft yellow faces of wild daisies and an occasional clump of primroses or daffodils gleaming up at the crisp blue sky overhead. To Dermott's left he could just make out the stone turrets of Stonewycke jutting up proudly into the northern sky. The thought crossed his mind of letting the old horse take him in that direction, for he knew his path must ultimately lead there, but instead he rode on, for the time for a confrontation behind the massive stone walls was not yet come.

He continued over the meadows another mile until their greenery began to give way to the moor called Braenock Ridge. Dermott had grown up not far from a moor very similar to this one. It was not unusual he was drawn to the desolate heath. As a boy he had often sought the somber comfort of the lonely countryside to be alone and work out the difficulties of growing up. As he rode, the way became rockier; he directed the gelding up the rocky ridge to the dreary peat bog.

At length he stopped his horse and gazed all about him. No thoughts of Ian were present just now, only nostalgic memories of his own past and of long walks on land just as this. He sighed deeply, then urged his mount slowly forward, aimless in his destination, soaking in the essence of his aloneness. *Lord,* he thought silently, *what do you have to say to me today? What would you have this place tell me?*

The heaps of granite boulders lying in seeming haphazard fashion escaped his notice as he passed them at a distance of some hundred and fifty yards. Instead, his eye caught sight of a lonely figure crossing the moor some quarter mile distant. His drab, peasant garb and browned skin would have made him blend perfectly into the landscape had it not been for the wild shock of wiry red hair. From a distance Dermott could not rightly judge his age, but wondered if the figure was one, like he himself had been so many years ago, who sought comfort from the land, beautiful—as the old groom had maintained—in its sheer tenacity.

Dermott flipped the reins and moved toward the distant figure. As he drew closer and the shape took on more definition, Dermott saw it to be a tall gangly lad of about fifteen. But he carried himself like an old man with the cares of the world resting upon his shoulders. Immediately Dermott's heart was drawn to him.

Stevie Mackinaw had also sought the peculiar peace of the moor that day. And as the man and the boy slowly approached each other, both would probably have been surprised to discover their thoughts flowing in a similar current. Stevie thought often of those past days when the healthy bleating of sheep followed him home to his dear mother and father, where also on an especially bright day he might be blessed to find the sweet countenance of Lady Margaret. But now such happy thoughts were gone and he, too, was struck with the loneliness of the place. Yet where else could he go for strength? This land was all he knew.

He looked up at the tall stranger approaching on horseback. And if his wary look was less than friendly, perhaps he could be forgiven. Gentlemen such as this one seemed always to bring nothing but trouble. Yet this man's eyes bore something different than he had been accustomed to lately, something that told him perhaps his mission was different, too. If Stevie had known the man better, he would have known it was love which looked out of those eyes upon him.

"If ye'll be wantin' directions," Stevie said as they met, "ye'd best be veerin' t' the left away from the boulders and takin' the road back down there off the ridge. There's nothin' up here but moorland, an' it'll lead ye no place."

"Why would you think I'd want directions?" asked Dermott.

"Any gentlefolk sich as yersel' who get this far up on the moor are usually lost," Stevie replied honestly, taking in a closer look at this stranger as he spoke.

"Perhaps you are right," Dermott said. "But in my case," he went on, strongly compelled to continue the conversation with this burdened young man, "I have come here to think. The place drew me simply by its solitary loveliness."

"Ye maun hae strange sight, sir," replied Stevie. "I've only known the moor t' be lovely once . . ."

His voice trailed away and his eyes seemed to scan the horizon as if he expected that lovely vision to appear once again.

"Then you must not be too familiar with this country," Dermott suggested, hoping to lead him into further speech.

"Na familiar wi' it! I were born an' raised but three furlongs from here, as were my daddy and his daddy too. Here all those years we were, until the laird turned me oot twa months past."

"I'm sorry to hear that," said Dermott, dismounting and taking the reins lightly in his hand.

"I thought ye was one o' his men when I saw ye ridin' up."

Dermott laughed. "No, not hardly. I have business of my own. But tell me, what could have happened to end all those long years of service?"

"My daddy died," Stevie said, his voice bleak as the moor itself. "An' fer the laird, I'm guessin' that be crime enough." The bitterness of his last words were unmistakable.

"And then the moor lost its loveliness?"

"Somewhat, maybe, but 'twas long before when the life was taken awa'—when my mither died and she on her black Raven no mair rode o'er this country."

"Your mother was a horsewoman, then?"

"Na, na. Not my mither. The *lady*. She was the rider."

As they spoke Stevie's initial wariness had subsided. If he had asked himself why, he would have decided it was something in the quality of the man's voice, in addition to the look in his eyes. Almost unconsciously they began walking together over the rocks through the wiry, bare heather brush whose blossoms were yet dormant. As Dermott gently questioned him, Stevie told about the days when his mother and father were both alive, about tending the sheep for them. The boy talked of his mother's faith and how it had always seemed to carry them through even the hardest times and coldest winters. Dermott said he would like to have known her, wondering silently if she did not somehow symbolize the essence of what was good on the Stonewycke estate. Then Stevie told of the day she died.

"The lady were there wi' us that day," he said wistfully. "My mither loved her. Some o' her last words were fer the lady. 'Always keep the hope o' the Lord in yer heart,' she said. I'll ne'er forget that day."

"Who was the lady, Stevie?" Dermott asked, realizing now that God had indeed led him out onto the moor for a purpose.

"The Lady Margaret, o' course."

"Lord Duncan's daughter?"

"Aye," he replied. "An' 'tis a sorry thing that an angel like as her maun call sich a man her father. If she would hae been here, he wouldna hae turned me oot. She was always friend t' the likes o' us. But she wasna here."

"What happened? Where is she?"

"She went off wi' him."

"Ian Duncan?"

"Aye. But I canna say mair aboot it," Stevie said pointedly, the former sadness returning to his tone.

"I am a friend of Mr. Duncan's," Dermott said. "I have come here to try to help him."

"He'll be needin' na help whaur he rests noo."

"Stevie," Dermott said, pausing and placing a firm hand on the boy's shoulder. "You must tell no one else this. But Ian is alive, and I have promised to help him. And I have promised to try to find her for him too. She has disappeared somewhere in America. Stevie . . . can you help me?"

Stevie stared blankly at the lawyer. They stood for some moments as the wind blew over the moor, tousling red and black hair alike.

At length Dermott spoke again, gently but urgently. "Do you hear me, lad? I need you . . . *they* need you."

When Stevie spoke again, the shock had disappeared from his face and his voice droned on sadly. "We didna see her o'er much after he came. An' she didna come t' oor cottage. She still rode her fine mare, but mostly wi' him. Then one day he came t' oor place."

"The young Mr. Duncan?"

"Aye. He came by himsel'—alone. He asked my daddy an' me t' tell na a soul—for her sake, he said."

Stevie stopped, as if he would say no more.

"I know why he came," Dermott said. "Ian told me himself that he sent Maggie to your brother in America."

"Then why would ye be needin' me?" asked Stevie.

"There was a great deal Ian could not tell me," Dermott replied. "Both time and his memory prevented him. He has been badly mistreated in prison and it has not been good for his mental powers. If I don't help him soon, I fear for what might happen to his mind. That is why I have come here, to try to fill in the gaps of what happened. And there is one most important thing that only you can help me with. I have tried to contact your brother in New York. But it seems he has left, moved west. If Margaret Duncan ever did reach him, I must find out where she is now. But there is no hint of her whereabouts. If you know anything . . ."

"I hae na heard from my brother in nigh t' four years."

"Didn't you notify him of your parents' deaths?"

"I ne'er wrote a letter in all my life. My mither used t' write sometimes. But I ne'er could learn. An what good would it hae doon anyway?"

"It might have gotten us closer to Lady Margaret," Dermott replied thoughtfully. "But I will have to pursue another direction for that."

They began walking again. Both remained silent as they pondered their own thoughts. Gradually their steps led to the foot of a small rise, over which sat the sod hovel where Stevie Mackinaw had been born. As they approached, Stevie veered away from the rise and back toward the road, for in the two months since his eviction he had never returned to the old cottage with its bittersweet memories of happiness and loss.

It was some time before Dermott finally spoke. "Did Mr. Duncan ever speak to you of anything else besides going to America, Stevie?"

"Na o'er much," Stevie replied, glad to have his thoughts diverted from the painful memories of his home. "He didna come t' visit wi' sich like us, not a London gentleman like himsel'."

"Do you remember anything about the death of Master Falkirk?"

"The likes o' me!" Stevie said with something resembling a smile on his weathered face. "The lairds keep even their deaths t' themselves. That's what made the Lady Margaret so special. She wasna afraid t' be one o' us, if ye ken my meanin'. But I do recall, noo that ye mention him, askin' the laird Falkirk the same question once that I asked ye a while ago."

"What was that?" Dermott asked.

"Weel, I asked him if he was lost."

"Do you mean out here on the moor?"

"Aye. But like yersel', he said he wasna lost. But he wasna as kind as ye were, sir. He told me t' mind my own business an' tore on past me on that golden stallion o' his. It wasna the only time I saw him here. But 'tis a free country an' a man, 'specially a laird, can ride whaur he wills. 'Tis the only time I laid eyes on Master Falkirk up close. I dinna ken what might hae been between him and Mr. Duncan. But Mistress Rankin might ken aboot that, fer Mr. Duncan stayed at the inn fer a spell. He said that if we ever had any messages t' git t' him, he told us t' leave them wi' the mistress o' the inn, that she could be trusted."

Dermott's face brightened. "So she *is* an ally! I thought as much."

"A friend t' some, na doobt," remarked Stevie. "But not a woman t' be crossed when she's standin' her ground. But Mr. Duncan thought she was a friend o' his, that much is certain."

"That explains her cool reception," said Dermott almost to himself, reflecting on Queenie's hostile looks the moment he had begun asking questions about Ian. Undoubtedly the woman was only being protective of the lad who had become her friend while staying at her inn, and had assumed him an enemy.

By now they had reached the road again, if that narrow rocky path through the peat bogs and over the rough landscape could be called a road. When Dermott extended his hand, large and warm and grateful, the lad responded awkwardly and shyly. But Dermott took the coarse, dirty hand and uttered a deeply felt *thank you*.

"Do you have a place to stay, lad?" Dermott added before they parted.

"Whaur the heather be soft an' dry, 'tis good enough fer me," Stevie replied earnestly.

"But the heather won't be in bloom for months. And it's hardly the dry season yet."

"An' till then, 'cept when it *is* warm enough t' be oot, I stay wi' friends in Strathy who was kind enough t' open their home t' me."

Dermott studied the boy for a long moment, satisfied at least for the present that the boy had a dry roof over his head. The bitterness he had occasionally seen rise to his face had now been replaced by a guileless simplicity. It was as if both emotions were struggling within him, even as boyhood still continued its losing battle against coming manhood, and young Stevie did not know which to give place to.

Finally Dermott took a sovereign from his pocket and handed it to Stevie.

"Nay, sir," Stevie protested. "I'll na take what I hae na worked fer."

"Neither would I expect you to," Dermott answered. "But you have been of immeasurable help to me, and I expect to call upon your service again. And so this is payment for those services. You will make yourself available to me in the future?"

"Weel," Stevie replied, rubbing his chin thoughtfully. "Since ye put it that way . . . I suppose I could that."

"Thank you," Dermott said, swinging himself up on Queenie's horse. "What's the name of the couple you are staying with?"

" 'Tis the Hawkins. Their place is aboot a half mile east o' the village, on the road up t' the summit."

"I shall be in touch," said Dermott.

He turned and directed the gelding north and toward Port Strathy on the road by which he had come. His keen lawyer's mind was already working meticulously over the details of his conversation with Stevie. By appearances he had learned very little. Yet he had a strong sense that this would prove to be of inestimable importance later. For now at least it had directed him to another who might help still further. The next order of business would certainly seem to be a candid talk with the mistress of Port Strathy's inn.

Dermott did not forget that he had been led out to the moor. God had indeed been faithful in providing the guidance he had sought. And on the way back toward the village Dermott Connell, in the quiet of his own heart, gave thanks to his Lord that he was not responsible to order his own steps throughout the perplexities of life.

30 An Evening at Queenie's

The cheery fire of the Bluster N' Blow's common room was inviting after the chill of the moor. Dermott settled down before the hearth and gratefully accepted a steaming mug of coffee from Queenie.

"We don't get much call fer that drink in these parts," the inn's mistress said as she stepped back to watch from Dermott's expression whether she had prepared it to his satisfaction.

"It tastes as if you are quite an expert with it, nevertheless," said Dermott after a sip.

She smiled, one of the first Dermott had seen, and said, "I learned it in the city, where they go fer such strange customs. Dinna touch it mysel', but I've always kept a small supply from those days. I'm surprised it didna lose its flavor."

At that moment the door of the inn opened and three fishermen walked in, diverting Queenie for some time. Before long, however, she returned to her softspoken customer where he sat in front of the fire.

"Would ye be wantin' more?" she asked.

"Yes, I'd like that," Dermott replied.

Queenie left him and returned with another mug of the brew. She tarried a moment longer than was necessary, then made to leave, but then turned again, clearly indecisive, and said in a casual voice. "Were—were the horse t' yer satisfaction, Mr. Connell?"

"Quite so, Mistress Rankin," Dermott replied, noting the uncertainty in the innkeeper's bearing. "I should like to make use of him once or twice more in the next few days if he is available."

"That it will be," she replied. "Then ye'll be stayin' a bit longer?"

"Yes, it seems so, for I have not yet been successful in my purpose. I had hoped to locate some friends of a certain lad in grave trouble. But it begins to appear I may be his only friend."

As he spoke Dermott registered the woman's reaction to his

veiled words with his keen lawyer's eyes.

" 'Tis a sorry pass," she replied noncommittally. "I had a friend in a fix like that mysel' once," she continued, still offering no clue to what lay beneath her thick black eyebrows. "In grave trouble, as ye put it. But where that lad is now, he needs no friends. Still, if he was alive, a body mightn't be able t' trust a man's *words*—fer anyone can *say* he's a man's friend."

As she spoke Dermott thought he detected an imperceptible squinting in her inquiring eyes.

"But if someone had tried to convince everyone that a lad was dead," Dermott argued softly, "and another came along to declare that he was alive and in dire need of help, would that not be proof enough of the latter's sincerity? Who else but a friend would risk provoking the powers which had feigned the man's death?"

"But no one has yet declared the man of whom you speak to be alive," Queenie said, fastening her shrewd gaze on Dermott now more fixedly. As she did so, she slid her bulky frame onto the bench next to the lawyer.

Dermott held her gaze and spoke in measured, precise tones. "I declare to you, Mistress Rankin, that Ian Duncan is this moment alive. I have seen and spoken with him less than a fortnight ago."

Yet even with the words Queenie did not relent of her wary suspicion. "Why then were ye lookin' fer friends, sir?" she asked as if she had caught a thief in his own trap. "Fer if ye had known this Mr. Duncan, ye would hae known where t' look fer his friends."

"He spoke to me of you, Mistress Rankin. But after your initial reception, I too felt caution was necessary. Deceit abounds in this case. Even old friends can turn—or be turned—away."

"Not I!" Queenie exclaimed, showing her emotions for the first time. "There's nothin' that laird up on the hill could do t' turn me against the lad!"

"Then let us put aside our caution," Dermott entreated. "Let us trust each other, for the sake of him whom we both care about."

"He's truly alive?" Queenie breathed. "Somehow I was sure all along he was."

"What can you tell me about him, Mistress Rankin?"

"First, I can tell ye, he called me Queenie, an' if ye be a friend o' his, then ye can call me that also," she said as she propped an elbow on the table and began rubbing her ample chin. "He enjoyed a good time, he did. But I always had the feelin' there was more t' it than jist that. Mostly I only saw the lad after all his troubles began. That is, the troubles here in Port Strathy."

"He told me of the day and night of the murder," Dermott said. "But it was so sketchy, as though he was remembering it through a fog. What do you remember of that day?"

Queenie glanced around hastily toward her other customers. Satisfied that they were well provided for and were paying no attention, she lowered her voice and said: "He had that sprattle wi' Master Falkirk, an' everyone swore t' the constable later that the lad had blood in his eye. But I ken that's no true. He couldna kill— not murder wi' oot good cause. But what's an auld innkeeper's opinion against what came oot o' the lad's mouth? Fer he swore he'd kill Falkirk if he touched the lady again."

"But neither of us believe he followed through on that threat."

"We're the only ones, Mr. Connell," said Queenie gloomily. "Time was when I thought it'd all turn oot right. Constable Duff seemed t' be believin' the lad. But then suddenly he was gone."

"Constable Duff?"

"Used t' be the constable o'er in Culden. But then jist aboot the time I thought he an' the lady was aboot t' get free o' their troubles, some new man's sniffin' around an' no one's heard o' Duff since."

"What happened?"

"No one's sayin'. But I hae my suspicions," returned Queenie.

"It seems no one is willing to speak of Ian Duncan at all, either for good or ill."

" 'Tis the laird, sir," said Queenie, lowering her voice still further. "He controls everythin' an' the people are afraid o' him. I sure wish I knew what Duff knew, an' that's fer certain, fer Ian told me the last time I saw him that Duff believed him. But the laird won't tolerate even the sound o' Ian Duncan's name in his hearin'. An' so most folk jist as soon na speak o' him at all. The laird has eyes an' ears everywhere."

She paused for a moment deep in thought, and when she began again, it was slowly and cautiously. "Noo that I think o' it, maybe he's better off wi' folks thinkin' he's dead. The laird's got people t' believin' 'twas Ian that killed Falkirk an' made his daughter run off. If they knew he was alive, I'm thinkin' he'd only end up at the gallows."

"I can't figure why Lord Duncan—for it is certainly he who has perpetrated this hoax—has done this to Ian, his own son-in-law," said Dermott thoughtfully. "What could he have against him? What motives are hidden from our view? But whatever the cause, Queenie, no man should be forced to live under the awful pall of guilt and shame that Ian faces with each new day. And though I fear exoneration alone will not give Ian the peace he needs, it might at least set him on that road. But for true healing to come to his soul, the changes will have to go much deeper."

"Deeper? What changes would ye be speakin' o', Mr. Connell?"

"Forgiveness, Queenie. I'm speaking of forgiveness, the one true road to forgiveness for all men and women."

Queenie did not respond, lost in her own silent reminiscences which Dermott's words had triggered. When she did speak, it was to ask perhaps the most practical question of all. "An' what if he's na cleared o' the crime?" she said, voicing the fear that had always haunted Dermott.

Silence once more descended upon the two and they sat staring into the fire for some time. Dermott's thoughts sought both comfort and guidance in silent prayer. At length he spoke. "He will be exonerated, Queenie," he said. "Only a moment ago, I was not so sure. But I now believe God has given me assurance that such is His purpose."

"Weel then," Queenie said, her practical nature once again asserting itself, "if that's t' truly be, then God might be wantin' a suggestion from an auld woman."

"And what would that be?"

"As things stand wi' the lad, it appears t' me the only way he'll be cleared is when we find who *really* murdered Master Falkirk."

At that moment several of Queenie's customers began clamoring for refills of their ale. She rose and busied herself about this task for most of what remained of the evening. Dermott finished his coffee and leaned back against the wall, his eyes focused on the dancing flames in the hearth. His mind ranged in many different directions, but before long it could not help settling on the conversation between certain of Queenie's guests whose words had grown too loud to ignore. A small group of farmers and fisherfolk, they were seated in a cluster about one of the larger tables in the room, bandying about small tidbits of daily news and local happenings. Dermott doubted he could learn much concerning the affairs of the laird or the neighboring gentry from their talk, which centered mostly on the state of their crops or the running of the fish. However, after some time, as their voices became louder, Dermott could not help his interest being drawn in their direction.

"He's got nerve comin' back after a' these months!" one was saying with mild indignation in his voice.

"I'm plumb surprised his wife had'm back, leavin' her as he did t' the mercies o' frien's an' neighbors," put in another.

"Weel, I'm tellin' ye straight oot," added a large imposing man with graying beard, "I'll na take the likes o' him on my boat again! He's a no account guid fer nothin'—an' them's the *kind* words I hae fer'm!"

"What goads me," one offered, "is jist afore he slithered oot o' here, he was actin' so high n' mighty like—"

"Aye!" agreed another. "Braggin' aboot becomin' a wealthy man an' all that talk aboot wrappin' some gentleman 'round's finger."

"That's Marty Forbes fer ye!"

"Tellin' tales. All yammer an' little t' back it up."

"Why do ye think he left so almighty hurried like?"

"I saw him the day after that young lord from Lonnon killed the Falkirk fella. He looked none too good that day, I can tell ye."

"Aye. That's when he left, it was. I never saw him after that, until—"

The speech was stopped suddenly as the door of the inn opened and in walked a tall, bedraggled man. From the looks on the faces of the men he had been listening to, Dermott could only conjecture that the very object of their conversation had entered. They welcomed him, if a bit stiffly, to their circle and the conversation slowly regained its momentum, drifting toward other topics.

Dermott paid little heed, soon rose and stretched his tired limbs, and decided it was time to turn in for the night. Before he climbed the stairs to his room, he took Queenie aside for a moment to apprise her of his intentions.

"Sometime I'm going to have to ask you what you know about this Marty Forbes who's now seated in the other room. And I think it's of some importance that I locate the man Duff to learn what light he might be able to shed on this."

"If he's to be found," added Queenie with cautious concern.

"Yes, you're right," said Dermott with a grave sigh. "But to-morrow," he went on, "I intend to ride out to Stonewycke."

"An' what can that accomplish," she argued, "but t' maybe in-cite the laird t' further injustices against the lad?"

"Sooner or later I must confront the man and try to find out what happened that night, from the laird's own mouth. I have de-layed meeting him as long as possible. I had hoped to obtain some solid evidence first, to see how things stood. But if he knows more than he would readily admit, then it may be that I can discern it from his speech."

"Weel, I wish ye godspeed," Queenie replied with resignation.

"Thank you. I shall need it."

Dermott turned and mounted the steps to his room. He fell asleep some time later to the sound of crashing waves on the shore, a prayer still lingering on his lips for the man he must con-front in the morning. In so many ways he was the man who seemed to be at the very core of all the events which had swept him into their path. *Was he*, Dermott wondered, *destined to be the man who in the end will prove to be my fiercest adversary?* Only the Lord could know that. So with a prayer for the Lord's hand to prepare his way, he drifted away from the world of the waking.

31   The Laird's Match

Dermott studied the castle a long while before beginning the ascent up the wooded hill to where it sat—somber yet majestic in its strength. The mighty estate known as Stonewycke had stood thus for some three centuries. It had weathered the awesome currents of history—the rise and fall of kings and chiefs, the victories and defeats in gruesome battles between Scotch and English, the passing of great and lowly alike. Dermott's present business might seem insignificant in comparison to the magnificent and inexorable march of history. But such a mission could never be insignificant to one like Dermott. For no matter how great a building or the persons within its walls, nothing was to Dermott more significant than the life and soul of a single human being.

As he rode up the hill and through the great iron gates standing open as if welcoming an honest breath of air, Dermott's mind and heart had never been more firmly set upon an unwavering purpose. Earthly might did not stir him, for beside the grandeur of his God this edifice before him was the same as a broken-down hovel. He kept the image of that God before his mind's eye, for he knew from years of hard experience that his own strength would avail him little.

A white-clad maid, breathless from hurrying down from the second floor, answered the brisk clap of the door knocker.

"I wish to see Lord James Duncan," Dermott said crisply.

"An' who might I be sayin' is callin'?" asked the maid.

"I am Dermott Connell of Glasgow," he replied, and as he did so he took a small card from his pocket and handed it to the woman.

She studied the card for a moment, then said without much enthusiasm, "Weel, I'll give him the card, but I canna say he'll see ye. Keeps t' himsel' these days, he does."

"Kindly tell him I am here on prison business," Dermott said.

She sighed heavily at the prospect of having again to negotiate the stairway, motioned for him to enter, closed the door, then turned and left him.

Soon she reappeared at the top of the stairs and beckoned him to follow her. With mounting anticipation Dermott took the stairs two at a time, then followed as she led down the wide corridor past several rooms, till they at length paused before two thick double oak doors. The maid opened one and stepped aside for Dermott to enter. He saw immediately that he was in a finely appointed library. Shelves of countless volumes lined the walls, in several places two books deep. The furnishings were as rich as he had seen, and for a moment he failed to note the slight figure seated behind the huge carved desk.

As his eyes fell upon his host his attention was instantly diverted from its external trappings to the source of Stonewycke's power. Here was a man who had unleashed all the wrath of his person and position against his own family and still held them firmly in his grasp. And yet to the first-time observer he seemed withered and spent, a mere shadow, a poor misguided wretch rather than an evil tyrant.

But James Duncan had not lost all his fight yet.

"I have never heard of you," James began without benefit of any social preludes. "What business could you possibly have with me?" If he quailed inside it was only because he feared a creditor may finally have caught up with him. But he maintained his outward composure without flinching an eyelid.

"If your maid relayed my message correctly," Dermott said, trying to ignore the man's haughty manner, "I said I have come on prison business."

"I have nothing to do with prisons," replied James, somewhat confused.

"But I have," Dermott stated. "I am a lawyer."

"What is that to me?" James stated, pulling himself up straight in his chair.

As he spoke Dermott began to see that this man could indeed pose a threat.

"During the course of my duties," he went on, "I made the acquaintance of a poor unfortunate young man imprisoned some months ago in the tollbooth in Glasgow. Imprisoned, I might add, for a crime he did not commit."

James laughed lightly, almost delicately. "Excuse me, Mr. Connell," he said with something of a half-smile on his face, "but don't *all* those malcontents *claim* to be innocent?" He was so greatly relieved to find the course of the conversation moving in directions other than toward his own debts that James's first reaction was toward an attempt at humor.

"Be that as it may, Lord Duncan," Dermott continued, "this man has not even had the benefit of a trial. The right to a speedy hearing is guaranteed to all British citizens, is it not?"

"Sounds like that freedom drivel from the colonies in America!" replied James, gathering strength for the resumption of his anger once he saw that the barrister's attacks were apparently not going to be aimed at his weak financial underbelly.

"But true, nonetheless," Dermott persisted.

"And?" was the only acquiescence James made.

"I should like to see justice done by my client."

"So see to it!" The finality in James's voice indicated that the interview had ended as far as he was concerned.

But Dermott had only begun. "That is what has brought me to Stonewycke."

"I fail to see how either I or Stonewycke could be of any assistance to you," said James, his impatience growing. If this man had not been sent by Browhurst or the others, then he needn't bother himself with him.

"My hope would be that you would offer your assistance for the aid of your *son-in-law*."

Dermott said the words slowly and calmly, letting them fall over James with the subtle power of understatement.

James's poker-straight body sagged slightly, nearly escaping Dermott's notice. But he could not fail to note the growing agitation in the man's eyes.

"I have no son-in-law!" James replied with only a hint of the emotion churning inside.

"And you have no daughter either?" Dermott rejoined.

"How dare you bring my daughter into this?" cried James, rising from his seat. "Whatever ill-advised commitments she may have innocently been duped into, they have all been annulled."

"Legally?" queried Dermott.

"Yes, legally! Of course legally!"

"By the court?"

"I am the court around here, do you understand?" retorted James, unable to mask his anger.

"Then perhaps you might be able to direct me to where I might find a certain constable by the name of Duff?"

"Duff! What in the name of—what could he possibly—why you—" thundered James. "What could Duff possibly have to do with—why, I replaced Duff months ago! The incompetent fool!"

"Well, I intend to find him with or without your help," said Dermott.

James turned back toward his desk, swallowed hard, and walked to a nearby sideboard where a decanter and several crystal glasses sat on a silver tray. This man would not so easily be intimidated. As his initial anger receded, a different approach occurred to him. He grasped the decanter carefully to conceal his shaking hand, then poured a portion into two glasses.

Handing a glass to Dermott, he said, "I hope we may be able to discuss this—ah, this, er—this case like gentlemen."

Declining the drink, Dermott answered with great earnestness. "That is very much my wish."

James tossed back his head and did away with the contents of his glass in one gulp, set it down on the table, then took the one meant for Dermott and began sipping it more easily. "This is most excellent brandy," he said. "You really should avail yourself of at least one small glass," he added in his most gracious social tone.

"I like to keep a clear head about me," Dermott replied.

"Yes, yes, I see your point," said James, taking another swallow. "Now," he went on, as if the brandy had renewed his strength, "you have come upon someone claiming to be my erstwhile son-in-law. Very interesting, indeed. Especially in light of the fact that he was declared dead by the prison authorities some months ago. For no matter what you may think, Mr. Connell, I have been genuinely concerned for the boy and have kept close track of him."

"You and I both know that not to be true. You know as well as

I that the boy is alive." Dermott's eyes, like blue ice leveled on James in an unrelenting grip.

At that moment, perhaps for the first time, James noticed that the stranger's imposing figure towered over his own by some ten inches. In addition to his stature, the lawyer's muscular frame was nothing to be disregarded even by one who held lofty notions of his prowess in less physical realms. James had always prided himself in his uncanny ability to stare down an adversary, and he tried desperately to hold Dermott's eyes. But after several moments he dropped his eyes to the table, finished off his drink, and poured another. Carefully avoiding Dermott's piercing gaze, he spoke.

"I see your game now, Connell," he said. "And I see no reason why we cannot arrive at some sort of mutually beneficial agreement. You see, this so-called son-in-law of mine has not only proved an embarrassment to all concerned, but he has also shown himself to be of most unstable character. His sole purpose has been to get his hands on my daughter's inheritance. It was especially for my daughter's sake—"

"Have you no conscience?" Dermott exclaimed, at last losing his patience with the pointless verbal sparring. For as the other had spoken, a picture had risen in his mind of Ian's wretched agony in his dungeon cell. But almost the same moment he calmed, breathing a hasty prayer that he would—in the midst of heated emotions—be able to see this man as Christ saw him.

"Come now, Mr. Connell," James said in his most condescending manner, "I thought we were going to be gentlemen. And in that vein, I think, and indeed I hope, you can understand my position. I greatly regret the circumstances which have led me to do what I have done. But I can assure you it was all necessary. If that alone is not enough to insure your—ah—your discretion in the matter, then I'm sure more, shall we say *tangible* inducements can be made available."

"You cannot understand, can you, Lord Duncan?" If Dermott felt deep pity for this man, he did not let it escape in his tone. "A man is dying, if not in the physical sense as you would have everyone believe, then surely he is dying in his soul. He has lost all hope and believes that the one person whom he feels has ever loved him is lost to him forever—as perhaps she may be. Can you feel nothing in your heart for him? Or at least for his wife—your own daughter? Imagine how deserted and alone she must feel? How can you in good conscience allow this deception to continue!"

"There are some matters," James replied without hesitation, as if he had not heard a single word of Dermott's impassioned speech, "that are more important than the *feelings* of a murdering reprobate."

Dermott gasped. The words were to him as bitter in his face as a physical blow. He was not innocent of men with such cold and callous motives. But his nature could never confront such evil intent without it stirring a passion toward righteousness within him. If he had prayed to view this man with the mind of his Lord, even Christ would not tolerate the falsehood of the moneychangers in the temple. If the lawyer's sharp response sprang from this passion, none could blame him—none except perhaps Dermott himself.

"There is no reprobate," he seethed, "except the one who refuses to turn from his selfish ways! And you, James Duncan, are dangerously close to occupying that position! For if you had a heart within you, it would this very minute cry out against the agony of one so helpless, if not innocent!"

"How dare you!" James shrieked in a rage. "You have no right—"

"Do not speak to me of rights!" Dermott cried. "For if Ian Duncan dies—as surely he must, in that miserable hole to which you have condemned him—his blood will be upon *your* head. As surely as if you had cut him down with a sword!"

"Then I'll live with it! Why you godless—"

"If you can live with such a thing, then you truly are a lost man," Dermott replied, cooling noticeably, then sighing with heavy anguish. He turned on his heel and started toward the door. If James had shown but the tiniest flicker of repentance, Dermott's heart remained so hopeful that he would have turned back immediately and made every effort to minister to the man. But the sounds which reached his retreating ear were far indeed from the sounds of a repentant heart.

"How dare you turn your back on me? You—you—By Jove, I'll see you—"

"I'm sorry, Lord Duncan," Dermott said, turning as he reached the door. "I'm sorry it has come to this. But I must do as my conscience—and my God—lead me. I can do no other."

James's only further response was a violent stream of imprecations at Dermott's back as the door closed behind him, ending with one final and pitiful attempt to regain the upper hand. "Do not set foot in my house again, Connell!" he yelled. "Do not even let me hear of you setting foot on my land, or I'll have *you* arrested and see you hanged!"

James Duncan shook with his own kind of passion—a passion far different than what drove Dermott Connell into the thick of battle. After so many years spent striving for the wrong things, being right was the only thing that mattered to the laird of Stonewycke. For if he once admitted to being wrong about anything, his life itself would instantly begin to erode from beneath him. How could he know—after all these years looking in the wrong direction for the happiness he had never found—that the only way out of the dungeon which so tightly imprisoned him, the dungeon of his *self*, was death to that very self which had sustained him in its evil ways all his life? How could a man in his advanced state of spiritual decay summon the courage to lay the axe to the old foundation in order to begin forming a new? To take even the first small step forward out of his bondage, the admission of one insignificant wrong, would have been of incalculable difficulty to one such as he. Such is the point where repentance must begin, but for a man like James Duncan, such an admission would have been to swallow a vial of pure gall.

The moment the lawyer was out of the room, James turned toward the silver tray and crystal decanter. The liquid sloshed into the glass as he filled it to the rim. Even now, completely alone, he made a vain attempt to steady his hand before grasping the glass with eagerness. The ruse of his life was as much a show for himself as it was for outsiders.

Slowly, purposefully he brought the glass to his lips. Then, as if his steady patience had worn thin, he tossed it back and emptied it with two greedy swallows.

"The nerve!" he spat, slamming the empty glass onto the table.

It splintered beneath his hand. Quickly he drew back, but the shattered glass had done its work. Blood dripped from several gashes in his palm.

"Curse him!" James cried.

Not even pausing to bind up the wounds, James stormed from the room. He sought the passages leading to the back of the house so as to avoid any chance of meeting the lawyer or any of the servants, but his menacing pace did not slacken until he reached the stables. There he ordered Digory to saddle the chestnut mare.

"But, my lord . . ." protested Digory, knowing the prowess of the chestnut, especially since she had not held a rider since her last master had fallen into such misfortune. James shoved the groom aside and began to saddle the horse himself.

Seeing that his master was not to be dissuaded, Digory stepped back, while James mumbled that "the old fool of a groom would take too long about it anyway!"

He mounted Maukin with a vengeance, as if riding the horse which had been so dear to the man whom James had wronged was the final assertion of his lordship. He would keep the man in prison! He would destroy this lawyer Connell! And he would prove his superiority by mastering the murderer's own horse! He was lord! No one else. And more than anything, that made whatever he chose to do right.

"You'll see who's right!" he cried as he lashed the mare's flank and lurched forward into a frenzied gallop. *Right . . . right . . .* the words echoed in his mind as he tore from the stables.

The iron gate was but a blur as he passed it. Somewhere in his confused mind must have been the thought of getting the constable in order to follow through on his threat to have Connell arrested. For James was a calculating man, even in the midst of his present frenzy. Yet his one-time cool character was presently on the verge of cracking.

He turned sharply to the left a furlong past the gate, away from the road into Port Strathy. At breakneck speed and for no apparent reason he tore down the steep path, normally a footpath leading into a rocky gorge and thence to the valley.

It was here, while negotiating the gorge, that Maukin stumbled. A rider of James's caliber would have had little difficulty maintaining his seat under normal circumstances. But Maukin hit the trail at a full gallop, and besides being in a white wrath, James had had far too much brandy already that day. Both horse and rider fell hard onto the stony ground. Maukin pulled herself up and shook her head with a horsey whinny, fortunate indeed to still have four unbroken legs beneath her.

The rider had not been so fortunate. James lay still, his face pressed against the dirt and stone of the path. Digory found him some time later. As the groom hastened down to where he lay, James had just begun to come to himself. He groaned in agony, rudely rebuffed the groom's efforts at assistance, and attempted to pull himself up, only to fall helpless back onto the ground with a dull moan.

In the end, Digory had to hobble back to the house for help. And thus the once proud James Duncan, lord of Stonewycke, was borne back to the castle in the arms of his servants, with his old groom constantly by his side.

32   Maggie and Stoddard

As the small wagon train had left the rugged hills, many had been the prayers that their fortunes would improve. Tommy Joe had some color back in his face, and the day's rest had worked magnificently upon Maggie. Though Gil Stoddard would never have admitted it, the stop had proved a boon for the entire train. However, the cheerful spirits about the camp did not sense the menacing thunderclouds of fate hanging just over the horizon toward which they were headed.

Truly, God's providence shields the future from the eyes of His children. As Ellie had prayed for her son and had assumed he was on the mend, she had no way of knowing how serious the injury had really been. No one, not even Dr. Carpenter, had known that.

But since the day of the accident, infection had been masked by more outward symptoms, and by now it was surging through the boy's weakening frame. Even as Ellie prayed, she had no way of knowing that before they had traveled another day, he would be dead.

That night they camped again within sight of the Platte. It was like returning to an old friend, for they had followed the river on and off for weeks. But this night it held no comfort for the weary train. Its only contribution was the soil from its bank for their first grave.

If grief over the loss of their son were not enough, Drew and Ellie had to face the harsh reality of their situation, which prevented even a crude outward release of their pain. Drew attempted to fashion a cross for his son's grave. He had not wept since the boy's death, but as he worked, his face was drawn and taut, his lips pressed firmly together in mute anguish.

"What're you doin'?" asked Stoddard.

"I'm makin' a marker fer my boy's grave," Drew answered simply, continuing on without looking up.

"Listen, Mackinaw," Stoddard replied, making a genuine attempt at sincerity, "this here is Sioux country an' we all know they're on the warpath. If you want your kid to rest in peace, you'll toss that thing in the river."

Drew glanced up, puzzled. "My wife wants a proper cross on his grave," he answered listlessly.

"I'm just givin' you advice," Stoddard said. "Take it or leave it. But I'll say this much—them Sioux is just as liable to destroy the grave as leave it alone if they see a marker. I don't think your wife'd be wantin' that, neither."

Drew stared blankly at the wagon master, then heaved his frame slowly up to his feet and lumbered to the river. He stood for a moment on the bank, perhaps in indecision, weighing Stoddard's words, perhaps offering a silent prayer of awkward grief and frustration. Then with one mighty motion he flung the wood far into the gray depths of the surging water. There was no one to see, but then and then only did the tears glisten on the rims of his eyes. To Drew this was one further reminder of the tragedy he had called his family to. He had brought hardship and death upon them, and now his wife was robbed even of the shallow comfort of a grave for her child. By the time he returned to his companions and the wagons were ready to move forward, Drew Mackinaw's tears were dry and he was ready to take command of the task that remained ahead.

But perhaps there was, after all, some latent sensitivity deep within Gil Stoddard's heart, for after the wagons were moving smoothly along, he fell back and brought his horse alongside the Mackinaw wagon. Normally a taciturn man, he managed to keep up a steady stream of conversation with Drew. Even Maggie, listening from inside the wagon, could tell he was purposely trying to distract the grieving parents with the only sympathy of which he was capable.

"Ain't much to look at on the surface," Stoddard was saying, "but that river can be a real—" He paused with a glance toward Ellie. "Well, it can be a killer. We're lucky there's a bridge now, but I crossed three times by ferry. I was there back in the summer of '52 when fourteen Mormon men from one train were swept away in one shot! That water's cold and ugly this time of year."

"Why do we have to cross the river, Mr. Stoddard?" Ellie asked.

"For one thing, the grazin's better on the north side for the animals. But you'll soon see even that ain't much to speak of."

"How so?" asked Drew. Were there *more* hardships in store for them, he wondered?

"Well," he replied, noting the concern in Drew's voice, "it's best to take one day at a time. And now we got at least one day of smooth traveling ahead."

It was well the trail master said no more of what lay ahead. By this time tomorrow they would embark across fifty miles of the worst terrain yet—high bluffs, broken and barren, combined with a semi-desert of endless scorched brush. But this was not all. Heat and dust would choke the travelers and their animals. Alkali filled the dust and stung the eyes and throats. Any water to be found along the way was a sheer deathtrap to the unwary or unprepared. Stoddard made certain that all the water receptacles were filled from the Platte before beginning the trek across the arid wasteland. But even he could do little to prepare against the hot, thirsty stock trying to drink the poisonous water. It was a constant battle, and littered along the trail were innumerable carcasses of animals whose masters had lost that battle in times past.

Fifty miles. Stoddard was determined to make it in two days—nothing less than a forced march. This time the travelers gave little resistance to the hard-bitten but experienced trail master. Once the stinging, stifling air began to assail them, they quite agreed it was necessary to get past the desert as rapidly as possible.

Hurrying over one of the slate-gray bluffs, the Kramer wagon lost one of its front wheels. For an awful moment the wagon teetered precariously and would surely have slipped to disaster over the edge had it not been caught by the jagged teeth of the rocks beneath it.

The nearby wagons stopped immediately and Stoddard rode up in a cloud of dust.

"Get a rope!" he yelled, dismounting and running forward. "Kramer," he instructed Pete, now standing on the ground after getting his family out of the wagon, "you get back up in the wagon and take the reins. We'll need a few more men. Williams, run back down the trail and get as many as you can."

By the time reinforcements had arrived, Stoddard had a rope attached to the undamaged side of the wagon with a crew of four men pulling. He and another were bracing the other side where the wheel was missing, while Kramer was furiously *geeing* and *hawing* his weary oxen.

Steadily the wagon inched toward level ground. Just then Stoddard's companion lost his footing on a piece of loose rock, fell, and slipped several feet down the edge. At that same moment, while Stoddard's attention was distracted by the falling man, the wagon suddenly lurched forward throwing the unprepared trail boss under the wagon. The shouts of the onlookers warned Kramer of the trouble and the wagon ground to a halt, but not before Stoddard's arm was caught under the rear wheel.

The lurch had brought the wagon up onto level ground. But there was no way it could now back up to free Stoddard's arm without repeating the earlier mishap. Now the men had to lend their strength to lift the cumbersome wagon straight up while one dragged their leader out from under it.

Shouting all manner of oaths and curses, Stoddard lay on the ground while several of the men milled around him, the others assessing the damage to Pete's wagon. In Stoddard's defense, most of his curses were aimed at himself and the wagons and any other inanimate objects within sight. When Dr. Carpenter arrived at the scene, the curses began wandering in his direction also, but he took no heed of them.

"That's my arm, Doctor!" he yelled. "You let *me* move it! I tell you, I can move it!" But one attempt forced him back with a groan and a curse. "This is going to set us back all day. Kramer, you get that wheel fixed! We still got four or five hours of daylight left." Then turning to the doctor, he said, "I want you to know, Doc, I practice what I preach. We ain't stayin' no longer on my account than it takes to repair that wheel."

Dr. Carpenter made no comment, but signalled three of the men who weren't immediately occupied to help carry Stoddard clear of the wagon and out of the others' way.

"It's my arm!" Stoddard grumbled. "Not my legs! I can walk!" He tried to pull himself to his feet, but immediately his vision blurred as objects began to spin before him. Catching himself from falling by grabbing for Samuel's arm, he let loose another string of frustrated oaths.

Supporting him between himself and Drew Mackinaw, Samuel at length managed to transport the surly wagon master to his own wagon—the closest thing on the train to a hospital wagon—where he could begin setting the crushed arm.

"I'm sorry," Samuel said as he began his work, "there's no more whiskey."

"Just my luck! The one time I could have a drink for all to see. But I been through worse—without whiskey," he added.

Before long Stoddard succumbed to the pain. His cuts were not severe, yet the blood lost contributed to his weakened state. He awoke several hours later to the eerie glow of a lantern illuminating what must certainly have been an angel. Even in his groggy condition he knew it was not the doctor standing over him. For an instant of disorientation his blurred mind was sorely perplexed. Then almost immediately his vision began to clear and he realized the ministering angel was none other than Mrs. Duncan—a fact perplexing enough in itself.

"Why ain't we movin'?" he asked with a hoarse attempt at a shout. "Never mind," he added almost immediately as if he had just realized the fact, "it's night. We couldn't get far, anyway."

He lay still for a moment as if deep in thought, then continued, as if Maggie had answered him, "Yeah, but *what* night? How long have we been sittin' here? If that dang fool doctor—"

"Mr. Stoddard," Maggie interposed. Though she had intended to greet him softly and gently when he awoke, she could not now keep a scolding tone from her voice. "That doctor saved your arm—and probably your life. I'll thank you to speak more respectfully about him in the future."

Suddenly Stoddard shot a glance at his injured arm. "I half-expected it to be gone," he said in a moderated tone—relief mingled with some apparent esteem for what the doctor had done.

"Well, it's not," replied Maggie, and her tone also softened. "Dr. Carpenter worked very hard to make sure it would heal properly."

"What're you doin' here?"

"The doctor had to tend Mrs. Keys. She burned her hand on the cookfire tonight. He asked me to watch over you. Are you thirsty?"

Stoddard licked his dry, dust-caked lips. "Yeah, as a matter of fact."

Maggie brought him a cup of water and placed one hand under his neck, lifting his head to help him drink. "And to answer your previous question, this is the same day as your accident—or rather, night. Mr. Kramer's wheel is repaired and we should be able to move on in the morning. We are all no less anxious than you to get through this wretched place. Though I doubt we've anything better to look forward to anywhere else."

Maggie's final words were spoken almost before she realized it, and then only because they had been an ever-present thought in her mind.

"No one ever said it was goin' to be a picnic out here," Stoddard said. "It takes some doin'—yeah, and some hardships sometimes—to be able to start a new life in a new country. And that's what this is all about, isn't it? But when we get through this stretch, we got the Sweetwater and then the Pass. And as places go, they ain't half so bad. There ain't hardly a sight to match the Rockies! Nothin' like 'em in Scotland, I don't imagine."

He paused as if his mind were trailing back over the four other times he had crossed the Continental Divide. In a moment he brought his attention back to the new young mother sitting at his side, and focused an intent gaze upon her. "But that weren't what you meant, was it?" he asked after a moment of silent reflection.

"What do you mean?" Maggie replied, taken somewhat aback by the question, especially coming from one such as Gil Stoddard.

"Well, it sounded like maybe you figured that with your husband dead and all, you sort of didn't care anymore. 'Course, maybe it's none of my business."

"I don't mean to be rude, Mr. Stoddard"—Maggie was not quite sure how to take this unusual display of interest on the part of the rough westerner, and she was in no mood to discuss Ian with anyone—"but you're right: it isn't any of your business."

"Oh, I know you ain't the rude type," he said airily, apparently ignoring her previous words. "You won't offend me by anything you say. But it seems to me that with a kid and all that you'd have a mighty lot to be lookin' forward to." Then his voice fell into a pensive tone. "I used to have a kid—two of 'em, in fact. Can you picture that? Me, a father. I was never much cut out for it, though."

"What happened to them?" asked Maggie tentatively. She hesitated to pry into another's life, especially as she was unwilling to discuss the inner turmoils of her own. Yet simple curiosity drove her on.

"Things . . ." he began evasively, yet thoughtfully, "things is different out here. It's a hard life. People get torn apart. Things happen, you know. Sometimes you have to leave your past behind. That's what it takes to build a new country like this."

He paused, clearly not having intended to say so much. "Yeah . . . things happen," he resumed at length. "But you got your kid. And it seems to me you got everything to look forward to, a reason for living, for starting over."

Perhaps Maggie would have agreed with Gil Stoddard's coarse

wisdom. But just at that moment Dr. Carpenter poked his head into the wagon and Maggie's mind was diverted for a time.

Later that night, as she lay in her own bed nursing little Eleanor to sleep, her thoughts once again were drawn to the trail master's words.

Had she indeed given up on life, without even realizing it?

She gazed down at the child, a constant wonder to her. The tiny round face was so smooth and soft. And those sweet eyes with their long pale lashes, closed now as she sucked contentedly with her little hand grasping Maggie's nightgown. Here was a part of her own self . . . a part of Ian . . . cradled now in her arms. And as she stared at the newborn child a well of joy surged within her. Was this baby indeed reason enough to go on, to face the future in a rugged new land? Even without Ian?

Yes, she thought, *I did give up when I had learned of Ian's death.* And yet she was moving forward. Living again. Now here was little Eleanor in her arms as a sign that all does not end with death. Life goes on, Ian still lived, even if only through their daughter. Did she not owe it to him, to the child, and even to herself, to go on, to make something of her life, to maybe give Eleanor the chance to find love, even if she and Ian had lost it? Could not the love she and Ian had shared be passed on to the next generation . . . and then the next? Was their love meaningless because they had shared it so briefly? Or could she not still—even though Ian was dead—add to its meaning by passing it along to their descendants to come—to Duncans and Ramseys yet unborn?

How can I feel this joy in my heart over this tiny child, she thought, *in the midst of my grief and this wilderness?* And yet the moment Eleanor had been born, something had begun to change. Maggie hardly knew what the change was, but the bitterness which had so filled her heart had begun to subside that day. Without Maggie's even realizing it, the words of a tough, half-disoriented, thick-skinned trail boss had somehow triggered a yearning after a deeper inward life, a yearning to start new again.

But with a kid and all, it seems to me you'd have a mighty lot to be lookin' foward to.

She could not erase Gil Stoddard's words from her memory.

All at once Maggie recalled her thoughts immediately after the child's birth: *Eleanor was a gift from God.*

Was this precious little gift, this bundle of life, meant not merely to give her joy—for that she had already begun to do—but to awaken the numbness which had consumed Maggie, to give her a reason to go on? Before she reached any conclusions, Maggie had drifted to sleep—the peaceful slumber of one who is beginning to feel the approach of dawning freedom from the bitter chains of the past.

When she awoke in the morning the joy remained, and so did the questions. A vision of Atlanta rose in her mind, and with it came tears at the memory. Maggie loved her mother. Yet she knew, too, that her mother had allowed herself to shut off her deepest feelings—especially those toward her children—and had in the end become a hard woman, unable either to give or receive the delights of love which should have been able to pass between her and her daughter. What had caused this, in addition to the codes of her upbringing, Maggie could not guess. But the marchioness of Stonewycke had kept her emotions steadfastly hidden to the very end, and the love which she and Maggie harbored each for the other had never found vent for its expression.

Tears rose to Maggie's eyes. *Yes,* she thought, *I love Mother dearly, but I do not want to be like her.* She did not want to become a hard woman, growing old with the bitterness she knew she had every earthly right to cling to. No, she wanted something different for herself. And for her daughter!

Maggie rose, laid the sleeping baby down in the bed, and left the wagon. The bustle of morning had begun. She strolled about, unconsciously seeking the closer approach to some kindred soul to whom she might draw near in order to give expression to the vague feelings rising within her. After a short walk she returned and approached the wagon. All was silent even though Ellie and Drew were making preparations for breakfast. The thought of opening herself to Ellie about her own thoughts in the midst of her friend's grief was inconceivable. Therefore after lending what assistance she could, Maggie found herself—almost without realizing it—wandering toward Samuel Carpenter's wagon.

The bustle of activity about the train grew steadily; parting preparations multiplied the closer the moment came. Samuel had just completed checking the harnesses on his brace of oxen and looked up, smiling at Maggie's approach.

"Good morning, Mrs. Duncan," he said cheerfully. "You look well today. I'm glad to see it."

"Thank you, Dr. Carpenter."

"And how's little Eleanor?"

"We had a restful night. She's sleeping now."

"A restful night? After I had to compel you into service so late last night here in my makeshift hospital!"

Maggie laughed. "And how is our patient this morning?"

Samuel answered with a knowing look of exasperation, then said, "I can't remember when I've had such an ornery man under my care!"

"Now that the arm is splinted," said Maggie, "will he have to stay in bed all day?"

"It would be best if he kept it immobile for a week. But I doubt that's possible. In Stoddard's case, if I let him up, he'll be out driving the cattle and loading wagonbeds and carrying on within an hour. My only hope is to keep him under my thumb at least for the rest of today." He sighed, "And Lord help me!"

Maggie laughed again. "He is an unusual man, isn't he?" she said. "Last night while you were gone, he spoke rather freely to me. There's more to him than I would have thought."

"I've seen that, too. I think he's suffered a great deal in his life. People who carry about a gruff exterior like that usually have. They're only hiding deeper hurts they don't want to expose."

"Why do people suffer?" Maggie asked reflectively.

"Everyone suffers," replied Samuel. "That's part of life. The Bible says that man is born to trouble."

"But why? Why does it have to be that way? Why does life have to be cruel? Why does man have to be born to trouble?"

"Because we have turned from God's ways. Apart from Him, there can't be anything but grief."

"But couldn't God erase the pain and trouble and grief of life?"

"That's not His way," replied Samuel. "Besides, the troubles of this life aren't really that significant to God, I don't think."

"That doesn't make them any easier to bear," said Maggie.

"Just think of what poor Drew and Ellie are going through right now."

"I know," said the doctor. "And my heart grieves for them. But the Lord has Tommy Joe in His hands. And Drew and Ellie's loss will pass and they will go on from this time of mourning."

"But then, what's the purpose of it all? How can you say the troubles we face don't matter that much to God if He's supposed to love us so?"

"It's not that God doesn't care; He's interested in what we do with our difficulties. Time heals the pain of our hurts and eases the anguish. But only the Lord can heal the deepest wounds. He wants us to take our hurts and griefs and bitter memories to Him so He can wash them from our hearts. Trouble comes to all of us; God wants us to give them to Him. That's how He is able to fashion us into the kind of receptacles which can then contain the love He has to offer us."

Maggie was silent a moment. "Then why do you do what you do, Dr. Carpenter," she asked at length, "if God is the only healer?"

"Because I care about people's hurts and pains. And if by tending their surface wounds—their cuts and bruises and infections and broken arms—I am sometimes able to pray for them and point them toward the Healer of their deeper hurts, then I will be a happy man. I offer what healing I can on the physical plane, and as I do I always pray that God will take care of the inner man or woman. Because that's where true life is lived. The troubles of this life are only the means God uses to get us to face the real weighty issues of pride, unforgiveness, and selfishness. Once we have faced those, we can be reborn into the life of joy He wants for each of us. But no man—or woman—can truly face the need to forgive without first experiencing bitterness and hurt. There is no other way."

Maggie looked down at the ground and did not reply. The doctor's words had suddenly probed dangerously close to home in her own heart. They had been talking so earnestly that they had all but forgotten the clamor of activity in the background. Gil Stoddard jarred them back into the present realities.

"Hey, why ain't we movin'?" he yelled.

Maggie turned toward the voice to find the irascible trail master standing outside the wagon with a scowl on his face, clad only in his long underwear, his arm hanging limply at his side, its sling dangling around his neck.

"Stoddard!" Samuel exclaimed. "What do you think you're doing?"

But before Stoddard could answer, Evan McCollough raced up to the doctor's wagon.

"Doc," he said, gasping in the stifling dusty air, "my missus is taken poorly. Do you think you could come and have a look at her?"

"Of course," the doctor replied. "Is it an emergency?"

"I s'pose it can wait a bit."

"I should see to getting Mr. Stoddard's arm tended to first. What are her symptoms?"

"Just kind of weak, you know, and a bellyache."

Samuel had learned that all internal complaints were referred to as bellyaches. From Evan's description it could be anything from indigestion to premature labor.

"I'll be there in a moment, McCollough," he said. "It could be the alkali in the air."

"Okay, Doc," he sighed wearily. "But I don't know what I'm gonna do. I got to get the wagon hitched an' the young'uns are runnin' all about ..."

"Mrs. Duncan?" Samuel turned to Maggie. "Could you possibly lend a hand?"

"Yes, of course," Maggie answered without hesitation. "You go on back, Evan. I'll be right there. I just have to make sure Eleanor is still asleep."

Within a few minutes Maggie was seated in the McCollough wagon with the three McCollough children next to her as she read them a story. Rebbekah McCollough looked dreadful, lying motionless on her bed. Maggie mused that they had spent nearly four months traveling together, and yet she still barely knew the young woman who was now so frail and sallow in appearance. Yet she had to admit to herself that the fault had been entirely her own. She had been so withdrawn and unapproachable. But she determined that would change.

She had little time to dwell on such thoughts, however, for the children were agitated, and Rebbekah's "bellyache" was in reality stomach cramps so violent that when the woman did move she was assailed by severe nausea.

Maggie did whatever she could, which amounted to keeping an eye on the children, cleaning up after Rebbekah, and bringing her water which she demanded frequently. Still the doctor did not come.

At length the wagon jolted forward. It was not like Dr. Carpenter to neglect a patient, although there could be no telling what complications Gil Stoddard had thrown his way.

Maggie had no way of knowing that while Samuel was finishing with the trail master, two more freak mishaps had occurred. In the rush to get underway, one man had been pinned against his wagon by a nervous ox and had suffered a cracked rib. Another received a nasty gash in his arm while securing a loose wheel. These two men had barely been tended to when the first of the wagons began to move. And in the flurry Samuel, who indeed was not a man to forget a patient, did forget Mrs. McCollough and the nurse he had sent to help.

33 New Crisis

The train planned to stop at a spring Stoddard knew of, the one supposedly good spring in the fifty mile stretch of desert. The water there, however, turned out to be as foul as the rest and two more cows were lost from drinking it. After conferring for a few minutes, the men decided to move on. Willow Springs was still a day and a half distant, the next water source of which they could be certain. Their water reserves were getting low; the sooner they got to the springs, the better.

It was not till the wagons had stopped that Samuel remembered his oversight. He hurried to the McCollough wagon, calling out a greeting, and climbing up and inside before even receiving an answer. The experiences of his profession notwithstanding, the putrid odor that met him nearly sickened him.

"Dear Lord! Mrs. McCollough, I'm so sorry it's taken me so long. And Mrs. Duncan—can you forgive me?"

"Doctor," Maggie said, "she's so sick."

"And your own child?"

"I'm sure Ellie is caring for her, though it's long past her feeding time and I ought to go to her soon. I'm afraid I haven't been able to do much for Rebbekah."

"You've done more than you know," Samuel replied. Then he turned his full attention to his patient. It was immediately obvious that she did not have long to live. Her skin tone evidenced dehydration, though Maggie assured him she had been drinking water despite the fact that it only seemed to make her all the more ill. He listened to Maggie's description of Rebbekah's other symptoms with an apprehension which grew into horror. The past several days had been so tragic it seemed impossible they could cope with another crisis so soon. Yet the doctor feared this could be the beginning of something far worse.

He laid down Rebbekah's hand, whose bluish nails finalized his awful diagnosis. He sighed heavily, but it seemed more a shudder than a sigh. Only one word could he utter: "Cholera."

He needed to say no more. Maggie fell back against several crates in the crowded wagon, the color drained from her face. But Samuel Carpenter was a medical man; his acute instincts were only temporarily daunted, but not overpowered by his complete dismay. Before another moment passed he sprang into action.

He did not know how to cure cholera, nor even what caused it. No one did. But he did know that it could spread like a prairie fire, and he was determined that should not happen. If it did, the entire wagon train would be wiped out and the hopes and dreams of its members along with it.

"Mrs. Duncan," he said, "go to my wagon and draw some water and wash very carefully. Then go get your Eleanor and return to my wagon immediately. You must stay there, do you understand?"

In a daze Maggie obeyed.

The moment Maggie had left, Samuel called Evan and calmly explained the situation facing them. "I will inform the rest of the train, but you and your family must keep to your wagon." Samuel did not relish the task of carrying such tidings to the others, for he had more than once seen superstition and panic overcome good sense and prudence. And if there was one thing they didn't need out in this wilderness, it was to have panic split the train apart.

Making sure Rebbekah was comfortable, Samuel left the wagon. He found Stoddard in the process of mounting his horse. The doctor suppressed a rebuke at the man's flagrant neglect of his orders, but there were suddenly much more urgent matters on his mind. *It's just as well, anyway,* he thought, *now that Margaret and Eleanor will have to stay in the wagon.* When he imparted the news to the trail master, even Stoddard blanched.

"Good God!" he swore. "That's all we need!"

"Only our good God will protect us through this," Samuel responded.

"Well . . . are you going to tell the rest of them, or am I?" Stoddard asked, choosing to ignore the doctor's statement. Without waiting for an answer, Stoddard rode off to round up the men for another conference.

Samuel presented the information medically, logically. For the moment at least he pushed from his mind the fact that the woman would soon die an awful death. He tried to convince the others that if they worked together they could isolate the dread disease to the McCollough wagon. But even if it proved too late for that, there was still no reason to panic.

"They're all going to die anyway!" someone cried. "It's best to save as many as we can right now."

"That may not help," Samuel tried to reason. "We can't even think of splitting up the train, not in this wilderness."

"That's better than all of us dying!"

"We've got our own families to think about!"

"Folks . . . please!" implored the doctor, but by now the general confusion had spread to the wives, who had gotten wind of the trouble and were approaching one by one.

"Listen to the doc!" commanded Stoddard.

"We've got to stay calm," urged Samuel. "Now, how many of you have been in close contact with Rebbekah McCollough these past few days?"

Rebbekah was a quiet, retiring woman and kept mostly to herself; no hands went up. Samuel could not help breathing a sigh of relief, but this did nothing to bolster his argument. Inside he was sure the train would reject his pleas and would, in the end, move on. He recoiled at the thought and would fight against it. But perhaps the others had that right. Yet even if the McColloughs did manage to survive the plague, how could they possibly hope to survive long in the middle of hostile Indian territory? And what of Margaret's exposure already, and his own? Only a miracle would keep the cholera from spreading.

It was an unexpected voice that assured the decision. "Listen, folks, I don't want to get too close . . ." It was Evan McCollough, standing some distance from the group. "But I ain't expecting you to make such a hard choice. We been through a lot together, helpin' one another out of one scrape or another, and, well . . . now it's my turn. My wife just died, and now my daughter's ailin', and I don't know which one of us might be next. You gotta go on ahead. Maybe when this thing's run its course, what's left of us will catch up. But that's the way it's got to be."

He finished his speech, overcome by the tears which were rising in his eyes, turned sharply away, and walked back toward his wagon, saying not another word and clearly expecting no argument from his companions.

A somber silence settled over the group, only to be broken by another voice that spoke as if it felt no pain at the man's terrible sacrifice. "Weren't that Duncan woman with the McColloughs all day?"

"Yeah, Doc," said another. "Ain't it possible she got it too?"

"It's possible we *all* could catch it!" shouted Samuel in frustration.

"Well, maybe she ought to stay with them."

"This is madness!" Samuel cried, rubbing his hands across his face as if when he removed them everything before him might have changed.

"Dinna worry, Doc," came Drew Mackinaw's slow foreign drawl. "We come wi' Evan an' Rebbekah all the way from New York—" As he spoke there was a certain mournful ache in his voice. "We've all had our hardships. We knew when we set out t' find a new life that it wouldn't be none too easy. That's the chance

215

we took. Now we both have lost someone dear t' us an' I don't intend t' leave my friend here alone, even if it means my dyin' by his side. We Mackinaws ain't leavin' them. I'm na sayin' this t' make ye others feel obliged t' stay but what e'er ye do, I ken my own duty, an' we're stayin'.''

Sorry as they were to lose a good man like Drew, very little resistance was offered. Bound as they had been together, suddenly life and death confronted them. Though such decisions were loathesome, they had to be made for the greater good of all, each tried to convince himself. As if in unspoken agreement, the party of travelers began to silently disband and husbands and wives slowly made their way back to their families. Before ten more minutes had passed, the line of wagons was again moving on under the scorching prairie sun. Only Stoddard and Frank and Leila Wooten remained with Drew and Samuel Carpenter.

"I thought you would move on with the others, Stoddard," said Frank.

"Thought I'd be worryin' about savin' my own skin, is that it?"

"I just thought that with seven wagons goin' on ahead, and only four stayin' here, you'd figure the others would be most in need of a guide."

"Not to mention getting the rest of your money, Mr. Stoddard," put in Ellie. "If you stay with us, we may all be dead before two weeks are out."

"It's become more than for the money by now," said Stoddard slowly. "Before I agreed to sign on, I said this'd be my last train. I said to myself I was going to make this one count for something—make myself count. Well, now I've decided this is where I do something that matters. So I've got to stay with the people who might need me the most, no matter how many of you there are."

"Weel, Mr. Stoddard," said Drew with a smile, approaching the trail boss with outstretched hand, "we're proud t' hae ye with us. An' we thank ye!"

When Maggie heard what had taken place, she could hardly speak. Since she had come into the Mackinaws' lives, a complete stranger, they had never ceased from the first moment to give to her. What she would have done without them she hardly knew. But now she knew she could ask no more of them.

Climbing down from the doctor's wagon, little Eleanor in her arms, she spoke out. "No," she said with a hard edge of determination in her voice. "I can't allow you to jeopardize your families like this. Not for me."

"Maggie, you've got little choice if we decide to stay," said Ellie, speaking more firmly than anyone had heard her since her son's death. "And we're not just doing it for you alone, although I'm sure we all would. But we must stand by Evan now too. He needs us more than ever."

"Drew," Maggie said, turning her argument toward him. "If it were just you and Ellie, maybe you'd have the freedom to do such a thing. But you have your children to think of. And, Dr. Carpenter," she now looked in the doctor's direction, "isn't it true that they could well escape it because their contact has been limited?"

The doctor nodded reluctantly.

"But I have been close to Rebbekah. I'll probably come down with it, won't I?" Maggie pressed.

Samuel swallowed hard. He could not forget that it was he who had in ignorance sent Maggie to the McColloughs' wagon in the first place. "No one can be certain . . ." he offered at length.

"Please!" Maggie pleaded. "Go on with the others. You have to protect your children. Let me stay and be of what help I can to Evan. But there need be no one else. There is no more danger for me. Whatever is going to happen to me is already determined. But *you*—Drew, Ellie, Frank, Leila—you must go on!"

Maggie turned and in the silence that had fallen upon her friends, she climbed back into the wagon. She feared that if she remained a moment longer she would allow them to stay, even beg them to stay. It was some moments before she heard another sound, and then it was Ellie's broken, sobbing voice.

"At least let us say a proper good-bye!" she cried.

"We will see each other soon," Maggie replied. "It won't be long. If we ever have to say a proper good-bye, let it be later. For now we will just have a brief parting."

"No . . . not long," Ellie managed to say. "Oh, Maggie . . . I love you! God be with you!"

Maggie could not reply. Her voice was strangled with tears. Worst of all, she could not even give her friend one last hug. She simply held her hand up and watched them slowly turn toward their wagons. They realized, painful as it was, that Maggie had spoken truthfully. They did have to consider their children, even more than their friends.

As the two wagons finally rumbled down the road, Maggie saw quiet little Bess waving vigorously from the back of the wagon. Maggie tried to smile, then waved back so the child could see. She was glad Bess could not see her tears. For she wept in the conviction that it would be the last time she would ever see the sweet little girl who had been her dear companion through the most difficult months Maggie had ever faced in her life.

As Maggie turned her head away and swept her sleeve across her eyes to dry the freely flowing tears, her attention was quickly arrested by the two remaining figures standing beside the wagon. Dr. Carpenter and Gil Stoddard remained side by side, an unlikely match in any but the most tragic of circumstances.

"You had better not let them get too far ahead of you," Samuel said.

"And what about you, Doc?" Stoddard asked.

"I'll be staying," Samuel answered. "A doctor will be needed here, hopefully not with the others."

"That's fine," Stoddard stated. "I was plannin' to stay, too. You'll need another gun."

Both Maggie and Samuel stared in unmasked surprise.

"What're you gawkin' for?" Stoddard snapped. "What'd you take me for, a dirty sidewinder that'd leave you to the vultures?"

"We never doubted your intentions," said Samuel, clearly touched. "But the train still needs you."

"They'll manage," he replied, glancing toward the cloud of dust that was by this time all that remained of the retreating Mackinaw Party. "It's like this, Doc. I owe you. And you too, Mrs. Duncan. After the way I treated you, you still sat by me when I hurt my arm. And you, Doc, you kept me in your wagon. Not many folks through the years have stuck by me, or shown me much gratitude. So now I got a chance to pay you back."

Samuel opened his mouth to speak, but Stoddard hurried on, "There's more, Doc. You got a right to know. And, anyway, I think I want you to know. I lied back there in Independence when I said

I wasn't drunk the day of the massacre. I was, or at least hung over so bad I couldn't see straight. We'd just lost my son to the smallpox. And when he died I just couldn't handle it and went out on a bender to try to drown my sorrows in the bottle. But even that don't give me no excuse, 'cause I was the boss and they were all depending on me. There'd been rumors of Indian trouble. I was just plain stupid . . ."

He paused and looked away from his two listeners as if he could not continue if he had to face them.

"My wife and daughter were still with me—and I lost them too. I lost *everything*!" He sighed deeply, fighting back the tears that were none too familiar to this tough-skinned man of the prairie. "But I can't let that happen again," he resumed, "—not where there's something I can do about it. Maybe you don't want me to stay, and well . . . I couldn't blame you."

"Mr. Stoddard." It was Maggie who spoke, her voice shaken anew with emotion. "I am honored that you would want to do this for us . . . for me. But I could never ask it of you."

"No one's asked," Stoddard replied gruffly, attempting once again to bury the emotion which had surfaced beneath the tough exterior. Then he continued more briskly, "Well, I expect we got work to do."

With that he strode to the wagon box where he took down a shovel, then walked some distance away and began digging a grave. This one would be Rebbekah McCollough's permanent resting place. He hoped he didn't have to dig too many others.

Samuel gathered up Maggie's carpetbag and few other belongings where Ellie had left them. And after stowing them in his wagon, went to continue his vigil at the stricken McCollough wagon.

34 Attack!

The following day was one of waiting. For what, the little party did not know. Death, perhaps. Indians, maybe. But certainly there would be more suffering and grief.

Two McCollough children were now sick, and it looked as though the youngest would not make it through another night. Samuel kept all but himself and Evan as far removed from the wagon as possible. Maggie had taken up residence in the doctor's wagon, while Samuel and Stoddard slept in the open air.

Stoddard kept himself occupied foraging about the area. He returned late in the afternoon with the announcement that he had discovered some good water. The remainder of the day he spent filling up every available container, a job which took him twice as long since he still had the use of but one arm. He had also located a more secluded campsite down the road, but the idea of harnessing the oxen and repacking all the gear was so overwhelming to the weary band that they unanimously decided to stay put. As it turned out, that decision would save their lives.

In the morning another grave had to be dug; during the night Evan's youngest daughter died. Maggie wondered how Evan could hold up under the mounting loss, but she knew how apt men were to hold their painful thoughts inside. She prayed, as she hadn't prayed in some time, for Evan and what remained of his family.

After the others had dispersed from the little graveside service for Evan's daughter, Maggie spoke out to Dr. Carpenter.

"Dr. Carpenter," she said, then hesitated.

"Yes, Mrs. Duncan, what is it?"

"I wanted to tell you that I was encouraged by the things you said the other day; you remember, when I was asking about suffering?"

He nodded.

"I was really asking as much on my own behalf as I was for Mr. Stoddard."

Here a smile tugged at the corners of Samuel's lips. Maggie reddened slightly, realizing he must have guessed at the truth all along, but something in the situation also pleased her, and she continued. "I must be extremely dense. Of course, you knew all the time."

"Perhaps. But what I said applies to us all. And I didn't want to embarrass you by—"

He paused with apparent uncertainty.

"—but it appears I have done so anyway," he concluded at length.

Maggie laughed. "I can tolerate a little redness in my cheeks from time to time," she said. "But I want you to know that I appreciate your honesty—both then and now. It's—it's very difficult for me to talk about myself to others. Especially since—well, you know, since my husband's death."

"It's understandable. I'm a complete stranger."

Now it was Maggie's turn to smile. "Here I am living in your wagon, completely at your mercy. I would hardly call you a stranger any longer, Dr. Carpenter."

For a brief moment, the thought of Ian came into Maggie's mind. How amusing this awkward little interview with the doctor would have been to him! He had always laughed at her feminine discomfiture, and she would have become angry at him. Later they would have laughed over it together. But this time, the memory of Ian had come into her mind, unaccompanied by the awful, sickly emptiness which had so characterized her mood for the last six months. She found herself almost smiling at the thought of his laughing eyes and merry wit.

"You would have liked my husband, Doctor," she replied finally. "And I'm sure he would have liked you."

"I'm sorry I couldn't have met him," replied the doctor. "I'm sure he must have been quite something for you to love him as you did."

"He was unlike you in many ways—so boyish and gay. There was almost a delightful immaturity about him. But, then, I was young, too—only seventeen when we married. It seems I have grown ten years since then."

"Age and maturity are not always measured in years," he remarked. "Perhaps you have grown far more in the past year than you realize, although it'll probably take years to appreciate it."

"If I live that long," replied Maggie with a sigh.

"Don't worry," said Samuel. "You'll make it through this, you and your little Eleanor."

"How can you be so certain?"

"There's a certain tenacity about you, Mrs. Margaret Duncan. Nothing's going to keep you down forever. God has things to do with you, in you, perhaps through that beautiful child of yours. I have no doubt of that. A spirit like yours comes along only once in a family in many generations. No, I'm quite sure the Duncan family will live on and on through its American line."

Maggie was silent a moment, and her thoughts returned to Ian. When she spoke again it was about him once more, as if to pick up the thread of conversation which had been dropped a few moments back. "He was not like you ... and yet, in many ways, he was. He had such a deep sensitivity and a strong yearning after right. I know he would have respected you. For you stand up for the things you believe in."

"When there is something I believe in," Samuel said, "then I consider it worth fighting for."

"You believe in God like that, don't you?"

"Yes."

"I've been so confused these last months. There was a time when I could pray and feel I was being heard. But that was long ago. And I want to pray again, and I've tried. Little Eleanor has brought me such joy. I think that's a gift from God. But it's all so hard to understand."

"Perhaps understanding it isn't as important as we make it. Perhaps the most important thing is simply allowing the love God has for us to flow over us."

"But it's not something you can see or touch."

"Perhaps it's like renewing the acquaintance of an old friend, a friend with whom we may have had a bitter parting. The first steps toward coming together are slow, almost painful. But we know the friendship will be worth the wait, so we persist, and ultimately are rewarded."

"Maybe I just don't have enough faith."

"I don't think so," replied Samuel. "I don't think God cares so much how big our faith is, but whether we are willing to trust Him the little bit we are able. A little faith put to use is much better than a big faith sitting on the shelf doing nothing. No, I think we all have plenty of faith if we'll just put it to work."

By now they had walked a little distance from the wagons along the jagged rocky path. It was odd, Maggie thought. Traveling in the wagon with the awful alkali-laden dust all about, hot and dry and bumpy, this road had seemed ugly. But now it had become rather peaceful. Around them all was still and quiet. Even the dry sage and jagged rocks contained a certain beauty.

"Only you can judge your own faith," Samuel continued. "And only you can know how God expects you to use it."

"But how can I *know* if I have faith?" Maggie asked, her eyes intent on him for an answer.

"I'm afraid I can't answer that question," he replied. "Perhaps *desiring* faith is all we need do—all we *can* do, in fact. God alone is the giver of faith. If we desire it, and ask Him for it—"

He stopped short, for suddenly Maggie had grasped his arm. Her face had turned white and she leaned heavily against him.

"Margaret...!" he could hardly force the word out. "You're ill?"

She only nodded, barely cognizant of the fact that he had used her given name. He caught her up in his arms and raced back to the wagons.

Immediately new sleeping arrangements had to be contrived. Maggie knew she would have to be separated from her daughter, but she insisted that Eleanor be kept in the wagon out of the day's intense rays of sun. Stoddard rigged up a tent for Maggie nearby, for none could bear to put her in the McCollough wagon, now rank with the odor of death. Samuel and Stoddard shared the doctor's wagon and took turns caring for Eleanor as best they could. As she could now have no more of her mother's milk, they had no choice but to soak dried biscuits or jerky in water and then attempt to force some of the liquid down her through the bottle which Ellie Mackinaw had provided. Both men shared equally the inevitable task of changing diapers.

Had Maggie been able to observe the tender care given her daughter by the two men, she would have rested without a care. Samuel was not altogether inexperienced, for physicians often find themselves commandeered into a variety of motherly chores while caring for the sick. Not so with frontier wagon masters! But Stoddard accepted his duties gamely, picked up the tiny bundle of life with fingers no less delicate in that they were hard and calloused with years of hard work, and even—when alone—murmured little bits of encouragement to the infant in high-pitched fatherly tones. During and after feeding times, being the more experienced of the two, he was often in the position of tutoring the doctor.

"Give her back a good firm rub," he instructed. "Down low—that's it—down where it'll bring up the burp."

But if the good doctor was unsuccessful at the fine art of burping a baby, he was an expert at singing to it and rocking her to sleep as he hummed soothing tones. During one such moment, as he walked slowly about the camp crooning to the child, he heard Maggie calling him from her tent.

"Samuel," she said feebly as he approached. "Look in the bottom of my carpetbag. I have a small music box I brought from home. It plays a sweet little lullaby. Eleanor might like the sound."

The doctor did as instructed and found, indeed, that the strains from Brahms' most famous tune quieted the baby as nothing else could.

That evening another of Evan's daughters died and by morning he and his remaining daughter had been taken ill. But Maggie—perhaps mercifully—was unaware of all this. The dreaded disease—so feared by everyone—had indeed struck her down.

At first her consciousness could only focus on the pain, the fever, and the shock of her hopeless plight. Then suddenly it seemed to dawn on her that she would probably *die* from the disease. Rebbekah had died, and her daughter had died, and far back in her memory Maggie recalled the cholera epidemic in Port Strathy when she was a girl. Drew Mackinaw's sister had died at that time, and many others besides.

People *die* from this thing! Her mind seemed to pulsate with the thought.

Oh, God, I don't want to die! she said half aloud. For so long after Ian's death she had longed to die, but now she knew she felt that way no more. She had reason to live now. *Oh, God . . . please don't let me die! I want to live, God. I want to know you if you'll just show me how!*

All at once the words she had heard so recently tumbled into her fevered brain: *Desiring faith is all we need do . . . God is the giver of faith if we desire it and ask Him for it.*

"Dear Lord," Maggie murmured, "I *do* desire faith. Let me live long enough for you to give me faith. And let me use whatever little faith I have already."

Not far from where she lay, Samuel also prayed. Perhaps he prayed no more for Maggie than he had for any of his patients. But there was a fervency in his prayers that surprised even him. He trembled at the thought of Maggie dying. Why, he did not know, but being left without her, though he had known her so briefly, scared him as much as the dying itself. He had felt the same during the months of his wife's illness. On the other hand he told himself that he hardly knew young Margaret Duncan. She was but half his age. Yet through the rugged circumstances of chance they had been thrust together, he felt, to minister and strengthen each other. She could not die now.

"Oh, Lord," he prayed earnestly, "in the name of Jesus, the healer of bodies as well as souls, I ask you to spare her life and heal her of this dread affliction."

Maggie's sickness continued throughout another terrible day, during which Evan's last daughter died. Still Maggie did not know that only she and Evan remained, and that for reasons undoubtedly miraculous in nature, Eleanor, Samuel, and Stoddard had thus far been spared. The lack of activity was beginning to craze poor Stoddard, although the rest allowed his arm to heal nicely. But on the fifth day since their separation from the rest of the wagons—just as he was about to crack—cholera suddenly became the less significant of their problems.

Stoddard, ever the vigilant wagon master, first spotted the Indians shortly after sunup. Like a dreaded nightmare, they had appeared on the rise of a rocky bluff a mile or two south of their position. He had rubbed his eyes several times before he could be certain that the sight was, in fact, real and not a hallucination brought on by another unrelenting day in the burdensome heat. But there could be no mistake. There on their spotted horses sat a half-dozen Sioux warriors, outfitted, by all appearances, for war—regal feathers upon their heads, buckskin quivers hanging from their bronzed shoulders, paint adorning their stern tan faces. The sweat stood out on Stoddard's face, for he knew better than anyone what lay in store for them. He instantly roused Samuel and shouted warnings to Evan to stay hidden while he and the doctor quickly moved Maggie to what they hoped would be a safe position behind two large rocks. They had barely eased her onto the ground and readied their weapons when the warriors swept down upon them.

Stoddard had always been a crack rifleman, and even with but one good arm he picked off two of the attackers before the first arrow pierced through the canvas wagon top where Eleanor still lay sleeping. The remaining warriors raced through the camp with ear-splitting yells and continued past them and disappeared over a rock rise on the other side of the trail. Perhaps the rapid diminishing of their numbers discouraged them, or perhaps they had not intended a massacre in the first place, but for whatever reason, they were gone, and the two men fell back against the wagon wheel where they had taken cover. Samuel had not yet fired a shot.

"Thank God, they're gone!" he sighed.

"Don't be thankin' your God yet, Doc," Stoddard replied as he hastily reloaded his Winchester. "More'n likely they've gone for reinforcements."

"Maybe we should move away from here," Samuel suggested.

"Yeah, we might, but . . ."

He paused for a moment as he looked sharply out toward the horizon. Were those more war cries he heard in the distance?

"We'll have no time for that," he said grimly. "If only we could get the lady and her kid to safety."

But there wasn't time. Almost before Stoddard could finish his sentence, the Indians were on top of them again. This time the descent from the hills was made by ten warriors, two of whom were armed with rifles, the rest with bows.

"If you can't shoot straight, Doc," said Stoddard, "then maybe you better do some mighty fast prayin'."

"I'll do both," Samuel replied as he lifted his rifle in readiness. He had never killed another human being before. His hands trembled, for in fact he had never even hurt another, not even in a fist fight on the rowdy docks where he had worked with his father. But he would kill now, forsaking for a brief moment of time his calling as a healer of men, in order to save the lives of those he had grown to love. And as the attackers drew within range he began to empty his rifle at them, remembering whom he was protecting and that he would die before he allowed them to be harmed.

Samuel's first shot missed its mark. But Stoddard's did not and another painted warrior fell. Behind them a shot rang out from Evan's wagon and the doctor and trail master shot looks of hope toward one another with the addition of Evan's gun to the battle. How effective Evan would prove was debatable, for he could barely hold the rifle in his arms. But it at least served as one further distraction for the Sioux. But even this could not hold them off indefinitely.

Quickly they were approaching on horseback now, too rapidly and too many to stop. As one of the band rode past the campfire which the doctor had maintained for the sterilization of water, he swooped down with a torch in his hand. Instantly it jumped into flame. Brandishing the blazing wood aloft and screaming a hideous cry, he pitched it toward Samuel's wagon. The next instant the Indian fell from his bewildered horse, fatally wounded by Stoddard's shot. But the brand still found its mark. It landed on the front seat of the wagon and instantly the canvas top was ablaze, fanned by a light breeze.

Samuel and Stoddard both jumped up and leapt forward in horror. Stoddard was the quicker of the two and reached the flaming wagon first. Inside he could hear Eleanor crying and his heart pounded against his chest in fear he could not get her out in time. All around him arrows continued to fly and shots explode, while he beat against the flames with his jacket.

Just as he climbed up to reach into the back of the wagon he heard, rather than felt, one of the arrows pierce his back. The thud and awful screaming pain which followed stunned him momentarily and brought an unspoken oath to his lips. But he refused to collapse; he would not die in that manner. If he must die, it would be in a manner worthy of those who had become his friends. As his mind grew blurred and the sounds around him distant, the only other thought which remained was that he must save the child.

No longer could he hear the sounds outside—the shots, the pounding of hoofbeats against the dry earth, the shouts and yells. All around had grown dim and quiet, all except the faint sound of a crying child.

He stumbled toward the infant, oblivious to the fire raging all about him. "There, there," he gasped, as tenderly as his failing voice would permit. "No need to cry. Uncle Gil's got you now."

Quickly he picked her up and backed out of the wagon. The pain in his back was gone now. In its place there was only numbness. He could not feel his legs, though he could tell he was standing on them. The wagon was engulfed in flames and all around he was exposed to the attack. A piece of burning canvas floated down and landed on Eleanor's blanket. Stoddard brushed it away and tried to run, keeping his back always toward the attack.

Suddenly people were running about. Vague shouts penetrated Stoddard's dim consciousness. He could hear no more shots or warcries; all was a blur. He began to slip. He clutched Eleanor to his chest more tightly.

"You ain't touching her!" he cried in a barely audible voice, then crumbled to the ground.

When he awoke, Samuel was kneeling over him, his great tender eyes wet with tears. Eleanor was gone.

"Where's. . . ?" he tried to say, but his mouth was dry and his tongue too swollen to move.

"It's all right now, Gil," Samuel replied. "It's all right. You just rest."

"Did you kill 'em all, Doc?" he asked weakly.

"I didn't have to. A small company of soldiers heard our trouble."

Stoddard tried to laugh. "Your—your God . . . He done okay after all, huh, Doc?"

Samuel nodded as tears flowed unchecked down his sunburned cheeks. Stoddard did not have long. The arrow was too deep and the shaft had broken off in the fall. There had been a good deal of death this week, but this was going to be one of the most difficult of all for the compassionate doctor. But though he could do nothing for the body of the dying man, he gave him something more important than what lay in the power of his medical skills.

"He's your God, too, Gil," Samuel said.

"You think so? I never had much use . . ."

"I know He is," Samuel replied, the certainty of his statement broken only by his trembling emotions. "And He always has been."

"It kind of makes dyin' easier, knowin' that, you know, Doc?"

"I know." But the doctor by now could hardly speak himself.

"And the kid? You sure she's okay, Doc?"

"She's fine, Gil, thanks to you. You saved her life."

Stoddard smiled a thin smile. "And the woman. You'll take care of her, too, won't you, Doc?"

"Yes, of course I will, Gil."

"And no whiskey, either, Doc . . ." Stoddard said with a smile.

Samuel slowly shook his head and forced a smile to his lips also. But the weary wagon master did not see, for he had already slipped into eternity.

35 Respite

Maggie recovered slowly. Even after the contagion passed, weakness clung to her. The soldiers had been kind enough to provide protection to the stranded travelers—at some distance, to be sure. July was drawing to a fiery close before they deemed it safe to move Maggie and Evan to the safety of the garrison along the Platte. Although most of the contents of Samuel's wagon had been spared, the wagon itself had been burned beyond use and the oxen from both wagons had been scattered by the Indians. So the four made the trip on spare Army horses, brought out from the fort during the last exchange of those who had been on duty staying with them to guard against another attack.

On the morning of their departure, Evan began to succumb to the loss he had experienced. Six soldiers and the four civilians had departed the campsite, while two soldiers had been left behind to burn the wagons, eliminating the possibility of the Indians returning to pillage and picking up the disease. About a hundred yards away, Evan turned back, saying he had forgotten something. When he reached the two soldiers where they stood lighting their torches, he grabbed one away, and with a wild gleam in his eye flung it upon his wagon. Then he stood as if in a trance, watching the flames hungrily licking at the last remnant of his earthly possessions. The two men finally had to carry him from the scene.

They reached the Platte Bridge Army Garrison late that afternoon. It was a flimsy fort-like structure, a log wall encompassing barracks for approximately a hundred soldiers in addition to all the other buildings necessary to complete such a wilderness complex. Maggie and Eleanor were put up in the captain's quarters, hardly plush by aristocratic standards, but welcome and comfortable after months in the back of a crowded wagon. Space was made for Samuel, Evan, and Captain Hodges in the barracks.

Samuel ordered Maggie directly to bed where she was to remain for at least a week. Maggie did not protest. With Eleanor at her side and with strength once again beginning to flow through her weary frame, she was at rest. Samuel brought her meals and dropped in at least four or five other times throughout every day, ostensibly to check her condition; more often than not, he spent the time holding Eleanor or conversing with his patient. Maggie looked forward to each of his visits and could even tell that little Eleanor had developed an attachment to the kindly doctor.

On a bright morning during the first week of August, Samuel paid one of his frequent visits to Maggie's bedside. He wore a cheerful, almost buoyant expression and his step was unusually light. He caught up Eleanor with a single motion, and his mood seemed to infect her as she broke out in a grin.

"Look, she's smiling!" he exclaimed. "Why, that must be her first smile!" He lowered the child to the bed, where Maggie could also appreciate Eleanor's marvelous achievement. Maggie smiled and said nothing. He need not know that she had smiled the previous day for her.

"She's such a pretty baby!" he went on exuberantly. "She must be a month old already."

"She is. Today, in fact," Maggie replied, but her voice seemed far away.

"Well, I have a one-month birthday present for you, Eleanor," said Samuel with a grin. "How would you like to go for a walk with your mother today—outside in the sunshine?" He turned toward Maggie, anticipating her reaction to the news that her confinement was drawing to a close.

"That sounds nice, Samuel," Maggie said. But even as she spoke there was something missing in her tone.

"Aren't you feeling well today, Margaret?" he asked, peering at her with something more than medical concern.

"Oh, yes. I'm much better," Maggie replied, trying to put more enthusiasm into her voice. "It's just that I was thinking of . . . well, today is my birthday, too. And I was . . . thinking of what it was like this time last year."

Samuel drew up a chair and sat down at Maggie's side, still cradling Eleanor.

"Much has happened to you since then, hasn't it, Margaret?" he said.

"Yes . . ." Maggie replied, drawing out the word thoughtfully. "It's hard to believe that only a year ago I was whirling around a ballroom, dressed in an elegant gown, without a care in the world—"

She stopped abruptly as a sudden and unexpected vision of her father came into her thoughts. He danced with her on that night, she recalled, and even in the innocence of the remembrance, the thought was like a grim cloud passing momentarily over the sun. "There were cares, even then," she mused, nearly forgetting Samuel's presence. "But it seems like so long ago."

"I know it is said that with the passing of time, pain is eased and grief is softened," Samuel replied, his words expressing the depths of his own heart as much as they were intended to ease Maggie's burden. "But I believe there is some pain which never leaves us entirely; perhaps it is intrinsically wrapped up with much that is good within us. I wish there were something I could *do* for you to help lighten your load, if only it was to direct you to the

One who can bear the whole load for you."

"You have already done that, Samuel," Maggie replied softly. "Each day, each moment you are here brings me closer. God is giving me faith. I know it. I know that's why He saved me from dying."

Then, as if visibly shaking herself into a new mood, Maggie began again in a less pensive and more cheerful tone, "But the day of my first walk is quickly slipping away! Take Eleanor out with you now, Samuel, while I dress. Then I shall meet you in a few moments."

So the time passed, one day inching lazily upon the next. Each was filled with its own peculiar kind of peace even though very real burdens and fears still lurked on the edges of life. For when one can do nothing about one's own troubles or the troubles of friends far away, peace often forces itself upon us. And at such times, though the cares of life do not evaporate, such peace can be accepted, even enjoyed. For Maggie, this time of respite was a soothing balm to her soul, an unexpected break from the cares which had for so long engulfed her. In total isolation from any remnant of what she had known, she was able to look around her, as she and Ian had learned to do together, saying, "This rock, this flower, this horse, this tree, this land . . . they are beautiful. And life can be good again!"

Only one shadow crossed the tranquillity of those fine days. Evan McCollough had gone to bed one night in the barracks with all the other men; in the morning he was gone, and with him one of the poorer horses in the stable. A few dollars, probably all that Evan possessed, had been left by the captain's bunk for the animal. A small party of soldiers immediately set out on a futile search. But he was never found.

As if that desolate Army outpost had a spell over it, the peace continued to cover Samuel and Maggie; Evan's loss seemed to blend in with all the other losses they had weathered together. The heartaches stood at bay like a threatening wave held in place by some miracle—never far from crashing down, but for the moment at least, its fury checked.

If anyone had asked Maggie later what her clearest memory

of those days was, she would have immediately replied, "The leisurely walks about the grounds." Morning and early evening would usually find the pair, with Samuel carrying Eleanor, strolling just outside the flimsy enclosure of the garrison. Captain Hodges permitted them to proceed no further, for the Indian unrest was still at a high pitch. The tortuous, murky river and the barren, sage-covered hills surrounded the two as they soaked up all the peace that God had to shower down upon them.

As they walked, and talked, the ground of their lives was softened and before long they were able to tread the paths of their hearts as if the gates had long been open and the ways well-worn.

One day Maggie laughed at Samuel's abandoned play with Eleanor. They had begged permission from the captain for a picnic. Hugging the safety of the wall, they sat upon a blanket in the questionable shade of a scrawny cottonwood. Samuel was doing everything within the powers of his masculine persuasions to induce delightful smiles from the two-month-old baby.

"You are very good with Eleanor," Maggie remarked.

Samuel laughed. "I'm afraid Gil Stoddard would never agree. But I hope I succeeded in learning something from him." A cloud of sadness momentarily replaced the laughter in his eyes.

"I was so sick," Maggie replied. "I had nearly forgotten how you both cared for her. I wish I could have seen Gil with her."

"He was so gentle. He treated her like the most delicate flower on earth. And if she *looked* out of place in his scrapping arms, I know she never *felt* out of place there. It was a wonderful sight."

"How terrible that he had to die!"

"Yes. It was awful—but in a way, perhaps it was marvelous, too."

"How can you say such a thing?" Maggie exclaimed.

"I'll always miss Gil," Samuel began, then he paused. When he resumed there was a smile in his eyes. "When I first met the man, no one could have convinced me I'd ever feel a fondness for him. I will greatly miss him, and yet I cannot begrudge him the happiest moment in his life since he lost his family—a moment that seemed destined to come to him only in death."

"Do you think a man like that could ever, you know, be with God?"

"Do you think he could *not* be, Margaret?"

"I know he died saving Eleanor, and he shall always hold a high place in my heart for that. But isn't there more to it? Going to heaven, I mean."

"Yes, there is," Samuel replied. "And I believe that somewhere in those last moments, Gil Stoddard made his peace with God."

"Someone could go along his whole life scorning God," Maggie mused, "and in the end come over to His side."

"Have you not heard of the eleventh hour?"

"I suppose so—like the thief on the cross who repented?"

"Exactly! But how much better to turn to Him sooner if we have the chance. For as happy as I am for Gil, he missed so much that he could have had here on earth—if only he could have opened himself to let God cleanse him. Then he would have been able to forgive himself for his past."

"It always seems to come back to that, doesn't it?" stated Maggie. "Forgiveness."

"That's often what stands in our way before God," said Samuel. "Either not being able to forgive ourselves, or another. And sometimes not being able to forgive God. Yes, the approach to intimacy with God often does hinge on being able to forgive."

"But what if we're unable to?"

"Maybe I should have said being *willing* to. For like faith, forgiveness begins with the desire to make things right."

Maggie did not reply. The words hit too close to home.

She did desire faith. She knew that now. God had spared her life; to Maggie that was a sign He was with her and loved her. Since then she had tried more diligently to exercise the limited faith in Him she possessed. She had tried to accept His love and to pray and ask Him what He would have her do. But so many of the spiritual things Samuel spoke of remained a mystery to her.

Am I holding something back?

Yet even as she asked herself the question with Samuel's words still ringing in her ears, she recalled vividly the day she had shouted out—about one who was thousands of miles away but whose image could still bring a trembling to her lip—that she would *never* forgive.

With the memory rose an inner emotional wall to shield her

from its pain. If approach to intimacy with God, as Samuel had said, did indeed hinge on being willing to forgive, then perhaps she would just have to settle for a faith smaller and shallower than his. For that was a step she simply was not yet able to take.

Whether she wanted to take it was a question Maggie was unprepared to consider.

Soon September came, heralding autumn and the distant whisperings of winter. And as if the change of season contained deeper significance, the peaceful respite of those days at the garrison also drew to a close and the impending wave of trouble was at last released. But it seemed to fall more gently on the two who had been greatly strengthened and refreshed by the weeks of God-given peace.

36   The Winds of Change

As the cold autumn rains descended upon the high country around the Platte, the Indians began to take more seriously the Governor's call to them earlier in the summer. In gradually increasing numbers they made their way to the three forts deemed as *safe*. Many on their way to Fort Laramie, mostly women and children and old men, traveled past the garrison on the Platte. The soldiers stood watchful and not a little nervous on the rickety ramparts, guns poised. But there was no trouble. Some who were sick would stop, and there they found a compassionate physician in Samuel Carpenter. But most chose to ignore the outpost of the "long knives," perhaps praying to their Great Spirit that they might also be somehow spared the indignity of facing the white man farther on at Fort Laramie. But the rains were heavy and the snows would be deep this winter, and the white man had medicine for the terrible diseases that had come to the Sioux these past five years.

On many days Maggie watched the sad migration, often wondering if one of the brown Indian babies could possibly be the one she had cared for early in the summer. Occasionally she would assist Samuel in his work among them and she always found special joy in this—both from being needed and finding a great satisfaction in ministering, and simply from being with Samuel, who was such a source of peace to her. Throughout the weeks their friendship had grown and deepened. They had come to share things with each other that neither had ever expected to share with another human being again. In the end a mere word or nod or sigh was enough to communicate what the other was thinking.

One afternoon Maggie sat at the secretary in the room which had all but become her own since their arrival. She was reflecting on a conversation she had had that morning with Samuel. For one of the first times he had asked about Scotland, and for the first time in many months she had found herself speaking of her home. Samuel had known about James and Ian and their terrible conflicts. But somehow it had been more difficult to talk about the land itself. That morning, however, through tears of bitter joy and loss, at last she did. And now, alone again, she could not erase from her mind the visions of the heather hills and the craggy bluffs overlooking the sea.

Suddenly Maggie rose to her feet and found the carpetbag where she had shoved it underneath the bed upon their arrival. How vividly she remembered the day so long ago when she had packed it! She had wept, thinking she would never see her homeland again. And how much worse might it have been had she known those fears were to be true? Carefully she pulled out the stitchery she had sewn as a child.

"Oh, Mother . . ." she murmured, trying to visualize the grand tapestry she had tried so hard to copy. It was still so clear in her mind hanging regally above the little canopied bed in the nursery.

"But we moved it, didn't we. . . ?" she thought absently.

With deepening nostalgia sweeping over her, Maggie reached in and removed the brown envelope her mother had been so careful to give her the day she left Stonewycke. She had not yet opened it. But now, a year later, the time all at once seemed right. Out of respect for her mother and the heritage of Stonewycke in which her memory was steeped, rather than from sheer curiosity, Maggie carefully opened the envelope and pulled out the contents. Inside were two papers, both apparently very old, yellowed with age, and written in ancient script and archaic language. One was clearly a description of the Stonewycke properties and estate, for Maggie recognized names of many familiar places in the description of borders, boundaries, and distance. The other was . . .

She could hardly believe her eyes!

It was the deed to Stonewycke!

She had never even known such a thing as a written deed existed. Why had her mother taken such pains to give it to her? Obviously this explained her cryptic words before their departure—that Stonewycke was *hers.* Was this Atlanta's way to insure her daughter's return?

But, Mother, I cannot return! she thought, tears rising in her eyes. *There is nothing there for me now . . . without Ian. Even you . . . and the land . . . without Ian they—nothing left—Oh, Mother! . . . there would be no meaning to life for me there now . . .*

Maggie dropped onto the bed and wept.

At length, after her grief had subsided for the moment, Maggie sat up, wiped her eyes, returned the papers to the envelope and returned it to the carpetbag. Her hand struck another object. She wrapped a trembling hand around it and pulled it into the light.

"The music box!" she cried softly.

Slowly she opened the lid and turned the key, and instantly the delicate Brahms lullaby floated out as clearly as it had the first time she had played it as a child. Before the tune had played itself out Maggie had once again crumpled onto the bed in a rush of tears.

She was only vaguely aware of the soft knocking at her door; at length Eleanor, stirring from her nap with growing cries of hunger, awoke Maggie from the sleep of her sorrow.

"Margaret . . . Margaret . . . are you all right?" a voice was calling.

Maggie opened her eyes and gazed around, bewildered for a moment at her strange surroundings; then, coming to herself, she rose, picked up the crying baby, and went to the door.

"I'm sorry, Samuel," she said. "I was asleep. I had just . . .

been . . ." But the tears had not finished their work with her yet and began to flow again in earnest.

"Margaret," said Samuel, taking Eleanor in his arms and placing a tender hand on Maggie's shoulder, "is there anything I can do?"

Maggie shook her head, then caught up the music box from the bed where she had dropped it. She handed it to Samuel.

"Something from home?" he asked.

"My father . . . on my fifth birthday . . . he gave it to me. It came from London," she managed to say. "Oh, Samuel," she cried in an anguish of fresh weeping, "I wanted to adore him and for him to be my papa . . . that's all I ever wanted from him!"

"And you want it still, don't you, dear?"

"Yes!" said Maggie as she broke down into an agony of convulsive sobs.

Managing Eleanor as best he could, Samuel put his arm around Maggie's shoulders. She laid her head on his chest and continued to weep. Neither spoke for several long minutes.

At length Maggie came to herself and said, "Is there ever anything else that a daughter wants from her father?"

"Probably not," Samuel replied softly.

"Is it so wrong to want a father's love?"

"No," he said. "A father's love is at the center of everything. It's just that our earthly fathers don't always reflect the love of their heavenly Father as God intended they should."

"But it will never be, not with my father," said Maggie. "I'm afraid after what he did, the hate has gone too deep. Even if he were here I doubt I could love him again. I wish it weren't that way. But I know it is."

"Forgiveness can begin to cleanse away the hate."

Maggie was silent a long while. She knew Samuel's words were the key to the closer life with God and the growth of her faith which she desired. But the struggle in her heart could not let go of the past. Finally she did speak.

"What good would it do now, anyway?" she asked softly. "I'll never see him again."

"The healing of forgiveness begins in your own heart," replied Samuel tenderly. "Your father will have to answer to God for himself. And you are responsible for the attitudes in *your* heart. To draw close to Him, your heart must be clean. He alone can cleanse it, and the process begins with forgiveness."

"Oh, I can't," wailed Maggie. "I'm afraid ... the pain is too deep!"

"My dear, dear girl," said Samuel, holding her close to him. "Don't you know," he continued in a barely audible voice, "that God requires only what we are ready to give? You need only take a small step, as long as it is in the right direction. And He requires nothing of us that isn't for our best, because He loves us so dearly. It is for your sake, and for the sake of the love He would shower upon you that He requires such a difficult thing from you."

He pulled his handkerchief from his pocket and dabbed Maggie's wet eyes. She looked up, smiled, and whispered a soft, "Thank you."

"I'll help in any way I can," he encouraged.

"I must write ... somehow. I don't know what I would say, but the beginning must be a letter home," said Maggie.

For the first time since they had begun, Maggie seemed to notice her daughter. "Oh, Eleanor!" she cried, taking her from Samuel's arm.

"She must have known her mother needed more care right now than she did," remarked Samuel. "She stopped crying the moment I picked her up."

Maggie laughed and dried her eyes further. "Thank you, Samuel," she said warmly. "You are so good for me. I don't know how I could have made it through all this without you."

Before he could reply a knock came to the door. It was Captain Hodges.

"I'm sorry to intrude," he stated. "But I thought you'd like to know. A rider has just arrived from California. He's carrying mail east, and if you have anything, this will likely be the last opportunity before winter sets in. He'll be leaving in the morning. And he also has news from the West, if you'd like to come over to the mess hall and hear his report."

About thirty minutes later Samuel and Maggie entered the room with the captain. Clustered about one of the long, rough-hewn tables were eight or ten soldiers. At the center of the group was a dusty civilian dressed in well-worn buckskin with a battered hat still on his head, despite the fact that he was about to dig into a steaming bowl of stew.

"Hello, Jack," the captain called. "Getting enough to eat?"

"Sure am, Capt'n," the rider answered. "Best grub I've had in months!"

"Folks," he went on to his companions, "this here's Jack O'Reilly. He's been a sort of unofficial Army scout for years—best in the business, too. Jack, these are a couple of our other guests, Dr. Carpenter and Mrs. Duncan. They got separated from their wagon train a while back and we've been putting them up until they are strong enough to move on and have decided what they want to do."

"Pleased to make your acquaintance," returned the scout, rising partially from his chair and touching the rim of his hat toward Maggie. "What train was you with? If it wasn't too long ago, I might of run into 'em."

"Oh, if you could tell us anything about them!" Maggie exclaimed.

"We started out as Gil Stoddard's train, but he was . . . he was killed—" Samuel began, but O'Reilly cut in with a whistle.

"Stoddard, you say? I didn't think he was in the business anymore. Killed, was he?"

"An Indian attack," said the doctor.

"He was one of the best. That is until he lost that train out on the Humboldt . . . but anyway, you was sayin'?"

"Pete Kramer would probably have been in charge of the train," Samuel replied.

"Kramer . . ." O'Reilly rubbed his chin, trying to recall.

"Perhaps it might have been Drew Mackinaw," put in Maggie impatiently.

Gradually O'Reilly's face darkened and he dropped his fork onto the tin plate with a clank. "Them's your friends?"

"Yes . . . yes!" cried Maggie.

"Then I'm sorry I got to be the one to bring you the news," stated Jack with a somber face.

Maggie held Eleanor tighter and clutched at Samuel's arm.

"What news?" asked Samuel in what was barely more than a hoarse whisper.

"I'm surprised a small train like that made it as far as it did. It don't make no sense. They got clean through the Sioux territory without a scratch, but Bannock country's even worse these days. There ain't been many to make it through without at least a skirmish or two. But your friends' train ... well, bad timin' is all you can chalk it up to. And too few of 'em to hold off the savages. Only six survivors in the whole train."

"Dear Lord, no!" Samuel breathed. The look of shock on Maggie's face was her only response. There could be no words.

"I talked to 'em myself," Jack went on. "They wanted me to get word back to some of the relatives."

"Who ... who were they?" Samuel asked. "Whom did you talk with?"

"Mackinaw and his wife, though Mackinaw was wounded pretty bad in the shoulder. Then there was a fellow named Williams, a woman by the name of Wooton, and a couple young'uns."

"What children?" Maggie asked urgently, finding her voice at last.

"I don't know. We just passed on the trail. They was pretty friendly with them Mackinaws though. Seems as though I remember a little girl calling him Pa. What I can't figure is how the man and his wife, and their wagon, and their young'uns—if they was theirs—all came out of the scrape when most everyone else was wiped out."

As he spoke Maggie recalled, with tears in her eyes, how many times since their separation she had prayed for the Mackinaw family and their safety. God *had* heard her!

"But the other children ... the Wootons' sons," said Maggie, her voice pale with shock, "... I just can't believe it."

"I'm sorry, ma'am. But I helped the survivors hook up with another train. Least they're all safe in California by now."

"You mean they went on?"

"No choice, ma'am. Out there you either go on or turn back. It happened in the Bear River Valley. When you get that far, already across the Divide, there's no way you can turn back then. Even if you have the supplies, you can't risk traveling alone."

O'Reilly pushed his chair back from the table and stood. "Well, I'm going to get me another bowl of that stew and then turn in. I'll be leavin' before most of you are even thinkin' of wakin' in the morning. So if you have anything for me, I'll leave a sack right here and get it before I leave."

Later that same night, Maggie left the room and walked briskly across the compound. The night air was chilly and she had left Eleanor alone on the bed. There were a few soldiers about and they tipped their hats to her as she passed on her way to the mess hall. She opened the door and spotted O'Reilly's waiting pouch in the candlelight. She walked across the floor, opened it, dropped her letter inside, then turned and left.

As she walked slowly outside and looked up at the rising moon over the distant Rockies, all she could think of was the heather moor from which Drew Mackinaw had come. The news of that day, as well as her talk with Samuel, had prompted the letter she knew she must write. She hoped Atlanta would write back, although how the letter would reach her she couldn't think. But she missed her mother at moments like these, though she doubted she would ever see her again.

Braenock Ridge was so far away now. Drew would certainly never go back. And probably old Hector, if he still lived, and little Stevie would go to their graves never knowing what had become of their eldest son and brother.

Land of opportunity, they called it. She and Ian had thought it would be the place of new beginnings. But it was a hard land and it took its toll. For Drew and Ellie, though the price had been high, they had made it west, their bridges forever burned behind them. *And for me*, Maggie wondered, *what does the future hold?*

Even as she framed the question, she knew her bridges were burned behind her as well.

There would be—there could be no turning back. She had come too far. She had crossed the Great Divide of her soul. Scotland was another lifetime ago.

37 The Laird and the Marchioness

Gray clouds, heavy with impending rain, massed around Stone-wycke's even grayer stone towers. But rain and the approach of winter were far from James Duncan's mind that dreary morning. He lay between silken bedclothes and could only reflect despondently that he felt weaker by the day. He cursed aloud, though there was no one in the room to hear him. He swore at the chill emanating from the very walls themselves and cursed the fact that he could not even rise to toss another log on the fire. He cursed the sluggard of a servant who was supposed to be watching out for the state of the fire. And finally, he cursed that "devil of a horse" that had landed him here in the first place.

"That animal's had a spell on her since the day I first laid eyes on her!" he said, as he had many times before.

But all James's cursing only masked what he really felt like doing—cursing himself for such a foolhardy stunt. A broken leg had, miraculously, been his only injury. But it refused to heal, and inflammation had set in. Several doctors were called in, whom he had thrown out with their dour prophecies of gloom. Although when he tried to walk the pain was frightful, on numerous occasions he had disobeyed orders to remain in bed, thus thoroughly impeding any potential progress. And there was also his cough. It had grown worse since the fall, and now came from the deepest parts of his chest.

It had never been James's character to accept illness. And it was even more impossible for him to think of death. He would hang on to life with a desperate grip, for it was all he had. There was no hope of afterlife, and James had not even the small hope of immortality in being remembered fondly by loved ones. He was a practical man. He knew no one loved him. He had never sought love and he did not care that it would be missing at the end of his life.

Or so he told himself.

But lying in bed as the days dragged wearily on, robbed of everything which had once made him feel important, reminded every day of the swelling in his leg, and having to face the raw realities of his own impotence and mortality—his circumstance was beginning to work in an imperceptibly positive way upon James. He was just as liable to shout all manner of fierce imprecations to any soul who ventured near. But, simply, James Duncan was gradually beginning to believe less and less in himself.

This particular morning found him more surly than usual. His weakness was so acute that he either had to admit his failing condition or gloss over it with a harsh attitude toward everything in sight. He chose the latter and tugged angrily at the covers, finding a new victim upon which to vent his anger.

"Rotten bed!" he muttered. "It never stays in one piece! I say, where's that maid? If she—"

A knock at the door arrested his attention, and though he answered it gruffly he was in fact glad for the diversion. Part of him even hoped it might be the old fool of a groom. Digory had come to visit the laird every day since the accident. James would never admit that he was fond of the old fellow or that he ever listened to his religious babble. Instead, he tried to convince himself that the old lout was good for a laugh or two, which, in his condition, he needed from time to time.

The visitor this morning was not Digory, but the butler instead.

"Well, what do you want?" James barked.

"This came to the house a few moments ago, sir," the butler replied, holding out a dull white envelope. "The Lady Atlanta was in the kitchen with the maid and didn't see it, sir. I thought you'd be wanting it . . ."

"And what else do you think I've been paying you so handsomely for?" James snarled. Indeed, the man had been receiving generous gratuities from James to insure that any correspondence coming to Stonewycke arrived in James's hands first. For even in his weakened state the laird still kept up the precarious game of duplicity with Atlanta, a tug-of-war which had characterized the whole of their marriage, and even to the present day he fully believed he was maintaining the upper hand despite the serious handicap of his leg.

"Well, give it to me!" James snapped.

The butler stepped forward and placed the envelope in his hand.

Instantly the scant remaining color drained from his master's face.

"Are you feeling well, sir?" asked the concerned butler.

"Get me a brandy!" was James's only reply.

"But the physician said—"

"Do you think I give a bloody farthing what that rascal of an absurd doctor thinks? Get me a brandy, you swine, and be quick about it!"

The butler retreated from the room, knowing full well the futility of trying to argue with the laird.

The moment he was gone James looked again at the letter.

It couldn't be! Yet the fine hand and the return address—the absurd name, *Platte Bridge Garrison*—left no doubt.

Margaret ... in America ... writing to *both* him and Atlanta! What could it mean? What scheme was the little devil concocting now? No doubt something Atlanta had contrived. Was she now planning to return to stake her claim?

A cold sweat broke out on his forehead. His heart began pounding in his throat. Why else would she now break her long silence? *She will ruin everything!* he thought. He could never stand against Maggie and Atlanta if they joined forces against him.

"You'll not take it from me now!" His voice trembled.

More than anything he feared what would be exposed if his daughter returned. To be publicly disgraced would be worse than death; no one must ever discover the terrible lie he had perpetrated against the so-called husband of his daughter. He could not even imagine what retributions Atlanta would levy against him were she to find out. He had only just begun to be able to manipulate her. The return of their daughter would only strengthen the terrible resolves of the mother once again.

It must not happen!

He flung the bedcovers from him. With all the effort he could muster he edged his infirm body from the bed, groaning as he swung his injured leg over the edge and wincing in pain as he lurched to his feet. Bracing himself beside the bed, he staggered toward the table, then holding on to the back of a chair he made his way to the hearth.

Standing in front of the crackling logs, he hesitated with the unopened letter poised in his hands. The part of him that might once have been called a conscience—the part of him which subconsciously longed for love—that part of the father wanted to read the letter from his little girl. For the briefest of moments, as he had first glanced at the familiar handwriting, something had leapt inside him, touched by the fact that she had addressed the letter equally to him.

But fear overpowered the longing in his heart. He understood greed and ambition and deceit, but love was an unknown and fearful entity. To open that letter might somehow force him to look at things differently. James Duncan was not ready for that yet.

He pitched the envelope into the flames.

"I do not hate you, Margaret . . ." he murmured. "But I have gone too far to change now."

The creaking of the door behind him startled James. Nearly losing his precarious balance, he reached out for the chair behind him. Atlanta quickly rushed to his side and caught his arm.

He stared at her for a long moment, more stunned at the proximity of her body than at her sudden arrival. *When was the last time she touched me,* he wondered?

"It is just like . . ." he began, then paused, unable to find the proper words within him.

"You shouldn't be up," said Atlanta like a stern parent, but with a measure of concern in her voice.

"What do you care?" asked James, more sadness than bitterness registering in his tone.

"I am concerned for your health," she replied.

"Concerned?"

"What do you expect me to say, James, that I feel affection for you?"

"Have you ever had affection for me?" James asked distantly. "And whatever the past, isn't pity what you feel now? But I suppose all of that matters little now, even if it is contempt you feel."

"I have never felt contempt for you, James," Atlanta replied, almost forgetting in that moment all the bitter emotions of the past.

"It's odd," James remarked. "But despite what we have said and been to each other through the years, neither have I felt contempt for you—"

He stopped short, seized with a fit of uncontrollable coughing.

"Come back to your bed," Atlanta entreated.

Leaning heavily on his wife, James hobbled painfully back to the bedside.

"I, too, have maintained a respect for you, Atlanta," he said, settling himself between the silken covers.

"And yet ours has been the mutual respect of adversaries," she said, almost regretfully.

"Do you think it could have been different between us?"

"I don't know, James," she replied. "But such speculation is useless now," she added, with more finality than she had perhaps intended, for the same fears which had assailed her husband a moment ago were at that instant surging through Atlanta.

"So much for sentimentality..." sighed James as he laid his head back heavily on his pillow. "Where's that butler with my brandy?"

38   Unraveling the Mystery

Dermott had not expected it to be so long until he returned to Port Strathy. He had left the little village several months ago feeling as disheartened as he had ever been. He had made the trip with such high hopes, yet the only success he could point to was the finding of two worthy allies in the innkeeper Queenie and the lad Stevie Mackinaw. But all three together had not been able to penetrate the mystery surrounding the night of young Falkirk's death.

There were only a handful of persons who knew anything about that night. Of these, one was dead, one was lost in America, one would sooner die than aid the hapless youth in prison. Dermott had managed to see Lord and Lady Falkirk. But Lord Falkirk had degenerated into a senile old man whose only lucid moments came when his eyes glowed with the memory of his youth in the faraway world of India. And when he had temporarily wrested Lady Falkirk away from her bitter denunciations of the Duncans, it was clear that she knew nothing which could possibly be of help to her son's accused murderer. And even if she had, Dermott doubted that she would have revealed it anyway.

Dermott had counted heavily on the possible support of Lady Duncan, but she had been away during his visit—in Aberdeen on one of her extremely rare absences from Stonewycke. But though Atlanta Duncan may have been able to lend moral support to Ian's cause, Dermott doubted she could offer any concrete evidence. Had she known any pertinent facts, she would have brought them to Ian's defense long ago.

Now more months had passed. Several other cases had demanded Dermott's attention. He continued his visits to Ian, but it was clear the lawyer's unsuccessful excursion to Port Strathy had been hard on the lad. He, too, had counted greatly on Dermott's success. Many a dismal day had he occupied with daydreaming of the moment of his release—the moment when he would begin his own search for his love. He would book the first ship to New York and within two months she would be in his arms! He knew he would find Maggie, and he would never rest until he did! The brilliance of the dream kept him alive.

But every day since Dermott's return, the lawyer had seen him grow more and more detached. Not only from his friend, but from reality itself.

At last, however, there was a break.

Working late in his office one evening, a stranger came to Dermott's door. The man was coarsely dressed, a sailor—not an uncommon sight in Glasgow. But this seaman had just arrived in town, he said, by way of Aberdeen. He bore a message which had been more than a month in route, first upon the schooner running between Banff and Aberdeen, where it came into his hands. He was on his way to a new job at the Broomielaw, the great quay upon the Clyde, and had brought it the rest of the way himself. The faithful messenger handed the note—for indeed it was little more than that, now crumpled and soiled—to Dermott, who amply rewarded his great efforts.

Dermott opened the single sheet of thin yellow paper, held it up to the candle, and looked on the printing, which was as coarse as its bearer. *You are wanted,* it said, *urgently . . . in Port Strathy. Something important has turned up. Should say nothing more until your arrival.*

It was signed, *Queenie.*

Saying nothing to Ian, Dermott was en route north again the following morning. Within a week he was standing on the deck of the Aberdeen schooner watching the small harbor of Port Strathy draw near.

He walked immediately to the Bluster 'N Blow, and Queenie greeted him as an old friend. Looking around he was both surprised and delighted to see Stevie Mackinaw standing near the kitchen holding a broom.

"She has you working for her, eh, Stevie?" he said with a laugh.

"Mistress Rankin's been very kind t' me," he replied.

"Just some small-time employment," said Queenie. "I needed some help, an' the lad's a hard worker. But, Mr. Connell, I thought ye'd never get here!"

"I received your message less than a week ago," Dermott replied. "But I'm afraid its route from you to me was rather circuitous."

"I was afraid o' that. I knew I should o' delivered the note mysel', but I thought my goin' t' Glasgow might o' caused undue suspicion."

"Well, I'm here now, in any case," Dermott said. "What is your news?"

Queenie cast a look around the inn to assure herself they were alone. " 'Tis Stevie here," she said, "who should tell you, for it was his own discovery."

"Come then, lad, and tell me about it, for I have been waiting a week."

Stevie stepped forward and, clasping his hands behind his back as if about to recite his lessons, began, "Weel, Mr. Connell, 'tis a simple enough bit o' news. But when I made mention o' it t' Queenie here, she nearly flew through the roof. If ye remember when we talked oot on the moor, I made mention o' seein' Master Falkirk ridin' upon the ridge on his bonnie golden stallion. It all came back t' me sometime later when I was here in the inn and I seen auld Martin Forbes takin' his ale as he does some too much, if the truth be known. For I recalled that twice I had seen old Forbes himself ridin' on the ridge wi' Master Falkirk. And when I seen them I said t' mysel', 'What would a blighter like Forbes be doin' ridin' wi' the likes o' a laird?'

"Weel, it all came back t' me an' I made mention o' it t' Mistress Rankin. An' didna she go an' ask the very same question I had asked up there on the moor! *What would the two o' them be doin' t'gether?*"

"I did," Queenie put in. "I asked that very question. Sorry, lad. Go on wi' yer story."

"Weel, ye ken yersel', Mistress Rankin, that's aboot the end o' it. Except that mysel' an' ye, we been keepin' a hawk's eye on Martin Forbes."

"Have you approached this Forbes?" Dermott asked.

"Oh, no! I didna want t' risk him flyin' before we knew what ye would make o' this information."

"Is it so out of the ordinary for these two to be seen together?" Dermott asked. "Perhaps this Forbes was in the employ of Lord Falkirk. Or perhaps they met by chance on the moor and were simply riding together."

"I don't like the looks o' it, whether ye can use it or not," said Queenie a little stubbornly.

"I'm simply trying to look at it from a legal standpoint," said Dermott. "Two men riding together is not enough upon which to base an accusation. And it offers far less evidence than, say, one man's verbal threats upon another's life in front of witnesses—which is the predicament Ian is in."

" 'Tis lookin' like we made a mistake callin' ye all the way from Glasgow," said Queenie.

"Forgive me, Queenie," said Dermott. "And you also, Stevie. I know you meant well. And it may turn out significant in the end.

But what you have discovered is purely—in legal terminology—circumstantial. Before we can level any accusations against anyone, we must examine this from every angle. At this point the only one with a motive for killing George Falkirk is Ian. If only we could establish a motive for someone else! But I'm afraid riding together on a lonely moor is *not* a motive."

"Then we still have nothing," sighed Queenie.

"We may have more than we did a week ago, thanks to you and Stevie," said Dermott with an encouraging smile. "We will just have to see where this leads us. If Falkirk's body had been found upon the moor, we would certainly have opportunity, if not motive. But instead, it was found in the stables at Kairn."

"Forbes could o' been there as easily as Master Ian," Queenie said. "And," she went on, her face brightening as if suddenly remembering something else, "it strikes me as odd that Martin Forbes all at once turned up missin' less'n a week after the killin'."

"Now that *is* interesting!" Dermott mused. "And who would have thought anything of it since no public connection had ever been made between the two? You say whenever they met in the inn they acknowledged no acquaintance?"

"Like perfect strangers, they was."

"Curious. I wonder why they were so careful to conceal their relationship?"

"I'll warrant they was up to no good," said Queenie with a disgusted snort. "That Martin Forbes never did an honest day's work in his life. An' Falkirk—weel, I seen but little o' him. But what I did see, I didna like."

A short silence followed.

"I think I'll ride out to Kairn," he said at length. "Perhaps someone there might have seen something. The last time I only spoke with Falkirk's parents. And I must try to locate that man Duff, the former constable. Where did you say he was from?"

"Culden. But I haven't heard aboot him in a year."

"I must try, though. There may be a reason for his disappearance as well."

Queenie's old gelding plodded determinedly along the tree-lined road leading to the stately manor of Kairn. Dermott was making this trip uncertain how to procede, for his parting with Lady Falkirk upon his last visit had been none too cordial. But if there was anything to uncover here he must not miss it.

Soon the manor sprawled before him. Unlike the austere Stonewycke castle, Kairn looked the part of the country estate it was. Never had an army been mustered here nor a battle fought on these grounds. Nestled among its oaks and surrounded by its expansive green lawns, it offered the picture of peace and solitude, certainly no visible setting for a terrible murder.

Veering away from the front courtyard, Dermott steered his way toward the stables, where the young lord's body had been found. A year had passed, so clearly no clues were still to be found, but it was a place to begin at least. He dismounted and slowly walked inside the stone structure, where the dull winter's midday sky emitted a few streams of light through high narrow windows. The lazy snorts of horses mingled in a pleasant way with the drone of flies. A lad of perhaps thirteen or fifteen was busy currying the gray coat of a fine mare.

"Mornin' t' ye, sir," said the boy.

"Good morning," Dermott replied. "Do you mind if I have a look at the stock?"

"I'm seein' no harm in that," the lad answered, then returned, unconcerned, to his task.

Dermott ambled down the aisles between the stalls. Probably eight or ten animals were housed here, not as many as the stables of the larger estate of Stonewycke could boast, but each was a thoroughbred.

Then Dermott was struck with a thought.

"Lad," he called, "where is the fine golden stallion that used to be housed here?"

"Oh, him," the boy answered. "The laird had him put away right after the yoong master were killed."

"Dear Lord," Dermott breathed. *How much more anguish must there be?* he thought. *It has to stop. I must get to the bottom of this and end the heartbreak! Dear God, guide my steps through this maze.*

"Lad, how long have you worked here in Kairn's stables?" Dermott asked.

"Two . . . three years, sir."

"Then you were here when the young master Falkirk was killed?"

"Aye, sir," replied the boy, squirming perceptibly before this powerful stranger. "But I didna see nothin'," he went on—too quickly, Dermott thought. "Honest! Ye must believe me. I didna!" His voice had risen dramatically as he spoke.

"I always believe the truth," said Dermott slowly, fixing his eyes with all their intensity on the boy.

"Oh, God!" the boy wailed.

"What is it, son?" asked Dermott, fully intrigued. His bearing revealed more fear than could be accounted for even by the lawyer's steady gaze.

"He sent you, I knew it!"

"No one sent me, boy."

"Please don't hurt me, sir!"

"What are you talking about?"

"Ye can trust me. I won't say a word," the lad went on in the same high-pitched voice, ignoring Dermott's question. "Tell him I ne'er said a word t' nobody."

"I won't hurt you." Dermott's voice softened as he perceived the terror in the boy's appeal. "I don't know who you are talking about. Who is it that wants to hurt you?"

"He said he'd kill me if I told."

"But another may die if you do not," said Dermott. "If you are shielding a criminal, it will be God to whom you will have to answer."

"Oh!" the boy wailed mournfully. "I should o' told the other man an' then I wouldna had t' live wi' it all this long year!"

"What other man?"

"The constable what came aroun' right after, ye know, talkin' t' all the servants an' me an' the master an' lady."

"And you told him nothing?"

"I couldna, mister . . . I *couldna*! Oh, God!" the boy cried, "I was scared! He said he'd kill me!"

"So the constable left without any idea of the truth?" asked Dermott.

"He left, but I think he suspected me o' lyin'. I could tell from his questions that he guessed it all. But he said he had t' hae proof an'... Oh, God! I just couldna tell him! I was so scared!"

"And has this other man been around threatening you recently?"

"Na. I hanna seen him in a year."

"Well, the time may have come, boy, for you to tell what you know. Others are suffering because of your silence. Do you understand me?"

The lad stared blankly at Dermott, trembling. Then he slowly nodded.

"I am a lawyer," said Dermott. "I think I can protect you."

"But what'll I do if he finds oot an' comes after me?" wailed the boy.

"God will also be your protector. He always honors the speaking of truth."

A long silence followed. At length the boy slowly began to speak.

"I canna name the man," he said, his voice steadying. "He came here once before ... before that night. He left a note fer Master Falkirk an' told me t' give it t' him. Then another night—it were real late. I was asleep in Donnie's stall—he's one o' my favorites an' was a bit collicky that night. The voices woke me—they was talkin' awful aboot each other, aboot deceivin' an' lyin'. Master Falkirk spit in the other fellow's face an' told him t' git oot an' t' ne'er come back an' that he'd git nothin'. The other fellow flew off in a murderous rage. Then I heard a struggle an' a groan an' then all got deathly quiet. I'd been listenin' so intently that I was payin' no attention t' Donnie, who was restless and kind o' movin' aboot. All at once she stepped on my foot an' I couldna help lettin' oot a yell, as much as I tried t' hide it. That was when he found me. He came int' the stall an' held a knife t' my throat—still red wi' blood it was—an' I knew he was goin' t' kill me right then. But he jist threatened me an' said if I didna keep my mouth shut, he'd come back an' find me an' run me through wi' the knife right through my heart. An' I was so scared I couldna hardly sleep fer a week." He stopped, tears streaming down his cheeks.

Dermott placed his large hand on the boy's shoulder.

"I ne'er meant fer anyone else t' be hurt," said the boy, breaking into a fit of sobbing.

"I believe you, lad. And did the man ever bother you again?"

"No, I never seen him again."

"Only the constable?"

"He was here the very next day. But I was so scared, I couldna tell him. Then when the new constable came aroun', that was some while later, he didn't much seem t' care aboot talkin' t' any o' us."

"And you never saw Constable Duff again?"

The boy shook his head.

Dermott thought a few moments.

"What is your name, lad?"

"Neil, sir."

"Well, Neil, would you help me find this man and bring him to justice?"

Neil shrank back a step. He looked at Dermott a long moment, then sighed deeply. "I'm thinkin', sir," he finally said, "that I best help ye noo, so he won't come back an' kill me."

"That's fine, Neil," said Dermott. "You'll be safe. I just need you to identify the man with the knife. You're the only one who can."

By the following day, as he returned along the solitary country road from the inland village of Culden, a plan was forming in the keen lawyer's mind of Dermott Connell. After much searching and many questions, he had succeeded in locating former constable Angus Duff, exiled to what Duff had termed an "enforced retirement from public service." Dermott's suspicions were confirmed; he had gained Duff's firsthand account of how things stood the day after the murder—including Duff's own inclinations. Now Dermott returned to Port Strathy armed not only with what he hoped would be enough to free his client but with information sufficient to extract concessions, if not admissions, from James Duncan himself.

39 The Beginning of Justice

Dermott's plan was to commence at sunset two days later. When all the necessary arrangements had been made, he sent a message to Martin Forbes. He had to meet him, it said. Forbes could choose the place.

Forbes was initially suspicious. Then it crossed his mind that perhaps his fortunes had changed and that the appearance of this impressive gentleman from the south boded well for him. It was, therefore, with mixed and not altogether pure motives that he chose as their meeting place his favorite haunt at Ramsey Head. Many was the time he had retreated here with his jug of ale, and after the discovery of Falkirk's body he had hidden out in the cave for several days. If for any reason events should turn against him, he could easily elude the gentleman, who would be unfamiliar with the craggy caves and cliffs of the Head. Besides, if all else failed, he had his dinghy tied up on the rocks below. He didn't trust any man in gentle garb, but he was willing to take a chance if it might—for reasons unknown to him in advance—mean a few extra shillings in his pocket.

Dermott was unfamiliar with the place, it is true. But as soon as he had received Forbes's message, he had sent Stevie and Neil to reconnoiter the place and report back to him. He arrived, with Angus Duff and the two lads, an hour before sunset and easily found the mouth of the large cave—more a tunnel through the rocks, as daylight could be seen through from the other end—which Forbes had specified.

Nestled in one of the dark crevices midway through the tunnel, Neil trembled with fear.

As the sun began to set, the light in the opening facing east was quickly dimmed. All became dark and quiet as the setting sun descended in the sky. Dermott began to wonder if perhaps Forbes had gotten wind of the trap which lay in wait for him. Still he did not appear.

At length he heard the scraping of heavy boots.

"Hey you ... Connell!" Forbes shouted from just outside the cave's opening.

"I'm in here, Mr. Forbes," Dermott answered. "Come closer. I must talk with you."

He heard the approach of Forbes's unsteady footfall, and even before he could see his silhouette in the dim, fading light, the stale smell of Queenie's ale assailed him.

"Where are ye? I can't see ye in the dark. Come oot where I can see ye!"

"No, Mr. Forbes. It is I who want to see you. Come in still farther."

"What're ye talkin' aboot?" said Forbes, his confused and muddled brain growing wary of the commanding voice in the darkness. "Hey ... what is this? Connell, ye blighter, let me see yer face!"

"All in due time, Mr. Forbes."

"Where are ye, Connell? ... Why ye jist let me git my hands on ye—"

Forbes's words were cut short as suddenly a brilliant orange shaft of light shot through from the opposite end of the tunnel. Momentarily stunned, Forbes stood stock still, but the light of the setting sun which had receded to a point exactly on a line with the other end of the tunnel fully illuminated his face.

"It's him!" cried Neil. "It's him that killed my master!"

"Why you lyin', double-crossin'—" Forbes began. But he took no time to finish. He spun around to make a retreat, but Dermott stepped quickly forward and loomed in his path. Rage and the growing effects of the alcohol in his body combined to produce terror. Crying out at the sudden sight of what must be a giant in front of him, Forbes turned again and ran toward the western exit where the shaft of light was already fading. But Angus Duff and Stevie Mackinaw blocked his way.

Forbes stood momentarily at bay, his hand seeking the crude dirk at his side.

"Why did you do it, Forbes?" called out Dermott's voice behind him.

"He's a dirty liar!" Forbes snarled. "I didn't kill no one!"

"The lad will swear it was you."

"He didna see nothin'. He was asleep in a stall—" Hardly realizing his blunder, Forbes stopped.

"Perhaps you had your reasons," Dermott said. "George Falkirk was a hard man."

"A dirty, cheatin' rotter—but I'll git what's comin' t' me yet!"

"What did he do to you, Forbes?" Dermott asked, determined to get as much of the story as possible, his voice still calm, though his heart was pounding.

"What'd the likes o' ye care? Ye can't trap me. I know ye can't prove a thing!"

"You've already trapped yourself, Forbes," said Duff, speaking for the first time. "I've heard all I need to bring you to justice. And we have more than enough witnesses."

"I know that voice," snarled Forbes, but even as he spoke he dodged to the right and straight toward Angus Duff. In the darkness, Angus could only barely make out the approach of danger. He dived toward Forbes, but miscalculated the distance and landed only inches from the fugitive. Bumping his head on a projecting rock, the former constable fell unconscious while the fugitive shot through the opening made by Duff's courageous blunder. He had just made it to the western opening of the cave when Dermott caught up with him. Dermott threw his full weight against Forbes, knocking him to the ground.

"He deserved what he got! An' I'll kill ye too!" Forbes yelled. The gleam of metal flashed in his hand.

He slashed wildly with his knife, aiming it upward toward Dermott. In the darkness Dermott saw nothing until he felt the sudden pain of a deep gash in his arm. Forbes was on his feet now and running from the tunnel. By now Stevie and Neil had reached Dermott and were following the wild man where he was making his escape along the top of a precipice toward a trail leading down to his boat.

"No! Boys, stay here! See to Duff. The man's too dangerous. I'll go after him!"

They obeyed. Clutching his arm to stop the flow of blood, Dermott took up the chase.

Forbes had already reached the top of the steep path and was scrambling down the loose rocks toward the sea some fifty feet straight below him.

"Forbes ... Forbes. Stop!" called Dermott. "I didn't come here to try to hurt you. I'm a lawyer. Let me try to help you."

"Help me t' the gallows, ye blighter!" yelled Forbes. "I'll kill ye before I'll go with ye!"

Dermott reached the top of the cliff and could see Forbes struggling down the dark incline inch by inch. He dared not follow. In the gathering darkness it would be too dangerous.

"Forbes," he called out again, "even if you escape from me, you will never evade your crimes. *God* will always haunt you until you repent. Lay yourself at His feet, Forbes, where you will find peace!"

For a brief instant Forbes stopped in his descent, the sentiment of Dermott's unexpected words catching him by surprise.

"It's never too late with the Lord, Martin!" shouted Dermott.

"Ha!" yelled Forbes back up the cliff. "Who'd believe my side o' the story?"

"I would," replied Dermott. "I would try ... and would do all I could for you."

"An' I believe in Broonies!" scoffed the fugitive.

"Think of your family—they need you, Martin!"

Forbes had begun his perilous descent again, but suddenly the rock beneath his foot began to give way. Dermott could hear the rush of loose stones falling into the stormy sea below.

"It was fer them I did it all!" shouted Forbes as he scrambled frantically to regain his foothold, "that they might hae somethin' better in life than me! But now if they canna hae the fortune," he went on, his voice trembling in panic and desperation, "they are better off wi' oot me!"

"What ... Martin! Don't let this keep you—"

But Dermott's words were cut short by a long scream as Forbes's flailing arms and furiously struggling feet lost their hold altogether and he plunged down the side of the cliff into the violent and rocky water below.

Dermott lurched forward, then realized any attempt to descend was futile. He stood for a long moment gazing down into the darkness, staring into the foaming grave of the poor, dejected man, uttering a prayer for him even now. Then Dermott turned and, wrapping his shirt tightly about his wounded arm, plodded back toward the tunnel where the others were waiting for him. His quest was over; Ian would at long last be freed; but he could feel no elation at the successful conclusion of his mission.

40 The Truth Comes Out

The laird had called for Digory.

The long weeks of his illness had stretched to months, and he had never once done so. It had always been Digory knocking tentatively on James's door to ask how he fared. Sometimes the laird's only response was a rude insistence that the groom leave immediately. On other occasions, more and more of late, he would speak to the groom for a few moments.

"Well, come in," he would growl, "before you let all the heat escape into the hall."

Oftentimes James would carry the burden of conversation, talking mostly of the old days. What to him were the "good" days were the times when he was a lad before his father lost his fortune. He also reminisced about his days as a rising young bank executive. His speech became inflated with the arrogance he had carried as a young man. And yet such lapses were not total, for there were other moments when the laird grew pensive.

"That was all before I came to Stonewycke," he might say. "Ah, what hopes I had for this place! But look where it landed me. A fancy bed with silken sheets to die in!"

And Digory would gently reply, "Didna the Book tell us that the rich hae already received their consolation?"

"And so that is all I am to expect?" James would retort.

Then Digory would seize upon such an opportunity to turn the conversation toward the things most dear to his heart, speaking to his master about the love of the God he served. And if James did not fall asleep during the groom's speech, at least he would generally allow Digory to have his say, then gruffly dismiss him. How much he really heard, Digory had no way to guess. But he could not let his master die without having the opportunity to hear and repent.

This morning, as he answered the laird's summons, Digory expected more of the same. He never took offense at the laird's gruffness, especially now. He knew the Word of God would never return without accomplishing the work God had intended for it.

He knocked on the door and the feeble voice which answered from inside the room was noticeably weaker than usual.

"I was afraid," James said after Digory had entered and closed the door, "that if I waited for your next visit, it might be too late."

"What can ye mean, my lord?"

"I mean, I doubt I shall see you tomorrow."

"Oh, my lord, can ye be so sure?" Digory stepped close to the bed and knew when he saw the ghastly pallor on the laird's face that he might indeed have spoken prophetically.

"I doubt it will inconvenience anyone, except that they will have to hastily convene their celebrations."

"Ye canna mean that!" Digory exclaimed, a tender pity in his voice.

"You have been a faithful servant," James said. "Perhaps you shall feel some sorrow..."

"An' Lady Atlanta," added Digory hastily, the tears of grief rising in his eyes. "She will mourn ye."

"I doubt that, Digory. And why should she? I have been a monster in her eyes."

"Oh, my lord," implored Digory. "Ye mustn't talk so."

"It's true. You know it."

"But if ye feel so, then ye still hae time t' make it right, na only wi' Lady Atlanta, but wi' the Lord God also."

"Ha. An old rotter like me? Come now, Digory. I know you've had high hopes for me, with all your preaching. And I haven't minded it so much. But you know my heart is hard as stone."

"Only the heart that's dead, my lord, can be that hard. An' I know yer heart's na dead. I hae seen the longin' fer somethin' more in yer eyes, my lord. Why else would ye hae listened t' all my ramblin's so many times?"

James was silent for a long moment.

Through eyes that glistened with the mingled tears of sadness and hope, the faithful groom looked on, praying for this soul struggling so hard against the birth which would allow him to face death as his Maker had intended.

"If only I could die knowing someone cared," he said at length, in a tone which Digory had never heard from his lips before, a tone which reminded him of sorrow—not sadness, but genuine, remorseful, almost repentant sorrow at what he had been. But before he could continue, a paroxysm of coughing overtook him. When it was finished he lay back on his pillow exhausted. He could not speak for some time.

Digory reached down and took the feeble hand of his master and bowed his head. "Oh, Father, ye only know the mystery o' this moment yer Son called birth an' hoo it prepares us fer the other moment called death. Strengthen yer child, Lord, this child o' yers that ye love. Strengthen him t' give birth t' yer life within him, an' strengthen him t' meet ye t' yer face when that moment o' crossin' the river comes t' him . . ."

When he lifted his head, James was staring at him.

"Ah, I should be happy that at least you care, my friend," said James, his voice now barely audible. "But it is not enough . . . go, will you . . . and find Atlanta . . ."

"Of course, my lord," said Digory rising.

"You'll probably find her crying somewhere. She's become so touchy and sentimental lately . . . God help me, I swore at her this morning . . . Bring her, will you, Digory . . . please . . ."

Atlanta had completed her morning duties. After leaving James several hours before, in tears, she had buried herself in meaningless tasks for distraction's sake to divert her attention.

There had been a time she had believed that Stonewycke could not survive without her. For so many years, especially since her father's death, she had thought that the very earth itself depended upon her for its sustenance. But lately she had not been so sure. She had even begun to wonder if she were nothing but an old matron deceived by her own self-importance. It therefore did not surprise her when she realized that she needed Stonewycke even more than it needed her. The heather-covered hills would continue long after she resided beneath its black loam.

Mortality, she sighed, *is such a hard fact to face.* But at least with it comes the hope of the cares of life ending one day. *I do not deserve more than that,* she thought. But she longed no less for more—for the hope of eternity which makes mortality easier to bear.

"I *am* growing old," Atlanta murmured, shaking her head. "Now I have forgotten what I was about to do."

At that moment a maid hurried up to her.

"M'lady," she said, breathless from her climb up the stairs. "There's a gentleman at the door. He wanted t' see the laird, but I told him his lairdship were seein' na visitors. He said it were important."

"Thank you, Abby," Atlanta replied, "I will tend to it."

The tall, broad-shouldered man standing in the entryway was a stranger to Atlanta, but he knew her immediately. The stately woman in her austere black taffeta stood exactly as Ian had described her to Dermott on many occasions. But even had the lawyer not had the benefit of these descriptive introductions, he would nonetheless have known the marchioness of Stonewycke, for this woman could be no less than the mistress of such a grand estate. Her very bearing reminded Dermott of the stately walls of granite over which she presided.

"I was told you wanted to see Lord Duncan," Atlanta said as she reached Dermott where he stood in the entryway.

"I did, my lady," he replied. "It is a matter of some urgency."

"He is quite ill and receiving no visitors."

"I am truly sorry to hear that he is ill."

"Perhaps I can help you," Atlanta offered.

Dermott quickly appraised Atlanta as she stood awaiting his reply. He wondered how much she knew of James's deception, both with regard to Ian's plight and Duff's disappearance.

"I don't know if you can, Lady Duncan," Dermott replied after a moment. "Or if I would be within my rights to beg for your help. You see, my business concerns your son-in-law, Ian Duncan."

Atlanta sighed heavily. "Even in his death, he will not give us peace. But I suppose we little deserve it."

"Then it is as I supposed, that you are in the dark concerning Ian's condition. I had hoped after my last visit, the laird might have been induced to tell you."

"My husband is dying, sir," Atlanta replied. "We have not ... talked ... about Ian in some time. How can you be apprised of situations in my family of which I am not?"

"Forgive me, Lady Duncan. My name at least I can give you. I am Dermott Connell, a lawyer from Glasgow."

"Then, Mr. Connell, perhaps you should acquaint me with these conditions, as you call them, of which you are so well informed."

"I am reluctant, because I would not want it to appear I have come to speak ill of your husband behind his back."

Atlanta's taut lips bent into a slight smile, whether from humor, bitterness, or sadness Dermott could not immediately discern.

"You need not spare me, Mr. Connell," she said. "I well know my husband's shortcomings. And as he is thus indisposed, it is time I became familiar with his affairs, especially where they concern my late son-in-law."

"My lady, I came here to inform the laird that I have found George Falkirk's murderer. And it is not, as many have supposed, your son-in-law. Young Falkirk was killed by one of Port Strathy's more unsavory characters, who was apparently in the employ of Falkirk—although the motives are still obscure."

"Thank God!" said Atlanta, closing her eyes and showing more emotion than she yet had. "At least we can take comfort that she did not marry a murderer. But little good it will do her—or poor Ian—now."

"I do not know about your daughter, my lady. But Ian shall benefit greatly from this discovery. He is not your *late* son-in-law, Lady Duncan. Ian lives, and will be free the moment I reach Glasgow."

"Alive!" exclaimed Atlanta. "But we were so certain! There was an official document ... a fire ... How can this be?"

"It was carefully conceived—"

"Say no more, Mr. Connell," Atlanta interrupted, as the full impact finally struck her. "I understand now. I will not place you in the position of, as you say, 'speaking ill' of my husband."

She turned toward the stairs to hide her rising emotions. She laid a trembling hand on the oaken rail. "Even I could not guess at how far he was willing to go in order to secure his ambitions," she said softly. "And yet, I can feel no rage. Knowing he is dying . . . somehow I can no longer look upon him as the evil man in reality I know he was. And perhaps it is because I can scarcely any longer feel . . . anything."

"Perhaps it is also that you feel tender toward a man who now only has death to look forward to."

"How can you know that, Mr. Connell?"

"I can only guess."

"You are not far from the mark."

At that moment, Digory appeared at the top of the stairs. Atlanta glanced up at the bent frame of the trusted servant. She knew even before he spoke why he had come.

"The laird, my lady," Digory said. "He's wantin' t' see ye."

Atlanta closed the door softly behind her. She wondered if James was already dead; he appeared so gaunt and shrunken. A knot formed in her throat, but she bit back the rising emotion and inched forward. What were these feelings? Was it pity at seeing her once powerful adversary now so helpless, so wasted? It surely could not be affection for the man.

"Atlanta," came James's feeble voice. "You have come."

"Of course," she replied. "You called for me."

"But you did not have to come. I should hardly have expected it."

"James, let us not spar just now."

"I would not . . . not now . . . wife . . ." James lifted his white hand to her. "Come and sit by me."

Atlanta moved a chair near the bed, then seated herself and took the proffered hand.

"I have been the devil to you," he whispered at length. "Is it enough to ask forgiveness?"

"Don't, James. It is not necessary."

"Ah, but nothing is more necessary. I have been cruel. I grasped for all the wrong things—"

His voice caught on a cough. He gripped Atlanta's hand as if to gain the strength from it to live just a moment longer.

"...But I threw away the best things. And now...I shall never have them back...and that...is my terrible punishment."

"God shall make it right," Atlanta heard herself saying.

"Yes. So Digory assures me. And I can almost believe it now. But there is one more thing...I have—have...deceived you about—our son-in-law..."

"I know all about that," said Atlanta tenderly.

"And still you came?...will he...can it be—how can I undo it now?"

"It's all taken care of."

"Atlanta...will you see that Ian...is provided for?"

Atlanta nodded. It took all her strength now to maintain her composure.

"And Maggie..."

James swallowed as the words had become almost impossible to form.

"Little Maggie...what did I do to you?...how shall I ever ...Atlanta...wrote us...I've got to—"

"Yes, yes. James, I'll write her," assured Atlanta, now choking back the sobs.

"No...no—she..." he murmured. "She—oh, Atlanta. I'm going—I have to tell you...apology to make. Atlanta, she—"

He could not finish the sentence. The glow faded from his eyes as the last breath of air left his body forever. He was dead.

Slowly the grip of his bony fingers loosened on Atlanta's hand. But she kept her fingers wrapped around his, though she knew all life had gone from him. Finally, as a single desolate tear inched down her cheek, she bent over and kissed her husband.

41 Securing the Future

James was gone. Atlanta could accept that. But what continued to gnaw deeply at her was the awful reality that from the moment she had known James, she had never once told him she loved him.

Perhaps she never *had* loved him. But what consolation could there be in that? That only made the ache of the realization more painful. What might have been if they had loved each other? If only . . .

Atlanta sat in her dayroom and looked about.

Everything was empty now, barren of life. Even the elegant furnishings which surrounded her brought pain. She remembered when she had purchased them so many years ago. She and James had traveled to Italy—before Maggie was born. James, of course, had been absorbed with business and she had spent her time in the shops. She was younger then, and such things had held a magnetizing allure for her. After searching through a great many shops she had at last found a set she had fallen in love with and immediately ordered the delicate furnishings for her own little dayroom. James found the purchase frivolous but was indulgent.

Were we even vaguely happy then? Atlanta wondered.

No. For instantly she recalled how piqued James had become with her less-than-amiable reception of some duke whose favor he had been currying. The fat, double-chinned man was a pompous fool, and Atlanta had had no intention of patronizing such a person.

No, there could have been no love between them. They were pursuing their own interests and stubbornly refused to budge from their own ways to accommodate the other.

"Oh, dear Lord!" Atlanta agonized. "Why was I so selfish? If only I had given just a little then, I would have more than some spindly furniture to comfort me now . . ."

But she could not finish, for a choking sob rose in her throat, followed by another and another until terrible sobs shook her entire body. Atlanta held out her hands in confused supplication as one totally unaccustomed to the agony of tears. As they mounted she could not control them, and they issued forth unchecked. Tears continued to wash down her face as her shoulders convulsed. She clenched her hands and unconsciously began pounding her fists against the desk where she sat. But still the tears would not abate.

All her past failures rose to confront her. And now the most terrible thing of all glared at her with a stark reality she had never seen: For the sprawling parcel of dirt and trees and moorland and valley called Stonewycke, she had sacrificed everything—love, children, husband, friends, happiness. *Everything!* And in the end would even the cold earth comfort her? No, for she had sacrificed her right to be comforted. She had nothing!

If only she had been able to say the simple words *I love you.* Would James then have fought so hard to protect himself? Would he then have needed to strip her of his greatest threat—their daughter?

Oh, Maggie, it was my fault, not his! For I drove him to it. He was my husband and I refused to love him . . . all for what?

Suddenly Atlanta pulled her distraught frame straight in the chair. She allowed one more sob to escape her lips, then she tightened those white lips and would cry no more. *I have been mourning too long . . . a lifetime,* she thought. *Now I must give it up for at least one act of love.*

She rose from her chair, went to a nearby secretary where she pulled out a clean white sheet of paper. Taking her pen and dipping it into the jar of ink, she began to write. How it would find its way to her daughter she did not know. She would have to think of that later. For now all she knew was that the letter must be written.

"My dear daughter Margaret . . ." she began.

Thirty minutes later, Atlanta rose from the secretary. Tears had once more assailed her and she could not finish the letter. She carefully folded it and, glancing about the room for a suitable place to put it until she could return to it, finish it, and send it, her eyes fell upon the old family Bible on her shelf. She walked toward it and laid her hand upon it.

"Oh, Lord," she murmured, "you know we didn't make much

use of this. But Maggie used to enjoy my reading to her from it."

Slowly Atlanta opened the Bible. It fell open in the Psalms. She tenderly placed the half-completed letter to her daughter inside. "Protect her, God. And keep this letter in your care until it shall find its way to her. Amen." Atlanta closed the book, turned, and walked to a bookshelf on the opposite wall where she retrieved a key from among the books. She then returned to the desk she had been at earlier and unlocked the bottom drawer. She took from it an envelope containing a single yellowed document. Then she dropped the key in the drawer.

"No need to lock this; there is nothing to hide anymore," she said.

The paper she held in her hand was very old. She had discovered it a number of years ago hidden in an ancient chest. At first it had appalled her and frightened her. Yet it had also intrigued her.

As she had examined it and investigated its origins, she more and more realized what a powerful document it was, especially as a weapon against one such as her own husband. Ever since, she had held it over James as a constant threat and an ever-present reminder of the lengths she was prepared to go in order to keep Stonewycke intact, safe, and out of his greedy clutches. He had never seen the paper, and she had only hinted of its contents to him. But it had served her purpose well, and had kept James and his schemes in check. Her own grandfather Anson had drawn up the document, and Atlanta trembled each time she realized that he would have invoked it had not sudden death prevented him. The date on the paper was merely a few days prior to his untimely accident.

What made Atlanta tremble even more was how close *she* had come to using it. But now, as her final, perhaps her only act of love toward the man she had married, she would destroy the paper altogether. For James's sake she would allow Alastair his share in the inheritance. He had been a son to her almost since the moment of his birth; even he himself did not know she was not his mother. He was James's son, so if Maggie did not return one day to claim Stonewycke as Atlanta had promised she should, then Alastair would have it. For James's sake, she would not invoke the powerful document against his son.

From a drawer Atlanta took a match, struck it, and held it to the paper, poised to reduce to ashes all evidence of Anson's deed.

Anson . . .

Suddenly the thought of her grandfather swelled in her mind. She had always had such a deep loyalty and respect for him, though she had never known him. How could she destroy his legacy, how could she destroy something he had held dear? This paper was a constant reminder of how deep the love for the land ran in Ramsey blood—and a reminder, too, of the capability that very love had to destroy. She could never let it destroy again.

Atlanta blew out the match.

No, she could not burn this paper. Anson was blood of her blood, bone of her bone. He was a *Ramsey*, as she was a Ramsey. Whatever amends she might make in death to the husband she had despised in life, she could not thereby destroy the deepest petitions of her own grandfather.

Another sob of anguish caught in Atlanta's throat. She was torn between strong conflicting motives, uncertain where to turn. "Dear Lord," she cried, "if only my Maggie would return . . . But she is in your hands. Oh, God! And so is my Stonewycke. You love this land and its people, and you will always do right for them. If only I could have realized that long ago . . . *Oh, Lord, take care of Maggie and Stonewycke!*"

Suddenly a resolve came to Atlanta. She would neither destroy the paper nor invoke it. She would hide it! But not among her own things, where it would be looked for and could easily be found.

She left the dayroom, still clutching the paper. In the hallway she glanced in both directions, and finding it deserted, she stole down the short distance to the next room. There she opened the door and entered the room where Maggie had spent her childhood. The room sparked in Atlanta all the emotions she had been fighting so hard to ignore—pain, bitterness, love, loss . . . and now longing.

But this room also represented the small bit of happiness she had known. What better place to seal up the past and step into a future where love might somehow be found?

42 Ian

Dermott remained in Port Strathy long enough to attend James's funeral. He was buried quietly with only immediate family and household servants in attendance, laid in the Ramsey crypt— at which even the vicar registered some surprise. But Atlanta was firm in her resolve that at least his body should rest peacefully in the one place which had remained elusive to him during his life.

So the man was laid to rest and Dermott set out to fulfill his final wish concerning Ian's care. Atlanta considered going to Glasgow herself, but in the end she chose to stay. "The most I can do for him now," she sighed, "is to allow him the chance to forget Stonewycke and those of us who so misused him. Let him begin his life anew, perhaps even find his Maggie."

Inclement weather had beached the schooner, and Dermott was forced to take the snow-encrusted inland roads. The trip was a long and weary one, and a fortnight passed before he finally beheld the pleasant house at George Square. What a contrast to the grim granite walls of Stonewycke!

It was late evening but still a lamp burned in the drawing room. Elijah was sitting by the fire, a book in his lap, his head nodding in a restless doze. At the sound of Dermott's step he raised his head and turned toward his friend.

"Ah, good evening, lad!" The doctor greeted Dermott as if he had only stepped out for several hours rather than having been gone a month. "I've always been so intrigued by Apuleius's *Metamorphoses*, but I'm afraid in my old age it sometimes only puts me to sleep."

"It's good to see you, Elijah," Dermott said. Unconsciously tears rose in his eyes. He possessed so very much, and at this moment he realized how often he took it all for granted.

"Come and sit down, if you are not too fatigued."

"I have never been so fatigued," Dermott replied, taking a seat near Elijah's. "So tired that I long for the rest a conversation with you always affords."

"So . . . you had a difficult time of it then?"

"Sometimes I forget the hellish depths our separation from God can bring us to," sighed Dermott wearily. "It is both the price and reward of redemption to forget. Yet in His mercy God occasionally allows us to see again how those outside His love suffer, to remember how we suffered when we were without Him."

"But you and I both know the suffering does not end the moment we give our hearts to Him," said Elijah.

"That is true, my friend, but at least it is a suffering with hope. But for all the difficulty of my trip, God was glorified in a most marvelous way. I have confidence that one of the hardest of hearts turned to Him in the end. And"—here Dermott brightened as some of the weariness fell from him—"the best piece of news is that my young prisoner will be free!"

"God be praised!" said Elijah.

They both fell into a restful silence for some moments until Elijah suddenly jumped from his chair. "I nearly forgot! A message arrived for you some days ago. I set it on the mantel over there." He retrieved the letter and brought it to Dermott.

The message had clearly traveled some distance to reach him. He was reminded of the last letter he had received from Queenie. It too had been travel-stained and had borne good tidings. Perhaps this would do likewise.

He broke the seal and removed the pages of the letter. As he read his face grew somber. When he finished, he leaned heavily back into the chair while his hand dropped limply at his side, the paper falling to the floor.

"When will the heartache end?" he sighed deeply. "How can I bring this news to the woman I just left behind? It will crush her. Yet she will have to be told. Oh, Lord!" Dermott sighed again, then closed his eyes.

When Dermott had first met Ian, he had enlisted the help of an acquaintance in America to conduct a search for the young man's wife. After many dead ends and false leads, the man had at last learned of Margaret Duncan's fate through relatives of the Mackinaws whom he had located in central New York state.

She had, indeed, traveled west in a covered wagon with the Mackinaws. But they had been beset by Indians somewhere west of the Great Divide and, save for a handful of survivors, all had been killed, including Margaret Duncan and her child. A list of survivors had been printed in an eastern newspaper, which was included in the correspondence to Dermott. Drew Mackinaw and his family were listed. Margaret Duncan was not. *At least the news will comfort Stevie,* thought Dermott.

"I had hoped to bring a man the joy of freedom," he said at last, "and the hope, however slim, of being reunited with his wife. But now, what can I tell him? This will destroy him altogether!"

"Is he not in God's hands?" Elijah said. "You once said that God's higher purpose went beyond restoring Ian to his wife."

"Yes, but that was before ..."

"Before you knew of a certainty that was not God's purpose?"

Dermott sighed. "Yes ... you are right. My own shallow faith is revealed again."

"God cares more to reconcile Ian to himself than to his wife. God's purpose is higher, further-reaching. Who can know what healing He will work in Ian's heart through this heartache? And who can fathom what He might have done in Margaret Duncan's life through this tragedy? Many prayers have been prayed. And none will go unanswered. Forgiveness, Dermott, is one of the great lessons of life. People like Ian, or Margaret Duncan ... people like you and me. All people, Dermott, must humbly come to the point of being able to forgive others the wrongs they have done them, forgive themselves for their own sin, and even forgive God for what we perceive as the cruel hand of fate working against us."

Elijah paused and looked intently at his young friend. "It is this forgiveness which lies at the root of repentance and opens the way for the life He would give us. This is now Ian's great opportunity. After such forgiveness, out of the ashes of the fires of bitterness and remorse, one is able to rise up with new light in his eyes, then to move forward into the abundant life spoken of by the Apostle John."

"But how does one such as Ian forgive? Only God in a man's heart can make such a miracle happen. Yet without forgiveness, who can approach God?"

"Another of the mysteries of our faith, Dermott," Elijah said, his eyes reflecting the glow of the dying fire. "We *can't* forgive without God's help. Yet to avail ourselves of His power requires a letting go, a turning away from the past, an attitude of forgiveness. I suspect God's help is already there before any change is made—prompting, urging, strengthening. And then His presence grows ever more keen the more of our *selves* we lay at the altar."

"Ah, Elijah," replied Dermott, "deep indeed are the mysteries of walking with Him in faith. Deep, yet practical. The choices remain ours, do they not?"

"We shall never understand God's ways. But you are right, it is practical. The lad must have a chance to make his own choice in life, Dermott. And perhaps the lesson God desires to teach him is that to choose God during and in spite of adversity *is* the higher purpose. At least for this lad who seems so much like the 'wave of the sea' spoken of by the Apostle James. He has been driven to and fro with every variance of the wind. And the time has come for him to learn to stand firm in the midst of the storm. Perhaps he never could have learned that any other way. Only the Lord knows that. But is that not what life really is about, rather than fleeting happiness and worldly peace?"

"Thank you, Elijah, for speaking truth," responded Dermott humbly. "I think I fear telling Ian about his wife as much for the pain it will cause me as it will cause him. But he must know."

Dermott rose, left his friend, and climbed the steps to his room. There, notwithstanding the weariness of his body, he spent the next hour in prayer for the task which he would face with the dawn of morning.

Dermott glanced around him as he neared the corner of Trongate and Saltmarket. The stone walls of the shops and businesses with their soot-blackened walls were almost appalling in their ugliness compared to the lovely countryside he had recently left. Yet even their filthiness reminded him of Elijah's words and he was strengthened. A man's heart need not be affected by such temporal things as his surroundings or his lot in life.

Dermott had learned all too graphically that even a lovely countryside could breed pain and suffering. The circumstances of life were *not* in themselves life, but only the means through which a person finds true Life. Every person's unique life breeds distinctive circumstances—some pleasant, others painful. But it was the response of each individual heart to the circumstances confronting it which was the substance of life—the very essence of what that person was and was becoming.

Dermott turned into the ancient prison where first he sought out the warden. Feigning shock at Dermott's presentation of the case, the man denied any part in the deception. But once having seen the affidavit from the ex-constable, two or three other signed eyewitness accounts, and a brief letter from the marchioness of Stonewycke herself, the man quickly scurried about to make himself agreeable to the lawyer—especially after learning of James's death. Dermott had suspected the warden's role in the duplicity all along, but that was hardly his primary interest at present. It was enough that he gave Dermott permission to see the prisoner while he arranged the details of his release.

Jerry shuffled ahead of Dermott down the narrow, worn stairs, then through several long dark corridors until they stood before the iron door of Ian's cell.

The door creaked open and Ian looked up sluggishly.

"I thought you had deserted me," came his dry, rusty voice from the dim interior of the cell.

"No, lad. I would never do that," Dermott replied, his voice already choked with emotion at seeing Ian once again. "I have some good news for you, but there is terrible news as well—heartbreaking news."

"I have come to expect it," said Ian with forlorn resignation.

Dermott sighed, then went on. "Ian, I have been to Port Strathy again. That is why you have seen nothing of me for these past several weeks. I didn't want to tell you before I left for fear of raising your hopes. But, Ian, I have at last found George Falkirk's murderer."

Ian started forward. "Then I am *not* guilty! Thank God!" He bowed his head in his hands and began to weep. "I shall be freed?"

"Yes, Ian. As soon as the proper authorities are notified and the details are all arranged. I have already seen to it."

"Free! I can find her now..."

Ian stood, his weakened body pulsing with sudden energy. "We'll be together at last. You were right ... about God, you know. You were right! He *does* have His hand on us." A smile lit his face. "How can I ever thank you, dear friend?"

Dermott could not respond. His mouth had gone dry in the agony of what lay ahead.

"When shall I get out?" Ian went on.

"Ian ..." Dermott tried to say, "... Ian, please sit down ... there is more."

Surmising impending ruin from his tone, Ian slowly sank back to his chair.

Dermott drew a deep breath and tried to continue. "Ian, I have received a letter from America—from an acquaintance who was searching for Maggie ..."

He closed his eyes, but the tears had already risen in them. He sighed again. "Ian ... your wife and child have been killed."

For a moment there was no response. Then slowly Ian began to shake his head in bewilderment.

"No ... no ... it can't be true. There has been a mistake."

"I'm so sorry, Ian. Here's the letter."

"I don't want to see any letter!" Ian shouted. *"It's not true!* It's someone else! I had no child ..."

"The letter explains it. The child was born after Maggie reached America."

"Oh, God ... no!" Ian wailed.

Dermott rose and went to Ian, but Ian shoved him away.

"Leave me alone!" Ian cried. "You were supposed to find her. You liar! He has bought you, too! I knew it! You want to keep me from her. But you won't! He won't win!"

"Ian ... please," Dermott implored. "No one wants to keep you from Maggie. James Duncan is dead—he has nothing to do with this. Oh, Ian ... I'm so sorry."

Once more he reached out to the desolate young man.

But Ian tensed and moved away slowly until his back pressed against the cold stone.

"God!" The word choked past his lips with loathing.

"Don't, Ian!" Dermott pleaded. "God loves you. He will help you through this. He is the only one who can."

"Don't talk to me of love!"

But even as he spoke a terrible look of reproach stole onto his face. Even in the dim light Dermott could detect the anguish of some horrible guilt passing behind Ian's eyes in the window of his soul. "I'll tell you about *love*," he went on in a dramatically altered tone. "Love sent her away, alone, helpless ... to her death. It was *me*. I killed her!" he cried, and the words reverberated against the cold walls of the prison.

But before the echo had died away Ian crumpled to the floor. "I killed her," he whimpered. "I killed her ... I killed her ..." At last the only sounds from his mouth were helpless, moaning sobs and inarticulate whimpering.

Ian was released the following day. He had not spoken since Dermott had left him. The lawyer dressed him in the new clothes he had provided as if he were a child, then led him out of the prison as he might a dumb beast.

He was taken to the house on George Square where he was surrounded by all the love Dermott and Elijah Townsend could give. But still Ian did not speak. Guided by Dermott, he went through the motions of living. For two weeks there was nothing in his face or eyes to indicate life.

One night as Dermott drifted off to sleep, a vision rose before his eyes—a vision of himself, walking slowly through a cemetery shortly after dusk. All was still and quiet. Through the ancient tombstones he walked, not pausing to read the inscriptions, moving straight ahead as if with some mission. In the distance he saw a mound of earth. Closer Dermott walked. The mound of earth was freshly dug; beside it was a deep grave, awaiting its new owner. Near the grave was a long, flat, cold slab of white marble. But as he moved closer he saw that a body lay flat on its back on the slab. The body was cold as the night and as deathly still as the air around him. It had been laid out for burial. Closer he came. All at once he saw the face. It was Ian!—his youthful frame shrouded in death. On his chest were great splotches of blood! In his anguish at the sight Dermott tried to cry out, but no sound would come. Like Ian, his tongue was held in check. He reached out his hand toward the pale face ...

Dermott suddenly woke, breathing deeply, sweat pouring off his face and chest, his body trembling.

He jumped from his bed and raced from the room to that on the next floor where Ian slept. Dermott flung the door open and saw Ian poised on the edge of his bed with a knife aimed at his chest.

"No, Ian!" Dermott screamed, rushing forward.

Ian raised his head and turned toward the advancing form. In his eyes glowed the same confused desperation which had first arrested Dermott's attention the day he had come upon him in the hall of the prison.

Gently Dermott pried the knife from his clenched fist, then held the weeping boy in his arms. It was a long while before Ian's tears subsided. Finally Dermott helped him back to bed, where he fell into a troubled sleep.

Dermott did not leave his side again that night, or thereafter for three weeks.

One morning the sky dawned blue and the air was crisp with the hope of spring. As the sun streamed in upon him Ian sat up in his bed. He glanced toward Dermott, reading at the opposite side of the room. Without warning he swung his feet out of bed and walked over to the window and threw open the shutters.

"Ah, the sun is shining!" he exclaimed. "Soon the flowers will be in bloom!"

Dermott stared speechless.

"It was a dreary winter," Ian continued. "I shall be glad to see it behind us." Then turning to Dermott, he said, "Have you my breakfast ready yet? I'm starved."

Seeing no visible motion from Dermott's chair, he added, "See here ... are you awake? I'm not paying you to just sit there, you know."

Finally Dermott forced himself to speak. "Ian, are you ... are you all right?"

"Never better, my man!" Ian replied with a boisterous laugh. "Never better! But it must have been some drunk I was on last night—I can't remember a thing! Tell me, what time was it when they brought me in?"

Dermott rose to his feet and descended, followed by Ian's light step behind him.

"Funny, I don't exactly recognize this place," he said. "But I suppose it must be some design of my father's to keep me off the streets. Well, no matter, it seems pleasant enough. Do you work for my father, my good man?"

With noncommittal reply Dermott arranged for Ian's breakfast, then went to Elijah's room to explain the latest developments in Ian's behavior.

They concluded, at length, simply to continue caring for Ian as tenderly as possible, allowing time for his subconscious to work its way through the trauma and slowly back to present reality. For the remainder of that day Ian's mood remained elated yet subdued, and he spoke freely of past events in his life as if they had taken place that very week.

So day after day, in days that eventually stretched into weeks, Ian's conscious mind had obliterated an entire year and a half of his lifetime. He could not face the pain of loss; he could not face God; thus he went through the motions of life as if his sojourn to Scotland had never existed. At times he might lapse into terrible bouts of despondency, at which times he threatened violence, both to himself and to others. But like his youthful binges, these were usually slept off and were replaced by an exuberant mood the following day. He showed little inclination to read, yet seemed content to loiter about the house, taking walks from time to time. As spring gave way to summer Dermott exposed him to more and more of Glasgow, even taking him on an occasional call to the prisons. But no recognition showed on the lad's face, even there.

His father would not have him back in London, so he continued on for some time in Glasgow. In late summer Atlanta came for a visit. He greeted her as a stranger. His forlorn condition tore at the woman's heart. When she was about to leave the following day, he said, "I shall have to visit this Stonewycke of yours one day." She turned her face and nearly wept.

They did not often mention Stonewycke or Port Strathy, but when the words came out in conversation, they appeared to have no effect on him. One afternoon he walked into the library as Dermott and Elijah were speaking of Maggie.

"Who are you talking about?" Ian asked, and only a slight wrinkling of his brow in momentary confusion gave indication that anything had stirred within him at the mention of her name.

But along with the pain, Ian had also obliterated the good—that which might have been able to comfort him and lead him to the One who would never stop reaching out to him, no matter how far he tried to hide within his mind.

43 Maggie

Maggie gazed out the window.

What a wonderful sight it was to see Samuel and little Eleanor together! He rolled a bright red ball across the grass, and with squeals of delight she grabbed it—whenever she didn't tumble over in the attempt, giggling more than ever—to toss it back.

At two she was a beautiful child, with deep brown eyes and golden curls so like her father's. Sometimes Maggie's heart fluttered with a dull ache when she looked on her daughter. But more often she would just delight in her, thankful to God that she had been given such a blessed heritage from the man she had loved.

Three years was a long time. But it was not long enough to quell the pain that still surfaced in Maggie's heart. Yet healing was taking place—a healing of her heart *and* her spirit. With Samuel's help and the growing delight of little Eleanor, it was happening.

They had left the little garrison on the Platte the spring following the news of the Bannock massacre and had returned to the surer and somewhat more civilized protection of Fort Laramie. The Indian trouble that year had been so severe that it was unthinkable to leave the confines of the fort. During the winter of her first year, Eleanor had come down with pneumonia, and travel from the plains was again impossible.

Samuel had gradually developed a ministry among the Indians, teaching them what medical practices they could grasp. Although the majority of the Sioux were hostile, many came to trust Dr. Carpenter. But Samuel would no doubt have remained even without such work, for a great bond had developed in his heart for Maggie and her daughter. The terms of their relationship had remained unspoken, each gaining comfort and security from the other without burdening themselves with attempted definitions.

This hot, dry land was certainly nothing like Maggie's Scotland. But perhaps that change further hastened the healing process. For some time after her letter to her parents she had waited, first in anticipation, then in growing despair, for an answer. But as the months had passed and no return letter had come, a startling realization had slowly dawned upon Maggie: perhaps she really *could* begin a new life here in America, with all the pain from the past erased! Perhaps, after all, she was now a woman—able to stand fully on her own with the ties completely severed to homeland, house, even parents.

She continued to tell herself that someday she would return to Scotland. But yet when she learned of the death of the marchioness of Stonewycke from a Scottish immigrant working on the new railroad several years later, she realized there was no longer any reason to return. She would always love Stonewycke. But with Ian gone and her mother gone and her daughter growing up as an American, the estate would have no life for her any longer. Her future was here.

There remained, however, a dull ache in her soul. Something was still not right. She could not identify it. And though she asked the Lord to remove it, almost as a "thorn in the flesh" the melancholy remained. She had learned to smile again, but the smile was incomplete and still did not touch her innermost heart.

On this summer day Maggie was quietly reflective as she watched the play on the scraggly lawn draw to a close. Exhausted from chasing the ball, Samuel had caught up the child and was carrying her in his arms toward the house.

"This little bundle of energy has worn her old Uncle Samuel out!" he exclaimed, then sank into a chair at the table. To the accompaniment of Eleanor's pleasant chattering they ate lunch; though toward the end of the meal the doctor grew unusually quiet. When they had finished, Samuel pushed back his chair with a look of purpose on his face.

"Margaret," he said, "I have something I must speak to you about."

"What is it?" asked Maggie as she began cleaning up after Eleanor.

"We have known each other for some time now," he began. "It is amazing how circumstances—though of course we know *Who* controls circumstances—bring things about that might never have happened otherwise."

He paused, searching for the right words.

"Well, in the time we have been together, I have grown closer to you than I have been to anyone since my late wife."

Slowly Maggie returned to the table and sat down.

"What I'm trying to say, Margaret, is that—I—I wish to take care of you."

"You *have* taken care of Eleanor and me," Maggie said. "We could never have survived out here without you."

"But times are changing," he went on. "It was different when this frontier was peopled with only Indians and soldiers. But with the gold strike on, the Sweetwater has brought in hordes, not only prospectors, but families. Nebraska's near statehood. Wyoming's now a territory. More people than ever are moving west to settle. Don't you see what I'm getting at ... people tend to talk—"

"And you care about the opinions of strangers?" said Maggie.

"No, of course not!" he burst out. "Oh, I'm afraid I'm going about this all wrong," he sighed. "I don't care about what others think of *me*. It is *you*, Margaret, and *your* reputation I am concerned with. But it's more than that ... *Maggie, I love you!*"

With the words he leaned back in his chair, seemingly more exhausted than he had been from his play with Eleanor.

"I—I don't know what to say, Samuel." Now Maggie's color had paled too. It was lost on her that for the first time since the birth of Eleanor, he had called her by the name Ian had always used.

"Perhaps," said Samuel cautiously, "it is too much for me to hope for. And I know I can never take Ian's place. But, Maggie ... do you think—that is, could you ever want to spend the rest of your life with me? Could you ... would you be my wife?"

Maggie took a deep breath, but it did little to clear the whirling emotions inside her brain. She cared for Samuel, but this was something she had never expected. She had loved Ian so much that even after three years she could not let go of that love. She didn't *want* to let go of it. How, then, could she give herself to another?

"Otherwise," Samuel went on, "it seems that perhaps the time has come for me to move on. You and Eleanor are situated here and it might be best for you if I—"

"Move on!" interrupted Maggie. "Samuel, you're not thinking of leaving us if ... if I...?"

"I just thought it would be in your best interests, you know, so you and Eleanor could get on with your life without having to worry about me."

"Oh, Samuel, we need you. I—I don't know about marriage. It's so unexpected—but don't you know how much you mean to me? I don't care what people might say."

The doctor leaned back in his chair and was silent for a few moments. At length he spoke in a quiet and thoughtful tone.

"It's strange," he said, "how God brings people together. Here we are out in the middle of the American wilderness. I'm years older than you. You're in a foreign land trying to raise a daughter thousands of miles from your family. We're both so alone. And yet here we are. God has given me to care for you, and both you and little Eleanor to add a sparkle of joy to my life. Margaret, I know neither I nor anyone else can ever take Ian's place. But if you'll have me I would be honored to watch over you—either as a husband, or like the father and brother you left behind."

The mention of her father and Alastair sent Maggie's thoughts spinning once again. Suddenly she realized that she had grown closer to Samuel than anyone except Ian. Her real family had been left behind, and all at once she was aware of how deep had grown the bonds of attachment she felt toward Samuel. But she still loved Ian and could never let go of that love. How, then, could she commit herself to another?

But almost the same instant a tiny voice inside her seemed to say: *It will never be required of you to let go of your love for Ian.*

Just as I gave you this good doctor to see you through a difficult time, though you did not know he was sent from Me, so I will yet— though you know not how—use your love for Ian in that work I intended for it. In the meantime, I have given you into the care of this righteous man, who will watch over you and protect you in this new land which is now your home.

"Please stay," said Maggie at length. "But can you just give me some time? I just don't think now is ... that is, perhaps the time will come when—"

He reached out and touched her arm. "I understand," he said. "You don't have to explain."

"But do stay," Maggie continued. "I don't think I could face life here without you."

"You want me to keep being little Eleanor's 'uncle'—whatever people may think?"

"Of course I do," replied Maggie. "You are our family now— more a father and brother to me than even blood can make. You have helped me find contentment in my life. But if you should go away..."

"I don't want to."

"Then stay—if you do not mind sharing a part of *us* with Ian."

"I would be content to occupy whatever small corner he would leave me," said Samuel.

"Oh, Samuel!" said Maggie, "thank you. Thank you for understanding."

44 Journey's End

Three months passed, and Samuel sensed a storm brewing in Maggie's spirit. Then the crisis broke.

For two days the distress in her soul had been growing. Whatever lay at its root was clearly coming to a head, though Maggie was still at a loss to know the source of the trouble.

She awakened in the middle of the night, breathing hard, overcome with a great sense of depression. In vain she tried to recapture the peace of sleep, but instead tossed about until the gray dawn of morning began to light the eastern sky.

Throughout the morning the oppression grew. She became sullen and morose, irritable both with Samuel and Eleanor.

By midafternoon she became restless, almost frantic. She had to get out of the house—away. She asked Samuel to watch Eleanor, then headed toward the creek, running like one in flight trying to elude hounds on her trail. Across the footbridge she flew and up the rise on the other side, toward the distant hills.

Halfway up the nearest in the succession of steepening hills, she knew *Who* was chasing her. But still she did not slacken her pace. By the peak of the second hill she knew *why* He was pursuing her, His surgeon's scalpel poised to inflict the mortal wound in her heart which she so long had feared.

Still she ran on. *No . . . no!* she thought. *I can't do it! I shouldn't have to do it!*

A hundred yards farther she stopped.

She knew she could no longer hold His insistent Spirit at bay. She had told Him, in numerous prayers during the past two years, to do His work in her, to give her more faith. But whenever He had suggested *this,* she had quickly shut the door to His intrusions. Samuel had told her that the one thing we hold back, the one thing we refuse to give Him, is the one thing which can open the door to the richness of further blessing.

Still she had resisted.

But He was now finally—today—bent on having His way with her.

Maggie turned from the path and walked slowly toward a small grove of trees which shaded the grassy hillside.

"Oh, Lord," she whispered in quiet desperation, "I can't . . . I can't!"

With the words came the answer she dreaded. Yet she knew it was His voice, and that she could not escape:

You must, my child. It is the only way into the fullness of the life I have prepared for you. It is the only way.

On Maggie walked, groaning inwardly at the weight of the burden she must release to the One she had made her Lord.

Each step grew heavier than the last. At last she reached the trees.

"Oh, Lord, help me!" she pleaded.

I will help you, child, came the immediate answer. *Trust me.*

"I cannot do it, Lord! I have no strength to face it."

But I do, child. In your weakness is my strength. I have put my power in you. It is a cross you must bear alone, though I will be at your side.

In an agony of despair Maggie sank to her knees at the foot of a small birch tree, stretching out her hands above her.

"Oh, Lord . . . help me!" she cried.

Then, bowing her head to her knees, she prayed: "God . . . with you helping me—I—I—will try to . . . to forgive him."

She jumped to her feet and screamed, *"Oh, God—I forgive my father!"*

With those words all heaven seemed to explode about her ears. She fell prostrate on the ground and burst into an agony of uncontrollable weeping such as she had never known.

An hour later Maggie slowly approached her house. As Samuel watched her through the window, he could tell by the composure of her demeanor that the crisis was past. He opened the door and went to meet her. Though tears streamed down her face, her eyes sparkled with the radiance of peace and joy.

Without a word she approached him, gazing up into his understanding eyes, while she continued to weep tears of gladness and freedom.

"It is over," she said softly. "God has released me from the terrible burden of bitterness I have carried all my life. I have at last—I should say, at last the Lord has enabled me to forgive my father."

"I knew the day would come," said Samuel tenderly. "I have been praying that He would give you the strength to face it."

"He has been so faithful, Samuel. And now it is past."

"I am happy for you, Margaret."

"Thank you, Samuel. Now with the Lord's help, perhaps I can begin to do more to pay back all the patience you have shown me."

The doctor simply smiled, his eyes saying, "There is nothing you could do that would mean more than the pleasure of your companionship."

Together they turned and walked back toward the house, where little Eleanor's unmistakable chatter beckoned them.

Later that night, while Eleanor slept, Maggie rose and went outside onto the porch. The warm night sky was filled with the sparkling brilliance of the heavens. Across the compound the occasional snort of a restless horse revealed the nearness of the livery stable. Next door, Samuel's office was dark, as was the single room adjoining it to the rear where he kept his quarters. She smiled at the thought of what went on in that office from time to time—everything from veterinary emergencies to infant care among the Indians.

Then her thoughts turned toward Ian. Upward into the stars she gazed for some time, at last breaking out in spontaneous prayer: "Oh, Lord, I thank you for crucifying my bitterness on the cross of my pain. And now, God, somehow in some way I pray for Ian. In your infinite ways I pray he will be drawn into your presence, even as I have been. Let him release his bitterness to you, so that he might know the freedom of forgiveness—"

Suddenly she stopped, trembling.

"Do prayers avail the dead?" she finally breathed. "Only you know, my Lord . . . only you know!"

Still looking upward, in the new silence of peace within her soul, Maggie seemed to hear the Lord say, *It was I who gave you and Ian your love. And it is I who will perfect it in each of you. Trust me, Maggie. For Ian is now in My hands. And I will never forsake him.*

Content at last, Maggie turned back inside—to Ian's daughter, and to the promise of a new life with the God who had made her.